THE
HONOR

Prequel to the Honor Series

THE
HONOR

Prequel to the Honor Series

J.L. KELLY

FORT WORTH, TEXAS

WIDE BLUE sky long shadow publishing LLC
Fort Worth, Texas
www.JLKellybooks.com

Publisher's Note: This is a work of fiction. Names, characters, places, and incidents are a product of the author's imagination. Labels, Locales and public names are sometimes used for atmospheric purposes. Any resemblance to actual people, living or dead, or to businesses, companies, events, institutions, or locales is completely coincidental.

Scriptures taken from the Holy Bible, New International Version®, NIV®. Copyright © 1973, 1978, 1984, 2011 by Biblica, Inc.™ Used by permission of Zondervan. All rights reserved worldwide. www.zondervan.com The "NIV" and "New International Version" are trademarks registered in the United States Patent and Trademark Office by Biblica, Inc.™

Cover designed by Maduranga Nuwan of Mnsartstudio.

The Honor – the Prequel to the Honor Series/ J.L. Kelly 1st ed
ISBN: 978-0-9897745-7-4
Library of congress control number: 2016911538

THE HONOR

A NOVEL BY
J.L. KELLY

WIDE BLUE SKY LONG SHADOW PUBLISHING, LLC

tota gratia

Dedication

To you Love
Three in One
Father. Sovereign strong.
Son. Beautiful Savior.
Spirit. Power proclaimer.
Forming and founding relationship.
Furious in Your pursuit.
You. Love. us.
Loved. Saved. Sanctified.
we are the outsider welcomed in
the orphan finding family
commoners who are crowned
Love crowns us and crowns us and crowns us
with compassion and love
We are loved.
JLK

for JMK
the real 'John' in my life

Author's Note

God says, "If you will honor Me, I will honor you."

Most of us are just ordinary folks. We understand life in a cottage not a castle. We're the fans not the famous. But God's Word makes it quite personal that both the extraordinary and the ordinary are called to honor God.

But what does that mean? And how does God honor us in return?

We honor God when we make it our chief ambition in life to please Him, to love Him and to serve Him at all times and through all circumstances.

So how exceptional is it that we have the ability to honor God and have God honor us?

Jesus said in John chapter eight, "I honor My Father." And "I do always those things that please Him."

Jesus was our example and a complete contrast to the people that sought the honor of the world and their fellow man rather than the honor that comes from God.

Jesus told us we honor God by believing His Word and trusting in Him. God honors us in return by giving us eternal life.

We honor the Lord by serving Him. Jesus said, "If any man serves Me, him will My Father honor."

As we honor the Lord we surrender to His Sovereign Lordship; He will honor us by making our lives spiritually fruitful.

We honor God by setting our love upon Him. He promises to honor us by delivering us, by lifting us up, answering our prayers and being with us at all times, especially in trouble.

We honor God with our giving. God honors us with the same measure that we use to give, it will be measured back to you.

Honoring God isn't easy. In some circumstances, we think we just can't do it—believe, serve, surrender, love or give. When we're afraid, outside our comfort zone, or challenged, tempted, and opposed how do we find the faith and the strength to honor God?

It is my prayer that *The Honor* will help you believe that God's furious love and amazing grace enable a believer to honor Him no matter what is involved. Even our greatest failure is just a new opportunity to Honor God with the story of how He honored us with His love and compassion in our restoration.

May Psalm 103 mean more to you after reading this story.

Praise the Lord, O my soul; and all my inmost being, praise his holy name.
Praise the Lord, O my soul, and forget not all his benefits—
who forgives all your sins
and heals all your diseases,
who redeems your life from the pit
and crowns you with love and compassion,
who satisfies your desires with good things
so that your youth is renewed like the eagle's **Psalm 103:1-5**

Reviewers agree that my stories are raw, real, sometimes intense and might not be for readers who are looking for the classic "sweet" Christian story where characters do everything right and the story world is heavenly. Unapologetically my style is to write it real—meaning closer to life, tackling issues with universal importance in a God honoring way by telling the truth in love. My characters will never be perfect but they will proclaim to you the love, grace and mercy of a perfect God.

The genesis of my writing began in the early 1990s with this story about John and Stephanie Dake. As I went back to rework this book for release it was interesting to see how much the world has changed. In the early 90s email and cell phones were for the innovators not mainstream. Not everyone had cable TV and Newspapers were where we went to find out the news and we used the library not Google for information.

This is the time period of the Prequels to the Glory, Honor and Power series. You learn where Stephanie, Samantha and Blair began. From these characters my others characters originated and stories began to spin off. These character-driven books became interrelated, sharing supporting characters but each with their own stand-alone unique story and Biblical theme.

I share this so that you don't get frustrated, thinking there is a linear time line developing from one book to the next. In fact, if you started The Glory Series with *The Psalm of the Offended*-Cheyenne & Bennett's story-you have found you've back tracked in time as you begin to read *The Prequels*, and in the *FURY* series you move forward into the future with Jaxson Cooper's daughter, Jaclyn.

Confused? I hope not. And if you are, here is a character chart to keep everyone straight

Character Chart

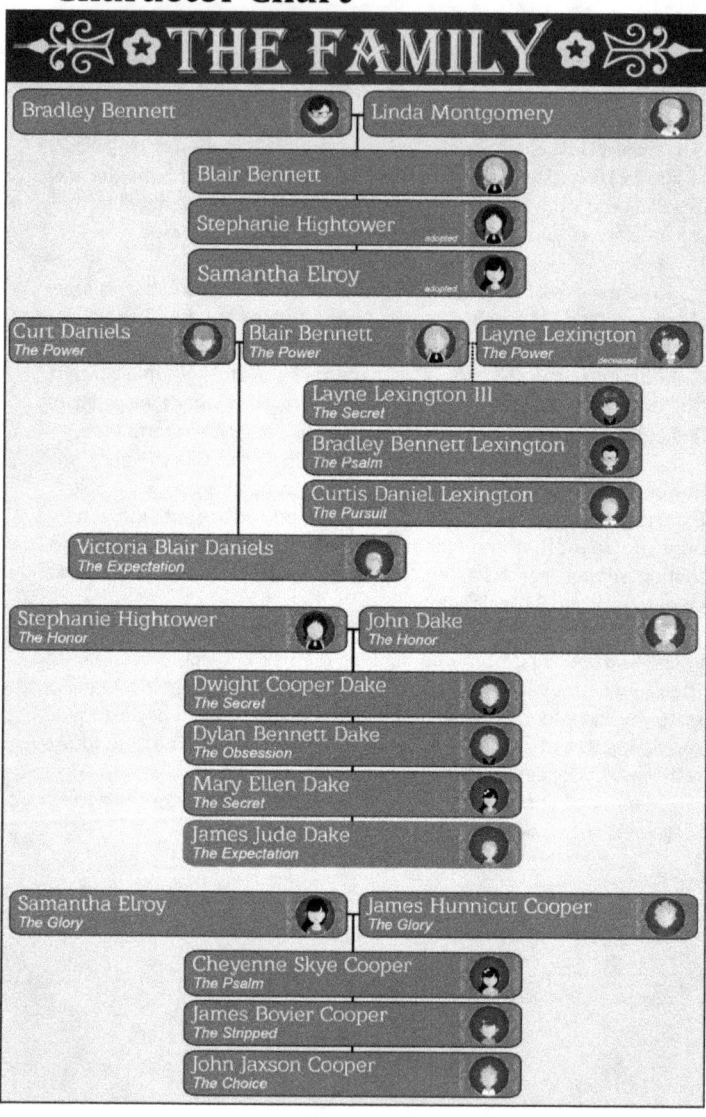

THE FAMILY

Bradley Bennett — **Linda Montgomery**

Blair Bennett
Stephanie Hightower *adopted*
Samantha Elroy *adopted*

Curt Daniels *The Power* — **Blair Bennett** *The Power* — **Layne Lexington** *The Power* *deceased*

Layne Lexington III *The Secret*
Bradley Bennett Lexington *The Psalm*
Curtis Daniel Lexington *The Pursuit*

Victoria Blair Daniels *The Expectation*

Stephanie Hightower *The Honor* — **John Dake** *The Honor*

Dwight Cooper Dake *The Secret*
Dylan Bennett Dake *The Obsession*
Mary Ellen Dake *The Secret*
James Jude Dake *The Expectation*

Samantha Elroy *The Glory* — **James Hunnicut Cooper** *The Glory*

Cheyenne Skye Cooper *The Psalm*
James Bovier Cooper *The Stripped*
John Jaxson Cooper *The Choice*

Books by J.L. Kelly

The Glory Series
The Psalm of the Offended
The Stripped
The Choice
The Glory Prequel

The Honor Series
The Secret
The Honor Prequel

The Fury Series
Book one Eros
Book two Echo
Book Three Effect

The Power Series

The Kingdom of God is like an orphaned daughter...

1

January 1991

"It's an honor."

There was a handshake. Firm and holding.

"Such an honor to meet you."

And a look, he found in their eyes, often awestruck.

Then the praise. The same sentiments said differently depending on the person who delivered them. Strangers telling John Dake their story in his story. As they pumped his hand. Held on. A little too long.

His mother had taught him to just say thank you. And smile. Give them the Dake smile.

"Thank you, Mark." He grasped the handshake and squeezed.

Over the last four years he'd learned the squeeze technique was a good way to get someone to release your hand. It worked again. Mark stepping back, pocketing his hands as he repeated, "It's really such an honor, Mr. Dake."

"No, it's all mine. I heard you were the best dog trainer in the state."

"Ah. Well. Matt McKinney really knows his business with English Pointers, now."

"But you know Golden Retrievers. And I appreciate what you've done to get mine ready for their first duck hunting outing."

"They're ready to go but I know you took a bad hit in that playoff game Sunday. How's the arm doing?"

It ached. Deep in the shoulder joint, like a haunting weakness that left his arm hanging wounded from the injury the doctors said would take surgery to correct.

If only...

And it started again; the replay of the play that ended their NFL season. With the clock ticking down the play call was a fade to the corner of the end zone. He broke the huddle with a clap. Twenty-two players faced off across a line and the pressure rose, vibrating from the volume for victory. It was on the line. Again. The demand shrouded in the furious energy of eighty thousand fans.

He did the quarterback crouch, his hands bracing against the spread legs of his center. He looked east then west, reading his enemy, evaluating their battle plan, seeing their defensive strategy. He pointed it out with confident authority to center the blocking scheme on player 54. "54 is *Mike*. 54 is *Mike*," he identified the middle linebacker, preparing the line for the onslaught as he saw eight defenders surging up to crowd the box.

Then he roared over the maddening chaos. "Hut!"

Hard leather snapped against his palms. Accelerated time stretched. It was slow motion, pressure howling to a dull buzz. He was already, one, two, three steps back as instinct took over. All those intangibles that had been repeatedly impressed into muscle memory went on automatic. Here the mysterious ruled. Fate and luck at war on the competitive edge of the clock. It ticked down, fueling the velocity of the internal enemy, pressure as the external opponent advanced with power. He had mere seconds and within each the defense rose like a tidal wave. Instead of backing up, he stepped forward. His gaze was forced to search his reads, find, decide. He scrambled now, throwing on the run, toward the post. His arm pumped back. Powerful muscles fired. The football was in flight as the enemy closed in from the left. Violent power collided with him as his body was helplessly spread wide. Instantly his view was gone. Time in warp speed. Ground rising. Gravity yanking. Body trapped to awkwardly fall beneath the attack. He heard the pop. Felt fire flare from his shoulder.

He'd rolled helplessly to his back. A whistle gave its shrill three syllable blasts and time broke to normal cadence. Two of his teammates were bending over him.

Did we win... win... win...

No one needed to answer. He saw their defeat. They had lost. One and done in the playoffs. Again.

If only he would have... Competed harder. Decided wiser. Thrown more accurately. Led more decisively. Trained longer. Been stronger. Faster. Watched more film. Improved his foot work, fundamentals, arm strength. Just taken another step to the right. Or forward. Just moved. Run the ball. Or braced. Turned his shoulders. Moved his hips. Kept his body loose. Avoided injury.

How's the arm doing?

Wasn't that the million-dollar question? And he gave a truthful answer, "It will heal," as he unclenched his jaw to give the confidant Dake smile. Then he asked, "How are my girls doing?"

"Fantastic dogs. My wife is bringing them in. She's dying to meet you. Got herself all dolled up when we heard you were coming this morning." John laughed along with him trying to hide the unease and embarrassment. "Thought I should warn you. Glenda's a big fan."

On cue Mark's wife came through the door in her Sunday best with his dogs tugging at their leads. His Golden Retrievers bolted to him with an assault of affection. Named after his two favorite quarterbacks, *the girls* were sisters, with silky bronze hair and eyes a loving rich brown. Bradshaw was the larger of the two, curious and affectionate. She sat right in front of John's face demanding continued attention as she rubbed and nuzzled the master she hadn't seen in weeks. The smaller Staubach ran around them both excitedly, stopping only for a quick bark, a pat and then a wet kiss for John or Bradshaw.

"Hi, Glenda," John stood, shook her hand and gave her his famous smile. "Mark's always bragging about his wife, but he never told me how pretty you were."

"Oh." Her face blushed beautifully, and a hand fluttered in front of her face as she gave a nervous laugh.

"Lucky man, Mark. And I'm lucky you gave my girls your time. I heard you were the best."

"Well—"

"He is," Glenda nodded. "The very best, just like you. We love you."

"Well," John swallowed.

She just smiled, batted eyelashes and said the infamous, "It's really such an honor."

And he said, "Thanks, Glenda."

"Can we get a picture?"

"Sure." He poised with Mark and the girls by the sign for their kennel. Then loaded the dogs up and waved as he drove away.

He stopped mid-way to the lake and let the dogs take a quick break then filled the car up with gas. He looked in the store, saw the handful of locals and wished the place had the new pay-at-the-pump system. But this Texaco was on a country road with old style pumps, so he pulled his ball cap down low, loaded the girls and walked inside. He grabbed a bottle of Gatorade and one of those new granola bars and went up to the counter.

"You're!" The middle age clerk stared as he pointed at his face. "I'll be! Alma," he hollered and John clenched on a smile. "Come see who it is."

A feminine shrill soared F sharp. "Lands sake, I don't believe my eyes. John Dake!"

"Hello," John tried to keep his patience.

"Where's the Polaroid Eddie? She ducked under the counter, muttering on to herself.

"Can I get your autograph?"

"If you'll ring me up." He smiled. "My dogs are in the car."

"Oh, sure thing. Right away." He yanked some cash register tape out and handed him a pen. "To Eddie."

"Eddie. Ring me up, please," he stated as he signed.

"Oh, right. Right." He grinned. A silver tooth winked. John held the smile, it was forced and fake and fighting not to frown with impatience as the man just stood there frozen and star struck.

Another man peered around. His eyes popping out, filling with the ever-present thrill. "It is him!"

"I got his autograph." Eddie held it up.

"Can I get a total?" John asked.

"Oh, yeah. Right. Sorry." He punched some numbers in and the total rang out on the register. "It's really you. John Dake." He told his friends, "John Dake at my filling station. Can you believe it?"

"Can I get an autograph?" Another man asked meekly. "My wife's just crazy for you, Mr. Dake."

"Sure." He quickly signed his name. Another fan was standing in line, he signed another one and handed it to him.

"Ah-ha!" Alma popped up. There was a rude flash that blinded him for an instant. "I got it! I got it!" She told the crowd.

John blinked, his smile lost. "Eddie, my man." He held out the money.

"Eddie, take one with me." She jumped on the counter, two hundred pounds of woman sliding toward him and he dropped the money, could care less about the change.

John backed away, quick and famous for it, avoiding the coming threat of contact and supporting his right arm because the shoulder was suddenly screaming with pain. "My dogs!" He pushed through the door and made a dash for the Bronco as an F sharp wailed in the distance, calling his name.

He got back on the highway, fighting a headache now along with the piercing throb in his shoulder. He couldn't find a comfortable resting place or position for his injured arm. Irritation had anger brewing just under the surface and he didn't want to deal with it yet. Sensing his distress Bradshaw showed up suddenly between the front seats. She nudged him with her nose. He leaned toward her and was lavished with love. With just a word she curled up in the passenger seat, resting her head on the console as Staubach showed up with more dog kisses. John invited her into his lap and she quickly curled into the space providing a perfect arm rest.

The three of them filling the front seats of the Bronco like one happy family. He chuckled, so much for two months of discipline and training with Mark, they were right back where they started. Over size lap dogs. He didn't care, he wasn't much of a duck hunter anyway.

An hour later he arrived at his cabin on the lake. He just looked at it for a minute and exhaled before he opened the door. The rustic place was tucked back into the forest, the lake behind it in the background. It was quiet and private. And it was his sanctuary. He was free. Finally. He exhaled again. He'd be alone here, could take the time to deal with things.

He jerked away from a nose that hit his arm in the sweet spot of misery. Both girls were surging toward the door over his lap, ready to go as he sat oddly on hold. "Okay," he told Bradshaw as her tongue lapped his face and her body lunged at the closed car door. "Let's get out and start dealing with things."

The dogs jumped down, noses to the ground, circling around. He cradled his right arm and tried to relieve the throb by finding that magic position, bad to worse to better. The loose, weak feeling drawing down his heavy arm just as the dread filled his body with tension.

If only... He wanted to rehearse the play again. Be back there. Third and goal with seconds left to make something happen. But he was here now—the loser, out of the playoffs and starting his off season. His jaw clenched. The pain real and raw and throbbing with his angry heartbeat as the truth rang. He was injured. His arm a mess. He couldn't fix it. And God had allowed it. He was mad about that, really mad. Which made him feel guilty and afraid, because he needed God to fix this. And his mood was dark, brooding, his attitude wrong.

His mom was the one that said he needed time to deal with it, alone with God. They could do that here. He could reboot and prepare for what was ahead—surgery, rehab—get ready to play through it and answer all those coming questions, with that confident smile. Honor God. His mom had reminded him again, his life was to honor God in everything he did—the winning, the losing, the highlights and the mundane. His injury was just another opportunity.

He frowned his way into a pout as he said, "Hell of an opportunity."

He unlocked the door. Hattie, his Dallas housekeeper had obviously found someone to come in and get the cabin in shape. The heat had been turned on and the scent of pine cleaner met John at the door. There were a half dozen brown paper bags on the counter, an overabundance of food waiting to be unpacked. He picked up an armful of bags and his shoulder screamed out, "Stop!"

He just dropped the four bags. The thud of tin cans and the crunch of dry goods an underscore to the one word that hissed from his lips. He looked at the sacks, cradling his arm for support against the pain. And just turned away. The bags could wait or stay right there. He didn't care.

He went out the back door, hugging his waist with his right arm as he walked the pain off and watched the girls run through barren winter trees. Leaves littered the ground, the January sky late afternoon grey, the air cool enough to cloud his breath. He felt the damp chill creep through the flannel of his shirt as he watched Bradshaw find a tennis ball tucked under fallen leaves. She came running to him and John threw the ball with his left hand and watched it sail down the shore of the lake. As the girls raced after it he wondered if he could retrain his body to throw a football left-handed. He squeezed his right fist, felt the corresponding twinge of weakness and the increase of pain. He'd be worthless left-handed.

He looked at the lake, still and deep and dark, and silently prayed. Random thoughts were expressed, he just let the story come with the questions; the why of this injury, the timing, and the uncertainty if he'd ever be the same quarterback. Pity taunted his thoughts, bringing on self-hatred. And then there was the stalking impatience. That time was his enemy and it was tick, tick, ticking. Year four in the NFL over. One and done in the payoffs when he should be peaking. Winning. He had maybe eight years left, ten if he was lucky. Or this could be it.

He cradled his arm, feeling the loss of strength and the growing fear as Staubach loped up to him with the ball. He took it from her and in a burst of rebellion he sent the yellow fuzz bulleting into oblivion with his famous arm.

Pain doubled him over and then just as quickly fury raged. He nailed a tree trunk with his right fist. One. Two. Three times before he writhed away and walked it off. His eyes tearing up, he blinked letting tears come, fall. Pain set the deeper emotions free to finally be released. There was grief and it was bitter and deep and joined with odd memories of deeper losses in his life. He propped himself against a tree, trying to breathe. He was cold and hurt, bad. He felt weak. Powerless. Shamefully pitiful.

And that's when he heard the dogs, saw the woman. A small shape tucked into a huge coat. Dark hair veiling her face. The dogs danced around her excitedly, then barked, calling him out. He stood still, stoic and silent, staring at the woman, daring her to come any closer, wondering if she'd seen his tantrum.

Dark green eyes widened. She took a step back, then another. Her gaze took him in, glanced at his fisted hands, then his face. He recognized fear, he moved, began to deny it.

But she fled.

He watched her go. The dogs standing by his side now, watching too.

2

The pain was constant. Nagging at him only to spike up any time he moved his arm the wrong way. Which is why they invented slings. He thanked his ego once again for leaving it at home and it answered sarcastically that the damage was already done, why make it worse by advertising the weakness. He couldn't sleep so he watched television, sitting in a recliner, petting Staubach—his ready armrest—and sipping his drug of choice, whiskey, until he finally faded off. In shallow dreams green eyes stared back at him as the only fan to watch as he played the game, going through that last play again, and again in a cycle of failure.

The next morning, he woke to a mess. The pain had sent him searching for medicine. He stubbed his toe on a misplaced can of chili, turned on the kitchen lights and moaned. He'd failed to unpack the groceries and food was everywhere. The four grocery bags on the floor chewed up, their contents scattered about and mixed together. There was a strong scent of coffee. The finely ground treasure like a trail of gun powder leading to a gnawed open bag.

Staubach sprinted in behind him, sniffing and further scattering the mess. Left handed, he grabbed her by the collar, lifting her clear as his bare feet smacked with sticky footsteps. "I know you had a part in this, but I doubt it was your idea." He led her to the closest bedroom and shut the door on her whine and called, "Bradshaw!"

His left heel stuck to the floor and he grimaced as it gathered a layer of grit over the sticky. "Bradshaw, come." He whistled, Staubach barked from the bedroom. He glanced at the scattered pile of groceries, was there anything left. "I know you're hiding, Bradshaw. Don't blame you. I'm pretty upset, girl. This is a heck of a mess and I'm alone here with one good arm to clean it up."

He paper toweled off the barbeque sauce on his heel and started to search.

"Bradshaw you know you're in trouble." There was food all over the kitchen, soggy chewed up packaging laid scattered among a variety of foods. Even a stalk of celery had been gnawed on and lay on the rug.

"Bradshaw." John exhaled in annoyance. "I thought we'd outgrown the puppy stuff, you're supposed to be a big girl now." He spotted her curled up in the pile of large floor pillows. She was shaking and whining. His tone changed. "Hey, now girl, John loves you." As he reached for the dog she yelped. He stopped before he touched her. "Bradshaw?" Her tail didn't move, her eyes were dull and full of pain, she laid her head back down and a soft whine wheezed out. Then she jolted up, her body began to retch as she coughed and dry heaved violently. She was acting like she needed to vomit but couldn't. He gently touched her head as the convulsion slowly ceased and she whined softly.

"Bradshaw, you okay girl?" He gently pulled the dog towards him and she yelped loudly, cowing down in pain. Violent shakes vibrated her body as she began another round of dry heaving and crackling coughs.

John looked across the living room. How much had Bradshaw eaten? It looked like a lot. She was in pain. Her behavior wasn't normal. Something was wrong; in fact he was starting to realize it was serious. John softly stroked Bradshaw's head. "It's okay, girl. I'm going to help you now."

He noted the time as he dialed the phone. Called Brad Bennett. Not every player had the home number to their owner, but Brad was more than a boss, he was a mentor and close friend.

"Come on, Thelma, pick up the phone," he said impatiently, waiting for an answer from the Bennett's housekeeper as he pulled on yesterday's clothes.

"Hello, the Bennett's residence." Thelma recited politely.

"Thelma, hi, it's John Dake."

"John, how nice to hear from you. I'm so sorry about the—"

"Thelma, I don't mean to be rude, but I have an emergency. Something is wrong with one of my dogs. I need to get her to a vet fast. Do you know where the closest one is?"

"We've got Dr. Hightower here now checking on a horse. Hold on and let me get Mr. Bennett."

John paced as he waited.

"Hi, John, it's Linda," Brad's wife said. "He just sent the vet to meet you at the office in town. It's on Main, right next to Annie's Cafe. Do you know where that is?" she asked.

"Yes, I'm leaving right now."

It wasn't a town, just two intersecting parish roads on the edge of horse plantations on the way to the lake. Commerce had been at the crossroads for a hundred years, but the recent population growth had the entire humble parish expanding with new construction. Streets were either congested or blocked off by road work. Amidst the detours, John saw the sign for Annie's Cafe and searched for the veterinarian's office.

"There it is!" he said out loud in relief as he saw the building. A modest sign hung above it reading, *Caddo Animal and Equine facility.*

He swung into a parking space not caring if he was between the lines or not, then led Bradshaw through the glass door with S.B. Hightower D.V.M., etched on it. Inside was a very small and very empty waiting room, with no visible sign of any employee.

"Hello," he called out from the reception area. Bradshaw was sniffing the ground and slow to follow him. "Is there anyone here?" he shouted.

"Yes! I'm coming." A young voice answered. A girl of about sixteen walked out into the hall toward the reception area and rounded the counter. She wore a blue scrub top over tight blue jeans that were anchored to the ground by a pair of bright red boots. "Sorry, I was in the rest room." He waited for the standard *Oh my God you're...*

"I'm Melissa, Dr. Hightower's assistant." Her eyes scanned his body and a pert smile appeared. "You must be the dog we hurried back in town to treat."

"No, I'm ... well yeah; I guess Bradshaw is the dog. Where's the vet? My dog's in a lot of pain."

"Hello, Bradshaw." Melissa leaned down to greet her. "What's the matter sweetie?"

"She got into some groceries last night and has been dry heaving and coughing."

"Got a stomach ache, huh girl? Bradshaw's a funny name for a girl dog, pretty as you." Her hands petted her, one traveling over her body. Bradshaw yelped and sank low. "Okay, sweetie," she pulled back. "Mister, what did you say your name was?"

"John," he said, glad that the girl didn't know him. He was in no mood to deal with a star struck young fan.

"This way, John." She walked down the hall and led them into an examining room with a table in the center.

John picked up his dog and gently set her on the exam table as pain rocketed up to explode through his shoulder. "Is the vet here?"

And Bradshaw jumped down as she explained there was no parking. Anywhere in town.

John quickly caught the dog by the collar as she darted toward the door. Picked her up and set her on the table again. "Sit," he commanded in a grunt as pain screamed into his chest now.

Bradshaw obeyed, looking at him only a moment before she stood back up.

"Stay," he added as Bradshaw looked down again at the floor, beginning to realize she wanted down, out, away.

The moment he looked at Melissa, Bradshaw jumped. John caught her up again. Tried to hoist her with his left arm but she was struggling now. He lifted her quickly, using hands and wrists and hip and waist and collar for leverage as his arm began to spasm into his chest muscles. He held on to her. Telling them both, "It's okay."

"She can stay on the floor. You can sit in the chair."

John didn't think he could get her back on the table again. He just shook his head, held his dog, ask again, "When will the vet be here?"

"As soon as a parking place opens up. Dr. Hightower dropped me off to open the door for you. We were treating some of the two-year olds out at the Bennett's place today. I'm the vet tech. We handle mostly horses," the girl stated as she put a sheet of paper onto a clipboard. "This is our only small animal treatment room." Her gaze swept the two of them and she smiled. "You and your dog sure look alike, most owners and their pets usually do. The blond hair and—"

"You handle mostly horses?" John interrupted, becoming annoyed with the small talk because his pain was at a screaming level 10. Then Bradshaw began the dry heaving again and John let go. "That's what she's been doing!"

"Huh." The word was odd. "That's probably not good."

He'd been consoling Bradshaw, now he looked up at Melissa's confused expression and demanded. "Does this vet do dogs?"

The young girl giggled, smiling again. Her immaturity pushed John's patience to the limit. "I meant handle dogs. Where is this vet? Did he stop to have breakfast or what? I told Brad this was an emergency. She's in pain. Something's wrong and I doubt you know what to do."

Her annoying giggle had curled into a coy coolness, "I'm sure Doctor Hightower is coming as quickly as possible. Parking's a nightmare and *someone* took both of the reserved spots." She pulled off the cap to a ball point pen and shoved it onto the other end with a click as she asked, "Now, what's your dog's name?"

He stared at her, knowing she knew, answering in the same flat tone, "Bradshaw."

"Bradshaw," she repeated as she wrote it down.

"Is she a boy or a girl?"

"She's female." John heard the pen make a flamboyant circle just as Bradshaw tried to slip her nose into his right armpit. Immediately there was a jolt of pain, then a firestorm of it as he fought her and tried to move her around.

"And how old is Bradshaw?"

"Fourteen months," John answered, still wrestling her into another position to hold her securely and keep her away from his right arm and his right arm in a position that didn't have him wincing.

"Golden retriever?"

"Obviously."

"And what's the problem with her?"

"She ate a bunch of food. And she's been dry heaving and whining. She's in pain. I already told you all this."

"I have to fill out the signalment for the Doctor."

"Can you get him on the phone?"

The jangle of the bells on the door signaled the anticipated arrival.

"Melissa!" A female voice shouted as the young girl hurried out of the room.

John frowned. It was probably the teenager's Mother. He heard the sounds of the start of a conversation. As he averted his gaze to the door Bradshaw darted under his right arm. The pain launched up. John stepped back to handle it and Bradshaw jumped down. He grabbed her collar with his left hand and just swung her up on the table. Cursing her by name and gasping from a pain brilliant enough to void his vision a moment as he forcefully swung his dog around and anchored her with his left arm and a harsh demand, "Bradshaw, Stay!"

"I have her. Let go," a woman said.

It was a command and he followed it.

John stepped back, feeling the awkward silence in the room as his pain and anger echoed, guilt escalated. He crossed his arms, holding himself, feeling in this moment like the world was tipping at an odd angle and everything he understood life to be was in the midst of a violent shift. He suddenly felt as dislocated as his shoulder with all the sudden changes. He was powerless to do a thing to stop any of it any more than he could shift the path of a tornado or stop the blind side hit from taking him to the turf in defeat.

He was suddenly hot. Bothered. Irritated. And very entitled to some VIP treatment here.

He swept the doctor who wore black insulated coveralls over mud-splattered boots. Read the red embroidery that stated *Caddo Equine Facility, S.B. Hightower DVM* like his own jersey said Dallas, Dake, #7. She was rookie young. Female. Smelled like horse. And had caught him in one of his worst moments ever.

He frowned, broke the silence with, "You're Doctor Hightower?"

And two green eyes looked up at him from a ridiculously beautiful face.

"Yes, I'm Doctor Hightower."

"I'm John Dake," the man stated. He had his muscular arms tightly crossed over a wide chest and his dark blue eyes were staring at her with noted hostility.

He was the same big, angry guy from the lake who apparently liked to use his fist on trees and his muscles to toss his dogs around. She tried to swallow; the suspicion and distrust. The skittish anxiety about as welcome as the sore throat she was fighting. Stephanie looked back at the dog, focused on her job. Then nodded for Melissa to hold the Golden.

She needed to wash her hands. Turned to the sink. As she washed up Melissa stated behind her, "She does do dogs."

She glanced at the teenager. She had her chin tucked and her gaze locked on the owner, wearing a smirk full of attitude. The look was like a mirror reflecting her own attitude that immediately convicted her. "I'm sorry you had to wait on me. What's the signalment, Melissa?" she asked in a tone that said cut it out.

"Fourteen-month old female golden retriever named Bradshaw is owned by Mr. Dake—" The teenager stated looking up from her clipboard at the client. "Ate a bunch of junk food. She's been dry heaving and whining with pain."

"Hello, Bradshaw." She talked to the dog now because it had always been easier to deal with animals than people. Keeping her gaze on the Golden's and one hand on her head, the other slowly began to travel over her body, she stopped when Bradshaw began to tremble. "It's okay, Bradshaw." Her voice was soft and kind, her hands slow and gentle. "Do you know what she got into?"

"She chewed through some brown paper sacks I left on the kitchen floor and made a mess."

Don't judge. She glanced up at him. He was frowning. His brow strong, his jaw square and ticking since he had it clenched so tight, along with crossed arms his body language was screaming, 'I'm really angry about this.'

"What did she eat?"

"A little bit of everything. Cookies, chips, bread, fruit, celery, some gourmet coffee and the paper or plastic it was all wrapped in."

"Do you know when this happened?"

"Sometime during the night." John looked past her. "I picked her up at the kennel late yesterday. Could she have gotten sick there?"

"Possibly. But I think this is related to her eating binge last night."

Her hands stroked down her spine and back legs then slowly up to her belly. Bradshaw yelped moving toward John, ducking her head into the safety of his body.

Immediately the man pushed back, pulled the dog out from under his arm and whipped her around to face her again.

"It's okay, Bradshaw." Stephanie regathered the dog.

"What's wrong with her?"

"Her stomach is full of..." she didn't say your unpacked groceries. She would not condemn the owner or judge. She swallowed the words. Began to cough, into her shoulder, trying to wrestle the urge to silence. She had no time for this head cold. Winced because it hurt, throat and chest and body. Everything hurt because of this sore throat she was fighting. She took a shallow breath when it ended. "She's full of gas and the stomach is enlarged. Mister—" She started coughing again.

In the midst of it, he said with a certain tone, "Dake." That square jaw ticked, twice before he said, "I'm John Dake."

She nodded. "Mr. Dake, I'll have to take some x-rays and depending on what I find, possibly surgery."

He blinked. "Surgery?" Shook his head. "No. She's just sick to her stomach and needs some medicine," he demanded.

"I won't know for sure until I look inside. She'll need some x-rays."

"Do you know about dogs?" He'd narrowed those hot blue eyes.

"Of course." She gave a smile. Saw he was serious. And a chauvinist. Now her head hurt too. She swallowed again. Her words frank. "I'm a Doctor of veterinary medicine, Mr. Dake."

"Your assistant said you're a horse doctor."

A cough sprang up. It was a fit this time that she fought with her mouth spewing all its germs into the fabric of her coveralls at her shoulder. She tried to shorten it and it made her eyes water and her throat just scream from the friction.

"I know... about dogs... Mr. Dake."

"If she has to have surgery, how long can I expect her to have to stay here?"

"Depending on what I find, it could be anywhere from a couple days to a week."

"I'm just here for the weekend. This throws a major curve into my plans." He thought out loud, "I was going to hunt this weekend then get out of here by Monday. My bad luck just keeps continuing. This is unbelievable. Tell me how else we can fix this?"

"Well, we could just put her to sleep and you could—"

"Do what!" John leaned toward her, towering over her with size and strength and a sizzle of outrage as he clenched his jaw and reclaim possession of his dog. "Look lady—"

"It's Doctor." She interrupted quickly.

Suddenly Bradshaw darted under his right arm again and John Dake jerked, man-handling a dog that was determined to get down, away, under, around, through him to the door. But the man had Bradshaw in hand by the collar, used it to whip her away and around as he commanded her to, "Sit. Stay." Then he looked at her and she saw rage, "This dog is irreplaceable!"

"Duck hunter, right?" she interrupted calmly as she crossed her arms and didn't let him answer. "Well, I'm sure she is irreplaceable. You probably paid premium price to acquire this living and breathing, addition to your duck-hunting portfolio of guns and equipment. No doubt another couple hundred after that, to get her trained to retrieve."

"Try a couple thousands. The best isn't cheap and Mark Parr's the best."

"Thousands? Oh, well that explains it. By the way Mr. Dake, retrieving is a God given instinct that needs little human training for Retrievers. I would guess that the fact that your irreplaceable asset is not going to be able to swim out and retrieve your downed ducks at the command of a whistle does throw a major curve into your hunting plans."

"Retrieving my downed ducks doesn't have anything to do with it. I don't want to lose my dog. If you're not willing to help her I'll drive all the way back to Dallas to find a real veterinarian, not some," those blue eyes swept her, "Cajun back woods country horse doctor."

"Well, Mr. Dake you wouldn't need a Doctor of Veterinary medicine if you hadn't carelessly left a bunch of junk food out, been irresponsible—" Her rebuttal was interrupted with a round of violent coughing. Finally, she caught her breath, and her manners, said, "She has a good nose, doesn't know any better than to break into the bags on the floor. And I guess I should give you a break since you're used to having your *pet* kept at a kennel accept weekends between December and February. I know about Golden Retrievers and I know duck hunters—"

"You. Know. Nothing."

She stopped, blinked, saw he was angry. Very angry. And she knew she'd gone too far as that anger seemed to curl up and he pulled it all in. Arms that were crossed seemed to cradle his dog now as he repeated, "I love this dog." And in that moment, she saw that the dog loved him. Bradshaw seemed to comfort him with a kiss and a cuddle, snuggling her body into his protective embrace as he exclaimed, "And this is just unbelievable." He looked at her. "You've taken everything the wrong way. You don't know anything about me or my dog. I have the sister to this one back at my cabin. They've never been hunting or separated and I'm sure she is tearing the place apart trying to get out. If anything happens to this dog, assume you've also been the cause of Staubach's death too." He just shook his head. "I'll call Brad Bennett get the name of—"

"I'm sorry." But she began to cough again as her apology was sprung free. "Forgive me." More coughing. Her throat closing up with pain. She tried to swallow, fight it. "I shouldn't have said any of that." More coughing. "I'm not myself." And another round. As he watched her fight it she felt her face flame. "Have this horrible sore throat. And a nonstop drip—" Some more coughing. "Down the back of my," she shook her head. "And none of that matters."

"No. It doesn't. My dog matters right now. Can you treat her or not?"

"Yes. I don't think it's a good idea to move her, and I can assure you, I'll do all that I can."

"You're sick."

"I'm fine."

"Can she get your cold?"

"No."

And Bradshaw chose that moment to rise and dry heave violently. Both of them moved to her, both of them soothed until she was quiet again. "This is critical, Mr. Dake. Please, let me get an x-ray so we know what we're dealing with."

"Fine." He gave a nod.

"Why don't you go next door and get something to eat, some coffee maybe. In about half an hour I'll be able to tell you what we'll have to do. Okay?"

"No. I'll wait here. I don't want to leave her."

"I need to take films and run some tests. It will take thirty minutes.""

"I'll wait here."

When the door closed John cradled his arm, felt the sting in his eyes and the tick in his jaw and the weakness in his shoulder and just sank down into the chair. He wanted to cry but suddenly he just laughed, that sick and tired kind of sound that comes out when you've had enough. Because he was weary from the fame and when he suddenly found himself in need of its privilege, he got no special treatment. Instead he'd been told the truth, given a rebuke and been totally misunderstood.

He couldn't remember the last time someone was angry with him, even disagreed with him at a level that showed any kind of emotion or conviction other than a coach. And she was right. He'd been irresponsible. And he didn't want to explain why his groceries were on the floor and he hadn't been watching his dogs close enough or that somehow when he couldn't sleep he'd slept through the kitchen invasion or that the pain and the weakness had him at his worst. And now, Bradshaw was sick. And it was serious.

Melissa opened the door, held out a phone. "You have a phone call."

He took the phone and said, "This is John."

"How's the dog?" Brad Bennett asked him.

John stood up and started pacing as he demanded, "Why in the world did you send me to your horse doctor? She's got a serious chip on her tiny shoulders about hunters. Wanted to put Bradshaw to sleep! Can you believe that? Put my dog to sleep! Does your horse doctor know a thing about dogs, Brad?"

"Hold on a minute, that doesn't sound like Stephanie."

"Oh, Stephanie? You do mean Doctor Hightower, right? She corrected me when I accidentally called her a lady. It's Doctor, Brad. She must be a Cajun witch doctor with her manners and that temper. Flashing those green eyes at me. The little thing bowed up to me. Me! And tried to put me in my place." He laughed arrogantly. "She obviously has no idea who I am. This place is the Twilight Zone, Brad. Must be why you hide out here half the year. They have no idea what football is or who plays it." He cradled his aching arm. "She says this is serious. Bradshaw might need surgery, and then she tries to get me to go next door and get some coffee like this is no big deal. Surgery, on my puppy, no big deal? Brad, I wouldn't put up with that lady. Excuse me, Doctor."

"Hmph," Brad made that noise John had heard in a lot of meetings.

Brad was considering options and John wasn't giving all the details, felt immediately convicted so he added, "She said she had a sore throat, wasn't herself. And God knows I'm not myself with this pain. No wonder she didn't recognize me."

"You're in pain?"

"I'm irritated." Now he sighed, added, "Worried. I love that dog."

"She's a very good veterinarian, top in her class. Bradshaw will be fine. I can assure you, Stephanie will take excellent—"

"I thought Mark would too, but now I'm wondering if Bradshaw didn't get something at his kennel. The doc says it's probably from the food. But, I'm going to call Mark, get his take on this. He knows Golden Retrievers and she said this was serious. Bradshaw's too critical to move." John rubbed the ache in his shoulder, squeezed his eyes shut against the headache as Brad continued to reassure him. When the call ended, John looked down at his watch, it had been twenty minutes.

He was cold again. His shoulder throbbing. He cradled his arm, frustrated with its uselessness and pain and fisted his right hand. The knuckles were scarred and now there were new cuts, harsh and raw red from yesterday's foolishness with that tree. He closed his eyes and prayed. Tried to relax his body.

The door opened, and he stood. She no longer had on the black soiled coveralls. A thick black turtleneck was tucked into a pair of well-worn blue jeans. She was tall, and John noticed that her height was the result of some very long legs.

"I want to show you her x-rays, so you understand what's going on." She put the films on a box on the wall and flicked a switch that illuminated the x-rays.

She looked him directly in the eyes and stated, "Bradshaw is suffering from GDV, Gastric Dilitation Volvulus. In layman's terms it is called Bloat. It happens in deep chested dogs like retrievers. The cause of GDV is really not known but in most cases, they come in with their bellies full of a lot of food." She pointed toward the x-ray. "Here is her stomach. It's about six times as big as it should be. And the stomach has turned or twisted. That's why she can't get anything to come back up."

"Okay, she's got this GDV, bloat condition. So, what do you do?"

"I'll be frank Mr. Dake, the only option she has is surgery. I'll have to go in and untwist the stomach and tack it back down. Her spleen could be involved, so we'll evaluate that. And I'll have to check her bowel. If she makes it through the surgery, it will take a good two days before she's out of the woods. A lot of these dogs don't make it through surgery. The ones that do, sometimes die of cardiac arrest while they're recovering. The risk level is very high, and the surgery is expensive."

"The cost is irrelevant. I don't want to lose my dog. She's a pet not just a hunting dog. She lives with me. I love her, and if you think she has a chance, I want you to do it."

"I'll do all I can for her." Her eyes had softened. "No one really knows why bloat happens, but it wasn't from just eating a lot of groceries. It wasn't your fault, Mr. Dake."

"How long will the surgery take?"

"A couple hours then we'll keep her sedated most of the night. I want you to go home to your other dog and come back in the morning. I'll call you when we're finished. Is that acceptable?"

"I really don't want to leave her."

"I know you don't. But there is nothing you can do for her here and like you said, your other dog needs you. I'll have Melissa give you all the forms to sign. I'm just waiting for my regular assistant to get here before we start the surgery."

"You'll call if anything happens, or as soon as you finish." There was a hoarse emotion in his voice.

"Yes, the minute we finish."

"I need to see her."

"Of course." She led him down the hall to the room. John walked in and petted the young dog's silky coat. He couldn't believe it had come to this. That this beautiful animal, he'd raised from a puppy was in such danger. He felt overwhelmed, fiercely fought a rare rush of emotion as he buried his face into the fur near her face, whispering nonsense and love words into the ear of a dog as he held her gently.

He said a prayer for her life, then told her, "You'll be okay, girl. I love you." He looked into her eyes and smiled as he gave her one last, long stroke before he left the room. John quickly read through the paper work and filled it out. Not listening to the rambling of the teenager's stories about her boyfriend named Charlie as he penned his famous signature on the dotted line.

"I'll talk to you in a few hours, Mr. Dake," Doctor Hightower said as she walked to the front of the clinic.

"Please, do whatever it takes."

"Everything I can, and God will do the rest."

He paused as if he wanted to say something else but then he just nodded, turned and went out the door to his Bronco that had taken up the two reserve parking places for the clinic.

Stephanie let out a breath and stood for several minutes staring out the glass door.

She should have apologized again. She'd never lost control like that, never been rude to a client. She'd recognized the dog from her walk yesterday at the lake. Recognized the man. He'd scared her yesterday when she'd seen him; the anger in his eyes, the authority in his stance, the overpowering size of his strength.

He'd man-handled the dog on the table when she first walked in. But the dog was frightened and in pain, and that combination made animals hard to control sometimes. So her conclusions had been wrong, that he was just a hunter when Bradshaw was really his pet. And her words had been rude, when she'd given him the option of putting the dog down. She'd been inconsiderate and uncompassionate. She rubbed her throat. Swallowed painfully. Even being sick was no excuse to act with such hostility to a client. Even if he made her incredibly defensive and anxious, she'd dishonored God and her testimony.

She confessed it; then the fear. The man made her nervous. That was the root of everything, even if she didn't understand it yet. He made her nervous, impatient and edgy and cautious—she frowned—and afraid. She'd been afraid and handled this poorly and he was a friend of Brad's.

She cringed, squeezing her eyes shut. That made it all the worse. She needed to... she started coughing again. The sinus drip just triggering the response. The fit lasting long enough to exhaust her and set the throat pain on fire. She heard Melissa. The call was from Brad. She answered the phone.

"How you doing?"

She fought off the cough.

"Sounds like you need another cough drop." He'd given her one this morning at the barn. It had helped.

"Yes, sir," she answered then just told him, "I was rude to your friend."

"Oh?"

"I apologized but I was rude. I'm sorry, Brad."

"You're not feeling well."

"No excuse."

"How's the dog?"

"Critical." She explained it.

"Linda and I are praying. God's grace is sufficient, Stephanie."

She agreed. As she hung up she said her own prayer, *God, please get me through this. And please, don't let his dog die. Deliver us both...* Then another cough seized her.

Melissa stepped up beside her and Stephanie confessed, "No matter how the clients act we have to be professional. Their pets are hurt, and worry comes out in different ways. I didn't handle Mr. Dake very well. I'll need to apologize."

"He's so cute, I don't think that will be too hard."

"Who's so cute?" Mary's familiar voice called out as she walked into the clinic and smiled.

"I'm glad you're here. I want to get started." Stephanie was already walking towards the back to scrub up.

"Who is so cute, Stephanie?"

"I didn't say that, your daughter did, and I'm sure Melissa will tell you all about him." Stephanie took off the turtleneck and pulled the blue scrubs over her head. The two of them shared the sink washing their hands and arms, as Melissa was getting the Golden ready in the other room.

They were barely beginning the surgery before Melissa was giving Mary the low down on what had occurred earlier. Stephanie tuned out the conversation, pumping the stomach, bringing up all the groceries the golden had eaten.

"Mom, they were like Grace and Michael on L.A. Law. Did you see the episode last night." She began to recap the hit show. Then she linked it to Mr. Dake. "Stephanie let him have it good for letting his pup get into all these groceries. Told him we could just go ahead and put the dog to sleep. That really got him. You could tell he loved his dog. I watched his face get so tight I thought it was going to bust and this cute little vein in his jaw kept twitching. He's got this great square jaw. He is soooo cute. And he was *sooooo* mad at Dr. Hightower," Melissa said.

"Really? I'm not sure I've ever seen a client get mad at Dr. Hightower."

"And muscles, momma. You should have seen his muscles. When he crouched down to talk to his dog I thought his thighs were going to bust right through the seams of his Wrangler jeans."

"I like Levi's myself on a man," Mary commented.

"Wait till you see this John guy." She sighed. "Blond hair, curly right here—"

"This spleen is going to have to come out," Stephanie interrupted as she continued to work. "There," she said aloud as she dropped the removed organ into a stainless dish.

"That is so gross," Melissa scrunched her nose.

"You better get used to it Melissa, if you're going to be a vet."

"I don't think we're supposed to get used to that, Mom."

"Well, bumble bees aren't supposed to be able to fly either but they do. We can do all things your Christ," Mary declared. "If God wills it."

"Should I save it to show John?" Melissa asked, a giggle escaping from her mask.

"I don't think that would be too wise after everything I said today. I was rude," she told Mary.

Cue the alarms. That high pitch signal was bad news. Bradshaw's pressure was dropping. Stephanie started praying, out loud, as she gave out instructions and worked to save the dog. When the room finally fell quiet, the three just watched the monitors. The beep a slow but steady pulse that signaled the crisis was over.

"I'm going to run the bowels," Stephanie looked at Mary and she nodded, her gaze on the monitors. She ran the intestines through her hands checking to make sure there were no obstructions as she silently kept praying. "Let's hope this dog has a strong desire to live." Stephanie commented checking the tacks that held down the correctly turned stomach one last time. She dabbed any trace of blood to make sure she didn't have any hidden bleeders in the abdomen. "Okay, let's close her up and let God work now."

"I'll stay with her," Mary volunteered.

"Thanks, but I need to do it." She started another IV and administered antibiotics, praising the two women and their help. "It's been a long day. Thanks for your help, Mary and thanks for hanging with us Melissa."

"No problem, it was my pleasure, believe me." Melissa smiled. "John was a doll."

A doll? Maybe G.I. Joe. She rubbed her sore throat and felt the pain begin to spread out to the rest of her body in an exhaustive ache.

"That throat's not getting any better is it, Steph?" Mary asked.

"No, it's not. In fact, it's starting to hurt so much I can't swallow those huge horse pills I've been treating it with."

"I'd say it's time to go to the doctor for some people pills."

"I will tomorrow morning." She saw Mary didn't believe her. "I promise Mary, I'll go tomorrow."

"Will you go home?"

Stephanie shook her head no.

"Then let me stay with the dog. You need to go home tonight."

"I have to stay tonight, Mary. I can't let this dog die. Not if I can help it. You go on and I'll see you in the morning."

"Please try and get some sleep. It's the reason you have a sofa in your office, right?"

She only nodded.

"I'm worried about you."

"I'll feel better tomorrow." After I apologize. There was nothing worse than carrying a load of guilt and nothing quicker than an honest amends to lighten the load. Until then she'd just have to deal with the consequence of feeling horrible. Her throat was screaming, and she was exhausted. She was watching the EKG read out as she laid on the floor beside the Golden and gently laid her hand on the dog's body to pray for it.

3

"Horse pills don't cure everything, Doctor Hightower," the Pharmacist stated with a straight face. "Occasionally you animal docs have to break down and take the drugs designed for people and if it's Mononucleosis—which is going through the high school like the flu—only sleep and time will get you to feeling better."

"I don't have time for Mono." Stephanie shook her head but wondered if that's what Melissa had suffered with last month when she was out for three weeks.

"You need some rest even if it's Strep throat."

She just nodded because rest would have to wait until tomorrow. She had a very sick Golden Retriever, plus a dinner tonight that there was no backing out of. And she needed to call John Dake.

Stephanie turned around and walked right into him with an awkward, "Oh!"

He had some deep blue eyes. And really quick reflexes as he took her in hand, steadied her balance, already pivoting her to his right away from his body into a turn like a dance move and she thought of Bradshaw, how quick he'd whipped the large dog around on the examining table. "I'm sorry, I didn't see you."

"Feeling okay?" John Dake asked. "You're pale, Doctor."

"I must look horrible," she thought out loud, remembering she wore yesterday's makeup. She tried to tuck the lose curls back into the messy knot at the nap of her neck.

"I wouldn't say horrible. How's Bradshaw?"

"Stable but not out of the woods yet," she repeated her words from earlier this morning. "If you like, I'll walk over there with you to see her."

"Let me buy my drugs." He held up a bottle of Ibuprofen then added a bag of cough drops to the purchase. "Brad swears by these." He handed her the bag of menthol lozenges.

"Does he?" she asked as they began to walk.

"Scotch would be better but they haven't put that in a melt away yet."

"I'll have to try that if things get worse. Thanks."

"Sure."

They crossed the street and went into her clinic. "Mary, it's me." Stephanie called out as the bells on the door clanged an arrival.

"Stephanie, I told you not to show your face in here again today!" Mary bellowed back from down the hall. "You stayed up all night with that pup and I'll not let you..." Her voice trailed off as she appeared, turning red as she saw him. "Excuse me; I didn't realize you had someone with you."

"I ran into Mr. Dake."

"John," he introduced himself to Mary.

"Bradshaw's resting well," Mary assured them both.

Stephanie led him into the room. As John greeted his dog her heart softened. Her gaze focused on his hands as they loved his pet. They were large and full of strength yet in contrast they carefully and tenderly stroked his dog. She thought of the stranger by the lake with clenched fists, and the irritated client from yesterday. Then his statement, that she didn't know anything. She knew he was right. She'd made a lot of assumptions. Despite his size and obvious strength, this man was gentle, caring, and compassionate but he had also been furious and angry and dangerous; just as she had been proud, presumptuous and judgmental. He'd caught her at her worst and maybe she'd done the same thing with him.

Without realizing it her hand was also petting the dog's beautiful face and she found herself looking into John's eyes. She addressed the worry she saw. "She's doing great. Really. Just great." She saw the relief, watched the love pour out in his affection for the dog. "How is your other dog doing?"

"Staubach? She's a little confused but I think she'll be all right." He nuzzled close to his dog and said softly, "I'll be back to see you later, girl." John patted her one last time then stood up. Together they walked toward the door.

"You'll call me if something should happen?" John asked as they reached the reception area.

"Of course, we will," Mary answered from behind the desk as she looked at Stephanie. "Doctor Hightower is going to go home and get some sleep. But I'll be here. There will always be someone here to watch over Bradshaw."

"Thanks." He nodded then looked at Stephanie. "Not bad for a country horse doctor."

"Cajun back woods country horse doctor," she reminded him with a small smile.

"I'm sorry for all that yesterday."

"You were just concerned. And I was rude. Please forgive me."

"You saved my dog, Dr. Hightower," he gave her a magnanimous nod. "Keep me posted on her condition." He walked toward the door.

"Bye, Mr. Dake," Stephanie said.

He quickly turned to correct her. "Please, just John," he pulled on the brim of his baseball hat.

"John," she echoed with a nod.

As she said his name a smile appeared. It changed his face, brought light into his eyes and a dimple to his cheek and a symmetry to his face that caused a terrifying flutter to her heart. Yes. He was handsome. In every way your eyes could take in but there was power here too, inside this man. A certain charisma that robbed her heart of a beat and made her just stare in appreciation at a beautiful smile that became a fond memory to the woman who saw it for the first time.

"Bye, doctor." The bells jangled as he walked out.

"Melissa was right." Mary fanned herself. "That man, the way it all comes together when he smiles, about gave me a heart attack."

"Hmm."

"You definitely need to go home, right now. *Hmm?* He gets a, 'hmm'? After almost forty hours you get home and into bed. Maybe tomorrow he'll be looking a lot better to you, once you've rested."

"I'm not even going to argue with you, Mary."

"You stay home tomorrow. I'll look after the dog. You hear me."

She wasn't about to tell Mary she had to be at the Bennett's tonight for a dinner party with who's-who in the Louisiana horse world. If there was any way she could get out of that tonight she would, but Brad had called her again this morning, requested that she be there, and he didn't ask her for much. She had to get some sleep.

Brad had asked him to come tonight for dinner. He'd said Linda wanted to see him and something about not hurting her feelings and this being a huge favor to him, so John arrived early that night at the Bennett's Louisiana house in a dark suit and tie, planning to skip out as soon as it was politely possible. Thanks to Tylenol 3 and 800 mg of Ibuprofen, the edge of his pain had been pulled back enough for him to grin as the huge front door opened only a crack. There, between the hardwood and the frame, lashes batted over pretty eyes. Only Blair Bennett Lexington had her father's violet blue eyes and they looked up at him as she stated in a very serious tone, "I'm trading the left tackle."

"Henderson?"

"Henderson." She gave a quick nod. "I've hired Viking-son and Sparta-son. Huge, vicious, giants-among-men bodyguards in the trenches kind of linemen to protect you."

"We've already got a Viking-son, Paul Anderson."

"Now you've got two left tackles with Sparta-son added."

"There's only one left tackle." He smiled now. "The other is the left guard."

"Well... there should be two left tackles. No wonder there's a blind spot issue."

"Is there a blind spot issue?"

"Are you having surgery on Wednesday?"

"Not Henderson's fault. It was my bad."

"It's the personnel manager's bad. All his fault is what those NFL insiders are reporting in the papers. I fired his bad self."

"You fired your father."

"Yes, I did. Mother and I have sent him back to the oilfield. We're running the team now. Changing the team colors, getting updated uniforms, letting those sexpot cheerleaders go too."

"Okay."

"What do you think of chartreus?"

"Is that green? I like green." And he smiled at her.

"I hate this for you." She took his hand, ushered him inside. "Surgery dad said."

He just nodded.

"Well were not going to talk about it. No football talk tonight in mother's house, just horses. Would you like to be a partner in a new race track?"

"Ah..."

"No," she whispered as they began to walk. "Just smile and tell them, 'No thank you.'"

"No, thank you."

"I've got a race horse you might be interested in. *No, thank you*," she cued him again.

"No, thank you."

"Add the smile. There you go. My daughter is single—"

"Daughter?" He swept her slim body.

"It's a walk through; I'm preparing you for the defensive schemes ahead. They say, 'My daughter is single.' And you say?"

"No, thank you, Ma'am."

She smiled. "Now, I do have a very beautiful single friend you might like."

"No. Thank. You."

"Did you see my bride's maids?"

"I think I need Sparta-son, I'm being blindsided."

She smiled. "I think you've got it now." She slipped her arm tighter into his. "How is Elise by the way?"

"Ah, no thank you."

"Really?"

"We're not dating anymore. It was over last summer."

"I know," she grinned coyly, "I just wanted to hear the tone in your voice, to see if it was really over. Supermodels can be entitled to retakes."

"Entitled to retakes," he laughed. "Yes, they can be. It's over. How's Layne, Mrs. Lexington?"

"My husband is marvelous." Blair answered with a dreamy newlywed kind of tone as they strolled into the plantation home. Her petite frame carried the elegant southern graces that made a man want to tuck her close, spoil and adore. She even pouted pretty. Looking up at him as she said, "He's working a lot but that's part of the assistant district attorney gig. So that leaves me with the fund raising and philanthropical social events. Did you bring your checkbook John Dake? You're always generous."

"No, thank you?"

She laughed. "We've switched to offense. Now the answer is, Yes! Absolutely."

He smiled. "You know I keep a check written out with your name on it."

"And I haven't even pitched the cause to you."

"Viking-son and Sparta-son was sounding pretty good actually. You'd make a great personnel manager but don't fire the cheerleaders. They're a tradition."

She snorted. The sound outlandish female swagger only a very few women could pull off. Her gaze locked on his as she looked up and that thick shoulder length blond hair fell back, and she lifted feathery fair brows over those magnificent violet eyes and pursed her lips into a teasing knowing smile. There was the daring look of her father, the alluring femininity of her mother, the smooth Bennett manner that was subtly and thoroughly classy. "We're picking Sparta-son in the first round. Going to have two left tackles on our O line. Start a new tradition. See if we don't."

"You've missed your calling," he whispered. "*You* should be the politician not the future First Lady."

She laughed, "Not a word of that to Layne, now, he'd be undone."

"John Dake," Linda Bennett called his name as she approached. "I'm so glad you could come so I could see you for myself. Bradley says it's nothing to worry over, but your shoulder and that puppy have been dominating my prayers. Bradshaw's doing fine but, how are you?"

"Glad to be here." John hugged her affectionately.

Linda held him close, whispered privately that she was here if he needed anything and praying. "I'm so glad you could come. You'll sit by me at dinner." Her eyes were a deep mahogany brown and her dialect was as soft and soothing as a lazy southern afternoon. She smiled, and John felt blessed, like when a favorite teacher affirmed you back in grade school.

The doorbell rang, and Blair said, "While you greet the guests, I'm taking John into the study to pick his pockets, Momma."

Together they walked into the masculine room suited for business. The walls were paneled in a deep maple and there was a large desk in the same wood. One solid wall was shelved with an expanse of rare and first edition books that bookended a glowing fireplace. There were two large oxblood sofas and several chairs positioned precisely for conversation. Several men were well involved already in conversation around the desk as Blair poured John's favorite drink.

"Whiskey. Neat."

"Thanks."

"Blair, could you explain the zoning change you're proposing again?"

"Sure, Herald." She handed John a crystal tumbler with a wink as she turned to discuss the plans. John sank down in a wing back leather chair, listening as he took a sip of the aged liquor.

The house had come alive with activity. The clanking of trays and glasses, various conversations, and the intermittent ringing of the front door bell mixed well with the smell of hors d'oeuvres and hint of oak in his whiskey. He felt it was a rare thing for a rich man to make a house so grand feel so much like a home. But that's what the Bennetts had done. They were people who downplayed the external and always concentrated on the eternal—people and the riches of relationships. Even now he watched Brad meet and greet the varied men and women who came into his home. His voice was always soft and sure, talking less and listening more as he made each conversation personal. His violet gaze kept eye contact despite the chaos of activity that waged for his attention. His hands weren't afraid to reach forward in handshakes or past personal boundaries for subtle confirming touches to arms, shoulders, backs. Not everyone liked Brad Bennett, but even his enemies respected him and to John that was the mark of a great man.

Suddenly, standing in the crowd by the door, he saw those green eyes. She was here—John leaned to the left to see a little better—standing with some guy that looked like a banker.

Hmph. He watched her introduce him to Brad Bennett then Dr. Stephanie Hightower dipped down and...

Wow!

He leaned a little further to appreciate the view. She was wearing a simple dark green velvet dress that made her eyes catch fire and a neckline that was conservative until you leaned over to greet the household pet.

Big double wow.

John hid his smile behind a sip of whiskey, watching as she pet the Bennett's Schnauzer. She was paying more attention to the dog then the people around them. She picked it up, walked away a few steps to snuggle the dog, smiling and whispering secrets before she greeted the Bennett's housekeeper, Thelma, handing off coat and handbag as the two moved out of his line of sight then he saw Brad Bennett.

As the man smiled at him John realized he was leaning so far to the left he was about to fall out of his chair.

4

"Is this your beautiful single friend, Blair?"

John Dake broke in on their private conversation wearing that same smile. It shocked her system, Stephanie's mouth just opening and her words freezing up as her heart jerked and then pounded so loud Stephanie was sure he heard it.

What in the world is he doing here? Here, at the Bennett's, smiling that smile and looking so... charming as Blair links arms with him like... allies, and goes into dangerous mode with that calculating gleam in those violet eyes. Ut-oh...

Stephanie stepped back only to have Blair draw her tightly into her side until they formed a nice little circle. "Why Stephanie is," she glanced at her and smiled, "Like a sister... and my very closest friend. I would just love to introduce you. She was one of my bride's maids, John."

"You said they were beautiful." John spoke directly to Blair as if Stephanie was invisible.

Blair's smile widened. "Why John Dake, aren't you being charming."

Stephanie interrupted, "Mr. Dake is being sarcastic. He obviously enjoys teasing me."

"Teasing you?" He'd taken a step, the circle closing only tighter. "It's obvious you're beautiful, Dr. Hightower."

"Wait. You know each other?" Blair whispered curiously, stepping in so that the three of them were even closer.

"No," Stephanie said quickly trying to step back.

"Oh?" John's eyebrow rose in lazy arrogance even as his hand blocked her retreat.

"What's up?" Blair shook her head as she looked back and forth at them.

"Introduce us, Blair," John instructed, staring into Stephanie's eyes.

"Okay, I'm confused but I'll introduce you. John Dake meet my—"

"Friend," Stephanie finished.

Blair frowned then repeated, "Ah, yes, my friend, Stephanie Hightower. Stephanie, John Dake."

"It's very nice to meet you Stephanie." He extended his hand and his face broke into that incredible smile again.

The shake of his hand was soft, but the touch was like a spark, and as his hand lingered it kindled a fire of nerves. She was suddenly hot, and the warmth was spreading, her body reacting to this man in ways she couldn't even begin to identify and in his eyes she saw that he saw the affect. Suddenly she found her back bone. Smiled, for self-preservation, because if he wasn't still holding her hand she would have turned and run the other way as fast as she could.

Instead crazy words were coming out of her mouth. "I came with someone."

"Yes. I met him. Tim—"

"It's Phillip," Blair smiled at John.

"Banker or something. I think he plays, tennis."

"Golf," Blair corrected John with a grin. "And polo. Stephanie tends his ponies. He's here to talk to Dad about the Equestrian Center. Isn't he, Steph?"

She just nodded. John was still holding her hand. And she was just nodding, leaving it right there in his gentle strong hand as Blair stared at them and someone called her name. It was Brad. And John let go of her hand. Then Blair excused herself and said something about getting together soon that had Stephanie nodding again. Then they stood alone.

"You're a friend of Blair's, know the Bennetts," he stated.

"Yes," she answered. "You?"

"Yes," he echoed. For a moment they just looked at each other. The silence stretched out into a standoff, neither giving up any more information or looking away. Finally, John suggested sincerely, "Could we start over?"

"Sure." She'd been holding her breath with a frozen smile.

"Do you mind if I call you Stephanie?"

She nodded.

"How did the cough drops work?"

"They kill the cough, but the sore throat is the real problem."

"Have you tried whiskey?"

She looked at his drink and smiled.

"This is Bourbon. All bourbon is whiskey, but not all whiskey is bourbon."

"Okay."

He smiled. "There's a difference." He explained, "But whiskey was originally invented by the Scots as a medicinal cure to numb throat pain."

"Really?"

"No." He grinned. "But it's the Toddy part of a Hot Toddy which does numb throat pain. Can I get you a drink?"

"It's worth a try."

He led her forward with a hand at the small of her back. They walked straight into the middle of the Bennett's kitchen, receiving several puzzled looks from the busy staff.

"Don't mind us. Carry on." He was helping himself to a plate of finger food which he handed to her before he took a coffee cup from the cupboard and placed it on a saucer then into her free hand with a, "Hold that too. How do you like your tea?"

She told him, and he asked for a tea bag and a few lemon wedges and a pot of honey before he stopped at the instant hot water spout and dispensed the steaming water into a china tea pot he handed to her on a tray. Then he swept her out of the kitchen and through another door saying, "This way," as he guided her along by the waist. He stopped them at a bar in the large billiard room. As she put down the tray John pulled the barstool out and reached for her hand to help her into the high seat. She crossed her legs as he found the bottle he was after behind the bar.

He'd done it all as he explained to her the difference between Scotch-whiskey made only in Scotland, Whiskey-fermented from grain mash, and Bourbon-which follows strict labeling rules and must be more than half corn mash and aged at least 2 years in new charred oak barrels in the United States to earn its name.

"Here's your Scotch." He showed her the bottle.

"Glenfiddich." She read the label, "Made in Speyside, Scotland."

"Very good Scotch," he advised. "Brad thinks it might be the best made but let's see what you think."

He opened it as she watched. Then poured two fingers into her tea cup of the rich walnut colored liquor. He held the cup to her nose, asking, "Do you smell the cloves and cinnamon. Cedar and toffee are in there too."

"My nose is dumb with this cold, but I trust you."

"It will be good," he promised as he dunked the tea bag into the steaming water then added the lemon and a lot of honey before he finished it all with the Glenfiddich.

"Let it sit a minute."

"Steep, they call it," she told him, "I drink tea in the morning."

"Then you'll like this." He poured just a finger of liquor into his own glass, smelled it as he said, "I'll try it neat and let you know what I think. Here's to your healing and mine."

"To better days," she told him.

He smiled. "To better days." He clanked his glass to her cup and drank. Told her, "This is good."

She bobbed her tea bag a few times, then set it on the saucer. Tested a small sip, the steam rising up, the heat soothing, the honey sweet, she expected a dark bite of liquor that would be hard to sip. But instead it was warm and smooth as a pad of melting butter as it gently coated her aching throat with a soothing heat. Surprised, she took another sip as she looked at him over the rim of the cup. "It's smooth and warm. Easy to swallow. Nothing's been easy to swallow lately."

He gave her a nod and took another drink. His eyes were a dazzling kind of blue. His golden hair highlighted by the dark suit. He was tall and broad shouldered with a golden weathered tan that finished off his rugged good looks. A man at ease in this masculine room, leaning against the bar, looking back at her as they both just drank in the silence. Her body could feel the sweep of his gaze and stiffened under his observation as she lowered her eyes, drank some more tea. She didn't know if it was the liquor or the man standing so close that was making her feel suddenly flushed, but she didn't like the uneasy feeling he was causing again. She glanced at the door, felt out of control and took a controlled breath, demanding herself to stop being so nervous. What was it about this guy that had her so... rattled?

Immediately she could think of about a dozen reasons. Drank again. "It's good," she finally gave him a smile.

John edged closer, turning the bottle for her to see. "It should be. This is one of the top ten Scotches ever made. Older than both of us."

She glanced at the label, noted the date as he talked about the brand. His voice was as deep and rich as the aged liquor. He had a slow southern pattern to his speech. It drew her gaze to his mouth. His lips were full, smiling as he lifted the glass to drink with those interesting hands. She'd never noticed a man's hands before—they were large. The tops of his long fingers were lightly lined with swirls of bronze hair to the second knuckle of each finger. The hair was also on the back of his hand and then swirled around thick links of a gold watch that edged his white cuff. There was a weave in the cloth of his suit. The yarn had a very subtle twist to it, like the strains in his blue eyes. There were lines at the corner of those eyes, smile lines. And distinct proportions from the squared jaw to the wide shoulders to those defined leg muscles that had been wrapped by Wrangler jeans that now wore the fine fabric of suit pants without even stretching the fabric. He must have a good tailor. She looked back at his hands, large but somehow gentled down from her first impression. The palm of one cradled the lead crystal highball, his thumbnail blunt and fitted to a deep cut of the glass.

There was a very male chuckle coming from a slanted smile as he asked, "Checking me out?"

She choked. He watched her. And this time the cough was fake as she forced the words out. "You clean up nice."

She expected a laugh, instead he said flatly, "You're very beautiful, Dr. Hightower," then he took another drink as he studied her face.

Beautiful, there was that word again. A compliment she never sought, never worked for, didn't really care about. It had once been annoying and a handicap to her intelligence. But suddenly it wasn't. For the first time in her life she liked the fact that he had noticed.

What was happening? I must really be sick.

She tested her temperature at her forehead as she reminded her sudden glee that beautiful didn't matter. She didn't want to be seen only as beautiful to him or anyone. She wanted to be labeled with intelligence and respected for it, not beauty. And she'd never admired someone else's beauty. Looks never attracted her before. It was what was inside a person... She looked at his eyes and what she was seeing was tilting her world.

Where was Blair? She could use her help here. She couldn't think of a thing to say. He smiled, and it made her throat close up with a feminine sigh that she immediately drowned with a huge swallow of Toddy.

"Bradshaw is doing better." She blurted out then began to babble nervously. "I talked to Mary late this afternoon. She said she had stayed quiet. Which is good. No complications. So far so good." Stephanie smiled nervously at him as her pulse continued to escalate. "She's doing good."

"I'm glad. I love that dog."

"Tell me about her." She needed to keep him talking.

"Bradshaw tends to be a little mess most of the time. She's too curious for her own good. I can usually tell when she's getting into trouble because my other dog will get as far away from her as possible."

"How's Staubach doing?"

"She doesn't understand where Bradshaw has gone, keeps looking around for her sister. I keep assuring Staubach that Bradshaw has a great vet and will be back soon."

"Interesting names for female dogs."

"They were named after famous quarterbacks." He took a drink. At her blank look he explained, "Roger Staubach and Terry Bradshaw. Do you know Mark Parr?"

"I don't follow football."

He smiled. "Mark is their dog trainer. Before you say anything," John touched her leg softly and all her senses rushed to the point of contact. "I know how you feel about spending money to teach a Golden Retriever to retrieve, but I didn't have enough consistent time to spend with them in training, so I asked Mark to do it for me."

"I need to ask you to forgive me. I said several things that were very disrespectful. I made a wrong assumption. I know now, you're not typical Joe-blow-hunter."

"I take it you don't like Joe-blow-hunters?"

"I'm a vet. I try to help preserve animals' lives."

He dismissed the conflict and said, "Some of the things I said weren't exactly nice either."

"We forgave each other, started over, right?"

"We did." He squeezed her thigh this time, then took his hand away. She watched as he lifted his glass and said, "Brad told me you weren't yourself. Didn't feel well." He took a sip of the Scotch and studied her eyes.

"You talked to Brad about me?"

"This morning. We went hunting." He smiled. "Staubach did great."

"You talked about me?"

"Yes." He put the tea bag into the cup, added more hot water, honey and lemon, then Scotch. "He seems to think very highly of you. Let that steep a minute." He smiled at her. "I like your hair." He touched it. "It's pretty. Wavy... curls."

She was hot again. Heat racing up from the roots of those wavy curls. She could actually feel her roots. And the curl he'd tugged. With those hands.

He was still smiling as he asked her, "Does that bother you?"

She shook her head in denial as she bobbed the tea bag, stirred the water, gave the cup a lot of attention as he continued to stare at her and wait patiently for her to take a careful sip, looking at him over the rim.

"I respect Brad. He's a great man."

"I was talking about me, touching your hair."

"No, that doesn't bother me," she answered quickly. The lie unsettling. She was seriously bothered by the warm glow that seemed to be spreading out from her scalp.

She drank as John reached for the bottle, poured himself a little more, his body moving closer into the insulating personal space that separated them. He looked up at her and asked, "Sure?" before he took another drink, watching her. His hand went to her hair, pulled a bit on an end until the curl straightened out as he studied it. "It's not really curls, it's more like waves." He looked at her now. "Do I bother you?"

"What did you tell Brad?"

"Umm, Brad told me you're driven and demand excellence, a bit of a perfectionist it seems. But you have a kind heart and he says you've got a lot of spirit. That you're tops in your field, stubborn at times when you're passionate about something. Anyway, Brad likes people that are passionate."

"Really? Brad said stubborn, Mr. Dake?"

"It's John, and you are passionate."

"Passionate?" She questioned.

"Definitely driven." His gaze moved over her face, slowly studying every detail. "Kind hearted." He nodded. "Tops in your field—you saved my dog." He covered her hand, squeezed it. "Thank you." His eyes were a brilliant blue, sharp now as they looked far too deeply into her own eyes and she watched attraction overtake amusement. "Obviously beautiful."

Their gazes were linked, and she was captivated and so was he. Something in her knew it instinctively, and she took a breath. His smile playful as he said, "And I think I remember a little demand to call you—"

"A Cajun back woods country horse doctor wasn't it? But we're forgetting all that."

"It's just John, right Doc?"

"Yes, call me Stephanie."

"Stephanie." He lingered over the three syllables in a way that brought another flush to her cheeks and then he smiled. And it hit her in the heart.

"Besides being extremely charming—"

"Charming?" he interrupted, moving only closer. "You think I'm charming?"

"We could call you Mr. Charming with that smile."

"Is that the royal we for the female race?"

"Sure."

He laughed, a full easy laugh, relaxed and natural. It eased the tension and she smiled.

"You have a great smile, but I'm sure you hear that all the time, John."

She glanced down for her tea cup only to feel his hand touch her cheek, slide to her chin. His thumb brushed the tiny dip that was there as he lifted it up.

He was looking into her eyes as he said, "You have the most incredible eyes." They stared at each other as John echoed, "But, I'm sure you hear that all the time, Stephanie."

She could feel his words whisper against her skin he was so close now. Close enough to hear her heart pounding. She should be afraid, but she was strangely warm, relaxed and she realized he was holding her hand. There, oddly atop the bar, they were holding hands as he leaned down to her face. She realized almost too late what he was about to do as she whispered, "Don't."

"Don't?" he questioned not moving an inch.

"Please... don't kiss me... I'm—"

"Here with another man," he challenged drawing even closer. Their gazes were locked, as he told her, "He should know better than to take even a step away from you."

She covered her mouth now and told him, "John, I'm contagious."

He was startled to a stop. Drew back and just shook his head as he told her with a chuckle, "Dr. Hightower, I'd say you're about the most contagious woman I've ever come across."

"It's just Stephanie, right?"

He squeezed her hand before he released it. Picked up the bottle of Glenfiddich and poured himself some more. "Just how long are you contagious, Stephanie?"

She also took a drink of her Toddy. "It all depends on what results come back from the lab. If it's Strep throat, about six days. If it's Mono, which it better not be, since you can't take anything to treat it but sleep... the doctor says about six weeks. Either way I'm on antibiotics to cover anything in between. But it's not Mono. I'm sure it's not Mono." She was talking way too fast and saying way too much. She must sound ridiculous. But he had her body doing things that made her reckless and nervous and anything but in control. And she couldn't stop talking, and he'd tried to kiss her, and she'd stopped him. She drank because this was just too awkward. Finally found the courage to look into his eyes again.

And he was smiling, and she looked down again and took a long drink of the Scotch laced tea.

Lord, why did you give him that smile?

They were called into the dining room and John pulled out Stephanie's chair at the long table taking the seat beside her at Linda's end. Phillip was sitting at the other end of the table beside Blair and Brad. The guy looked like your typical yuppie to John. He was wimp skinny. Had more hair than muscle and undoubtedly the only sport he played was golf and he probably drove a cart when he did that. John thought women might find him attractive, but he better have one great personality if he was going to compete with John Dake—because

John Dake was suddenly very interested in competing for this woman's attention.

"Is Tim your date?"

"Tim?"

"The guy you came with."

"I invited Phillip." She glanced at John and he just looked down the table. Phillip, clearly thrilled to be in the seat of honor next to Brad, had no idea what was happening down the table next to Linda.

"So, he's your date."

"Why all the questions?"

He tossed his napkin in his lap and thanked the server for the salad as it was placed before him. "Maybe I'm interested, Stephanie."

They both bowed their heads for the grace, linking hands around the table as was the Bennett tradition before a meal, as Brad blessed the food and the guests.

Everyone answered, "Amen," then broke into conversation.

"Stephanie," a husky voice from across the table said, "Mary told me you had a case of GDV last night."

She nodded her head without even looking at John. "Sure did."

"Ever handle one before?"

"No, never had the misfortune."

"Had to remove the spleen, I heard."

"Yes," she took a sip of soup.

"Heard you almost lost her, that the Retriever went into cardiac arrhythmia, that true?"

"Yes," she answered evenly as she continued eating.

"And she's still hanging on?"

"She's doing fine," Stephanie answered evenly. "Thank God."

"You should have told me—" John started.

"I told you her chances were less than fifty-fifty."

"You should have told me not to worry," he said sincerely. "You obviously do, do dogs."

"I pray too."

"I'm so glad we got the two of you together. We were very fortunate Stephanie was still here when you called, John," Linda stated. "How is your throat feeling?"

"I'm so glad you ask me that, Linda. I have to take some medicine, excuse me while I find my handbag." John stood up and was glad he had her arm when she swayed. He caught her eye as he whispered discreetly, "Drink a little too much throat tonic, Dr. Hightower?"

"I stood up too fast." She gave him a soft smile.

"You want to sit down?" he asked, now a little concerned. "You're looking a little pale."

"No, I'll be all right." She nodded, touched his arm. Said confidently, "Really. I'm okay."

And he watched her walk away.

Linda was smiling when he took his seat. "She's quite something, isn't she John?"

He nodded. "She's a great vet."

And he'd call her a cheap drunk if that Scotch wasn't so expensive.

It had been almost half an hour when John walked into the kitchen looking for Stephanie. "Have you seen Dr. Hightower?" he asked one of the staff.

"Yes, sir. She's in Thelma's room." She tilted her head in the general direction of the housekeeper's quarters and whispered, "She's real sick, Mr. Dake."

"Sick?"

"Yes, sir."

"Oh John, you are heaven sent. I was about to come get you." Thelma said as she rushed into the kitchen. "Stephanie's so sick. Poor child." Thelma shook her head.

"Sick? I hope it wasn't that Scotch," John said with concern.

"Well of course it was that whiskey," Thelma scolded. "Besides lifting a wine glass for a special toast that girl has never been much for alcohol, Mr. Dake."

"What?"

"Stephanie doesn't drink." She fluttered by with a wet wash cloth. "She's done getting sick, and she refuses to go on upstairs. Stubborn as a mule," she muttered. "She insists she's going home. I think you should get her there before she takes herself. She's in no condition to drive." She commanded, "Pull your car up by the back door."

John was starting his Bronco before he even realized what he was doing. Nothing with this woman had gone right yet. He was only trying to be nice when he offered her the Scotch for her throat. Now he'd gone off and served up a Hot Toddy for a teetotaler. He was making a great impression.

"Stephanie," he whispered as he crouched beside the woman lying on Thelma's bed. "I'm taking you home."

"John," there was an irritated groan. "No, I don't—"

He interrupted, "I don't care what you don't want to do, Stephanie, I'm taking you home now."

"Stephanie, don't you worry. John is a good man, he'll take good care of you."

"I'm not worried, I'm just," her pale face flushed, "so embarrassed about this whole thing."

"Thelma will tell Phillip and the Bennetts that you didn't feel well, and I offered to take you home." He gave her no time to object as he bundled the blanket around her and started to pick her up.

"Don't you dare be picking her up, Mr. Dake or Brad will have us both." Thelma glared at him, gathering Stephanie up herself. "Miss Stephanie can walk. In fact, it will do her good." She assisted her up and gave John a stiff warning. "Walk her now, she's not a baby to be carried in your *arms*."

"I can carry her single-handedly, Thelma."

"I can walk," she insisted.

"And I can be very discrete about this whole situation," Thelma said as she walked behind John out the door. "I got your handbag and your coat Stephanie. Here's my trashcan if you feel you're getting sick again."

"Thanks," she muttered, totally humiliated.

John placed her into his already running car. "If you start to feel bad at all, you tell me, and don't be embarrassed about it. This was not your fault." John pulled the seat belt across her lap.

"Well, I am embarrassed," she argued softly.

He looked into her eyes, frowning. "I'm the one that should be, for filling a teetotaler full of Hot Toddy."

"You're mad again."

"At myself." He looked at her mouth. "And you're extremely contagious."

"What does that mean?"

He just shook his head and closed the door.

"You should have told me you don't drink, Stephanie," John said firmly. "I wouldn't have poured you a second cup. And I should have said something when you mentioned taking that medicine. You're a doctor, you reminded me enough times, remember?" He laughed. "A veterinarian should know not to mix alcohol and medication." He teased as he drove away from the Bennett's. "Where do you live, Doc?" There was no reply. "Stephanie?" He gave her a glance. Then a soft shake. Then another.

John suddenly realized she was out cold.

"How am I supposed to get you home?"

He had no idea why that problem made him suddenly smile.

5

"*Sleeping Beauty* finally wakes up."

Stephanie lurched back into the head board. Holding the blanket like a shield as she swept the strange room. Nothing seemed familiar but the aching pain in her throat and the residual deja vu from her years in the foster care system. "Please don't hurt me. They know where I am. Thelma and—"

John Dake had been leaning toward the bed from a leather chair with that charming smile. Now there was a fierce startled frown. And the word "What?" held both shock and sympathy.

Her gaze fled, darting over the room. It finally landed on a dog. The Golden looked like Bradshaw. As their gazes met the dog quickly surged to her with affectionate kisses.

"Staubach. Stop. Come here."

There was silence. In it they stared at each other. The dog between them. John's face hard to read. Serious and stoic. His dog jumped down to come to his side. A wide distance between them.

"Staubach and I went duck hunting this morning. Brad sends his best by the way. Hopes you're feeling better? Said to call if you need anything. He knows you're here. I told him what happened."

"Brad." She swallowed. Heat flared. Embarrassment ripe as she tried to get her words out of a sore throat and her body down off the headboard. She settled back down into the bed. "You saw Brad this morning? Told him I was here?"

He nodded. He'd stood up. Turned away. "I told Brad that I took care of you last night after you passed out in my car from the Scotch I'd talked you into drinking. That you were still fast asleep, alone in the guest room. Is that a problem?"

She shook her head.

He was stroking his dog. Staubach had reared up to his waist with her paws, her eyes full of affection for him. "I'm sorry if I scared you, Stephanie."

She was nodding. Rapidly and repeatedly, still trying to catch up and come to grips with everything. She was still in her dress. Tucked in tight to a large four poster bed under an avalanche of down comforters and pillows.

"How do you feel? You didn't move all night."

Her eyes darted to him. "You watched me sleep?"

"Well, you did it for Bradshaw."

"I wasn't in danger of dying."

"Maybe just dead tired. You were really pale. I was worried. How is Sleeping Beauty feeling?" There was concern.

"I feel better."

"You need some fluids. Food."

"What time is it?" she asked.

"It's about two o'clock in the afternoon."

"Two!" She repeated in alarm. "In the afternoon? No. I've never slept this late."

"I don't think you've ever been drunk before either. I'm sorry about that."

"It wasn't your fault. I have this cold. I'm not myself."

"I brought in the Tylenol." He nodded to the bedside table. "But you should eat first." He nodded to a pile of sweats on the chest of drawers. "And change out of that dress if you want to. I'll meet you in the kitchen, Sleeping Beauty." He walked out closing the door shut behind him.

Sleeping Beauty?

She looked at the closed door. Saw her high heels neatly set along the wall beside it. She slipped out of the bed, drawing up the covers and finding the decorative pillows on the floor, fluffing them until the ensemble looked right.

Then she looked at the pile of clothes he'd left. Soft gray sweats and a pair of socks. She slipped her feet into the thick white tubes, drew the two stripes up to her knee and turned them over in a cuff because they were so long. The sweatshirt was big and the pants, huge. She'd pulled a good yard of string out, trying to get them cinched enough to circle her hips. She was still working the material around when she walked into the ensuite bathroom and got a look at herself in the mirror. Her face was pale, her dark hair wild curls in disarray. She wet her hands and worked the waves into some kind of hopeless order. Then used the new toothbrush and mouthwash he'd left out for her to find.

She looked at the closed door and an old prayer sprang up. The one that asked for help and guidance and protection against the unknown that was on the other side. Then she opened the door and walked forward again into another unfamiliar house.

She was obviously in a cabin. She could see the lake through wide picture windows and a fire was going in a large stone fireplace as a basketball game played out on a big-screen TV. The Golden rushed up to her, circling about her legs.

"Hi, sweetheart." Stephanie gently rubbed the Retriever's silky coat crouching down to her level. "You must be Staubach. You're such a sweet girl." She said running her fingers between the dog's ears and under her collar. Staubach nuzzled into her hand.

"Do you have this kind of effect on every dog that sees you?" John asked walking toward them.

"Not when they're in my office getting their yearly shots."

"I fixed my specialty for you. Coffee," he said, smiling as he handed her a cup. "I can do eggs, soup or a sandwich in the kitchen. I'm better on the grill but—"

"I can cook." She led them into the kitchen. Staubach right beside her, John just watching. "What would you like?"

"I'm not sure what I have to work with."

She opened the refrigerator, pulling both it and the freezer open. Next, she walked over to what she thought would be a pantry and opened it, looking at all the can goods. Then she began to open each cabinet pulling something out if it suited her purpose. Midway through the kitchen, she reached up into the high cabinets over the breakfast bar.

"You want some more bourbon?" he asked sarcastically as soon as she realized that particular cabinet was where the liquor was stored.

"There's some sport on TV. Go watch it and I'll call you when it's ready." She closed the cabinet with both hands and looked at him. "You're making me nervous."

"I would never hurt a woman. Any woman, Stephanie."

"Not that kind of nervous."

"Hmph." Now he smiled, and it shocked her system as his blue eyes became amused.

"Just go. Please." She shooed him away. She worked methodically. Chopping, slicing, browning sausage. She used his house phone to call her clinic while she worked, getting an update on Bradshaw and a 'that's my girl' from Mary who thought she was home resting. She was too much the coward to call Brad. He'd ask her questions and she didn't have answers yet to why she was still in John Dake's cabin cooking.

She finished the gravy about the same time the timer went off for the biscuits. She arranged the browned quail breasts, biscuits with gravy, and cheesy sausage omelet on his plate and filled two glasses with orange juice. She put her own plain cheese omelet and buttered biscuits on her plate.

She walked up behind his chair and squeezed his shoulders.

Immediately his hand bolted up to hers, intertwining their right hands.

She gentled at once, felt the swelling, sensed his pain. "What's wrong with your shoulder?"

He just shook his head, watching the TV, holding onto her hand. "One second, it's almost half time."

"Come on Staubach, you can have John's plate since he's not hungry." She slipped her hand free, her nerves dancing wildly.

"You are the most demanding woman I've ever met."

As the recliner retracted she found herself grinning behind his back.

"Come on Staubach, you might just get some of this meal. I have a feeling Doctor Hightower doesn't cook much."

"We'll see, Mr. Dake," she replied from the kitchen table.

He lifted a brow as he sat down and tossed his napkin in his lap. "I had all this stuff?"

"You did," she answered and secretly sighed as she sat down. Her energy was nonexistent. All she wanted to do was eat and get back in bed. She was surprised when John took her hand. Squeezed it as he said, "Thanks," then said a simple grace. There was small talk as they ate. An update on Bradshaw then the weather, the lake, the meal—he thought it was fantastic. There was reoccurring eye contact, smiles, and spaces of silence.

"This was really great," John said eating the last of the omelet. "How did you learn to cook like this?"

"Necessity." She said taking their plates over to the soapy sink already filled with the dirty pans. "If I wanted to eat when I was growing up, I had to cook it myself."

"Latch key kid?"

"Something like that." She was clearing the table.

"Let me clean up. You sit."

"I'll dry if you'll wash." She handed him the sudsy wash rag.

He smiled rolling up the sleeves of his flannel shirt. He was glad she hadn't said anything about wanting to go home yet. He put several pans up on the drain board teasing, "You're getting behind me here, I'm almost done."

"That's okay you can wipe off the counters and the table while I finish up."

"We sure do like giving instructions out."

"That's the way you have to treat people who need to be led in the right direction." She looked at him with a straight face and then turned away, but he saw her grin.

"A woman has never led me in the *right* direction, Dr. Hightower," he teased, placing the last of the dishes on the drain board and rinsing out the wash rag.

"Then you've been following the wrong kind of women, Mr. Dake."

His mother would agree with her, but he bantered back wanting her take on the matter, "And what woman is the *right kind of woman?*"

She shrugged, drying the remaining dishes.

"Eye of the beholder, then?"

Now she shook her head. "There's your problem, you've being using your eyes instead of your heart."

He was looking at her now, not with narrowed eyes but a definite careful study.

"It's what's inside not outside that matters," she advised.

"Hmph."

"Hmph?" She shook her head. "God said you needed help, not me."

"Help?"

"In the beginning. It wasn't good for Adam to be alone, so God gave him a helper. Later He says a good helper is noble. Her help is always to do him good and not harm, so she is trustworthy. Finally, He tells us a noble wife is the crown of her husband."

Things clicked. A hundred things from his past just came together and he said, "King me."

"What?"

He shook his head, motioned for her to go on.

She crossed her arms, shrugged.

"Come on, God said I need some help."

"You believe in God?" she asked.

"Yes," he replied. "Don't you?

"Yes," she answered, "Yes, I believe in God. I'm a Christian."

"So am I. What else does God say about these noble women that crown their husbands? They must be hard to find, like rubies I think Solomon said, right Beauty?"

"If you've read the Bible then you know women are called to be modest."

"That does make them hard to find." And he thought about last night, the modest cut of her dress and the way he'd responded when she'd bent over and revealed more. He hadn't averted his gaze but looked his fill until he almost fell out of his chair like a fool. He felt the conviction; it stung in a place he'd grown numb to for a while. He liked a woman's body, wanted to see more of hers for sure but he also liked the fact that she was modest. Most girls weren't, so he asked, "Why modest?"

"Beauty has a responsibility. God's people understand they shouldn't be sensual. Peter warned women that their adorning should be inward not external. The eternal beauty of a gentle, quiet spirit but women are also told to be strong. Physically and emotionally they should have dignity, a kind of poise or posture."

She said this as she stretched up to the overhead cabinet. She was trying to position the large frying pan under the smaller ones above her head. He grinned as he saw the struggle taking place that her height didn't allow her to witness.

"Not too strong, physically or you'd never need a man." John stepped behind her and took the pan from her hands. "Let me help." He trapped her gently against the counter, easily putting it away.

"So that's what God designed men for," was said with marked sarcasm as she turned to face him.

"If you weren't so contagious I'd show you what God designed men and women to do together," he told her softly. "But we'll have to wait for that. Come sit down and let that food digest with the medication while we watch the last half of the basketball game."

"I really should—"

He took her hand, gave it a tug. "We can't miss this. The Spurs and the Celtics, Sleeping Beauty."

"Look, I'm smart not beautiful—"

"What?" They were walking, he leading her by the hand into the living room with a little tug.

She rushed on. "And if you only knew that I have insomnia and get up every morning by five, you would know that name really doesn't fit me."

"The name fits—S.B... Sleeping Beauty. But I'll compromise, settle on what fits. Come help me out a little while longer, Beauty. God says I need it."

John added some logs onto the fire. She thought he'd sit back in his recliner, but he nudged her and Staubach over on the wide chair and a half and drew up the ottoman, instantly slipping his arm around her to pull her close as he covered her up with a blanket and Staubach settled in at her side. He seemed so relaxed, so comfortable with all this touching and silent staring and whatever it was that was going on between them. She was anything but relaxed; tense and uncertain and exhausted in contrast. But he was warm. And this was cozy. And his dog was sweet. And the basketball game had a rhythm that lulled her to sleep.

Sometime during the game, John also fell asleep. The restlessness melted away as she naturally settled into his arms. He slept deep and dreamless, nurturing his need for companionship as she stayed close to him. John woke up slowly. His right shoulder was throbbing from being kept in the same position so long. He'd shifted and Staubach rose and Stephanie's eyes opened to look up at him. "I'm glad you woke up." He moved her off his shoulder. "My arm fell asleep and it hurts," he explained with a grimace as he moved it, trying to get the blood to circulate into the joint again by flexing his right hand.

"I'm sorry."

"Don't be. It's not your fault."

"What's wrong with your shoulder?"

"I injured it."

Her hands were there, touching gently, feeling, finding the injury. "Here at the AC joint."

"Everything's all loose inside and weak."

"You've got a separated shoulder, John. You're collar bone is completely detached from your shoulder. You should be in a sling."

"Won't help." He shook his head. "I'm having surgery, Wednesday."

"Surgery?" She was massaging the blood back into the muscles with careful, gentle pressure. "This Wednesday? How in the world did you carry me?"

"Single-handedly. You're little. I am strong, Beauty."

"Strong and foolish. Don't tell me it didn't hurt." She was up. "Don't move."

Then she was back with ice. "Cold therapy isn't going to help right now," he told her.

She ignored him and unbutton his shirt, applied the bag, holding it as she sat close beside him again and told him, "You should be wearing a sling."

He frowned.

"Ice helps reduce inflammation and a sling would keep your arm in a comfortable position. Hanging like this must hurt. And the damaged ligaments—"

"Both the AC and the CC are completely torn."

"Which means your arm just hangs heavy." She adjusted its position. "And throbs. It wouldn't do that in a sling."

"Hmph."

She looked at him and said, "You do need help."

It had been sarcastic truth, but he smiled.

"Do you have pain meds?"

"Tylenol 3. Whiskey helps."

She was up again. Then back with a glass of whiskey. "It's Bourbon which is whiskey someone taught me yesterday. And you like it neat."

"Thanks." He took a drink.

"Your chest hurts I bet."

He showed her where. Her hand carefully rubbed out the tired knots formed from over compensating for the joint. "Now I understand why you were so concerned about the timing behind Bradshaw's surgery. Why didn't you say something when you brought Bradshaw in? It certainly would have made everything clear." Her eyes were soft and concerned. "I'm sorry how I mistreated you. This weekend did throw a major curve into your plans." Her hand was still stroking and soothing. "I can keep Bradshaw until you're fully recuperated," she added, "if that's okay?"

"Are you sure Stephanie?"

"I'm sure. I'd love to do it for you."

He smiled. "You would?"

"Absolutely. Is your family going to be with you during the surgery?"

"My Mom will be there. My dad died a long time ago."

"I'm sorry," she said, understanding his pain.

"He was killed in action in Vietnam the fall of 1967. I really never knew him."

"Any brothers or sisters?" she asked.

"No, just me, Mr. only child."

"Um-hm, no wonder."

"No wonder?"

"You're a little spoiled."

"A little," he admitted. "More impatient. I didn't have to wait much or share anything. How about you, tell me about your family."

"A younger half-sister, Samantha. She's getting ready to graduate from law school."

"Your parents must be pretty proud of their daughters. A doctor and a lawyer."

"My mother died twelve years ago."

"I'm sorry. What about your Dad?"

She shook her head. "I have his eyes she said, but I never knew him. He was killed before I was born."

"Then your mother died?"

She nodded. "We spent six years in the system until I gained guardianship of Samantha," she answered, closing the subject. "Are you close to your mother?"

"Yes," he answered simply, then told her, "I'm sorry, Stephanie."

She nodded, accepted. There was a silent moment again, when they simply stared at each other. Her hands working over his injury.

"You're good at this."

"It's getting the blood flowing again."

"By the way, I think your eyes are the most beautiful eyes I've ever seen in my life."

"Thanks. You've got great muscle tone. You'll heal fast." Then she smiled. "If you listen to your doctors. Wear the sling."

He nodded. Finished the drink. Let her keep working.

A loud rumble of thunder sounded outside. John raised his head and looked out the window. Rain mixed with sleet pelted the glass. "Beautiful night. I'll stir up the fire. You hungry?"

"A little," she felt the cold the minute he pulled away and rose, adding wood to the fire, letting Staubach out.

"Soup?"

"A little soup sounds good. I'll help."

"No, you made lunch. I got this." He walked away, and she pulled the blanket tighter around her, glanced at the windows, at the dark night surrounding them. Staubach was back at the door. She rose and let her in then walked to the kitchen. John was standing over the stove and cradling his arm.

She touched his back and said sincerely, "Let me finish this. Can you go find something on the television? I can't work your system."

He gave her a little grin. Poured himself more Bourbon while she stirred the soup. She made him some grilled cheese sandwiches. Found a box of crackers. Served it all up to find he'd switched the channels on the TV to another basketball game.

Staubach came up in between them ready for any handouts and some attention. John told her to quit begging and Stephanie sympathetically pulled the dog into her lap lavishing her with pleasurable strokes.

"I'm not going to take you home tonight." The words were matter of fact as he ate his soup.

"Excuse me."

"I want you to stay here tonight."

"John, it's not good for you to be around me with this sore throat, especially when you're getting ready to have surgery next week."

"I think we're past that now. Besides, I'm not sharing any drinks with you or even kissing you for that matter. I'm not in any danger of getting your Mono."

"I don't have Mono."

"You can sleep in my guest bed again. You told me last night it was the most comfortable bed you'd ever slept in."

"Really, John," she said annoyed.

"Did you sleep 15 hours?" He asked the question as he watched the game, enjoying the banter they were beginning to volley back and forth. "Plus, you don't have much choice in the matter. You're stuck with me."

"I always have a choice. I can walk. There's a trail. I live around the lake."

"I saw you. Thursday. Walking."

She nodded.

"I scared you."

"I didn't know you. And you were angry."

"I couldn't throw the girl's tennis ball. I was frustrated. Hit a tree."

The corner of her mouth curled up. A little smile. Like she knew a secret.

"It hurt. Sang up my arm. I was mad at myself. Was having a very private temper tantrum."

She took the soup bowl, set it aside. She opened his right hand, touched the scars on his knuckles, kneaded his palm muscle then both thumbs worked up his forearm. Her hands moved on to his bicep, a light pressure, careful soothing up to his shoulder, softly going over his chest. "It's sore here," she told him. "You're compensating with these pectorals."

He nodded. She worked the muscle. Fingers careful over the collarbone. "You're completely detached."

His eyes were closed. "That feels good."

She'd moved to his back, deep strokes of careful pressure. "You're tight her too. I'll be careful," she assured as she came close to the joint. "Just let me feel."

"It's a type three injury."

She was still touching him, now under the arm along his side.

"You've got great hands. Should have been a doc, doctor."

"I'm better with animals. People make me nervous." She massaged the muscles in silence then arranged pillows, propping them and pulling him back. Then she moved a small pillow under his forearm, pulled his wrist up. Smiled. "How's that?"

"Horrible." His eyes were staring into her own.

"Horrible?" she countered. "No, physics says if I move your back forward and your arm up—"

His left arm reached out, touched her hair. "If you sit over here, under my left arm and cuddle, I'll feel even better."

They looked at each other, into each other.

"Sit over here," his voice was soft. Softer still he said, "Stay tonight."

She rose with the dishes, went to the kitchen. Worried as she loaded the dish washer and wiped a clean counter cleaner, then prayed because she knew common sense said she shouldn't stay. There were moral reasons and practical ones. But she heated water, waited for it to boil as she looked at his bottle of Bourbon. She didn't drink but she wanted a Toddy. It had felt good. And so did John, the talking and the touching. Her nerves had quieted and now they were rising up again with the uncertainty.

She heard Staubach then she saw John. Leaning in the doorway as his dog rushed up to her by the counter. She pet Staubach, looking at him.

"Please stay." It was the way he said it, softly and a bit uncertain. He didn't look so big standing there in the shadows or so confident. She heard the need. It linked to her own and she just nodded.

"You want to watch something besides basketball? There might be a movie on." The big screen television had two commentators talking about the games of the day as they walked back into the living room.

"Basketball is fine," she answered, drinking the hot water. The taste was plain, but the heat felt good. The thunder sounded in the distance, the sleet singing against the glass. She looked at the dark windows, for a moment thought of the thousands of nights she'd been in a foster home with that acute pain of isolation she'd had to deal with alone, looking out the window and thinking of a day when she'd be old enough to settle in one place and feel safe and secure.

He turned her chin to him. "What are you thinking about?"

"I wanted a Hot Toddy." She gave a little laugh.

"Sorry I don't have any tea."

She poured a splash of his Bourbon into her water and lifted her glass to his. "To your health and mine, I think you said."

Now he smiled. "To better days," he quoted her back. "I liked that better."

"It's what I used to tell myself," she confessed. "That better days were coming." She finished her drink, put the mug on the table and pulled the lap blanket up.

When she sat back, he drew her to his side. "Did they?"

She nodded. "I try to live in the moment now instead of the future." She could hear his heartbeat, feel his breathing. Her hand moved to his chest, to the knot she'd found there as she settled against his side and slowly worked the muscle with careful hands.

He took her hand, interlaced their fingers there against his chest.

She couldn't hear the thunder anymore. She couldn't hear the television either. She could only feel. Feel his arm around her. Feel his warmth, his strength. She wasn't afraid. She felt safe. She exhaled and relaxed. Despite the pain raging in her throat that should have distracted her, or the storm raging outside that should remind her of her unsettled conscience, she let go and experienced the moment. Not the past. Or the future. Just him, holding her, here in this moment. Nothing had ever felt like this.

She didn't understand it and she didn't want to. It wasn't like her to let herself be so completely taken care of. It wasn't like her to let a man this close, to be vulnerable and needy. Weak.

She was just sick, she decided, that's what this was about. She fell asleep telling herself she just needed to be babied.

Later that night she woke up when she felt him place her in bed. The linens were cold, and his warmth was gone. Her hand caught his arm before he released her.

"John, your shoulder—"

"Shh, go back to sleep." He tucked the blankets around her, touched her hair. "Sweet dreams, Beauty."

6

He didn't know who he hated leaving more Bradshaw or the woman, but he knew he had left more than just his dog behind with Stephanie. And amidst his entourage of VIPs, that had gathered to pre-game his surgery and encourage him that everything was going to be fine, his mind kept drifting back to her.

Somehow just being with Stephanie had eased his tension about his surgery. She had explained the medical details of what they would do, and he had listened, appreciating the clear precise way she described things. Her touch had been gentle on his shoulder, testing the injury carefully, feeling precisely the areas of weakness and the strain on the muscles that were compensating. Then she had assured John once everything healed he'd regain his strength and range of motion and leave behind the pain. She promised to pray just that.

Somehow knowing her prayers would include him connected with something untouched in him and her confidence in God had given him peace. She had told him not to worry about Bradshaw and to call if he needed anything. Then there'd been that look in her deep green eyes. Complicated and yet contrasting the normal star-struck idolatry most of the world cast his way. There was interest and intrigue and still a surprising hint of irritation.

There was a mystery to solve here, of who she was and who he really was as well. He'd been found at his worst and maybe so had she. Two strong people suddenly made weak who were learning how to handle things and none too well. She didn't like being sick any more than he liked being injured. He'd been irritated, entitled, superior and a bit pouty and pitiful with his demands. She'd been angry, direct and critical, proud and a bit nervous and skittish. But there'd been a strong mutual attraction, and, in the end, the whole thing had mysteriously only drawn them together. Maybe it was easiest for strangers to find that kind of safe reserved intimacy in their weakness.

"What do you think, John?" His head coach, Mike Merrill ran his hand through his curly chestnut brown hair and cupped the base of his thick former linebacker neck. John had seen that stance a hundred times on the sidelines. Coach was fretting through the options yet seeking his opinion.

"Ah..." John just blinked. He swept the crowded room. A ring of familiar faces and beside his mother stood his best friend.

Honey Cooper gave a chuckle. "Did that cocktail kick in, John?"

And John suddenly felt it. Some soother was moving into his system through his IV line.

"We were talking about changing up the offense," the offensive coordinator, Rob Richardson joked.

"Going with the Option so you can use your legs instead of the arm," his quarterback coach added.

"Disagree with that," one of the players voiced. He was the captain of the offensive line and Paul Anderson reminded them all, "You're forgetting, Dake is turtle slow."

"And you didn't bat an eye at that insult," Neil, his tight end remarked with a chuckle.

His mother smiled, said something in his defense. There was talk about the Wishbone and the Spread offense. But John knew the coaching staff had already been thinking out all the what-ifs in case the news went from bad to worse. Teams lost players to injury every season. It was the nature of the game. And managing those diverse and sudden setbacks was what set teams apart.

Brad Bennett was a master at the personnel managing process. He'd bought the team after the former owner went through a scandal. Returned the organization back to an old school philosophy that success grew out of discipline instead of entitlement and ego. It was no longer an every man for himself superstar philosophy but you were a teammate who had the privilege to play the game of football at the professional level for this city.

And he'd let them down... One and done. Again. The replay started of his last play. He went through all the what-ifs one more time. Then the fear came that this could be it. He could be done. There would be life without football. Or worse yet, seasons playing behind a starter. He'd seen it happen, to some of the best. Knee injuries. Neck and back surgery. Multiple concussions. Shoulder injuries—

"John," Brad called his name. His eyes, that odd purple blue, were full of assurance and they held his, understanding exactly what he needed. "Let's huddle up here and pray."

In a few steps the men drew together. He felt their hands rest on him as his mother took his hand. Then Brad prayed. It was humbling to be in the center of their circle, lying in a bed. Assuring to hear Brad worship God as sovereign and express that they were surrendered to His will in the surgery today. He thanked God for the skill of the surgeon and the compassion of the nursing staff and asked that God work through their hands to heal and protect John from any complication, risk or infection. He voiced his concerns for John's faith to grow through a greater dependence on God's Spirit.

Then he petitioned, "We need a godly woman, Lord, a daughter of the King hand-picked just for this son of yours. John is incomplete. You've said this isn't good. In his weakness honor him with the strength of Your grace with a wife. And let us each live to honor you through Christ our risen Lord. And God's men said—"

"Amen," the group answered and filed out until John was left with Brad Bennett, his mother and Honey Cooper as two nurses walked in and cued it was time.

His best friend leaned in close and promised, "I've got your mom. We'll wait together then see you when you wake up."

They clasped hands, squeezed.

He kissed his mom and assured. "I'm good, mom."

"I know you are." She kissed him again. "You're in really good hands. Trust God to do his work."

"Yes, Ma'am."

He looked at Brad. "Those drugs must have me hearing things. I thought you just prayed for my wife."

"I did." And as they rolled him away Brad said, "*He who finds a wife finds a good thing and receives favor from the Lord.*"

"How was the R&R this weekend at the lake?" Honey asked sitting beside his bed. James Hunnicut Cooper had been his best friend all his life. They knew each other like brothers. Their parents friends before they'd been born. The location of college and careers the only thing that put time and space between them the past eight years.

"Ask Bradshaw," he gave him a goofy smile. His right arm was numb, weak, set in a sling and completely useless now. He was terrified and high as a kite, but Honey was talking him down.

"Alright, alright. Just what did my favorite pup do this time?"

"She got into the groceries."

"She's got a nose now."

"Ate more than her stomach could hold."

"And an appetite."

"First morning there and I had to rush her to a vet."

"Oh?" Honey settled in for the story.

"Who turns out to be- one; a female, two; immune to my smile and three; living in the twilight zone of backwoods Louisiana with no idea of who John Dake is."

Honey laughed. "No special treatment, huh?"

"None." He told him the story.

"Is Bradshaw okay?"

"Fine, thanks to the vet. She's a superstar surgeon."

"What a weekend."

"Oh, it gets better. The vet shows up, guess where? The Bennett's dinner party that Brad coerced me into attend by telling me Linda would get her feelings hurt if I skipped out."

"Alright. Alright." He smiled.

"I try to be nice to the doc, start over, right? I offer her some of Brad's best Scotch; I'm talking the good stuff, because she had this sore throat. She forgot to inform me she didn't drink. Throws up everything."

"You got her drunk?" Honey chuckled then scolded, "Dake."

"Wait, there's more. Stephanie falls asleep in my truck before she can tell me where she lives. So, I take her back to the cabin and put her in bed. Then she proceeds to sleep through the rest of the weekend, contagious because she's got this cold, so no kissing or anything like that allowed. I dropped her off Sunday. She's keeping Bradshaw. Told me to take Staubach so I wouldn't be alone."

"So, I guess now you've got to go back and get Bradshaw."

"Well, Bradshaw's recuperating. Needs to be quiet. Better without Staubach and Stephanie knows what she needs right now. Another vet said most dogs don't survive Bloat and we were lucky to have her as the vet."

"And I'm guessing this little vet is real homely looking too?"

John just gave him a smile. "Drop-dead natural beauty that makes you stare opened mouthed like you were some sort of knuckle head. She's got green eyes." There was a lot more he could say but instead he laid out the problem that was bothering him, "She doesn't know I play ball. Doesn't know anything about me at all, Honey."

The two men looked at each other, there was silence and in it understanding. Honey told him, "There's time for all that."

"She's a Christian, said she'd be praying for me."

"Then she's probably waiting for the good news." Honey held up his phone. "Got her number in your fancy cell phone yet."

"Yeah. It's under S.B."

"Alright." He was thumbing down the list. "Alright." He found it, handed it to him. Stood up and smiled. "It's ringing, Brother."

John shifted immediately. Sitting up a little as he held the phone to his ear.

"This is Doctor Hightower," a voice answered.

"Hi, it's John."

"John." She cleared her throat. "How are you feeling?"

"Pretty good. You don't sound good. Your voice is raspy. Feeling better?"

"Umm. I've been thinking about you. Did the surgery go okay?"

He smiled at the sentiment. "The doctors say it went great."

"Great—that's doctor language for perfect. I'm so glad. Are you in pain?"

"I'm groggy."

"Are you home?"

"They're keeping me one night." His right hand flexed carefully, and he said honestly, "I'm numbed up. Weak."

"That's normal. Everything's asleep right now and needs to rest."

"I don't like weak."

"Then I'll pray for patience," she answered. "Bradshaw is standing right here. Say something to her John."

"Hey, Bradshaw. How's my girl?" He said feeling very stupid that he was talking to a dog on the telephone, feeling that sense of peace again that Stephanie was praying for him.

"Yes, it's John, girl. She's wagging her tail and her ears just went up. She's healing up fine. I've been bringing her home with me, but she really misses you, John."

"She does huh?" He smiled wondering if Stephanie missed him as well. "I miss her. It will be three more weeks before I can get over there. If that's going to be a problem, I can get Linda Bennett to take her—"

"Bradshaw is so sweet she won't be a problem."

"Are you sure? I don't want to put you out."

"I'm sure, John."

"I want to see you when I come. Take you out."

Silence.

"Stephanie?"

"Ah... that might be a problem," she answered.

"Problem? Why because your dating Tim?"

"His name is Phillip."

"I want to see you again."

"I've got Mono, John." There was a pause. "And I'm worried I've exposed you."

"We never swapped spit," he assured her, "Drank after each other—"

"I shouldn't have stayed with you. It was selfish, and I feel horrible."

"Hey," he stopped her, hearing the anxiety he started teasing. "You felt horrible because you were drunk and got sick—"

"We're not talking about that again."

He smiled now. "I can't believe a woman can sleep fifteen hours in my guest bed."

"Are you really going to talk about that again?"

He laughed. And it felt good. "Yes."

"Really."

"I think we should rehearse the whole weekend."

"Should we start with you nailing the tree with your fist?"

"Sure."

"And how pleasant you were in the clinic when we met?"

"Definitely, back woods Cajun country horse doctor, tell me all about duck hunters."

"And..."

"Keep going. You're getting to the good stuff."

"Me and the Hot Toddy."

"It got you to the cabin."

"It probably got you Mono."

"No one but myself to blame for that. And it was worth it."

"You say that now. It's horrible, John. My throat is even worse."

"Why are you at work, Beauty?"

"I can't just stop working."

"Listen Dr. Hightower, you get your sore little throat home and to bed. Who's taking care of you?"

"I'm fine."

"You need somebody—"

"Really, I'm okay. I'm trying to sleep my way clear of it."

"Sleep at work? I doubt it. Do I need to hire you a nurse? I'll call the lady that takes care of my cabin and ask her to help you."

"Don't be ridiculous."

"That's not ridiculous. I don't want you alone and sick."

"I'm okay."

"Yeah. Well, expect me later this week, we can rest up together. We figured out how to do that pretty well at the cabin. I never slept better."

"John." She laughed, and it delighted him. "You really don't need my germs right now. You have to protect yourself from infection to get better," she said with sincerity. "Being around me wouldn't help you heal. I'm sure your mother is good medicine right now."

"Look, I want you over this Mono so I'm not waiting half my life to kiss you."

There was a stretch of electrified silence.

"Stephanie?"

"I'm here."

"Just mark your calendar—John Dake. I'm taking you out to dinner. And Mono's not going to stop me."

"I'll think about it," she answered. "I was thinking about you... I'm glad everything went well today. Will you do me a favor?"

"Anything," he told her.

"Practice, being still. For seven days. Keep your arm as still as you can. Don't compensate with the chest or the biceps. Keep the sling on, ice it on schedule, and just rest. Will you do that?"

"For you. I will."

"Okay. Good. I won't worry then. I'll pray for the time to fly and you to be extra still as God heals. He will, so trust Him and do your part."

"Thanks for caring."

"Thanks for calling. I'll let you get some rest. Don't worry about Bradshaw, she's fine. And take it slow, okay?"

"You take it slow too. I mean it. Resting, at home, no work. I'll check up on you tomorrow, okay, Beauty?"

"Bye, John. I'll be praying for you."

"Beauty, huh?" Honey was giving him a look as John handed him the phone.

"Nickname."

"Already?"

"Her initials; S.B., Sleeping Beauty." He shifted his body carefully. "I watched her sleep and... it just fit. I can't believe she has Mono."

"Who's got Mono?" his mother asked, concern in her voice as she came into his room, Brad Bennett walking in behind her.

John glanced at Brad. "A friend."

"What friend has mono, John?"

"Mom, don't worry."

"I will worry if one of your girlfriends has Mono. It's a highly contagious virus and it wreaks havoc on your body. I had it in college. Fever, chills, a sore throat I will never forget and the worst fatigue, I couldn't even walk up a flight of stairs without collapsing at the landing. Do you know how serious it would be if you got Mono, you could just plan on staying in bed for a good six weeks." Her hands planted on her slim hips.

"Then me and my friend will just hang out together and recuperate."

"You get around that girl and get Mono and you can kiss more than just your off-season goodbye."

"I won't be seeing her for a while so don't worry."

"Well, who is she?"

"She's a striper, Mom," John said, the right side of his mouth curling up.

"That's plain bunk." Helen crossed her arms over her chest. "Honey, do you know this girl?"

"No, ma'am but Mr. Bennett might."

"Well?" She prodded.

"John, I think you might as well tell your Mom. She's not going to rest till she knows."

John took a deep breath. This was just what he didn't need, his Mom finding out about this girl. But Brad was right. She wouldn't rest till she found out now that her curiosity was aroused.

"She's the vet that has Bradshaw."

"The veterinarian?" Helen questioned.

"She specializes in horses and works for Brad."

"And a lot of other stables," he added.

"What's her name?" She looked at Brad.

"Stephanie Hightower," John answered.

"Stephanie . . . what does she look like? James Hunnicut, why are you smiling?"

"I'm sure she's a beauty, Miss Helen."

John told his mom, "She's sick, really sick and alone." He looked at Brad. "Think Linda would check on her?"

"I'll guarantee it," Brad answered.

"Linda, I'm fine," Stephanie assured from behind her desk before she broke into a fit of coughing.

"Oh? I'm not sure you are," Linda replied, coming around the barrier to sit on the edge of her desk and feel her forehead for fever. "I want you at our house until you're feeling better."

"I can't do that. I've got John Dake's dog."

"We've got Sasha." She shrugged. "She'd love the company."

"I can't."

"You won't," Linda countered, crossing her arms. "And it hurts my feelings, Stephanie."

"I don't want to impose."

Linda frowned. "You don't want to slow down. You're going to run yourself right into the hospital."

"I'm only working from noon to four and I've got two vets covering my clients right now."

"You're sick. And you need someone to look after you. Please let me." She held up a hand to silence her. "If you don't, Brad is going to insist on sending someone over to care for you."

There was a look of horror.

"Just a week. Okay. Then we'll see how you feel."

"Linda, I—"

"You're not comfortable imposing, I know." Linda touched her cheek, feeling the dry heat of her fever under the chalky pallor of her skin. "Please don't try to do this on your own. You don't need to anymore. You're not alone. You have us, and we care about you. I'm worried, Stephanie."

"Okay." She nodded. "But I'll warn you, I'm a horrible patient."

Linda kissed the top of her head, stood. "I'll see you after four then."

Stephanie laid her head on the desk. She felt horrible. She wanted to chase after Linda and go crawl in one of her big, soft beds. She swallowed, blanching at the pain. Popped yet another throat lozenge in her mouth. Two more hours.

"Are those for the patient?" Brad asked his wife, drawing her near in the silence of their private sitting room.

Linda showed him the three pair of flannel pajamas she'd found. Each was covered in a silly pattern—the blue with dancing dogs, the mint with singing swans, the yellow with flying cows. They were soft as butter and thick as a blanket. "If I leave them on the bed, do you think she'll take them?"

Brad grinned as he touched a dancing beagle dog. "She'll smile when she sees these. They're perfect, honey."

Linda sighed. "I hope she'll wear them, the fever leaves her chilled."

"How is she?"

"Prickly," Linda answered. She yielded into his embrace, resting her head for a minute on his chest. "She doesn't want to be here."

"Deep down, she does. You know that."

"She's not like Samantha."

"No. She's not like her sister." Brad soothed. "Since her mother died, Stephanie has been the caretaker. She doesn't know how to be cared for, but we're teaching her."

"She's so sick," Linda's voice was soft with worry. "And she just keeps getting up and going on to work."

"That's in her blood too—the drive, the work ethic. She's a survivor, she doesn't know another way." Brad held her closer. "Keep loving her, teaching her, Linda. You're doing a good job. I see a difference, a softening. Life's been hard, it scares her a bit to hope, to trust us, to trust anyone that she's not alone anymore."

"I wish she'd relax, let me help her. She's in so much pain, I see it every time she swallows and she's not eating much. She doesn't have a lot of weight to lose before she's nothing but bones. I know I can't push, but I'm worried," she told him again.

"I'll get the doctor over." He assured. "You know the Lord works in mysterious ways and this Mono might be just the thing to get our Stephanie closer to us."

Thelma stepped into the room. "Mrs. Bennett, I've got Stephanie's soup ready. Want me to take it up?"

"No, I will." She squeezed her husband's hand and went to take another go at it.

She knocked first then opened the door. "Stephanie?"

She was surprised to find her curled up with John Dake's Golden Retriever on the bed. Her green eyes were dull, her face very pale. Linda put the tray on the table, sat softly on the bed. She knew Stephanie was horribly ill, or she would have been sitting up and pretending otherwise. She stroked a hand over her, felt the warmth of the fever then the tremble of her chills.

"I picked up some warm pajamas for you." She showed her, and a small smile did turn her lips. "It will help stop those chills. Which animal first?" Linda grinned. "The dogs or the cows?"

"Dogs," she answered softly. "Thank you. I was about to come down for dinner," she explained.

"I brought it up tonight. You looked tired when you came in." Linda helped her rise then watched as she went into the bathroom to change. She'd seen her take the stairs tonight, stopping halfway up before she gripped the bannister and slowly made her way to the top. All the while the Golden had been right beside her. Now Bradshaw stood up, waiting beside the bed as she watched the bathroom door.

Stephanie came out and said, "These are great. Thanks." She smiled as Bradshaw immediately circled her legs as she walked toward the bed.

"You've still got a fever. Let's take some more Tylenol." She held them out.

Stephanie swallowed painfully.

"Can you take a spoonful of soup? It's warm."

Stephanie nodded. Linda counted five agonizing swallows. She handed her the Gatorade, was pleased that she got another long sip of fluid down.

"Do you want this?" She held out the medicated spray. Watched as she coated her throat then sank back into bed with a sigh.

"Thank you," she whispered.

Linda stroked her hair back, soothed, "Thank you for letting me help you. I want to. I want to take care of you, Stephanie, be here for whatever you need."

Stephanie nodded.

"Can I do anything?"

"No." She squeezed her hand. "I'm sorry, I'm just so tired." She swallowed painfully.

"I know." Linda watched her curl up with John's dog. "I'm going to have the doctor come out tomorrow. There must be something he can give us for your throat. You don't need to be in this kind of pain."

"I just need sleep." Stephanie closed her eyes, took Linda's hand, whispered. "Thank you."

Brad found them that way—his wife holding his adopted daughter's hand.

"Never thought I'd see the day when I'd find you sleeping at noon." Blair's violet eyes danced above her mocking smile. "Much less sleeping in this bed. Don't!" She pressed Stephanie back down with a no-nonsense firmness, tucking the covers up to her chin. "Never mind that *this* bed is *your* bed and mom decorated *this* room just for *you*." She glanced around at the gray walls, the pastoral painting of the hunt, the Chippendale furniture and gorgeous velvet bed linens. "If it takes Mono to get you to spend a few nights here in mom's house, then praise God for His intervention."

"Blair—"

"Don't talk!" She ordered. "I've heard it's painful just to watch you swallow. Anyone with half a brain would know they needed to be home in bed and not trying to work an eighty-hour week with Mono. Your own fault they had to flush you with an IV yesterday for dehydration."

Stephanie sighed. Even that looked like it took effort to Blair. Her mother wasn't kidding—this Mono was serious business. Her sister looked horrible.

"Samantha's worried. I promised I'd come check on you since she has school. She says you're stubborn, but I tell you it is pride." Blair shook her head. "You need to work on getting rid of it before it kills you, Steph. I mean it." They locked eyes, Blair's were compassionate. "I love you enough to tell you what you don't always want to hear, that's part of the sister deal. The solo act is pure pride and completely unnecessary now. You've got a family and we love you. You've got us all worried, okay?"

Stephanie nodded.

"I brought you a smoothie. Want a taste?"

She held the spoon to her mouth. "Try to let it slide down."

"Umm," Stephanie moaned, getting a taste then tightening her face around a swallow. "Thanks."

"So, where'd you go the other night at the party? Heard you got a little sick." She snorted not giving her sister the opportunity to respond. "Dueling shots of Daddy's best Scotch with John Dake, huh? I heard ya'll finished off a fifty-year-old bottle."

"Is your dad mad?"

"He's your dad and John gave him the bottle for Christmas. So, no." She fed her another bite. "But can you believe anybody would pay that much for a bottle of Scotch. You could buy a car for the price of that whiskey. Every shot is like taking a flight to Paris." She snorted then frowned. "I freaked you out. Calm down. It's okay."

"How much was the bottle?"

"Forget it."

"I won't."

"Well, it is hard to forget I guess. Not near as tasty coming up, is it? Wish I could have seen it. You, hugging the toilet." She grinned. "Fooled me good. You looked just fine across the table at dinner. I'm surprised you could eat a bite as close as the man watched you. Those blue eyes of his didn't leave your face. And John Dake has some kind of blue in his eyes." She slipped another spoonful of smoothie between her lips.

"So, what did Phillip think of you sneaking out the back door with Mister Tall, Blond and Gorgeous? Ut, don't talk." Stephanie glared. "Did he kiss you good night?" Stephanie shook her head. "Really?" Blair frowned. "Did he try?"

Now her sister shook her head and mouthed, "I can't talk."

"Um-hm and he's obviously not a bit interested, and neither are you. He means nothing to you, right? Just a client. Since you're treating his dog... oh wait, is this huge teddy bear under the covers snuggled up to your side Bradshaw Dake? And this phone, that's been attached to your hand, is John Dake still on the other end."

She reached for it and Stephanie's pale skin actually blushed a soft pink.

"I heard Mom found him still on the other end again this morning."

"We fell asleep talking."

"Talking," Blair snorted. "All night when you both need to rest. Mom said you were watching television together on the phone, he was explaining the plot of L.A. Law to you since you never watch TV."

She nodded.

"Oh, you're hating this. Stuck in bed with me to play nurse and drill you about John Dake." She suddenly had a thrilling thought and her eyes went as wide as her smile.

"No!" Stephanie saw it and the road those thoughts had traveled.

Blair frowned. "What? Don't talk. I'm not up to anything. You met on your own, I had absolutely nothing to do with this. Besides its obvious he's nothing to you." She shook her head then whispered, "Let him down easy when he comes in, okay? He's waiting in the hall with a dozen roses. Don't talk!" She laughed, seeing the look of shocked horror on Stephanie's face as her gaze darted to the door and a hand stroked over her horrid bed head of curls.

"Blair—"

"I'm kidding! I'd never let a man in here right now. What kind of sister do you think I am?" She laughed harder. "Of course, now that I see he is something, I'll make sure to... okay, don't glare like that. Geez, I thought I could get away with something since you're so sick. Have you told Samantha about John Dake?"

She shook her head.

"She's ready to share that kind of stuff. You know that. Don't talk," she challenged. "And don't think this is nothing. I've got eyes in my head to see it's something. I know you both, and John is just as interested as you are. Don't wait too long to tell Samantha. It will hurt her."

She took her hand, dropping the subject now that she'd gotten her answer. It was thrilling to know a man had finally captured Stephanie's attention. "I'm doing these nails. Ut! Don't talk. I brought blood red." She couldn't keep the snicker from slipping free as Stephanie yanked her hand back. "For your toes. We'll keep your fingernails neutral like you like. How 'bout a bath, you can soak in a bubble bath while I paint your nails?" She tugged her gently. "Come on," She slipped her arm around her. "Oh, I love these cow pajamas! Did I tell you about the ACS luncheon? I was head of security. They gave me an ear piece radio and everything. It was a blast. I busted Sharla St. James cheating on the silent auction." She snickered. "She'll never live down the fact that she thought she could erase Hillary Simon's name and steal a day at the Crescent Spa for a hundred bucks." She snorted twice just remembering the thrill of it and spent the rest of the afternoon lifting her sister's spirits.

It was three full weeks before she was out of bed. Time a blur. The days spent cuddled under the covers with Bradshaw and coddled by Linda. Conserving the small strength she had to go to the bathroom, take her medicine with meals and talk to John Dake on the phone. He'd called every day, checking on Bradshaw. Every conversation starting with, "How's my girl?" She'd answer, "Fine." And he'd say, "I was talking about my dog?" And she'd say, "I was talking about your dog." It was strange that you could hear someone's smile over the phon,e but she knew when he was smiling and when he was impatient. Helping him be still to heal had also forced her to take her own advice and rest. Sometimes at night she'd just silently hold the phone and they'd watch television together, saying little, and if she tried he'd say, "Shh, Beauty don't talk," as he told her a story or read her the paper or an interesting article, usually about sports. She'd often fall asleep holding onto the phone and he teased her she snored, was still there when she woke up. She'd commented about the phone bill and he told her if she mentioned it again he'd just come over and recuperate with her. And she knew he was serious, never brought it up again. She'd often hear people in the background. He had a housekeeper and his mother was there, friends stopped by. And she had Linda tending her and Thelma's cooking and Brad checked on her every day.

He'd offered her an outing on the golf cart down to the barn. Linda had bundled her up and she'd enjoyed the fresh air and the sight of her horse. Her mare was almost ready to foal, and Bradshaw found a friend at the barn she'd brought back to the house. It was something to talk about when he called that night and asked, "How's my girl?"

"Bradshaw found a kitten in the barn. We brought him back to the house." She told him the story.

"Hmph, not much of a cat guy."

"He's cute."

"You like cats?"

"I'm a vet. You should see him chasing this yarn."

"Yarn?"

"Cats can't get enough of yarn. Or catnip." She laughed.

"What's catnip?"

"It's like Scotch."

"Ah. Catnip."

"He's adorable. Bradshaw thinks so anyway."

"I didn't think cats liked dogs."

"He's a kitten. Bradshaw is babying him. She'll be a good mother, will you breed her?"

"Haven't thought that far yet. Do you want kids?"

"A full house. You?"

"A house full. Eventually. Catnip or yarn?"

"What do you mean?"

"Am I like catnip or yarn?"

"Are you catnip or yarn?" she repeated the question. Watched the kitten bat at the fringe of the blanket as she wiggled it above her. "Yarn."

"Yarn?"

"Charismatic, Mr. Charming."

"Ah. Then I guess you're catnip."

"Am I?"

"Like Scotch you said. Is catnip like catwoman? I always liked catwoman."

She laughed. "Meow."

"Say that again."

And she smiled and said very slowly, "Meow."

"Hm, maybe I do like kittens."

"You can take him home next weekend."

"Or you can take him to work with you tomorrow. Half day, right?"

"Yes. Bradshaw's going to make sure we're home early."

"Shouldn't you be at home in bed, little Miss Mono?" Phillip asked from her office door.

Stephanie's eyes rose quickly from her work on the desk, she had piles to go through. "I've been in bed for three weeks straight."

"I heard the Bennett's had to take you in you were so sick. IV and everything."

"I got dehydrated," she nodded.

"Mary said it got critical. Good thing for the Bennetts, huh?"

She remembered Linda's constant presence. It still made her feel warm inside and weepy. She knew Linda cared. She'd seen her great tenderness with Samantha after all hell had broken loose against her sister and Brad and Linda stepped in to adopt them both. She had felt Linda's encouragement and respect as she worked toward her own goals in Vet school. Linda had always been there, for the small and the important. Giving her a listening ear, or imparting her wisdom, or sharing the perfect gift. She loved those pajamas. She'd felt so safe and warm tucked into that bed, tended by the forever-family presence of adopted parents she knew cared deeply for her. She blinked. She loved Brad and Linda Bennett and like Linda said, the last three weeks had been worth the illness for the bond that had been created.

"I'm finally feeling close to normal now that I can swallow again."

"Who's this?" Phillip greeted the Golden Retriever that stood between them.

"Bradshaw." John's dog circled her legs and she stroked her head. "She's recovering from Bloat."

"What?"

"Stomach problems. What's up with you?"

"I want you to meet someone. Got a minute." He waved, and she got up and walked out to the lobby with him.

"Stephanie Hightower, this is a friend of mine from Norman, Oklahoma. Lance just started breeding Arabians."

"Arabians? Takes a lot of blood work to raise good Arabians." She stated with a smile as she shook his hand.

"I'm quickly finding that out."

"I thought maybe you'd be interested in helping Lance get started?"

"I'd love to, once I get over this Mono. I'm still not a hundred per cent. I barely last half a work day."

"Or a dinner," Phillip teased. "Steph left me high and dry at Brad Bennett's dinner party."

"I got sick."

"John Dake took her home," he told Lance.

"Really?"

Phillip gave a nod. "I'd have been jealous, but she really was sick, and I had Brad Bennett's ear so it all worked out." He smiled affectionately. "I'm investing in the Equestrian Park, Steph."

"Great," she just answered.

He'd wanted the connection, asked her if she was going to the dinner with the horse association. She'd invited him, made the introduction. Thought it was business. That he understood this was friendship, but she was sensing a shift as he said, "I know we just started dating but I really appreciate the invite. I made more contacts at that party than I do in a year of business. I owe you for that Steph. Since you're feeling better, I'll take you into Shreveport and say thanks with dinner. Let's go out this weekend?"

"I've got plans." She just smiled.

"Then I'll call you. We'll go out soon, okay." He'd taken her hand, gave it a squeeze as he leaned over to kiss her.

She pulled back, "I'm still contagious."

He kissed her cheek anyway. "I think you're over that now." Squeezed her hand. "I'll call you."

She just nodded. Stepping back. Frowning after he left.

"That was smooth," Mary said.

"It felt awkward."

"I didn't know you were dating Phillip."

"I didn't either." She frowned. "He said he was looking for a business connection. It was a favor not a date. He thinks it was a date." She looked at Mary. "I don't date."

"Then what are you calling your plans Saturday night with John Dake."

"Dinner," she answered and walked back to her office.

John fingered the new mustache and beard. He wondered what she'd think. He'd been growing it since he left her, and he'd been telling himself it was just because he couldn't use his right hand to shave, but he had a barber who could keep him clean shaven and a stylist who kept telling him lumberjack wasn't a look they were after to get magazine cover shots.

John didn't care. It was a disguise. And looking at himself in the mirror he felt the guilt and the sense of urgency that it was time to come clean. He and Stephanie needed to talk about who he was and what he did. He needed to tell her tonight. Before someone else did.

But he didn't want to talk about football. He wanted to keep this going a little longer. Stay in the Twilight Zone of back woods Louisiana and shut the rest of the world out. Just be normal. He was entitled to a little normal.

And she was entitled to the truth. But the truth was, he wasn't sure how Stephanie would handle it. And that made him nervous. He took a deep breath as he pulled into Stephanie's long drive off the Parish Road. It led to a small house with a covered front porch on several wooded acres near the lake. He had asked her over to his house for dinner. She had suggested a steak house that had an attached dance club. John had agreed. Foolishly, agreed, to go out in public when he'd wanted to bring her to his cabin and... did he really want to admit the word that filled in that blank was—cuddle. Yeah, he was thinking about just that, how long it would take him to get her and his girls all snuggled up. Just the four of them. Alone. In that wide chair. All cozy. And they were going out to a steak house with a dance hall...

Did he have a death wish? A John Dake sighting could definitely be the death of the very fragile beginning of this. She'd know who he really was. He didn't want that yet. So, he'd purposely grown the beard, changed his clean-cut famous look and camouflaged as best he could with cowboy hat and boots and the worn starched blue jeans with a plain shirt. He looked at the bouquet of flowers he had bought at the small-town florist. He didn't want the traditional roses, so he had selected tulips in a soft pink. He thought she'd like them, but suddenly he wasn't sure. He wanted to say thanks, the flowers seemed a nice way, would she understand? Read more into this? Was there more to this?

Good night, Dake, flowers... and nerves?

He was acting like a seventeen-year-old kid. He took a deep breath and stopped thinking. Just went on automatic, played through it, letting muscle memory move on as he grabbed his jacket and the silly flowers and knocked on her door.

Bradshaw flew out to meet him as she opened it. He crouched down lifting the bouquet safely up to her. "I got you a little something. Hey Bradshaw, how have you been girl, huh?" He loved on her, hugging her close with his left arm, his right still secure in the sling. Bradshaw was kissing him, excited and affectionate.

"Thank you, John, they're beautiful."

"You're welcome," he looked up. Smiled. So glad to see her. Watching her gaze sweep his face. Feeling oddly off balance and hesitant, like she could see right through him. And he wished he'd shaved, come clean on the phone. Told her weeks ago, or yesterday who he was, so there was nothing between them. He gave her his smile. "You look well."

"I feel great. Come in. Bradshaw," she called, and the dog obeyed. Leading the way inside the house as Stephanie walked into the kitchen and put the flowers in a vase. John was glancing around, staying back, needing to get himself together as much as he wanted to investigate her space.

Her house was cottage small and comfortably neat. All the furniture was antique, nothing matched but everything seemed to have its place and work together to look really nice. From the simple hardwood floors to the softly colored walls, her home was cozy. The living area had a pine chest that was placed in front of a small two cushion chintz floral sofa. A tall pine armoire stood against the opposing wall.

Glass French doors were opened revealing a study that had a desk with a tall backed leather chair behind it. Shelves of books covered one wall and a square window the other that looked out on the lake. John walked into the study noticing the wealth of reference books. He was surprised to find so little on horses and so much on God. She had a shelf of current best sellers too. The titles made him smile. So, she liked biographies and order. Everything precisely, alphabetically in place.

Squared to the corner of her desk was a single sheet of paper. At the top was the word, 'Budget', and he followed the columns of categories that started with a tithe and ended with an offering. She was a generous giver, a moderate spender. And the past month was about as close to zeroing out as possible. Brad said she was a perfectionist and it delighted him to tilt the paper a bit, then push a few books out of line as he strolled by, touching things. He had a curious need to leave his mark here and there within her house and walked through another set of glass French doors into her bedroom.

The pretty room fascinated him. A tall headboard rose almost three-fourths of the way to the ceiling. The double size bed was small and covered in a floral comforter. A mirrored vanity that matched the bed displayed only a silver brush and a crystal perfume bottle. John reached down and picked it up inhaling the fragrance. It was her and he noted the name on the bottle before he put it down.

A small chest of drawers had a single picture on it. Blair stood between Stephanie and another woman. The unknown girl had silk straight dark hair. Her eyes were an unusual golden green set in an exotically beautiful face. He decided she must be Stephanie's sister, Samantha. In the corner was a chair draped with a quilt. A brass floor lamp and small table with two books were next to it. One was a Bible, the leather really worn, the volume opened easily in his hand. Its yellowed pages fragile with inked notes scrolled throughout the pages in different hand writing. He read a date next to a Proverb with the words, "Promise kept. Hallelujah!" from April 29, 1956.

"There you are. I thought you decided to take Bradshaw and run."

"No, just snooping around." Finally ready to look at her now that he'd worked out the nerves, John smiled and carefully put down her Bible to meet her gaze. "Family Bible?"

"Yes. My mother's and before that, her mother's."

"Your place is... pretty," he decided. The way the neat and cozy and curious little feminine things all came together. Just like her.

He walked to her, his system quickening with every step closer. He remembered her like a china doll, pale, fragile, pretty. Now color had been added, a deep glow to her skin that washed out the pale and dismissed the marks of fatigue and sickness. Her skin wasn't pale at all but warm, peaches and cream and in those dark green eyes was an eminent energy and within it he saw intelligence, confidence, strength and a certain tenderness. He wanted to know more and more and here he stood showing only less and less of who he really was. He swallowed. His hands sweaty and his heart beginning to pound.

"You look... well rested," he finished, realizing suddenly how sick she must have been, how alive and healthy she looked now. A rush of belated concern made him step closer.

"I'm feeling much better."

He nodded as his gaze skimmed her face. He'd thought she was beautiful, he'd been wrong, she was more than just a pretty face and applauding her beauty would just seem to take away from who he was finding her to be, so he struggled to find anything to say.

"I'm glad," finally came out and he felt like a tongue-tied moron as he wiped his sweaty palms on his jeans and took her hand.

"Thanks." She had been ridiculous about this whole thing tonight, shot with nerves, restless and anxious as if this was the first date of her life. And maybe it was... she'd never been so... excited—is that what she was feeling—about a man. So, mixed up with trepidation and nerves, sweaty palms and a pounding heart. He'd handed up flowers, avoiding her eyes, almost anxious to be... gone.

Then why the flowers? To say thanks, of course, for keeping Bradshaw. Perhaps this wasn't a date, just a dinner, a friend saying thank you—and she was like Phillip, wanting this to be more than just an obligation. Maybe she'd read this all wrong, John was certainly acting distant. There'd been a stab of hurt and uncertainty as she'd filled a vase and turned to find him gone. She'd irrationally thought he'd left, but Bradshaw was waiting with her in the kitchen.

Uneasiness assaulted her again as she realized he'd toured her house alone and was now looking over her bedroom. She'd given the room a quick glance, knowing it was neat and nothing personal was lying around. Then he'd smiled and the jolt of it made those dreaded butterflies begin to dance inside her again. Attraction announced itself, loudly, clearly and doubt shadowed her heart with a little ache of dread. She'd read this wrong. He wasn't attracted to her. He was just here to claim his dog and say thank you.

Then he'd wiped his hands on his jeans. Was he nervous too? The thought made her relax a little. Then he'd taken her hand. And his gaze had caught hers and there was that moment as she looked into his eyes that she realized this attraction was mutual.

"You look really," there was a little male sound, half laugh and half growl before he told her, "good. Pretty. Beautiful."

"Thanks." She felt the heat of his hand holding her own, watched his gaze go fierce and probing and beneath it a small part of the John she thought she knew finally broke through the face cloaked with a well-trimmed beard. The word beautiful echoed and speared her mind. He'd called her beautiful again, but with a different tone this time, as if the declaration was for him instead of her.

"You look . . ." Her hand lifted to his cheek, stroked the finely manicured beard that covered his face. "Just like a duck hunter."

He looked away. "Like it?"

"It hides your handsome face."

He brushed his whiskers across her palm, his blue eyes dancing above it. "Handsome?"

"Yes," she answered, "I remembered something about a smile." He gifted her with it and she nodded. "That would be the one. I got us reservations. There's only one steak house in town. It's connected to a dance hall. It's always crowded on Saturday nights. And a band plays, so it can be loud. I asked for a quiet table, they laughed and couldn't promise anything. And the foods not very good," she was rambling because she was nervous. But she'd made a plan and she was sticking to it, so she told him. "So, I thought maybe we could just stay here."

"Yes." The word was pure relief as he stepped closer.

She said, "I cooked." At the same time he said, "I could grill."

He smiled. "What did you cook?"

"You told me your favorite was pot roast. I made pot roast."

"Seriously?"

She nodded. "Hungry?"

"Suddenly, I'm starving."

"Okay then. Let's eat."

She walked away. Tossed her hair over her shoulder to look back at him and caught him staring. "Coming?" Now she smiled at him. Bradshaw pranced to her, circling and excited.

And John just nodded, slowly smiled and followed her to the kitchen.

"Can I get you a beer?"

"Beer?"

"They don't sell hard liquor in town, so I got beer." She named his favorite brand. "It's what you like, right?"

"I thought you didn't drink and how do you know what I like?"

"It was in the refrigerator at your cabin." She walked away, and he watched her again. Those long legs in old denim, the stitching on the back pockets accentuating her subtle curves. Levi's had never looked like that before...

And dinner had never smelled like this.

"Is that bread?" he asked.

"Pillsbury," she answered as she served dinner. Her table was small, and the pot roast was steaming. There were small potatoes, little onions and baby carrots under gravy and in a basket were hot rolls. Beside his plate she placed a bottle of his favorite beer.

He gave her a one arm hug as he said, "This looks great, Stephanie," then pulled out her chair before he took his seat and held out his hand saying, "I'll bless the food, okay." She bowed her head and he prayed, "Father God, I'm speechless. Impoverished to properly give you praise so let me thank you instead for Your healing power. Thank you that Stephanie is well. That Bradshaw is alive. That my shoulder is healing. Thank you for this food and the hands that provided it, may it nourish us for your service to honor You for Your glory. In Jesus name. Amen."

"Amen. Thank you, John," she told him when he finished. He praised her cooking. The food was excellent. They lingered over the meal. The table cozy and the conversation catching up over events from the past two days. She had cobbler and ice cream and they left the dishes soaking in the sink to go enjoy the fire. John sat on the floor and she said, "Don't you want to sit on the sofa?"

He glanced at the small love seat. "That's not a sofa and I'm not sure it would hold me." He patted the floor. "Sit here, it's warm and the sofa is a better back rest."

She sat down beside him and Bradshaw immediately joined them, indecisively circling them both as she looked at John then Stephanie. "I think Bradshaw has become a little attached to you. She'll probably be mad when I tell her we have to go home."

"Um," Stephanie said rubbing the dog's head with both hands as she lapped at her mouth.

"Now, that's no fair," John pouted, "Bradshaw gets to kiss you? Am I ever going to be able to kiss you?"

"Is that the only reason you're interested in me?"

"Who said I was interested." He returned playfully, looking at her with a smile. Then he teased further, "Are you asking me what my intentions are, Miss Hightower?"

"I want you to be honest."

The word made him need to hide. He leaned to his left and rolled down to his back, looking at the ceiling because she was just so infuriatingly... challenging, yet vulnerable and just honest enough to disclose facts but hide feelings and the combination caused him to feel things that were foreign and frustrating, protective and irrational. He wanted to impress and woo her, seduce and claim her. There was a rising lust edging into his good and honorable intentions. As Bradshaw sniffed him out, he covered his eyes with his left arm.

And this whole problem could be solved if he just moved his arm off his eyes, sat up and started talking. But it was so much safer to stay just like this, with his arm over his face and his eyes closed as he told her the truth.

"Honestly, Stephanie, I'm attracted to you. I find you very challenging and I want to play this right—"

"Play this right?"

There was silence. He opened his eyes. Moved his arm. Looked at her. She was leaning over him with a look that had his inner dialogue going 'ut-oh'.

"You think this is a game? Well let me take the initiative and *challenge* you with some honesty. I'm not playing games. I'm not playing anything. I'm not like you, playful. I don't play. I'm serious. And smart. Seriously smart, honestly. And I'm honest." *Ouch.* "And you need to know if you think you're going to play this right and get anything more than a kiss in two weeks, I'm afraid you're going to be very disappointed."

Now he sat up. "Beauty—"

"No." She was shaking her head. "I've needed to tell you this." She looked him directly in the eyes and her voice was firm, but he could see her pulse fluttering in the slender column of her neck. It softened something in him, made him reach out to take her hand and steady them both. "Don't be charming. I'm serious."

"So am I. That's what I was trying to tell you…"

How did he tell her? That she was real, that this was normal and authentic and for the first time in a really long time he felt like someone was connecting with him and not with just who he was. She even got mad at him. Who did that anymore? And nothing would come easy here with her, he'd have to work. And the things in life you worked for mattered most. "That you interest me. The way you… interact with me. You say what you mean—"

"Then you should know," she told him frankly. "I don't," she waved, "date."

And he saw that little flutter in her neck again. "You haven't had a lot of time with your career, Dr. Hightower."

"Yes, I've worked hard to get where I am, but I don't date, John."

"You don't, date?"

"I don't believe in casual dating or casual sex or kissing that leads to casual sex."

"Hmph. So, you're that kind of girl. Well I guess I'll be going." He acted like he was going to get up but instead he wrapped his good arm around her and drew her in close to him. She wasn't laughing. She wasn't even smiling. But he was. It was a soft expression of understanding not of ego. "I'm kidding."

She wasn't laughing.

"And I see you're serious…" His eyes searched hers. "And honestly, I don't feel like this is casual. Do you?"

She just looked at him.

"I'm not after casual with you," he said it clearly. "And isn't this a date?"

"You told me you were taking me out to say thank you."

"Then I still owe you dinner."

"You gave me flowers. Said thank you and you're very welcome. So, there's no more obligation."

"Okay, then what should I do if I want to see you again?"

"You should ask me."

"Will you see me again?"

"Yes," she answered.

"How long are you contagious?"

"Two more weeks," she answered. "Why?"

"About the kissing, you know the Bible talks about kissing. When Jacob met Rachel. He kissed her. It's a biblical expression."

Her eyes narrowed a bit. "Is it?"

"There was a combination of feelings going on there. She was beautiful in form and face and seriously smart and honest. And her work ethic, family heritage of faith and willingness to help him was very attractive and challenging to Jacob. He fell for her. Right there at her father's well. Read it."

"Hmph," she mocked him. "I will. In the King James version."

And she was up, coming back with her family Bible. Sitting right down beside him again as he tucked her under his arm and she read aloud from Genesis. *"And Jacob kissed Rachel, and lifted up his voice and wept. And Jacob told Rachel that he was her father's brother and that he was Rebekah's son—"*

"See."

"After tricking his father, stealing his brother Esau's blessing and being forced to leave his mother, Jacob had been running for 400 miles when he happens upon family. This is more about weeping for joy than kissing a girl."

He carefully took the Bible and showed her. "And yet in just a few verses right here, it says..."

His finger swept the words.

"I know the story, Mr. Duck Hunter." She patted his check. "The question is, behind this beard are you Esau or Jacob, hmm?"

"I'm John Dake. Heard of him?" He pressed his face against her hand.

"I've heard a lot about him lately. I liked those conversations."

"Me too." And he told her honestly, "There's nothing casual about my intentions. I'm going to keep calling you. I want to see you again. And I respect you, Stephanie. But, how will we get to know each other if we don't spend time together? And when we spend time together, I'm going to do what comes natural, and you're going to have to set the guidelines. Is that fair?"

"You might not like my guidelines."

"You might like what comes naturally." His smile blazed.

She finally laughed. "John, that Mr. Charming smile of yours is up to no good."

"Mr. Charming smile?"

"You know exactly what I'm talking about. I can still see that smile underneath that beard. I'm sure you think you can get anything you want with that smile."

"Cuddle with me." He was still smiling.

"I knew it," she laughed.

"Cuddling came natural for us. Right?" She ducked her head now, waves of dark curls hiding her face. He just drew her closer to his body, whispered, "Right."

"I want you to be comfortable, rest your arm."

It was the first time she'd mentioned his shoulder, looked at his sling.

"You want to inspect the surgeon's work?"

"Absolutely." She helped him up and they settled on the sofa, Bradshaw on one side and Stephanie on the other. He let her investigate, her hand moving over his chest, shoulder, arm and back not letting him move his arm or remove the sling. She'd warned him how mad she'd be if he wasn't wearing his sling like he was instructed when he came today. When she was satisfied, she snuggled in, and he loved the way she softly clung when he drew her under his arm.

They talked long into the night. Stephanie told him about her job in more detail and shared her excitement about her own mare that was getting ready to foal at the Bennett's barn. John just listened, enjoying the rare occasion to hear about someone else's life instead of always being asked about his own. He kept waiting for the right moment to transition into his confession. Kept looking for the opportunity to tell her about his career, but it never happened. Tonight, he was just a man, exploring this wonderful woman.

He watched the firelight strengthen the depth of green in her eyes. There was a need to keep her warm, to keep her talking. He caught the edge of the lap blanket she'd covered up with, lifted it once again to tuck over her shoulder as she told him about her love of swimming. It was her exercise of choice. She'd competed in high school—free style and the breast stroke. He smiled, his fingers playing with her hair. Another woman, and his hands would have traveled at will. But with Stephanie, he was prudent—keeping his touch isolated to her hair, finding it was marvelous to play with and her face, intrigued with her bone structure and the softness of her skin, the lace of her lashes, the tiny indention in her chin that complimented the symmetry of her heart shaped face. His touch would stall her words at times and they'd fall into that warm silence of just looking at each other. Then he'd gently nudge them on with another question.

He'd never been so aware of a woman before—of how she responded to his touch, of what she liked, of what made her nervous, or would send her pulse to a flutter in her throat. He'd never listened with such focused attention before—not waiting to talk or assuming, or finishing or judging, he simply listened with a need to know her.

They talked about politics, Texas and their favorite places there. She preferred chicken to his beef, but they both liked Mexican food. She couldn't sing or carry a tune and she showed him by impersonating Elvis then he bantered back his talent by trying to harmonize until they both laughed.

She liked classic comedies, Lucy being her favorite. They talked about *I Love Lucy* episodes, then Sam's adventures in *Cheers*.

"You need your sleep," he told her when a clock softly chimed three times and she clung a little closer. He told her, "I'm going to leave Bradshaw here. Come get you both for breakfast tomorrow." She nodded, and he held her tight for a moment more then kissed her brow. How startling and simple that the greatest pleasure of his life thus far was to spend an evening before a fire with Stephanie Hightower.

The soft light of winter's dawn illuminated the room. She knew it would be early, just as she knew she'd never return to the hazy world of dreams with so much on her mind. But this morning she nestled under the covers instead of bursting forth to start the day. Bradshaw was warm and soft beside her. Tonight, she'd be back to sleeping alone. And this morning she was wondering when John would come and what would happen when he left with the dog?

She was clueless on how things worked in the dating world. Would days turn to weeks as she paced by the phone hoping he'd call? What were the rules? He'd annihilate her in a game she knew so little about... but this shouldn't be a competition or a game. Couldn't she just be herself? Did there really have to be games and strategy involved?

She'd told him she wouldn't play games. That meant honesty should be a strong part of this. Her heart beat faster. She was having trouble accepting the honest truth herself, how could she begin to explain it to him.

I'm attracted to you. You do something to me no one else ever has before— you make my heart race and ache and hope. I'm scared to death... but in your arms, I've never felt so safe. I love the way that feels—safe—I haven't felt safe in a very long time... since my mother held me.

Tears were being fought and she carefully slipped from the bed. She sank into her office chair, pulling the quilt she kept beneath the desk around her legs. She opened her Bible and read Jacob's first encounter with Rachel. There'd been a kiss. Then she went to the only place where she knew there was another, the Song of Solomon. For the first time she understood the lover's dream. She related to the anxious need of the bride, of the love-sick feeling that was so all consuming. When would the bridegroom come...

She turned to the window and prayed silently, deeply. She thanked God for her sisters, then Brad and Linda Bennett. They had been an unexpected blessing during the darkest valley. Would John be an unexpected blessing amid her mountaintop?

The main events of her life had come unexpectedly. Her mother's death. Samantha's abduction. The Bennett's support. John was yet another thing in her life she hadn't expected. He had caught her by surprise, and the feelings he was producing she barely understood.

She acknowledged the fear and stepped out in faith. She asked for wisdom and courage, protection, because suddenly she realized how harsh a broken heart could feel. She thanked God for the many blessings He was pouring out on her.

And then she paused, because there was a pain that could bear down on her—at how much her sister, Samantha still suffered and what she could have done to prevent it ever happening. The ache of grief made the bite of guilt all the stronger.

Bradshaw barked at the door and she looked out the window to the lake and saw his dog. Staubach was running after a ball, John walking behind her on the trail as he came toward her house. He wore a hat and a hoodie and a warm smile when he saw her come out the back door with Bradshaw.

"Morning." He smiled. "Sleep okay?"

"Yes. You?" Bradshaw was circling John and excitedly interacting with her sister. He tossed a ball. The girls raced to retrieve. They watched the dogs, smiled at each other as he reached out and took her hand, drew her close.

"Cute PJ's. But this quilt is hardly a coat."

"I should change."

"Do that. We'll walk to my cabin. Make breakfast at my place."

"I can cook."

"Yes, you can. I want a big breakfast. Biscuits and gravy. Omelets. The works."

"We'll be stuffed."

"Then we'll cuddle up with the girls and catch a nap."

"Will we?"

"Someone kept you up late last night."

The girls were back, Staubach had the ball. John took it and tucked it into his pouch as he walked her inside the house. "That's the plan. I thought about it all night. I didn't sleep," he told her as they went inside. "I want you to know I'm serious about this, you, breakfast, the nap. There's nothing casual about any of it and I want to talk some more today."

They were still just looking at each other when the phone rang. It took her a minute, to step back, away then she had to rush to catch the phone. "This is Stephanie. What? You're sure. Yes, I trust you to know when a horse is in labor, Brad." She gave a laugh. "I'll be right there."

She smiled at him. "My mare is in labor!" Then she frowned. "I'm sorry, John, I've got to go."

"I'll come with you."

"Are you sure?"

"Yes, but you should change first, doc."

"Are you sure you're good to do this, John?"

"Just takes one hand to hold the halter, Doc," he answered. He didn't tell her he'd been here before. That he'd been raised on a ranch and seen animals born. He didn't say a word. Just followed her directions and watched her work, kneeling in a stall padded with hay. He was stroking the mare's neck gently with one hand as he looked down the horse's body at Stephanie. All those long curls were in a crazy knot at her neck and she was in the black coveralls with the red embroidered on the left chest. Her eyes were bright with excitement and singly focused on her task, not noticing that Linda was even now videoing the event and Brad was standing ready with his Nikon camera. Brad had unhooked the rectangle of satin fabric with the large curvy double B's across the stall door to give the onlookers a better view. But Stephanie's attention was on the mare.

"You're doing a great job, John. Come on Runabout," she cooed to the dark bay mare. "We're almost there, girl. I can see the tips of her hooves. This foal is getting ready to make its debut. Remember, when she drops the foal she's going to want to get up pretty quick. Be ready." She glanced at him.

"I'm ready."

The mare rocked her powerful neck back and forth as if she was about to get up. "Easy, it's all right girl. Easy Runabout, easy," Stephanie soothed holding the mare's rear leg and backing away slightly. The tips of two small hooves were closely followed by a white tipped nose encased in a translucent bluish sheen sack. The foal seemed to just slide out, growing wider as it came. Stephanie let the foal come not aiding the natural process. She knew it would be just moments and the colt would be completely born.

"She's almost there. Come on girl, you're doing great, Runabout." She encouraged. "Okay John, let go of the halter. Keep your hand on her neck so you can tell when she's going to get up. I don't want you squashed by my mare."

As she instructed him, the rump of the foal softly fell onto the thick hay. The mare laid there for a brief instance before rising sluggishly to her feet, John aiding her up with his good hand on the halter as he too stood.

"There's the afterbirth," she announced as John came beside her to the stall wall. "Let's see what momma is going to do." Together they watched Runabout turn and sniff at her first born, nudging it slightly. She softly licked at the head of the foal peeling the coating from the newborn. Then as if the very taste of her babe relayed an instinctive message, she more aggressively began to lick and clean the colt.

Runabout nudged it, she whinnied softly as if to welcome him into the world. The dark foal batted his doe like eyes looking toward his dam. On flimsy and fragile legs, it tried to rise. His back side came up slowly and then he extended one front leg at a time. All four legs were marked with soft tan socks soon to turn white.

"That's incredible," he took her hand and squeezed. "I still can't get over the fact that these animals literally get up immediately. Look at Brad, Beauty, he wants a picture."

"What?" She saw the Bennetts. Gave a wave.

"Here." John pulled her forward, crouched down with her near the foal. The newborn standing, just as the mare reached down and Brad said, "I got it. That's great. He's beautiful just like his father. Look at those legs, Stephanie," Brad said excitedly. "He'll be winning some races in two years."

"Someone has high hopes now," Linda added.

"High hopes," Stephanie smiled. "I like that, Linda. What do you think?" she asked John as the foal slumped back into the hay. Runabout spoke again to the little colt, encouraging him as she smoothed his coat and stimulating his circulation. "That's it, momma. Get him up."

Slowly the foal rose shaking as he stood. Runabout softly nudged him to her supply of fresh milk. He suckled for a short period of time before his trembling feeble legs just gave out.

"That was well done, High Hopes." She reached out with her hand and very softly stroked the still damp coat. She spoke to the mare reassuring the horse of her presence. The mare snorted down at the doctor sniffing her hand as she touched the new creation.

"Okay I get a hint. You did good, girl." She moved her hand to stroke the mare's nose. Stephanie picked up the placenta and spread it out on the hay making sure none of it had been left inside the mare. Confident that it was intact, she administered a shot of antibiotics to both the mare and the foal. She took a final glance at the new colt and turned to leave the stall.

"We got the whole thing on tape," Linda told her.

"And some great photos."

"Let me take one more," John requested. "The three of you stand there." It was a little tricky one handed but he got the shot of her with the Bennetts and the horse and foal.

"Thank you." Brad smiled as he took the camera.

"Look at that," Linda pointed at the Goldens. They'd come out to greet them in the alley way of the barn and between them stood the little kitten.

"Is that Yarn & Catnip?" John asked her.

"That's him." She scooped the dark gray kitten up. He had one white paw and a white marking on his nose. She cuddled him and looked at John as she said, "Your girls love this little guy."

"His eyes are green." John gave him a stroke.

"Are they? Hmm. You should take him back with you." She tried to pass him off.

He slipped the kitten inside her coveralls, "You should take him home so you're not alone."

"Cats belong in barns not houses."

"Office cat. Take him. I'll feel better if you're not alone. And the girls can see him next time."

"Are you staying for dinner, John?" Linda asked.

"I wish I could." He took Stephanie's hand now. "But I have to get back. I have rehab early tomorrow morning."

"We'll see you soon then," Linda smiled, tucking her arm into Brad's as they made their way from the barn.

"Thanks for helping me," Stephanie told him.

"It was an incredible day, Dr. Hightower. A great weekend." He drew her closer. "I wish I could stay but I need to stay on schedule. I want out of this sling as soon as possible."

"I know." Under his left arm she settled against his chest and held him, confessing, "It was a great weekend."

"I want to see you again," he revealed. "I enjoyed last night. The dinner. The fireside chat. I kept you up too late."

"And I kept you here too long. You need to get home."

"I want to tell you something. Hold here. Just a minute more." And she surprised him, curling into his body as he tucked her under his arm. "I like holding you... it's been awesome to just hold you. You feel good." His voice was low and soft. "The way your hair smells, and your skin... here." He touched below her ear, brushed her neck, tipped her face up to look at him. "You're beautiful. Here." He studied her cheekbones with a tender finger then touched the place over her heart, remembered her words about what God said was a beautiful woman. "And here. Inside. It radiates from your pretty eyes. Did you know that?" His gaze came back to her and he stated, "There's strength and wisdom and... tenderness." He nodded. "Your heart is tender and a little bit unsure of me, my motives. Because we've taken this so slow I've seen that, Stephanie."

"I need slow," she told him in a whisper. "I need to know," she looked at him now. She wasn't a coward, but it took more courage than she ever imagined to speak the truth of her heart. "What this is?"

"We decided it's not casual," she wasn't sure if he was telling her or himself. "And it's okay to go slow. To talk and listen, I love hearing about your life, learning about you. And I need to tell you more about me. So, we'll figure out what this is in time." Then he whispered in her ear, "But I think most people call it dating." And he brushed a kiss there and promised, "So you might need to rethink the dating clause, okay?"

"Okay." They'd begun to walk, holding hands as the dogs kept pace.

"Call you tomorrow," he said at his Bronco. He'd fetched it midday, packing up and coming back to the barn while Stephanie stayed with the laboring mare. They'd shared lunch, waiting for nature to run its course through the afternoon. Now it was growing dark.

She said goodbye to both his dogs then he told her again, "Take the kitten home." He smiled when her eyes went wide. "He's still in your coveralls. Lucky fool."

"Oh! Lucky Fool where'd you go?" She drew him out, cuddled him up to her face. Both sets of green eyes looking back at him. Then she said, "I'll take him to the office with me. Be careful driving home."

John sighed when he saw the silver Cadillac parked in the usually empty stall in his four-car garage. He exhaled a long breath, glanced at the clock. It was eleven, maybe she went to sleep already, but he could hear voices from the television. He walked into the living area.

"Hi, Mom," he said.

"I was getting worried about you." She met him with her usual tight hug and kiss.

"I got off a little late."

"I see you picked up Bradshaw." She leaned down to pet her. "But I doubt this trip to Louisiana had much to do with these girls. How is your friend feeling?"

"Much improved. When did you get in?"

"I drove down yesterday morning. I'm helping Nancy Hilton in the United Way campaign on Monday, remember?"

"That's right."

"I have sandwiches waiting in the refrigerator and a pasta salad since Hattie took the weekend off."

He walked into the kitchen. "Want anything?"

She said no, but he knew better. The interrogation should begin any minute due to his lack of creditable information.

"How's Brad and Linda doing?" she asked, taking a seat at the bar along the kitchen counter.

Yep, here it comes.

"Great, Linda told me to give you her best."

"Does she know Stephanie?"

"The Bennetts took her in when she got so sick, so they must know her pretty well. I told you she works for Brad and is friends with Blair." He took a big bite out of the first sandwich.

"And she's feeling better?"

"Um-hm." He nodded, eating.

"What does she look like?"

The vision instantly came to John's mind and he took another bite despite the fact he still had a mouthful. "She's pretty."

"Elaborate for your mother. Describe her to me."

"Tall brunette. Green eyes. Spectacular body," he said bluntly.

"What's she like?"

"She's great."

"John Paul," she shook her head. "Why is it so hard for us to talk about some things?"

"Because women have always been a challenging conversation with you. No one's good enough."

"That's not been the problem with your women," she corrected. He took the last bite and quickly opened the refrigerator and stuck his head inside searching for the pasta salad that was right in front of him as his mother rebuked, "It's been your revolving bedroom door."

He braced for the lecture.

"I taught you better."

"Yes, Ma'am."

"I know the temptation is overwhelming."

"Sometimes."

"And the world continuously offers you its brightest and most beautiful, but those kind of women just bring you to destruction."

"That linebacker that destroyed our season wasn't female, Mom."

"And your father's smile should not be on your face right now, I'm serious."

"Yes, ma'am," he answered then said sincerely, "I'm not having sex with this woman."

"Because she has Mono?"

"We're taking it slow."

"Slow is good," she praised.

"We think so."

"Are you seeing her again?"

He just nodded.

"Tell me about her. Please, John."

"She's very bright and beautiful. Hmph, maybe I should steer clear." He began to fork up pasta salad, but his mother just waited so he gave her a little more. "She loves her job. She's worked almost all her life to get the DVM behind her name. I had a chance to watch her this afternoon at the Bennett's. She delivered a foal. It was incredible."

His mother smiled.

"She has this way about her, I can't quite describe it. Tough, yet sensitive at the same time. She lost both her parents by the time she was a teenager. Life hasn't been easy for her. She's alone, with one sister."

"Is she bitter or better for it?"

It was a line his mother had used all his life about tough circumstances and he proudly answered, "She's better for it, mom."

"She sounds like she's independent."

John just nodded, forked up more pasta. Thought about how much he wanted to call her, right now, tell her he made it home alright and how great the weekend had been. Just hear her voice as he lay down in his bed and kept her talking until he got so sleepy they just got silent and whispered they should go but neither one of them would say good night. And that seemed so ridiculous.

And something he didn't do. But that's all he wanted, even after a weekend with her, he just wanted to call her... maybe she'd had enough. He should definitely wait. Until tomorrow.

His mom had been talking and he hadn't been listening, until he heard, "Independent women are hard to have relationships with, especially when they're married to their careers, other things are more important than the relationship," his Mother warned.

"You're an independent woman," he countered, "And I was always important to you."

"The most important thing but..." She sighed. Smiled, "I'm not trying to dissuade you, John." She quickly added, "I'm just giving you some facts to think about."

His mother had hit the nail on the head. Stephanie was definitely independent. She wasn't the kind of woman to be charmed and seduced by her infatuation to John Dake or any man. But then, she didn't know that John Dake wasn't just any ordinary man. She only knew him for who he really was, not what he did. For a spilt second a ripple of fear went through him. What would she think when she found out who he was, what he did? Maybe she wouldn't like it. Maybe it would all be too much, and she wouldn't want to see him anymore...

"She doesn't know what I do."

"What?" His mother shook her head. "How could she—"

"Not everyone follows football, mom." He ate some more pasta.

"Well, that's true." She nodded now. "So, she has no idea you're famous?"

"No. It's been—"

"Refreshing?" she finished for him.

"Very. I spent all night listening to her life. Hers, not mine."

"I imagine that was nice for a change."

"She just talked, and I listened, really listened. There wasn't sex to distract us, or lust stealing all the attention. I mean, sure she's got a great body and I'm aware of it, but it's not the focus, in fact I wasn't even thinking about it." He ate some more and shared, "The only thing I touched was her hair. She's got curls, like waves really. They're long and soft, really soft. I love her hair."

He realized he was leaning across the counter and spilling his guts to his mother. He straightened and started in on the second sandwich.

"So, when do you think you'll tell her about your life?"

"Soon."

"You don't want her to find out from someone else."

"No, ma'am."

"Or hear your name on the television."

"Shouldn't be a reason right now."

"You can be all over the news in a minute if it cycles that way."

He looked at her, fear shooting terror into every muscle. "It shouldn't."

"Don't risk it," she advised. "Really. She sounds like a great girl, John."

He nodded.

"I'm glad you had a nice time together."

"I haven't had a night like that since..."

"You got famous," she answered again.

"Yeah. It's easy with old friends. But new ones," he shrugged, crunching through a pickle now. "You know."

"Yes."

"What's up with you, mom?"

"I'm thinking about looking for a small house here in Dallas."

He nodded. "Let me buy you something."

She laughed. "No but thank you."

"Really," he put his sandwich down. "I want to."

"When I sell the ranch I'll—"

"What?!" The word just came out in a panic. "You're selling the ranch?"

She laughed immediately.

"Seriously?"

She leaned toward him and said, "Actually, *I'm* having a very hot affair with a tall brunette with green eyes and one spectacular body." And she gave a nod. Like an exclamation point.

There was silence. He was just staring at her smug smile. And he couldn't tell... if she was kidding or not.

"I couldn't tell," he told Stephanie. He'd called. Told her he made it home okay. She said she was glad he called, actually thanked him because she was worried. And then he'd just told her what his mom had said, "I'm having a very hot affair with a tall brunette with green eyes and one spectacular body—she said that. To me." He was pacing. Far from ready to slip into bed and cozy up with soft small talk. "She wasn't serious, right? I mean, I'd been kidding around because she was working me over to get information about you, so she was just kicking it back. Right?"

"That's how you described me to your mother? Tall brunette with green eyes and a—

"Spectacular body. Yeah, I did. And before those pretty green eyes darken up, I also told her you're great at your job and watching you today was incredible. I loved it."

"She thinks we're having a hot affair."

"No." He carefully explained the conversation. "I told her we weren't having sex. This wasn't close to casual. We're taking it slow. That I'm serious about you and you're considering dating me. So, was my mom serious, Beauty?"

"Probably," she answered, "But not about the affair. It sounds like she's been thinking about moving. But it was just the beginning of an idea and when she saw it upset you, she reflected it off to something else, made it a joke and regrouped."

"Hmph."

"Maybe she's lonely?"

"She's got lots of friends."

"Or wants to be closer to you."

"I see her all the time. Maybe the ranch is too much for her now?"

They went back and forth with ideas as he lay down in the bed, struggled a moment to get his arm situated, the pillows propped up for support, the dogs curled up and quiet and everyone snuggled in for the night.

"Who would my mom be seeing and where did she meet him?"

"Don't know but he sounds great." She'd said it softly and he closed his eyes as she told him sincerely, "It will be okay. Don't ponder the past or call up the former things when God's doing something new. It's already happening, and He's just made you aware of it. God has a plan, He's even now carrying it out. Trust him. He loves your mother and I know you want her happy."

"Yeah, I do."

"Talk to her tomorrow and listen. Ask her what she wants."

John didn't wait. First thing the next morning he told his mom as he handed her a cup of coffee, "Mom, let me buy you a house, anywhere you want."

She laughed. "No but thank you."

"Really, I want to. Whatever you want, we'll make it happen."

"The ranch is your home." His mother had reached out and covered his hand. "I won't sell it," she assured him now, but he heard something in her voice, something he might not have been attuned to if he hadn't talked to Stephanie, been learning how to slow down and really honor people by listening.

"But you don't have to stay there. Move."

"I have a room here. And I love it."

"And you can live here."

"I could."

It hadn't been a question, but he answered it, "Of course."

"That's one way to stop that revolving door into your bedroom." She laughed, drank some coffee, promised him, "But I wouldn't do that to you. You need your own space and so do I."

"Let me buy you a house."

She shook her head.

"Okay, let me buy the ranch then you can buy what you want, but I'm taking care of you, mom."

"I can take care of myself."

"You're right, independent women are difficult."

"I warned you." She smiled. "The ranch is home, John." But he saw something there, an edge of nerves, a quick stepping back and securing herself with what was safe. He'd seen the same thing in Stephanie's eyes sometimes, a cautious almost uncertain indecisiveness.

John leaned forward and moved his hand, he turned it so that he held his mother's hand and softly squeezed. "Tell me what's going on."

She blinked.

"I see it. Behind your eyes and in the edge of your smile. Stephanie gives me the same look sometimes and I have to nudge her too. Mom?"

He waited.

Finally, Helen Dake just shrugged. "I don't know yet. For a while it was just a thought, now I've been thinking more about it."

"Okay." He accepted that then repeated what Stephanie said, "Don't ponder the past or call up the former things when God's doing something new. It's already happening, and He's just made you aware of it."

"Isaiah 43." Helen smiled.

"What?"

"That's a paraphrase from Isaiah 43."

"It is?"

She nodded. "*Do not call to mind the former things, Or ponder things of the past. "Behold, I will do something new, now it will spring forth; Will you not be aware of it? I will even make a roadway in the wilderness, Rivers in the desert."* God has a plan."

"That's what Stephanie told me."

Helen Dake just nodded because that's what God had told her too.

8

The familiar bells jingled as Stephanie pushed through her clinic door. She stomped her wet boots and wiped the sleet from her coat as she shivered from the cold. She was almost to her office before she noticed Mary and Melissa smiling like two calicos who had just eaten the canary.

"What's up with you two?" she laughed as Mary tried to conceal the amusement on her face.

"Nothing," Mary replied pressing her lips together tightly.

"Nothing," Melissa echoed with a giggle.

The kitten darted out to greet her and she scooped him up. "Hey there, Lucky Fool." Only a step into her office she stopped short. There was a tall crystal vase filled with long stem red roses on the center of her desk.

"They must be from your valentine, since it's Valentine's Day, right Dr. Hightower?"

"They're so beautiful," Mary said tilting her head down to sniff one of the velvety buds.

Stephanie rounded the desk to sit in the big chair. "Well, McNatt's three-year-old survived the colic."

"Don't you want to know who they're from?" Melissa interrupted. "We've both been dying for you to get back to the office."

"Read the card Stephanie," Mary urged.

"I'll read it for you," Melissa suggested.

Stephanie quickly took the card as the young girl reached for it. It was probably from Phillip, she thought, not wanting to risk a letdown.

She opened the small envelope and slowly pulled the white card out.

Happy Valentine's Day Beauty.
Love,
Mr. Charming

Her heart was beating frantically. She lifted her eyes to Mary and she no longer could hide her smile.

"Well, who are they from?" Melissa prodded.

"They're from John Dake," she answered as Mary's smile widened.

"Holy cow!" Melissa bellowed. "Well, what did he say? Is it romantic or what?"

"Just Happy Valentine's Day," Stephanie replied looking at the card again.

"He is so good-looking Dr. Hightower. Aren't you just dying?"

The bells announced someone had arrived and Melissa left to take care of them.

"Well? Are you dying or what?" Mary teased, drilling Stephanie with a knowing look before she headed toward the front. She heard her greet Linda. "Hello, Mrs. Bennett."

Linda had arrived for their lunch date and Stephanie stood.

"Hi."

"Oh! What beautiful roses."

"Aren't they. I love them!" Stephanie couldn't hide the smile as she held out the card for her to read.

"And Mr. Charming would be?"

"John."

Linda smiled, handing her back the card. "I believe John is taken with you. How do you feel about that?"

"Shocked."

Linda held up her thumb and index finger an inch apart. "Aren't you a tiny bit excited, though?"

"No." Stephanie shook her head, then let her smile explode. "I'm a huge bit excited, Linda." She couldn't hold back the laughter. "I am dying." She waved. "That's what the girls say. I guess it means you're shocked-excited. I can't believe he sent me flowers on Valentine's Day." She looked down at the card in her hand. "And he wants me to come to Dallas and visit him in two weeks. And..."

"And?" she prompted.

"I won't be contagious, by then. And..." She began to pace, her thumb brushing over the etched words of the tiny card. There were several steps of silence, a turn, several more. Linda waited patiently. "John is, well he's... " She looked over at Linda. "I just don't know how to keep my composure at times. I've never had a man make me get all nervous and spacey, Linda." She looked at the card, read the simple words again. "Now I won't be contagious. There won't be that excuse as a boundary to keep things platonic. And he makes everything so... well, I can't even think sometimes and I'm not sure I even know the rules when it comes to dating and relationships. I told him I didn't date... now we're dating. I told him I didn't kiss," She confessed, "I haven't kissed... anyone, ever romantically. And now in two weeks, in Dallas, I can and I'm a nervous wreck."

"Stephanie, do you like this man?"

"Yes."

"And we both know that he likes you. Just look at these beautiful roses." Stephanie smiled, the thrill surging through her again. Linda walked to her, took her hands. "There's nothing wrong with a man making you feel that way. I'm so happy that one has finally come along that does. For years you worked hard, took care of Samantha, focused on your goals, and now that you've reached them, and your life has more balance, the world has opened back up to you. John walked in and you noticed him."

"Yes. He either makes my heart race or melt."

"How wonderful," Linda encouraged.

"I'm not sure that it is when my mind goes numb and I'm constantly nervous. Most of the time I have no idea what to do."

"Do you think God will fail to help you now in this new area of life?"

"I know He won't."

"Then honor him by trusting Him in this, share with Him how nervous you are and ask Him to help you. Love and all that comes with it can be beautiful, and very satisfying. Just relax a little bit. You're the one who's setting the boundaries, John will honor them and God will help you both."

"Okay."

"I'm proud of you, Stephanie."

"Thanks Linda, I wasn't sure you'd be coming today since it's Valentine's Day but I'm so glad you could."

"It's Wednesday. We're meeting every Wednesday for lunch. I wouldn't miss it." Linda brought her into her arms for a fierce hug. "I want to be here for you. I want you to know how much I love you, care about you. What a blessing you are to me."

"Thanks."

They looked at each other and smiled. "I've tried not to push, to let our relationship develop naturally. Blair was my miracle baby. I wanted more, but they never came. Then Blair went to college and talked about new friends, Stephanie and Samantha. She was so impressed with how you were working through college and caring for your younger sister. She told me how Layne had helped you work with the university for optional housing with your scholarship, so you could keep guardianship of Samantha. We met for lunch—"

"Yes, I remember."

"Did you know God laid you on my heart that day? I secretly watched over you after that." Linda smiled. "I made sure you had the funds you needed, the little extras, the protection to stay together as sisters even though you were barely eighteen?" She sighed now with the grief of regret Stephanie often heard in her own heart. "I blamed myself when Samantha was abducted. Just as you did," she linked their hands. "Because I thought I could have done more, could have acted faster and been more deliberate. You were so strong, Stephanie, so capable and determined. It took a horrific crisis and God's own voice to convince you to trust us. I wondered if you thought we took advantage of you—"

"No, I was so thankful." She tried her best to explain what they so rarely spoke about. "We needed you. Samantha, of course, but I did too. I haven't known how to tell you or show you—except to do my best in school, to be successful in my job."

Linda nodded. "We're proud of you, Stephanie."

She smiled. "I know. I feel that all the time."

"But it's still hard to let us help you."

"I'm not sure I knew how until I got sick."

Linda smiled. "It was hard for me to watch you suffer with mono, but in my heart, I was so glad for the chance to be there for you. And to watch this relationship develop with John Dake. He would call, and your eyes would just light up suddenly, then you'd take my hand even as you took the phone."

"I have no idea how to deal with men. I've been keeping them at arm's length so long I don't know how to let them close just like I didn't know how to let you close."

"You're learning, one small step at a time, like we all do." Linda encouraged then handed her a gift. "Happy Valentine's Day. It's a book," she told her. "And it seems to be the perfect choice."

Stephanie unwrapped the paper covered with pretty hearts, carefully exposing Max Lucado's newest inspiration. The topic was love. "Thank you, Linda." She handed her a card.

Linda opened the envelop. There was a little sound of surprise. Stephanie felt tears burn her own eyes. There was only one word on the cover—Mom.

Linda didn't even open the card, she just gathered her up tight and close in a hug and whispered, "I love you," as Stephanie echoed it.

Then Linda encouraged her, "Why don't you call him right now and thank him? That would be a nice small step."

"What do I say?"

"Thank you." Linda smiled. "They're beautiful. I love them."

She took a deep breath. "Okay."

"I'll get us a table at Annie's, order the soup. It's your favorite today and you can tell me what he said." Linda winked as she shut the door.

Stephanie wiped her eyes then looked at the phone. She had never called him before for a social call. Why not, he would probably be at work anyway. She sat behind her desk, rocking her foot anxiously as she traced the beautiful cover of her new book. She listened to the rings and hoped for his machine.

"Hello, Dake residence." A Hispanic voice answered.

Stephanie paused a minute before asking. "Can I speak to John?"

"Who's calling please," the voice replied.

"It's Dr. Hightower."

"Dr. Hightower, the veterinarian?"

"Yes."

"I'm sorry, he's out. I'm expecting him around five-thirty. This is Hattie Chavis, his housekeeper, let me give him a message for you."

"Please tell him I called to say thank you... and that the roses are beautiful."

9

"King me."

They were the words John Dake said in the end zone when he scored a touchdown as he pointed to the sky then put an imaginary crown on his head. And just now his number one wide-receiver smiled wide, as he mocked John with the phrase. "King me, Dake!"

DeShawn added his own touchdown dance to the sentiment. The receiver stood head and shoulders above John's staff in the center of his kitchen and in his hand was a cookie. "This is food heroine now." DeShawn was passionate about everything he did in life and at the moment that was devouring Valentine's Day cookies. He was one of the three skills players the press had dubbed the Triple-D. Dake, DeShawn, and Dewayne, the running back. Dewayne was a quiet man, considering anyone standing next to DeShawn was considered quiet. He just nodded and smiled while he calmly ate a cookie, giving Dake that head's up look that DeShawn was revved up and rolling.

DeShawn had wrapped his arms around John's housekeeper and was nuzzling Hattie with affection. "I'm stealing this woman from you, Dake. I've got to have her, you hear me. These are the best cookies ever. I thought the brownies rocked, but these," he shouted now doing a little dance like he'd just scored a touchdown. "These cookies are heaven. Are you an angel?"

"DeShawn." Hattie chastised, she turned away, the timer sounding off that more cookies were coming, and the smell of sugar and spice invaded the kitchen as she opened up the oven.

"How you doing, man?" DeShawn was moving. He scooped up a stack of cookies, holding them in his huge hand before he came his way. Dewayne beside him.

"Good," John answered.

"Started rehabbing, I heard." He swept the sling then he turned to John's team and addressed the kitchen. "Glad to see all ya'll here. John's got his team on the field and we're all with him there, heading in the same direction. Vic-tor-y! And he's got his team here, in the house, heading in that same direction. What direction?" he called out the question like a drill sergeant now.

"Victory," John's manager, Carl answered.

"That was pitiful. What direction? Tell them Dewayne."

"Vic-tor-y!" Dewayne smiled wide.

"Vic-tor-y! Your hearing me. And right now, this is his huddle, hear me? You huddle up right here. It's not a time to be alone. No sir! It's winter. Buuurrrr. Feel me? It's cold and it gets dark early and our noses run and our head's they're a hurting, and no chance to wear sun glasses cuz the lights have dimmed. And these injuries just suck the life outta of an active man and make him wanna curl up in bed and hibernate till it's over.

"But... we're not going to let our king here head into that dark hole. We gotta keep him out here and you got to give him light. You got to do what you do, each and every one of you. You are his light. You gotta feed him cookies, angel. And keep your eyes on him, rockin' Rhonda. You gotta keep him up, Kenny! Get him going, Ryan! Make him look like the million-dollar man now and keep pushing the product. That's what team John Dake Inc. does! You don't need the world's respect. You got your own. You're manufacturing the sun here. Giving off light. And what you do, well you do it too well. Where are my sunglasses now? It's like August in here, Dewayne. I'm sweating. Blinded by all this light. I'm telling you it's enough to take us the distance. We're going the distance, aren't we? Vic-tor-y! Aren't we?! Are you all in?"

"Yes," they answered.

"What?"

"Yes." It was louder. Smirks and smiles and even Hattie was answering.

"Again."

"Yes."

DeShawn swaggered, nodded at him and said, "My work is done, Dake. See ya' soon." He held up a peace sign. "Happy V day. Tell them my man. We're ready for some real sugar now! All pre-gamed up. Gonna find my girl tonight."

Dewayne just held up the peace sign, smiled wide and the two were gone with most of the cookies.

"What did he just say?" Kenny, his publicist, asked. "It was like conflicting metaphors."

"I have no idea," John answered. "I never do. I just get revved up and answer yes and go play my heart out."

"It's like a sermon in a guru's rap song and you're singing along and don't know the lyrics but you're believing them. I'm all in by the way," he told John.

"I know you are." John snagged his cookie and with the first bite announced, "King me!" Then he moaned. "These are really good, Hattie."

He smiled at the group. He'd collected the best, starting with Hattie and his assistant, Carl. They took care of him, like an O line. He had the dynamic duo of personal trainer and physical therapist, one for nutrition and work out, the other for the recovery. Then there was the business side of the team, the front office people like the skills players on the team; manager, agent, publicist, stylist. They'd worked together now for four years because the nature of the game feeds the fame while the beast is hungry. It was a statement he didn't understand at first when he was still in the blessed early years of his college ball, but then he'd won the Heisman and a National Championship and in thirty days his life had changed forever. He was famous, and the clock was ticking. And like compounding interest, what they did today would build his name or deteriorate it. John Dake might play football, but he was a product that his team was diligently working to promote while the opportunities presented themselves.

"These are incredible," he praised again.

"Saint Valentine Cookies," Hattie told him.

"We should patent the recipe," Carl, his business manager added. "Dake treats."

Even his stylist had a cookie and Rhonda hardly ever ate sweets. She moaned as she told him, "These can't be good for you."

His personal trainer told the physical therapist beside him, "Fiber and protein. Oatmeal with black cherries and walnuts, dark chocolate. Great snack and the tart cherries fight inflammation."

They handed him another one as his therapist began to unwrap his shoulder from the ice pack. And a protein shake was placed before him and his chair was pulled out at the bar. And a squeeze ball was in his right hand and he was going through a set of isometrics that he did now every hour. And Rhonda had three sets of new workout clothes with the emblem of the athletic shoe company that paid him to promote their name and she'd selected the business suit for the luncheon tomorrow where he'd give a short speech. The words would be laid out on a single sheet of paper, written by his publicist. Kenny was a master at spin and statements and especially well versed at preparing answers to stupid questions he'd be asked multiple times in interviews. Even now he was flirting with Hattie for a fresh cookie being lifted off the cookie sheet. They were like a family and it was Kenny that held up the note written in Hattie's handwriting that was tucked under the phone.

"Who's Doctor Hightower?"

As everyone looked, Kenny flipped the note so the writing was facing them all.

"Thank you," Carl read the notepaper.

"They're beautiful," Rhonda finished.

"Give me that." Hattie gave Kenny a swat.

Everyone was waiting. He finished the protein shake. Asked Hattie, "I had a phone call?"

"Si."

"What did she say?"

"To tell you thank you and that the roses are beautiful."

"Good. What's for dinner, Hattie?"

"No date for Valentine's day, angel?" Kenny asked Hattie in a whisper everyone heard.

She ignored him. "Prime Rib, and I made you some mixed vegetables and a Caesar salad. A few more minutes and it will be ready."

"Sounds great. I'm going to go shower. I'll see everyone tomorrow." He pointed at Kenny. "You're going to the luncheon, right?"

"Of course."

"And that's the suit, Rhonda?"

"I'll be here at ten to get the tie right," Rhonda told him. "We're going with a Windsor knot."

John smiled. "Even with a good shoulder I can't tie a Windsor knot."

"We want your look to be confident the first time you're seen out of the sling. I'll make sure we pull that off."

"Is this event televised?"

"Local news but could go national so we'll be prepared."

"Let's try to stay under the radar a while longer. I want to get in and out. No side interviews if we can help it and if it happens, I'll need a fresh line or two on the shoulder update, okay, Kenny?"

"You've got it, boss."

When he was gone, Carl asked the group, "Who sent the flowers?"

Everyone shook their head.

"Okay, Hattie," Kenny nudged her. "We know you did it. Who is she?"

"I did not send the flowers."

"So, he did it himself?" Kenny took another cookie and handed it to Carl.

John's business manager announced, "He's never done that before."

The phone rang, and her heart jumped. She pulled the quilt up higher around her legs and held the receiver letting the phone ring three times before she answered it.

"Hello."

"Hello, Beauty. I heard you called."

"The roses are beautiful, Mr. Charming."

"I'm glad."

"Thank you."

"I wish I could have been there to give them to you myself and take you out to dinner. How was your day?"

"It was a little crazy. I got called out early this morning to look at a three-year-old with a bad case of colic. I was in the barn with him three hours before he started to turn the corner. It's still sleeting here. Needless to say, it wasn't too fun being in a cold stall for three hours with a distressed animal. Anyway, you made my day when I got back to the office and found the roses. How was yours?"

"A little long with two rounds of rehab today."

"Did you ice?"

"Yes, I just finished. And I know a way you could make my whole week. Tell me you're going to come see me in two weeks."

"Is that why you sent me the roses, to try and persuade me?"

"No, I sent roses because it's Valentine's Day, and..."

"And what?"

"And, that's what you're supposed to do on Valentine's Day when you're dating someone."

"Oh, it is?" she questioned, toying with him.

"Yes."

"Are we dating?"

"Are you going to tell me tonight that you're coming to Dallas, or am I going to have to call you up a hundred times a day until you relent?"

"I've got the kitten now, someone has to take care of him."

"And I've got yarn and catnip, bring him with you."

"And High Hopes—"

"Has his mother and a dozen grooms at Brad's barn to watch over him. Next excuse?"

"You want me to stay with you? I could ask Blair."

"You could ask Blair."

"It would be the right thing to do, to stay with Blair."

"We're going to do the right thing at my house. I've got four guest rooms with private baths. You'll have your privacy, I promise you. And I have a housekeeper, people in and out all the time, we won't be alone. I want to see you, Stephanie."

She squeezed her eyes shut, thought about what Linda said, knew this was the next step and that she wanted to see him too. She confessed that, "I want to see you too. I'll come."

"You'll come?"

"I'll come see you."

"In two weeks?"

"In two weeks." She echoed.

"I'll see if Blair and Layne want to join us for dinner. Take you somewhere nice so you can dress up. I can't wait to see you, kiss you." She was silent, he couldn't be. "I miss you. What are you doing, right now?"

"Just sitting here, talking to you," she answered softly.

"Where? Where are you sitting?"

"In my study."

"In that leather chair?"

"Yes."

"It's big for you. You look like a little girl in her daddy's chair. Do you want kids? I always wanted a big family. It was just me and mom." He moved on. "Have you got that quilt tucked around you?"

"Yes, it's a cold night here." Her voice was softer. "Do you have friends with big families? I had foster families that were large, but we never had enough time together to really merge into a family. It takes time for me to trust people, John," she told him something that was important.

And he heard her. "We're going slow. Taking that time. I want you to trust me."

"I'm coming in two weeks. I'll stay with you."

Layne Lexington held his hand out to her and smiled. "Wow, little sister."

Stephanie smiled at the nick name he'd called her since the beginning. She grasped hold of his hand again as she'd done many times in the last seven years and Layne gently brought her into a hug. He was tall with an athletic build and an elegant attractiveness. His hair was a thick dark bronze, his eyes an easy attentive blue. She'd met him at college orientation. Three years older than her, he'd been a student volunteer. A senior helping her to create her first freshman schedule. He'd learned she was on scholarship and then heard about her younger sister and the court's tentative decision to give Stephanie guardianship if they approved her student housing. He'd been the one to help her find alternative housing outside the dorm, so Samantha could live with her. He'd been her advocate; with the university and the court. Leading her to people who could help, because it just came so natural to Layne to help people and he'd kept promises and advised, and made the system work for them, earning her respect and trust. Now his soft confidence assured her again, "You look beautiful," he told her softy then his voice firmed and threatened, "Dake better—"

"Blair warned me you were going to go big brother."

"You better believe it when you walk out looking like this."

"You've seen me dressed up before."

He'd tucked her under his arm as he looked down at her. "I've never seen you dressed up before for a date. You're interested in John Dake."

It wasn't a question. She told him, "We're going slow. And I'm really nervous so please don't make it worse."

His gaze softened. A soft hug was given as he said, "How about a little wine. I know Blair will want some and there's this cheese she likes. It's smoked. Really good with this red. Try it."

She did. And she took the wine glass. He lifted his glass and they toasted as he told her, "You remember how precious you are, to God, to me, to your family and just relax, be yourself."

Their wine glasses touched, and she reached up and kissed him. "Thanks, Layne."

"See, you've kissed a guy before, Steph," Blair said as she came into the kitchen with her mother. "You've kissed Layne. Do it again. Get the nerves out."

"Blair." There was a tone to Layne's voice. It was subtle and strangely effective to lead his wife in another direction as he held out a glass of wine to her. "This cheese is smoked. Perfect with this wine," he started again then asked his mother in law, "Linda would you like a glass?"

"Blair your house looks great," Stephanie commented.

Blair smiled, looking toward her husband. "Thanks, we love it. It was worth all the trouble, wasn't it Layne?"

"If we ever try to build a house, campaign for DA and try to plan a wedding at the same time again, just shoot me."

"It was a little stressful to juggle." Blair caressed his neck.

"Thank God you're a master juggler." He kissed her softly on the nose. "And we made it through it all successfully."

"Your father-in-law and I second that, Layne."

"What am I seconding, Linda?" Brad asked walking into the Lexington's kitchen with John beside him. Stephanie looked at him, smiled. Conversation continued, but she wasn't listening, just looking into his blue eyes.

And neither was he as Brad asked again, "John, do you want a drink?"

"Excuse us for a second."

John took Stephanie's hand and led her out of the kitchen. He guided her around the corner into the formal dining room and out of view from the Bennett's. In one motion he turned her around, put his hands on either side of her face and kissed her fully on the lips.

She gasped in surprise, but his mouth was soft and gentle. It seemed to float over the surface of her lips so tenderly. He pulled a whisper away and she could see his eyes.

"I've wanted to do that since the first time I saw you," he stated, looking into her eyes.

"The first time? I think it was probably the third," she replied smiling and he sought her mouth again.

She tasted of wine, she smelled of romance, and in his arms she felt perfectly right. Very slowly he pulled away from her. "Hi," he said, smiling all the way to his eyes as he kissed her again.

"Hi," she replied breathlessly. She touched his smile, reflected it.

"That was worth waiting for." He feathered soft kisses across her lips between each word. "You're worth every second of the wait." He looked into her eyes, taking her hands, and the silence spoke as he smiled and lifted her fingers, pressing his lips there too, keeping his gaze on her own. "I'm so glad you're here." Then he squeezed her hands, asked, "Are you cold?" as he brought her closer.

"I'm nervous." She smiled, her hand glided down his right arm. "You've got both hands again."

"Yes. I do. And don't be nervous. It's me."

She nodded.

"And I'll need you to get me through the next ten minutes in there of socializing politely when I just want to get your luggage and run you home. Where's your bag? I don't want you to think for a second that I'm going to let you stay here with Blair when I want you all to myself this weekend."

"Maybe I should. I'm not here to be seduced, John," she told him. "And I fear you're going to try."

"No. I swear." His hand was over his heart. "We're going slow," he promised her. "Nothing's changed, except that I can kiss you." And he did, again, softly with his eyes open. "I'm not going to try to seduce you. Please, trust me." He was sincere. Seriously, sincere as he repeated, "Please, Stephanie."

"My bags are already in the car. You got a limo?"

"Layne got the limo. Blair's spoiled."

"Is she?" She laughed. "I'm not sure the socializing is going to be polite. Blair's also a master at satire. We're toast."

"You mean roasted. Hold my hand, I'm nervous too."

And she laughed, relaxed as their smiles blended into one more grinning kiss then they walked back into the kitchen.

They arrived at the Petroleum Club that looked out over the city from the top of a sky scraper. John let Layne take the lead, deal with the hostess as he helped Stephanie off with her coat, noticing the dress. It was like unveiling a beautiful piece of art. He'd given the dress only a glance earlier when his focus had been finding a private place to kiss her. Now he studied the sheer sapphire fabric that screened her bare back, arms and chest with a scrolling pattern that covered a solid sheath underneath. She was all legs, slender as a wand, her breasts a spectacular contrast, the blue dazzling against her dark beauty.

"Just what are you thinking about so intently?"

"You're beautiful."

"Thanks." There was a blush now, soft and so becoming he had to seize the opportunity and steal another kiss before they headed to their table. It was private, in the corner with a view out the windows of the lights of the city. She was relaxed, here among her friends. The food just the backdrop for the fellowship. After they shared dessert the girls slipped away to the restroom.

He was watching her go as Layne said, "John."

He turned to him smiling, but Layne said, "I told her she could call me, any time, for any reason and I'll come pick her up."

"Okay."

"I don't think she should stay with you alone at your house, but she says you're—"

"Serious. I'm serious about her, Layne. And I respect her, and you for saying something."

"Then you better prove it," Layne stated, smiling as the girls came back.

The Lexington's had tickets to the theater and the first acts of '*The Best Little Whorehouse in Texas*' flew by and Stephanie could hardly believe it was already intermission. She excused herself to go to the lady's room as Blair visited with a few friends and the men stretched their legs. She was having a wonderful time. John had kept her close, mingling kisses with whispered comments and teasing her about the Aggies in the show. She was still grinning to herself when they pulled through the gates into John's neighborhood. His house was at the end of a cul-de-sac behind another gate. They drove up the circular drive, Stephanie saying goodbye to the Lexington's as the driver got her bag. He carried it into the house as John escorted her by the winter landscaping of white pansies and up several steps to a massive front door. A woman met them there, John introduced her as Hattie and she guided the driver in with Stephanie's bag as the two Golden Retrievers greeted the couple. Stephanie dipped down to give each a minute of affection and when the driver left she asked, "Show me your house, John."

"Sure." He took her hand and walked toward the main part of the house. "My exquisitely furnished formal dining room." One corner of his lips rose in a smirk as Stephanie grinned at the huge empty room. "I'm still looking for furniture for a room I've never used. My kitchen table can serve dinner well enough and even then, I sit at the counter bar most of the time." He turned her into another room. "And this is the formal living room," he added, "I call it a furnished hall because I just pass through it. I'm not sure I've ever sat down in here."

"It's got a great view," she commented looking out the wall of windows that showed off the swimming pool. The floor was a checker board of light marble where two identical sofas sat on a plush area rug with a coffee table in the center and art and nick-knacks strategically placed to finish the room off via decorator style formality.

"Master is this way." He just stopped at the door. She saw a big bed and neutral linens and another wall of windows that looked out on the end of the pool. "There's a bathroom and a gym and stuff back there that I use."

He led her back through the living room to a hall that lead toward the front of the house. "There are four bedrooms back here. Each has a bath. My mom's room is in the corner. My best friend has a place to stay here anytime. He's in rodeo." He turned on the light and she saw the western décor in the room. There was a G. Harvey painting and an award saddle and a gallery of antiques that she'd like to explore.

"I like it."

"So does Honey. The decorator did it up right for him. I hope you like what she did for you. Your room was empty until two weeks ago. I told her a few things."

When he opened the door, there were antiques. A lovely carved four poster bed, the wood dark, the dresser, a feminine makeup vanity and tall mirrored wardrobe all matching. The linens were a soft silver scrolled with dark green and the art, pastoral paintings of horses. There was a picture of the two of them at High Hopes birth in a pretty frame. And a little pillow on the bed that was embroidered, "Catnip" the ends fringed with crazy colors of bright yarn.

She picked it up.

"Do you like it?"

She hugged the little pillow to her heart with a smile. "You didn't have to do this."

"But I did." He'd gathered her back to him. They looked at the little pillow. "It's scented with lavender. Helps you relax and fall asleep."

She breathed in the soothing scent. "Where did you find this?"

"I just told the decorator a few things. She did the rest." She set the small pillow down as he led her forward. Her suitcase was already placed on a chest at the end of the bed. The bathroom was large with a tub and separate shower. There was a chair and reading lamp with a stack of books by a few of her favorite authors. He'd remembered things, made the room personal and she looked up at him, reached up for the first time and pushed through the fear and kissed him because no one had ever done something this special for her in her life.

"Thank you, I love everything, John."

He smiled. "Good because I want you to come back."

"I know there's more to your house. Show me." They began to retrace their steps.

"It's a big house for just me," he said in an uneasy tone.

"It's beautiful."

"Hattie has an apartment." He pointed in a direction off the kitchen. "She's great. Totally gets the ebb and flow of doing her job; when I need her, when I don't. She'll have something in the refrigerator for us. You hungry? Thirsty? Wine, beer, Scotch?" He said the latter with a grin.

"Water would be nice." He reached into the huge sub-zero refrigerator as she asked, "Glass?"

"Right of the sink, Beauty." He pointed, and she chose a glass. "Want something to eat?"

"I'm okay, but you go ahead. You sound hungry." She grinned.

"The only thing I'm hungry for is another one of those kisses you just gave me." He reached over to gently bring her close to his body. He nuzzled her neck and whispered, "No wonder you waited so long to let me kiss you. You knew I'd never be able to stop." His lips covered hers in a slow kiss. It was like a dance, slow and easy, a movement of holding together and sharing, touch, taste, breath.

She just seemed to melt. Mind, heart, soul all merging together. And she made a little noise, both sigh and whimper, because this was all so new and wonderful and overwhelming. Everything seemed to be slipping and she held onto him breaking the kiss, reached for her water as he said, "And I love this dress, Beauty." His hand was a soft glide down her back and a thousand butterflies took flight. She was flushed, searching for stability, reaching back to step away.

"Thanks. I've had more people tell me that tonight." She leaned against the large kitchen island, putting some space between them, regaining the control, praying silently for more. Her heart was pounding, and it felt like her soul was on fire. "As a matter of fact, I overheard a remarkable conversation in the rest room tonight."

"The rest room?" he questioned. He took his tie off, undid two buttons.

She should help him, but she watched, stayed where she was and told him, "The ladies room at the theater. It seems two women were admiring my dress from their seats."

"Oh?"

"Not only did they comment on my dress, speculate on the price, but they seemed to question if my figure was natural or fabricated by plastic surgery and if my livelihood was from modeling. Not to mention the fact that my date, who they knew by name, has yet to be seen with the same woman at any performance this season."

He was just looking at her and the look on his face made her nervous and ramble on, "They were also vastly disappointed that you'd shaved your beard but seeing you all dressed up made one of them just 'bout melt into a puddle!"

She grinned at him, but John wasn't smiling. He wasn't bantering back, so she just went on, "I confronted these women and asked them just how they knew you. They replied, 'Every woman in Texas knows who John Dake is, but who are you?'" She grinned. "They weren't impressed that you were out with a Cajun back woods country horse doctor."

Stephanie took a sip of her water. She'd meant for the story to be something to spar about. To get them talking before she melted in a puddle at his feet after another one of those kisses. Instead, she noticed that look of frustrated fury building from that squared off jaw as a throb began to tick in the corner by his ear. He stood there looking at her but not really seeing her. There would be no bantering over this and that threw her off.

"John?" she asked him to explain.

"Stephanie, there's something I've needed to tell you." He took the glass from her hand. "There's another room I want to show you." His voice was gravel dry. He reached out for her hand and walked her around the breakfast bar past the long kitchen table to a wide double door.

He paused briefly before he opened them, "This room says more about me than I could begin to tell you."

His thumb brushed the top of her hand once before he released it and flicked the light switch on and led her into the room.

"This is why everyone knows about me. This is what I do, Stephanie," he paused, walking her further into the room. "This is who I am," he said stepping back to present a room full of athletic memorabilia.

She looked at him perplexed, then looked at the game room. It could have been a sports bar. They had just passed a long counter with several stools. Behind it three TVs were built into the wall and beyond it a pit of sofas sat before a huge wide screen television. An ornate pool table stood off to the side and around it all were photographs and sports paraphernalia with framed jerseys and trophies, footballs and helmets. She walked forward to the wall with all the photographs, keeping her back to him. Dake and number 7 were on the jersey in each shot. She touched one of him when he was in college at the Rose Bowl Game.

"I'm a quarterback. I play for Dallas. I'm famous, Stephanie."

"I know."

Then she looked back over her shoulder and her smile melted as she realized, "You didn't think I knew who you were?"

And her world tipped violently out from under her as she saw the truth.

10

John's world locked firmly back into place. It was like stepping onto a rock after he'd been wading through a bough. She knew. Everything. Knew who he was and what he did. And her knowing everything caused a paradigm shift in him that this wonderful taste of normal wasn't temporary. He laughed. Joy just springing up in him. "You know."

He reached for her and she backed up. Shaking her head. Heat in her eyes and more, he saw hurt as she told him, "You've been lying to me."

Talk about a pinprick to a balloon. He carefully answered, "No."

"Oh?" There was anger now, brewing into a boil. "It's called omission. You *omitted* the truth."

"You knew the truth this whole time. It's me who was deceived, Beauty."

And they were right where he thought they'd end up, but it was all upside down and he just laughed at the irony. This was so great, yet she was so mad.

"Are. You. Kidding."

"No. I thought you didn't know. Why didn't you tell me?" he asked.

"Why didn't you tell me?"

"Stephanie, this isn't something I can just rattle off at a simple dinner party."

"Why not? It's the truth."

He mimicked the imagined conversation in a sarcastic voice. "*So John what do you do? Oh, I'm an NFL football player, a quarterback to be exact. I work for Brad Bennett too.*"

"I knew you were *an NFL football player, a quarterback to be exact,* the minute Brad came to me and said, "Hey, my quarterback let his dog eat all his groceries and he needs a vet.""

"Really?" He crossed his arms. "Then you knew I'd just been injured when you recommended we put Bradshaw to sleep."

"I told you I don't follow football. I had no idea you'd just lost a huge playoff game and gotten injured. I saw you hit that tree with your fist. Thought you were an angry, abusive, arrogant spoiled athlete who thought he was entitled to special treatment and no kinks in his weekend hunting plans."

"And even knowing who I was and what I did, you got mad at me, bowed up on me, didn't give me an inch or any special treatment. No one does that. So, I assumed you didn't know I was famous, just thought I was a normal guy."

"You, a normal guy? You must think I'm unbelievably naïve."

"Seriously, I thought you lived in the Twilight Zone." He smiled.

"So, my ignorance and alienation from your cool famous world is your excuse for omitting the truth?"

"No," he said again, and his words turned serious. "You not acting like everyone else is what kept me from telling you. It was normal for once, you acted like yourself and you never tried to impress me."

"Impress you?" She glared as a laugh became intertwined with her words. "I hope you're kidding? I don't give a flying flip what you do for a living. Playing football doesn't *impress* me. You lying to me has left a definite impression."

"I never lied to you and I was planning on telling you this weekend, for weeks."

"I still don't understand why you lied to me. You didn't even know me."

"Exactly! And you didn't know me. Know anything about me. Stephanie, you don't know how nice it's been to be able to have someone else's career as the focus of conversations. To be able to laugh and talk with a girl who thinks of me as just a guy."

"John, a relationship can't be one sided. You know so much about me and now I feel like I don't even know you."

"Yes, you do." He shook his head. "You know the real me and what's between us has been pure, without any outside interference, until tonight with those women in the bathroom. I'm sorry about what they said. It's one of the things that goes along with the notoriety. People are curious."

"Don't worry about that, it's insignificant. I've dealt with mean girls most of my life, you ignore them." Then she said obstinately, "Besides, I'm perfectly capable of taking care of myself in a bathroom."

"I know you can, but I want to protect you and us. Stephanie, this relationship means a lot to me."

"Then you should have been honest. When you thought I was ridiculously stuck in the Twilight Zone, you should have enlightened me. Each chance you had to keep hiding was another lie. Didn't you feel guilty? Anxious? I mean anyone could have made you."

"I was so glad we didn't go out to that steak house for dinner."

"The beard." She looked at him and there was another stab of hurt. Another step back. "You actually grew that beard to cover this up. You are like Jacob, tricky and cheating people to get what you want."

"No." He defended himself now. "I'm not like Jacob." And he used another reference to prove his point. "I'm more like Solomon, in the Song of Songs. He comes to her vineyard and she thinks he's just an ordinary guy when he's really the king."

"Hmph." The sound was outrage.

"At least that's what I thought. Look, I was afraid," he confessed then he said, "See, I tell you stuff like that. I get vulnerable with you all the time. You know me." He patted his chest then waved to the walls. "This is just what I do." He took a step to her, trying to explain now, "And I knew I had to tell you, and I was going to this weekend. It's why I wanted you to come here. It was time to introduce you to this part of my life. But you already knew, so does it really matter that we had this misunderstanding?"

"You just don't get it, do you?"

"You need to trust me, and this looks like I lied to you, when really I was just holding something back. I'm sorry. Forgive me. That's all I can say. I can't change it, Stephanie. I honestly didn't want all this involved at first. I admit it. But, I think I explained my reasons."

She nodded.

"Stephanie," he said softly as he stepped toward her again. "You know me. I was at my worst the first day we met and then I served you Scotch and you got sick. You were contagious, and I had surgery and we were both recovering, and I was weak and so were you and we talked each other through it, didn't we? All those hours on the phone. You were there for me and I hope I was there for you and there's been real honesty. But there's still more to learn about each other. I want to know more about you, Beauty, and I want to tell you more about me. And I promise you, I'll never keep anything from you again. I swear you can trust me."

"*Let your yes be yes and your no, no.* You have to earn someone's trust. It doesn't just come from a pledge."

"I know," he said softly, longing to take her in his arms when he saw the naked hurt in her eyes. "I've hurt you and I'm sorry."

She shook her head. "I don't know anything about football but you're one of its top players. And this whole thing... it has been a big game with you. I've been a game of 'normal'. Well, I don't play games. I don't have the time or the experience. I'm not a challenge to be seduced and lied to and left."

"That's never—"

"I won't be seduced," she said over him. "I won't sleep with you."

"I know that. I respect that. Believe me, Stephanie. I respect that."

"Ever," she added, making a firm point then lifting a brow. "So now that you know who I really am, and we see each other clearly, let's agree the game is over. Say good bye and—"

"This isn't a game of what you think I want versus what you think you're going to have to defend. I respect you. I'm not out to seduce you." His jaw had that angry tick. "And I won't be the one to say goodbye. You'll have to do that."

"Goodbye." She turned from him and walked out of the room.

Anger had her cold. She was frozen and furious and focused on one thing, getting away from him. She couldn't think through the emotional confusion, so she went into action. Calmly undressed and put on the old jeans and the black sweater and the boots she wore everyday like they were a lifeline.

She felt the outrage, it was a controlling rush and beneath it was the horrible uncontrolled shame. She was embarrassed, feeling like an idiot that she didn't realize he'd been distorting his life, omitting the truth, lying and betraying her trust and playing her for a fool. Like the Andersons, the very first foster family after her mother died, who just acted like their home was a permanent solution and then came the brutal truth—it was temporary—her and Samantha weren't babies to be adopted, they were expensive, difficult teenagers. She'd trusted in them only to learn how untrustworthy the system could be. And the feelings were the same, the shame almost crippling, but life packed you up and moved you on. Like a roaring river you had to hold on tight to the life preserver of faith or you'd drowned trying to reach back to the safety of yesterday's shore.

She sent up a prayer, turning in a circle, trying to figure out what to do as a little whimper leaked out of a heart that was breaking and it was like a power surge. She was in the dark here. Not knowing what to do next. Stuck again, in a strange house. The situation flipping emotional switches that had anxiety only rising. The fight was gone, and fear was driving the need to flee. To get as far away from him as possible and freeze out the burning hurt that was consuming her heart.

She looked for a phone, she would call Layne. He'd come pick her up and take her to...

Wait, did Blair know?

And Brad certainly knew John had been hiding this. And Linda...

She sat down. The shame spreading. They all must know John was trying to hide his identity from her. They'd known about this game and switched sides, betrayed her.

There was pain now. The kind that takes hold of your heart and just squeezes it. Quickly, she did what she used to do as a foster kid. She was up, made her way into the bathroom, closed herself inside the smaller closet that held the toilet and locked the door. Slowly she sat down on the lid and just closed her eyes. Hiding in the dark so no one could see her, hear her, know she was terrified and overwhelmed because she didn't know what to do.

She was lost again. Lost in the dark. Lost to the past and to the pattern of her life that kept repeating itself. The grief reaching back to find the terrified, abandoned girl whose father had died, and mother had orphaned her. She'd lived in loneliness and used pride as a shield and intelligence as a sword to survive in a world that was never certain. Moving from foster family to foster family, her and Samantha separated for lengths of undetermined time as they grew up in a system that always changed and never felt secure. She swore no one would do this to her again. Yank the rug out from under her. Surprise her. Control her. Betray her.

She was done with this, him. She'd take a cab, would leave on the first flight home tomorrow. She never wanted to see him again. And it would be a long time before she spoke to any of the Bennetts. In fact, she would move, get another job. She didn't need them or John Dake. She didn't need anyone. She could do this alone... She was still... alone. And there was a terror in that awareness and an anxious pride that said, "So what." It was trying to rise up and take over, to claim control and convince her she didn't need anyone. Even God.

She shook her head because she knew what was happening, whose voice was lying to her and how quick this line of questioning could have her believing those lies. She began to pray the promises of God's word, "Lord, you are an ever-present help in times of trouble, please help me..."

The prayer skittered to a quick halt as she heard something. Anger fired up again. She came flying out of the bathroom on the attack until she saw the dog.

Bradshaw cowered down.

And Stephanie reached out, stroked and assured and accepted the unconditional love of the animal as together they curled up on the bed. Oddly the pattern on the new comforter reminded her of her childhood bedroom and the little flowers that covered her bedspread. She'd been taken from there with nothing but the clothes she wore and the family Bible she'd held on to, and over time she grew out of what her mother had given her until there was nothing left but memories and God's word. There were new clothes and new places, beds that she slept in at stranger's houses, days and weeks and years counted off until she was finally old enough to be on her own, in control and even then, she'd failed to guard her sister. God had rescued Samantha, but God had also let the whole thing happen. Just like He let her mother die. Just like He let John Dake show up.

You can't trust anyone. All you've got is you.

She heard the proclamation but at the same time there were memories. Of her mother's hugs and Linda's care. Of the haven of John's arms. Finally, she was crying, curling up and clinging to the dog as Bradshaw licked her face of the hot burning tears. And she felt the grief and the fury because love made her remember what it felt like to be home...

How could her mind be so mad at him and never want to see him again, yet her heart was breaking over what she would lose and finally her prayer came again, "God, please help me."

John plowed his fingers through his hair again as he sat in the dark kitchen on one of the bar stools. He cradled his skull as his thumbs tried to work the tension out of his neck. What had he expected? Not this.

She knew. She. Knew.

From the very beginning she knew who he was, and it really had been normal. She'd treated him like a real person and wasn't that what he loved about her?

He was really falling in love with this woman. He took a deep breath.

God... forgive me, I was selfish and fearful.

"I need You. Help me with this woman. I don't want to lose her. I don't deserve her, but I'm asking, begging you, God, to help me. Help her to see I didn't mean to hurt her. Help me fix this. She needs to trust me. She needs to trust You too... help us both. Talk to her

11

Early the next morning she quietly carried her bag down the hall toward the front door. As she turned the corner she saw him. Still sitting in the clothes he wore last night, he was cradling his head in his hands at the kitchen bar and at his feet Staubach rose and looked at Bradshaw beside her.

Then John looked at her. And it was a reflection of her own pain.

"Stephanie, I want to own my part of this. I blew it. Bad. Was selfish. Wanting to keep things normal for just a little bit longer. Wanting it my way at the expense of being honest with you. I should have told you. I had more than enough opportunities and I made the choice to keep it concealed. Grew the beard." His eyes were dry but she saw a certain pain reflected back at her that she understood. "I'm not ever going to be normal, Stephanie."

"Neither am I," she answered him honesty. "I got left as a baby by my dad. Was orphaned as a teenager. Had to learn how to survive in a system that's very unpredictable. I need to be in control or I get scared. And trust is earned—"

"And vitally important."

"To me, it is."

"I blew it. Forgive me."

"I forgive you."

"Don't leave." There was an ache in his voice, an authentic plea as he said, "Please."

She stood there holding her suitcase as he sat there on that barstool.

"I know you're spooked, want to run," then he begged her, "Give me a day."

"John, I—"

"You don't have to say anything yet. Just give us a day."

"Us?" She glanced at the dogs.

"Me and God." He looked at his watch. "I've got rehab in thirty minutes. My trainer will be here with my physical therapist. It takes a few hours, so I scheduled it early since you were here." He looked at her and said honesty, "I do it here because I'm weak right now and I'm really proud. And I don't want anyone else watching me rehab until I can get my arm strength back."

He stood up now and explained, "There will be some people in and out. They're part of my personal team," he explained, "They work for me. Help me do what I do and be who I'm supposed to be, and I trust them because even though I play a sport, this is business and I need to treat it that way to be successful. Hattie will be up. She can get you anything you need. I heated the pool for you because you said you like to swim and I knew you'd be up early. There are a few robes in the pool bath with the beach towels. Will you stay?"

She nodded.

And when he usually would have smiled he respectfully just nodded his head and she went back to the guest bedroom.

She didn't know why she'd agree to stay or where John had gone but his house was big, and the voices had carried only a moment after the door bell had rung. In her guestroom, she'd waited in the silence a few minutes then found the pool bath and a thick terry robe and went outside and quickly into the pool, leaving the robe close by on the deck as she began to swim.

It was eleven strokes to the other side. She counted. Moving from one end to the other.

1-2-3-4-5-6-7-8-9-10-11-turn.

1-2-3-4-5-6-7-8-9-10-11-turn.

The rhythm familiar and the routine putting her mind into that quiet space as her body worked and she closed her eyes. She often felt blind not really knowing how to navigate through a world that since her teenage years felt overwhelming. She'd learned to be the outsider even as she'd longed to be included. Hope was a fragile thing, stepping forward took courage. And yet she found herself once again back where she was comfortable, withdrawn, alone, mentally working through the issue and knowing she didn't have the answers again. But God always did.

So, she would close her eyes for the object lesson. She was blind, and here in the dark the warm water was smooth. The sounds muted. She felt the tension begin to wash away. Peace was here. She knew that. Not just in the quiet soothing water but in the solitude of her soul.

She'd learned loneliness was an emptiness, but solitude was often a filling.

Every day you could learn something new about God and yourself if you allowed faith to do its work. And in the water God had often come to find her and fill her. She could confess her anger. And the doubt. She could recall God's promises and let His word begin to transform her mind. But this morning she just kept reaching forward with her hands. Knowing Jesus was nearer than she could imagine, caring more than she could understand, loving her in her doubt and fear and pride. Peace was here. Christ was near.

And she needed to close her eyes for the visual effect to remember she was lost here in the dark. Her flesh was consoling her to go its own prideful way. Emotions fighting to protect her as she regrouped from the betrayal and shame. The fist of unforgiveness demanding that John owed her, the world owed her, God owed her, and it was a bitter taste.

"I'm lost," she prayed, "But God, *Thy word is a lamp to my feet and a light to my path.*"

She opened her eyes and kept reaching forward.

Jesus was near.

Lost, she asked for nothing but to be found and shown the way to go.

She cooled down with the back stroke. Eleven slow steady laps down the long length of his pool. It was shaped like a cross. The short sides shallow with the steps near the house and the opposite end a series of rising pools where water cascaded down in waterfalls. The long side was deep with an expanse long enough for exercise and at one end a diving board. After finishing the last lap, she just floated on her back, concentrating on her breathing. Taking air in through her nose until her filling lungs lifted her to float high in the steaming water. Slowly she exhaled through her mouth and her body began to slowly sink. She repeated it. Looking at the wide blue winter sky. The barren trees that cast their long winter shadows. Spring would be coming soon. Seasons changed. Time heals. The river of time moves you on and tomorrow it wouldn't hurt so bad. Better days were ahead... She reached for the side and rested her head on her arms as her eyes closed and the steam rose around her.

Today, she could just wait and see and trust in the only One who was faithful. It wasn't her. She confessed that she couldn't trust herself either. She told God, I'm selfish too. Scared of what I don't know how to do yet, have this relationship, kiss him. And that's pride. Just like John, I don't want people seeing me weak or afraid. And I act selfishly. Hide who I really am and show just a managed image of who I want people to see. A disciplined woman who swims...

She glanced at his large bedroom windows. Wondered if he could see her here in his pool. Wondered if she wanted him to see her. She turned her face away. His house was big, and he had respectfully left her alone. He'd given her space and she'd give him his day and God time to work. She invited Him to start. Just quietly told the Spirit to come and do His work. To recreate and renew her.

Then she grinned when Bradshaw came running out a doggie door and dove into the pool.

Matt, his physical therapist just pointed out the window. "One of the dogs just jumped in the pool."

"Uh-huh,"

Then he said, "Wow."

Stephanie was getting out of the water. She wore a one-piece but the simple black tank only accentuated long legs and a figure that had two guys staring with open mouths.

John felt his molars meet and his trainer knew the look. Closed his mouth. Nudged the therapist. "Get the ice, Matt, we're almost done."

"She's really—" Ryan shook his head now but Matt's words were already coming, the kind of phrases guys say when it's just guys. "Is this one a model too? Or another singer? Actress? No wonder you're worn out this morning."

"Get. The. Ice." John's words were blunt, and the man moved to the ice machine that was less indulgence and more of a medicinal necessity when he spent too many hours soaking sore muscles in an ice bath or icing his throwing arm in a wrap. It was what Matt prepared now while Ryan massaged him, deeply to break up any scar tissue then manipulating his right arm into a stretch then several careful bends, gently increasing the static stretch in the final set of the morning.

The ice came, a bag that was designed to sculpt around his shoulder and was tightly wrapped. The two men worked together silently while John stood waiting. He slipped his left arm into a zip up jacket and told them, "Thanks," as Ryan pulled it around his wrapped shoulder and zipped it up.

When Stephanie opened the bathroom door she heard a boy. He was talking to someone and Bradshaw sprang off to find him as she followed the dog into the game room, securing the long robe tightly around her. "Bradshaw! There you are." The boy hugged the dog, her tail wagging, his voice excited as he said, "I couldn't find you. Only Staubach."

The little boy was wearing a soccer uniform and eating cereal from a box as he watched cartoons on the big screen television. Bugs Bunny was making pizza with Daffy Duke.

She smiled and said, "Hello."

"Hey!" he looked at her with wide eyes. "Were you swimming?"

She nodded.

"Bradshaw's wet. She's not supposed to swim in the pool," he whispered it.

"Ut-oh," she sat down beside him on the huge pit sofa that surrounded the big screen. "Am I in trouble?"

"Big trouble." He looked off over her shoulder toward the kitchen. "But I won't tell. She's just damp and my Grandma is busy cooking."

"I dried her off in the bathroom with one of the towels."

"Not the good ones." His warm brown eyes were big again. He whispered, "With the big D stitched on them?"

She shook her head.

"Whew, we don't use those. Ever. Just the little one by the sink to dry your hands. There're towels in the cabinet. Big ones, for the pool."

"The beach towels."

"Yeah."

"That's what I used for Bradshaw. What are you eating?"

"Captain Crunch. Mr. John gets it for me. He leaves the box on the sofa every Saturday. It's my pre-game energy boost. You know about that?"

She just shook her head.

"Mr. John eats peanut butter and honey on wheat toast before his games but he used to eat Captain Crunch when he was a kid. Grandma says it has too much sugar but she's old Mexico. I was born here."

Again, she nodded.

"Want some? It will be awhile before we eat," he held the box out, his attention drifting back to the big screen. There was a fight on screen, pizzas flying like discus. She took a hand full of cereal and they watched the fight. Before long she was grinning, then giggled.

"Poor Daffy," she said.

"He always loses." He tilted the box. "You can have more."

She took another hand full. "This is really good."

"The best. What's your name?"

"Stephanie," she answered.

"I can't call you that. I only get to call Mr. John, Mr. John cause were so tight and all. Are you a friend of Mr. John's?"

"I'm a friend of Bradshaw's," she answered, stroking the dog.

He tilted his head and crunched on cereal. "How'd you meet her?"

"She got a stomach ache when she came to Louisiana."

"Yeah. She was really sick had to stay there forever to get better."

"I helped her do that. I'm a veterinarian. Do you know what that is?"

"I'm eight already," he told her with a frown but tilted the box back to her to share more cereal. "You're a dog doctor. We've got one for our cat."

"What's your cat's name?"

"Snowball. She's all white. My mom named her."

"That's a good name."

He shrugged. "It's okay. I like dogs, but we have to wait until Celia is bigger. She's my sister. Just a baby."

"What's your name?"

"I'm Roberto Chavis." He held out his hand. They shook.

"Nice to meet you, Roberto."

"Yes, Ma'am, you too. Have you been on that ride?" He pointed to the screen where an advertisement for an amusement park was showing off a ride.

"It looks scary."

"It's really not." He shook his head and told her. "It's like an elevator. You go up, up, up to the top. Then they hold you there—that's the scary part, you're just hanging there waiting for the drop, right?"

"Yes." She looked at the television and saw what he was taking about.

"My dad said that's called insecurity—that's when you're not in any control. That's what's scary. Cause you don't know when it's dropping, but you know it is." He shrugged. "The drop isn't bad at all. Weeeeeee, and your down. So, it's not that scary. Just try it." He ate more cereal and asked, "Do they have any soccer teams in Louisiana?"

"I've seen teams playing soccer on Saturday mornings at our park."

"I play striker."

"I bet you score a lot of goals, Roberto."

"Not yet." He offered her more cereal. "I pass to Nick, he's good at scoring."

"Well no one can score without the assist, right? Passing is important." Stephanie accepted another handful.

"Yeah, I got the passing down. My dad said if I get the chance I need to take the shot more often. But Nick says, 'I'm open!' and I just pass instead of shoot." He looked down into the cereal box and shrugged. "Then it's too late. I missed my chance and the game is over. I get home and I'm disappointed. You ever get like that?"

"Sometimes."

"Got to take the shot, Miss Stephanie. Oops."

"You can call me that." She smiled at him.

"Better not," he looked up and waved as a woman approached them.

"Good morning," Hattie smiled, joining them. "I thought I heard you." She was holding a steaming cup of tea and a glass.

"Is that chocolate milk?" Roberto jumped up and the dogs were at once circling and joining in on his excitement.

"Yes." She handed him the glass, cautioning him to be careful as she told the dogs to sit. "And John said you like tea. He got the brand you like and I added honey."

"You don't have to drink that tea. Mr. John has chocolate milk. It's the best. Really." He smiled with a chocolate milk mustache then he whispered, "My mom won't buy it. Ever."

"Roberto." Hattie chuckled.

"It must be good." She touched her lips as she grinned. "You have a milk mustache."

He licked it off with his tongue. "It is. You can have some. I'll share."

"I like you." She smiled. "Most kids won't share Captain Crunch and chocolate milk or a chance to score a goal, but you've learned the more you share the more you get to have to share and God just keeps giving you more and more."

"Like Mr. John, he gives a lot too. I'm getting a goal today for sure, right grandma?" he said looking at his grandmother.

"I think you will."

"I think I'll have a glass of chocolate milk," Stephanie told him.

Roberto nodded.

"Did you enjoy your swim?" Hattie asked, as they walked toward the kitchen.

"Yes, Ma'am. Thank you."

"On the side bar there is honey and lemon by the coffee pot if you want to add more to your tea."

"It's perfect," she took a drink then smiled. "But I will take a glass of chocolate milk."

Hattie smiled back and prepared it for her as she said, "I'll make breakfast for you. You like eggs?"

"Yes, but you don't have to."

"It is what I do." She smiled.

"How can I help?"

"No. You are his special guest. I get to serve you." Hattie began to prepare as she asked her, "Did you like the play last night?"

"Yes, I loved the scene with the Aggies, I went to school at Texas A&M. And the dancing was especially good."

She placed a placemat on the bar setting up the silverware with a space for the plate. "Mr. John, he so excited that you came. He worked for two weeks on your room." She laid out another place setting. "Did you like it?"

She could only nod.

"Then he made sure the fresh flowers match all the colors. It so nice to see him so," she smiled warmly, "Happy with you coming. He very excited."

Stephanie looked down into her milk glass and digested the information as she took a long drink.

"So last night you have fun?"

"It was very nice. Have you worked for John a long time?" she asked trying to move the topic from last night.

"Since he was drafted in the NFL. Now, he is like one of my own boys. I have four sons." She smiled proudly. "John, his life is a hand full but he's a man trying hard to do good."

Stephanie echoed, "He's definitely a hand full."

"I said his life is a hand full," Hattie corrected her softly and Stephanie saw the loyalty as she explained, "He just have so much world outside that know of him and want to get a look at him or have him do something. Where ever he goes, they calling his name, wanting his autograph or his money for some cause. People never let him be just John. It's been hard on him." She looked at Stephanie, "And it will be hard on you. Mr. Dake is very caring, and he do anything for the people he loves. He takes good care of us."

"You take good care of him, Hattie. He's blessed to have you."

"I am blessed. He is a good man who gives a widow renewed purpose." She touched Stephanie's hand softly. "I hope you take good care of him too. He is special."

"What I want to know is just how you got a bath this morning, Bradshaw?" John's voice drifted into the kitchen as he walked in with two men and both dogs. Bradshaw instantly darted to her, circled once, then reared up on her thighs with a 'help me out here' look.

She stroked the Golden's head, softly urged her down and recollected the robe, re-cinching it.

John looked at her, smiled and asked. "Good swim girls?"

She nodded, noting his right arm was under his jacket and a bulge was over his shoulder. He must be icing she thought as she told him, "We both enjoyed it."

"Dr. Stephanie Hightower, this is Matt my physical therapist and Ryan my personal trainer."

"You're a doctor," Matt stated.

"Veterinarian," she answered. "Want some coffee, John?" she asked moving to the side bar in the corner without waiting for his answer or making eye contact. She knew he was one handed. And this was awkward, standing in a robe in a kitchen with strange men. She took a long drink of her chocolate milk to hide the nerves as John walked over to her, handing her a coffee cup as he stood behind her. "My team will be here any minute. Rhonda and Kenny are stopping by. Everyone made excuses to drop by this morning because they know you're here."

"I should change."

"You're covered head to toe in that robe. Look beautiful." He tucked a curl back behind her ear, threaded it into the crazy knot at her neck.

"Here's your coffee."

He took her arm instead as someone's question proceeded them into the kitchen. "Are they up yet?" A woman asked, and her partner echoed, "Oops, they are."

"I'm going to change," she said as the kitchen filled with three more people.

Then two more were coming in with Roberto as he ran up to her and said with a grin, "You have a milk mustache."

She wiped it off. Glanced at John as heat flared into her face. He turned them back toward the corner, acting like he was stirring something into his coffee when she knew everyone in the kitchen knew he drank it black.

But he whispered, "I was about to do that, would have just used a kiss if I hadn't totally made a train wreck of my integrity last night. I feel like Bradshaw, deep in the doghouse."

"Um," she started stirring her own tea as she tried to figure out how she was going to handle the next few minutes. She glanced at Roberto, felt like she was on the tower ride, just hanging there, ripe with insecurity and anxiety.

"What do I need to do here Stephanie?"

"I don't know. I'm giving you a day."

He leaned in close. "I'll take it. God said to show you my life. These guys are a big part of it." He touched the corner of her mouth, a little sweep as he sincerely told her, "I've got everything to prove, you just be yourself, Beauty. Milk mustaches are really endearing by the way."

He turned them, tucking her under his left arm and it was so sudden all she could do was clutch her robe and curl into him as he protectively presented her to his team.

"Hey guys."

There was silence. Everyone smiling.

"This is Stephanie."

A woman holding an armful of clothes was the first to say, "Good morning."

"Rhonda, is my stylist. She started dating my publicist about a year ago."

"Two years." She gave Kenny a glance and the man greeted her with a wave. Then John just went around the kitchen sounding off names and titles until he got to the boy.

"And this is Roberto Chavis!" John announced, rolling the R and speeding up the last name dramatically.

"Hey Mr. John, I like your friend."

"What friend?" John asked not understanding.

"Your girlfriend from Louisiana, she likes soccer too. Want to come to my game? We're playing the Hornets!"

"Ah?" John glanced at Stephanie.

She said, "I love a good soccer game and Roberto is going to score today. It's a can't miss."

John nodded. "Sure, we'll come. Henderson Park, Hattie?"

"Si', at noon. Breakfast is ready for whoever is eating."

His staff began to move, getting plates and circling toward Hattie who was serving.

"Glad I brought these," Rhonda set down the stack of clothing on the island and Carl was already on the phone managing the outing.

"You'll need two guys at Henderson Park," Kenny advised, "Maybe three with a noon game and the crowd."

John just gave a nod. Rhonda held out a pair of athletic pants. "I got these in black or granite. With a full zip jacket and a long sleeve logo tee. Pick."

"Jeans and a USC hoodie."

She shook her head. "We're not getting paid to promote USC or Wranglers."

"We're working on Wrangler," Kenny interjected.

She held up the athletic gear. "These guys are paying you now and do your own job, Kenny so I can do mine."

"Ouch," Ryan said.

Rhonda gave Ryan a look that had him following Kenny to the stove for food.

"Beauty, what color?"

"Ah." She just blinked her eyes.

"I brought you this." Rhonda smiled at her as she held up a track suit by the same company. "The sponsors would love you to wear it."

"Rhonda gets paid by the sponsors too," John interjected, "So make her sell it."

"Really? You too today, huh John?"

"Stephanie's not under contract."

"Well legally, at an athletic event as public as Henderson park, she kind of is if she's with you. No competitor's labels. They could be captured in a photograph and we'd violate the contract. You'll look great in this."

"Ah," Stephanie just said again.

Rhonda went right on along. "And if you're holding hands with John." She glanced at John's hand on her arm.

"She's under no obligation to hold my hand."

Now Matt stepped up, "She's going to need to stay on your right, protect your shoulder. We can't have some kid accidentally hitting you."

"I'll be fine. She'll wear whatever she wants; jeans and boots are fine."

"It's a soccer game." Rhonda looked offended.

"She's like me, casual cowboy works for us."

"You're an athlete. We've gone over this, boots are for buildings, and athletic shoes are for fields of turf. And I got her these." She slipped a pair of women's shoes from a draw string bag and smiled. "Look, aren't they gorgeous. It's a new color. No one has these yet, they're a summer prototype."

"She's not impressed with that either."

"Are you taking the girls?" Rhonda just marched right on. "If she's in this track suit. Granite and green. You're right, she has great eyes. Then you go granite too, John, and we go with the cardinal red and these stripes across the chest that accentuate your wide shoulders, showing strength. You're just icing right? No, sling today."

"No, sling."

"He needs to be careful some kid doesn't grab him and extend his arm out," Matt's arm was showing them the move that was dangerous as he held out his arm, opened and swept it wide. "And no high fives," he held his hand up, "I don't want you going up yet either."

A beeping started on someone's watch. It was Ryan and as he moved his way John said, "Finally. That was a long twenty minutes. I'm starving. Beauty, can you get me unzipped." He'd turned to her and she just obliged him. Ryan helping him shed the jacket and unwrap the binding to take off the ice pack. His scar was pink and several inches long. Matt was warning John again about keeping his arm protected. Mentioning he might want to just wear the sling out to the park. Rhonda was still talking about the coordination of the outfits. Carl was asking if the dogs were going too and how big of a car they needed. And Hattie was holding up a plate, hearing John was hungry as Ryan helped him put his jacket back on.

"I'm going to change," she told him softly and slipped out of the busy kitchen.

Bradshaw was beside her and so was Staubach for a few steps then she circled back to John. Stephanie went into her room behind Bradshaw. Her luggage standing right inside the door, her small bag left open with the jeans and sweater on the bed. She was barely inside when there was a knock on the door.

"It's Rhonda."

Stephanie opened it.

"I asked John if I could follow you. He wasn't sure, so I want you to know this is on me, not him, okay?"

"Okay." She liked her honesty and smiled as she said, "Come in. How long have you worked for John?"

"I don't work for John. I work for JDi—John Dake Inc.—we're an incorporated team. We work furiously hard together in our various roles to build his name into a brand in the short time we have before John's career transitions off the field into broadcast or coaching."

"He said you're his stylist, I'm thinking that's more than a tailor?"

"Image manager. My job is about optics. Kenny handles the audible."

"And you're dating, Kenny?"

"Yes. We went to John first when it started moving that way. Loyalty is important, and the team comes first at JDi. He's been supportive, trusts us to keep to business—that's the easy part. I'm bossy and serious. Kenny's sarcastic and playful. He thinks some jock is going to turn my head and I used to think he was still looking for someone prettier. We both come from broken homes," she shared. "But that's the past. I'm crazy about Kenny, no one could turn my head now. We're good together. He'll figure that out eventually. You know how guys are? They blow it and we come in and help them regroup and the process hurts but it builds trust and, in the end, it makes the relationship stronger." Rhonda smiled and explained, "I know this is all new with John and strange and maybe the clothes seem silly and insignificant but every detail matters to us at JDi. John Dake is a brand and fame has as many challenges as advantages. He's scrutinized by the public and restricted by his business contracts. He's paid to wear this brand. And when someone else has studied what works and lays it out, it reduces the stress of what to wear when the spotlight is already on you. You can't go wrong with this." She held out the track suit. "It's comfortable, stylish and warm. You're a couple now. You guys will look great in these and it's the right look at a kid's soccer game at Henderson Park without being matchy-matchy. Just try the shoes. He gave me your sizes, so everything will fit. There's a bite to the wind today," she opened up another draw string bag that was color coordinate with the track suit and designed like a back pack. "There are gloves and a hat and scarf in here if you need it. Everything works together."

"Thanks, Rhonda."

"He did a good job on the room. Did you like it?"

She nodded. "It's beautiful."

"I'll leave a few things in the closet for you. Since you swim I'll get a few suits. Our sponsor has a great line of—"

"I just wear one pieces."

"Okay, they do competitive swim wear. Have a great sports bra too. I'll leave you a few."

"I'm not sure when I'll be back."

"You'll be back." She swept the room. "He's never done this before." Then she looked at her. "I didn't say that." She pressed her lips together tight then whispered, "Kenny says I need to stick to the optics and let him handle the sound bites." She smiled. "I'll let you change."

She showered, dried her hair, applied her makeup. She stared at the track suit, glanced at her old jeans and sweater. She was a rule follower and it was the guilt that overrode the anger and had her putting on the warm-ups and lacing up the new shoes. She filled the little drawstring bag with a few more necessities from her handbag and walked out to the kitchen.

"I kept this warm," Hattie told her as she set her breakfast plate down. "John went back to change."

In a few minutes, he joined her, wearing what Rhonda had recommended. He didn't comment on her outfit, just told her she looked great and that the car was waiting. He had sunglasses and a ball cap, a camera bag and two leashes as they loaded up the girls in the black SUV with three men.

During the drive over, he talked about the camera, showed her how to use it.

"Roberto's going to finally score today," John stated. "He's been shut out all season and its starting to bother him."

"Were you always the kid that scored all the goals?"

"Ah," he looked at her like it was a trick question. "Maybe?"

"I'm sure you were. Not everyone gets to score, some players will always be in support positions instead of the superstar, right?"

"True, but I want Roberto to score today. He's a good kid and I hate the disappointment on his face."

"We learn a lot through disappoint," she stated then said, "Tell him he's a great passer."

"Did you play soccer?"

She nodded. "I never scored in soccer, but I made a lot of kicks some people would call assists."

"What team?"

"We were blue. It was YMCA in elementary school. I wasn't very good."

"Assists are important, Beauty. It's a team sport."

"This is it," the driver told John as they drew to a stop at the entrance to Henderson Park. "Closest drop off point to field five." The parking lot was crowded, the fields a colorful showing of teams and parents. The park wide open with only a cluster of trees at the edges of endless fields and at its center was a building and playground.

"Okay girls." John gathered leashes.

"Let me." She took them from him. "You get the camera bag."

"Wait," he told her, "The guys will help you out. We follow their lead, okay?"

She nodded. The dogs were restless as they waited, crowding in front of her and looking at the door. She soothed them both. When the door opened, a man took the leashes, allowing the dogs to exit before he offered her his hand. His name was Nate and he told her he'd be close by along with Tim if she needed him. She just nodded as John met her. He was adjusting his ball cap and scanning the scene ahead as he talked to Tim.

"Let me have Staubach." He reached for the leash. It was blue. Bradshaw's gold.

"I'll carry the camera."

"I've got it, Dr. Hightower," Tim shouldered the camera bag.

They began to walk. John pointing ahead to where field five was located as both Goldens tugged with excitement. "Heel," John ordered and Staubach obeyed immediately, tucking right to his side. "Tell her," he suggested. "She'll obey you. Don't let her tug."

"Heel," she said then praised, "Good girl."

Just as someone pointed and exclaimed, "John Dake."

"Hey." The word was pleasant as he raised his left hand, smiled and kept walking. The excited man stalled his approach and just like the dogs, seemed to heal and pull back.

But his name had been like a cheer and people were turning to look at them as they walked by, then some started following them.

He smiled. "Great day. You warm enough, Beauty?"

She nodded. Just observing the crowd and how he was handling them by not handling a thing.

"Hattie's family will be here. They're great. And Rhonda and Kenny might show up." He smiled at her. Then looked at Tim, "I'm going to keep moving when we get to the field. Work with the kids," he looked at Nate. "You stay with Stephanie. The Chavis family knows how to circle up. We'll try that."

The men nodded, and John put his hand gently on her back as they came to a stop. Hattie welcomed them, introducing Stephanie to her family. The dogs greeting people. John passing off Staubach to one of Hattie's sons. Bradshaw circled back, and Stephanie had to turn to get untangled and that's when she saw the incoming surge. Dozens of people with cameras and pen and paper or scrambling to find them were like an incoming tide about to ascend.

John kept moving, leaving her and the girls in the center of the Chavis family and taking the field with Roberto's father. He was greeting the coaches before he began to move along the boys. Roberto at his side. The other team joining them at center field for a huddle. Then they were following John, all clapping in a rhythm. Stephanie watched him work both teams in simple calisthenics that started with jumping jacks. John just clapping as he walked among the kids. Then the boys were lifting their knees up along with John as they counted to twenty before they all dropped to the grass. He led them in stretches. Reaching for toes and holding as they counted off again before they moved to sit ups.

"He's showing off," Rhonda said beside her. She smiled as she used a video camera to film it all. "Wonder why?"

And so did she. She glanced at the crowd. It had grown some more. Parents were filming everything and she wondered if this was for them, the kids, her or perhaps it was just what he did. She didn't know yet. So, she silently observed, Bradshaw at her side. Her hand holding tight to the leash like a lifeline as she fell deeper into the rabbit hole of his world.

"You look great," Kenny smiled at her as he clicked off a photograph.

She just smiled back, and he took another picture of her.

"He'll love that one." Then he told her, "Don't take it personal but he'll probably stay across the field to avoid the crush."

He did. John stood with Roberto's dad between the two teams as the game started. Ryan, John's trainer, kept a low volume play by play going as he anxiously watched the kids run up and slap his left hand in never ending excited high fives as they came on and off field.

"My husband has him covered, Ryan," Roberto's mother encouraged. "He will stay on his right and protect his shoulder." The little girl in her arms pointed at the dog. The three of them crouched down and let her pet Bradshaw. Maria told her Celia was ten months old and had suddenly developed severe separation anxiety. "She only wants me or her daddy. Will hardly even go to Hattie."

"Can you say dog?" Stephanie asked Celia.

She just smiled at her.

"Bradshaw likes you." The little girl giggled as the dog gave her kisses. "She's beautiful, Maria."

"Thank you."

"Roberto has the ball."

"Oh!" Maria rose and began to cheer. He was dribbling toward the goal but when he got close instead of shooting he passed it to another boy who shot and scored. They all cheered. His mother calling out, "Great pass, Roberto."

John was high fiving again.

Roberto's team was outscored, but the kids didn't seem to care as the parents formed a tunnel and the boys came running through. At the end of the tunnel she linked a hand with Maria as she held Celia and Stephanie held Bradshaw's leash. Then John was beside her as the celebration moved off the field. Nate and Tim were there along with his team from JDi and they all seemed to know what to do as they casually circled around the couple. The dogs were calm, but the kids were everywhere, and unpredictable. She moved closer to John's right side, put her hand on his back. The Chavis family was grilling burgers and they were invited but it was a long walk to the concession area. Fans moved in as soon as the game was over. He signed autographs and poised for photos with kids and then a lot of parents.

She just watched it all patiently, holding the leashes of both dogs. Observing the way he greeted strangers. There was his smile and he answered their praise with a simple, "Thank you." At times people would just gush, others could hardly do more than kindly ask for his autograph. He was especially kind to the kids, considerate to the elderly, patient with the star struck and firm with the flirts. When a girl started moving too close he said, "Stephanie, are we late for lunch?"

She accepted his hand as he reached out and many were left disappointed as he waved goodbye. Kenny took the dogs and Ryan was on his right. Then John drew her tightly to his left side and as he moved it was like the parting of the red sea. People were moving with them. Kids running along. His name echoing forward and heard behind them. Nate having to spearhead the group through the throng at first until they reached the main path. People were everywhere. The park full. Every field had a game in progress. And in the middle of it all, as John held her under his arm, he said with a smile, "Great day."

They stopped at the center of the park where the Chavis family had gathered to grill. There were hamburgers and people handed them plates, moved so they could sit at the picnic table. John flirted with Celia, but she wouldn't leave Maria's arms when he held his hands out. There were jokes about it. Someone wanted to know if he'd lost his touch. Another asked why the magical Dake smile wasn't working. All the while Maria tried to explain her daughter had separation anxiety. Then they laughed as Celia reached for Stephanie. She held the little girl, the two of them petting Bradshaw and John snapped a photograph.

The wind had picked up and it was mid-afternoon when the group began the walk to the parking lot. Tim was on one of those new cellular phones. It was big as a brick with a thick black antenna rising from the top of the cream colored case. He'd called the driver to bring up the car. They had almost made it to the parking lot before another group of fans gathered up to swarm him twenty yards from the car. It was the first time she got bumped. Bradshaw barked and tugged her as she commanded, "Heel."

But John said, "Hey. Guys." His voice was firm and she was tucked under his right arm this time and he was using his left like a straight arm as he told them, "Back up," shaking his head as he moved. Tim had whisk Bradshaw away, loading both Goldens into the SUV as Nate moved to her other side. He was holding on to her as the three moved and it all happened so fast. In a blink of an eye the crowd changed from friendly fans to hungry foes.

"You okay?"

She just nodded. Reached for Bradshaw. Her hand shaking as she buried it into her thick curly coat. She glanced out the window as the car stopped hard and then surged forward. People were actually chasing his car.

"Wow," just slipped from her lips.

And she looked at John, saw the tick in his jaw. "Welcome to my world."

12

John walked in front of the big screen TV with a seven of clubs stuck to his forehead.

"What are you doing?" Stephanie asked.

"Forehead poker. Take a card." He held out a deck of cards. "Don't look at it and stick it on your forehead, like me." He directed.

She slid a card off the top of the deck and held it with her thumb and index finger on her forehead like he did.

"Okay, you can see my card and I can see yours, but we don't know what our own cards are, right?"

She nodded, looking at his seven.

"Whoever has the higher card gets to ask the loser a question. If you get an ace, you automatically get to ask two questions. And you have one joker," he handed it to her. "You can throw it out and pass on any one question," he finished. "But, you have to tell the truth."

"That might be hard for you." She lifted a brow. "Is this truth, or dare?"

"I double dog dare you to play," he challenged as he took a seat across from her. "Ask anything. Find out who I am."

"I'll play." She pulled down her card and frowned when she saw a six of diamonds.

"What size bra do you wear?" He questioned with a straight face.

Her mouth just opened. Then shut. She frowned. He lifted a brow, waiting smugly.

"34-D," she answered quickly. "Give me those cards I want to shuffle them."

He handed them over, boldly smiled.

"And that question said a lot about who you are." She pointed to his motives, shuffling several times. "I take it this isn't a game of what's your favorite color?"

"You'll have to win to ask me that?" he shrugged.

"I seriously overestimated your groveling technique to get out of the dog house."

"Hey, if you're scared to answer a few personal questions truthfully then we don't have to play," he said dryly, evoking a challenge he knew she wouldn't turn down.

"Draw, Mr. Dake." She set the cards down in front of them and took a handful of popcorn from the bowl beside him.

"No, ladies first."

"You won, winner draws first." She pushed the deck toward him.

He held up a nine of spades.

She pulled her card down to look at it, frowning at her four of hearts.

"Panty size?"

"X-large."

"That's a lie." He laughed. "You have to tell the truth, Beauty."

"I'm no Sleeping Beauty, that's the truth. And maybe I should practice lying while you practice telling the truth. Size small," she answered. "Draw."

Stephanie's brow lowered as she saw the Jack of diamonds on his forehead and John said, "You shuffled." She moaned at her two of spades.

"Lace or satin?"

"What?"

"We're still on the lingerie. Do you wear lace or satin?"

"Cotton."

"Another lie, I saw lace at the Bennett house."

"What?"

"You leaned over to greet the Schnauzer and I saw lace."

"I can't believe you!"

"Next time do this." He held his hand over his chest and pretended to bend over.

"Next time don't stare down my dress."

"You looked incredible in that lace bra. I couldn't take my eyes off you. Almost fell out of my chair you were so beautiful."

She put her hand over his as he reached for a card. "How is that question getting to know me better?"

"I know what you like now." He drew. Won again. "When do you wear cotton bras?"

"Sports bras to work."

He won again. "And out with me?"

"Last night I wore lace."

He smiled, and she nudged his card toward him as she said, "If you win again this is rigged."

He won again, and she threw a kernel of popcorn at him after seeing her five of hearts. He crossed his arms and began to smile as he swept her.

"What now?"

"Favorite color?" he asked.

"Blue."

"Blue? I thought it was green."

"No, it's blue."

"Hmph," he said. "I blew it on the room then."

"I loved the room. Take a card," she demanded.

He stuck the seven of diamonds to his head. She lifted her card up, waiting for him to nod. She became impatient as he looked at her forehead perplexed. "Okay," he finally said.

"Are you kidding!" She threw her six of clubs to the side.

"Are you a bad loser?"

"Yes. Draw."

He laughed and then asked, "Did you like the way I kissed you?"

"Draw."

"You didn't answer."

"Your question was, 'Are you a bad loser'," she prompted, nudged a card his way only to watch him win again. He looked at her, smiled.

"What?"

"I already asked my question."

"You're a good kisser, John."

"I didn't ask if I was a good kisser, I know the answer to that."

"Yes," she interrupted. Her answer brought out his smile as he drew another card. "It was mutually enjoyable by the way."

"I didn't ask you."

"I was just giving you some grace since you keep losing."

"You're going to be sorry in a minute."

He won again.

"Was it better than your first kiss?"

She blinked. Then wondered if they'd told him. Layne and Blair, Linda, all the people who knew her, had they told him how nervous she was, warned him maybe, like Layne, trying to be a big brother, protecting her even as he betrayed her. And Blair, with her wit and sarcasm, did she tell John she'd never kissed anyone. And Linda, all the things she'd shared with her...

"Stephanie."

"You know the answer to that. Draw." She pushed his card to him and picked up hers to hold on her forehead.

"I don't know the answer to that. Tell me."

"They told you already." She picked up his card. She'd finally won. And she boldly asked him, "Favorite color?"

"I don't know," he answered.

"First question and you don't know?"

"Blue. I don't know—"

But she'd already lifted the next card. Waited for him. He drew. Lost.

"Ah... where did you go to college?"

"I started at Texas. Finished at USC."

"What made you switch?"

He drew her a card. Lost again. "New coach after my freshman year. I didn't fit the offense. Transferred to USC. It happens."

She won again and asked him, "Favorite Bible verse?"

"I can do all things through Christ who gives me strength."

He drew for her and then waited. And she was out of questions.

"How many women have you slept with?"

"Enough." The answer was blunt.

"That's not an answer."

"Yes, it is."

She just waited.

He threw out his joker. "And you still haven't answered my last question."

"Draw a card." His six lost to her eight.

"What does the Bible call someone who sleeps with people before they're married?"

"A fornicator?" His answer was a question.

"An adulterer. You cheated on your wife."

He nodded. Drew a card. She won again.

He just looked at her and she said, "That made you mad."

"It made me sad." He sighed. "And I think you're mad and you have a right to be. I'm sorry, Stephanie. If it had been one girl it would have been too many, right?"

"It's my turn to ask the question. What does the Bible call someone who sits in the seat of scoffers?"

"I don't know what the seat of scoffers is."

"From Psalm One, *Blessed is the man,*" she was waving the air. "*Who walks not in the counsel of the wicked, nor stands in the way of sinners, nor sits in the seat of scoffers; but his delight is in the law of the Lord, and on his law he meditates day and night.* A scoffer is being a smart mouth judger."

"I think you've memorized a lot of Scripture."

"I think I was scoffing you and that's as evil and sinful as adultery. Scoffing is judging. It's counting your sin greater than mine. Only God gets to judge, so forgive me."

"Draw," he prompted. And he won.

"Is that your favorite Bible verse, Psalms One?"

"Ah... I'm not sure I have a favorite verse, there are so many I like."

"Have you memorized a lot of Scripture?"

She shrugged.

"If I called a book out could you quote something? Like from Revelation."

"*Blessed is he who reads aloud the words of the prophecy, and blessed are those who hear, and who keep what is written therein; for the time is near.* Revelation is easy."

"Hmph. Back to my question, What did you mean, they told you already?"

"I answered your question, draw loser."

"Scoffer." He flicked her a card. He won again.

"What did you mean, they told you already?"

"Blair, Layne, Linda—they told you."

"Told me what?" He covered her hand on the stack of cards. "That your first kiss was better?"

"You were my first kiss. Draw."

"What?"

"You have to draw."

"I was your first kiss?"

She threw the joker out. "Please. Draw."

He won again.

"As beautiful as you are, inside and out, how can I be your first kiss?"

"My mother died when I was thirteen. I needed to be smart not beautiful out kissing boys."

"So, you were smart enough to never date?"

She handed him a card. He won. And she answered, "We got moved around a lot in the system. It's hard to fit in when you're always the new kid in middle school or high school. My clothes were hand me downs, and out of style puts you on the outside. And I learned not to get too close to friends because we'd be moving again anyway. By college I was focused on my future not dating or fitting in."

She dealt the cards again and won.

"Who was your first kiss?"

"Vicki Veslage. Third grade. At recess. We got caught. Went to the principal's office." He grinned and somewhere in the conversation, he'd taken her hand, his thumb sweeping across the top. "My mother was the principal. She followed me through school. Was the principal at my middle school then moved to my high school, I have some serious issues, Beauty."

"I'm aware." She dealt the cards and he won.

"What do you like best about me, physically?" John asked.

"Physically?"

"Yeah, hair, eyes, smile?"

"Your hands," she answered immediately.

"My hands?" There was surprise. He looked down at them. "Why?"

"Draw a card."

He sighed impatiently when he saw her king of diamonds.

"Ah... how much money do you make?"

"We get paid by the week during the season—"

"I was kidding." She held her hand up for him to stop, "I'm not good at this game, I'm out of questions," she said but he had just kept on talking, counting it out loud, as he added on the bonuses and endorsements and sponsors until the number was ridiculous.

"Once the question is asked it has to be answered and we're both out of jokers." He drew her card and placed it on her forehead and this time he smiled. It was a two and his ten easily beat it. "Explain," he demanded.

"It was rude. You know I could care less how much money you make."

"No, my hands. Explain."

"Explain, is not a question?"

"Why do you like my hands?" he sweetly countered.

"They're strong," she answered matter of fact.

"Strong? Anything about me and it's my hands, my strong hands? My arms and legs are a lot stronger than my hands, Beauty. That's not the truth." He tilted his head waiting for an explanation.

"Sure, it is. You have strong hands," she defended. "It's impressive."

"Strong hands?" His eyebrows dropped, and he clucked. "You're a better liar than I thought you'd be."

"I'm not lying." She straightened to the challenge. "You have very nice hands. They're strong looking and yet they're... soft."

"Soft?" He nodded for her to go on.

"And, your fingers are nice... and um," she lowered her eyebrows trying to think of the right way to say it. "You don't bite your nails. And, I... well I guess I like the way the hair from your wrist kind of trickles down onto your hands and fingers. It makes them look soft... and nice. You have very nice hands." She nodded, that should satisfy him.

He looked down at his hands. "Go on," he said.

"That's it." She shrugged and quickly drew a card.

She won again. He was so much better at asking these stupid questions. She didn't know what to ask. Well she did want to know. And she could have laid money on the answer. She lowered her eyebrows. "What do you like about me, physically?"

"Your heart." He stated evenly, staring into her eyes. "You know who you are, what you want. You're confident, self-determined, independent. You're also compassionate and intensely merciful. Unpredictable and very challenging. You have a great heart."

That hadn't been what she had expected. It startled her. His unyielding gaze made her say something stupid. "I'm not confident," she corrected him. "I'm nervous all the time. Don't know what to do socially, always feel like an outsider. I'm great with animals but I don't really understand people. And my heart isn't something physical, John."

"Physical? Hmm. Your pretty eyes are the window to the soul, but your breasts are spectacular. And your legs were definitely in the running for the top spot in that dress Friday night, until you came out in the track pants today. I absolutely adore your size small fanny in those track pants... I should have stopped with the eyes, right?"

"That was another question that you already know the answer to, so I'm going to draw a card now."

She won and asked him, "How much money do you give away?"

His brow dropped, he shook his head. "I should know that, but I don't. My mom chairs my foundation, I'll find out and let you know, okay?"

"It's okay, I'm not good at coming up with questions."

"It's a good question. I donate a lot of my time too. Put my name and my money on causes for the military to honor my dad and children because that's close to my mom's heart. I'm still looking for my own cause, something I can be passionate about and really get behind."

"I know a lot of people are constantly holding their hand out to you."

"My mother told me I'll know when God is holding His hand out so to speak and I usually do. He also stirs my heart to give at certain times and I've learned to follow through, usually in secret. That's how I like to give, anonymously. Isn't there a Bible verse about that?"

"Matthew six."

He waved her on.

"Be careful not to practice your righteousness in front of others to be seen by them. If you do, you will have no reward from your Father in heaven. So when you give to the needy, do not announce it with trumpets to be honored by others. Truly I tell you, they have received their reward in full. But when you give to the needy, do not let your left hand know what your right hand is doing, so that your giving may be in secret. Then your Father, who sees what is done in secret, will reward you."

"Exactly. Matthew six." He smiled at her.

She saw him raise the ace to his head and tossed her card down. "Providence is on your side tonight, John."

"Providence... You being here with me. Do you think God brought us together?"

"I think all things pass through his hands. Don't you?"

"I think... when this vein right here," he touched her throat, a careful glide of his finger on the side of her neck. "Starts to flutter, then I've made you nervous."

"Is that the second question?"

"I think you're nervous."

"I told you I was nervous."

"And I think you want to be mad because anger is a feeling you can control but not fear. You don't like being afraid and I make you nervous. And that makes me sad because I know what anxiety does, how that building pressure tightens me up, makes me second guess myself, and the situation I'm in, instead of stepping up and confidently trusting myself to play through it. You're wrong by the way. You are confident but maybe it's not self-confidence, maybe it's God-confidence and that's even better."

"Ask your question."

"Are you going to forgive me and make up?"

"Yes... maybe."

"Is that maybe you'll forgive me and yes we'll make up?"

"I forgave you this morning," she finally said. "I don't know about the rest."

"What don't you know?" He gently lifted her chin to look at him.

"I don't know about you, anymore." Her pulse was pounding. Her throat drying up painfully. Fear was fluttering, and heartache was burning her eyes. "I don't know about... us anymore."

"Because I'm famous."

"Because I'm freaked out."

"By the fans. It was a lot to handle today. Even for me and the JDi team. That one woman got aggressive but that's a huge turn off to me. And there at the end, I knew better, should have waved and walked, got us in the car, but I didn't want you thinking I was arrogant."

"No," she shook her head. "You freak me out," she explained. "How you make me feel."

"How do I make you feel?"

"Crazy."

"Crazy?"

"Part of me is so mad at you I don't want anything to do with you ever again." Her emerald eyes glared then glanced away. "Part of me is..." she whispered looking away, "Disappointed, hurt, doubting everything. I don't know what it wants. I'm really confused right now."

"Stephanie." There was regret in his eyes, and the blue glistened with his own pain. "What has God said to you today?"

"Forgive John. And I did. I released you from any emotional debt to me. You don't owe me anything even though you promised me the truth."

"If you want to know how many women—"

"No."

There was silence and he sighed, told her, "No one told me anything about you. Layne warned me to respect you and Blair might have mentioned you were beautiful and her bride's maid and Brad told me a few things that first weekend, but nothing personal. I didn't know I was the first guy you ever kissed."

She blushed. He wasn't smiling, said very seriously, "Why didn't you tell me?"

"I didn't get a chance. You took my hand, led me out of Blair's kitchen, turned me around and stole a kiss. I didn't give it to you. Not that that's what people do, 'heads up, I'm about to kiss you, okay?', but I didn't know it was what you were going to do, then it was happening, and maybe that's the way it's supposed to happen because I was really nervous and then it was okay. It was okay," she told him.

There was silence. A long stretch of it as they just looked at each other and she saw honesty in his gaze as he told her, "Stephanie. I'm sorry. I'm really sorry you lost your mom so young, was put into the system and had to wear hand me down clothes when you were a teenager and move around a lot and couldn't keep friends. I know that was hard." He took her hand, squeezed it as his words just stilled to silence because his heart burned with emotion for her. She gave a little nod, brushed his hand with her thumb and he asked her, "What's the real reason why you like my hands?"

"I told you, they're strong."

"You're nervous again." He touched her throat.

"Great, you've got my tell. No more poker."

"Play through this, Stephanie." He touched her face. She closed her eyes. "Don't get mad when I tell you that you like this. You like it when my hands touch you and so do I. When you take my hand, turn to me, into me so I can hold you. It's what I think about. You. This. Not your body, or sex, or seducing you. Just this, holding you right here." He'd brought her head to his shoulder and he was whispering now, "So I'm glad you like my hands."

"I want to be angry," she admitted softly. "And run, just leave."

"I know. And I want to charm you, try to get my way but instead I'm being honest."

"You hurt me," she whispered, catching her trembling lip with her teeth. "Why did you do that?" There were tears and she hated herself for them. Hated the way her whole body seemed to tremble now with the growing fear of being vulnerable.

He said her name, holding her close, endearingly close. His arms were gentle but secure. His voice tender but sincere. "I told you why. I wanted you to know me without all the glory. I wanted to be me again, just me, Beauty. Without the legend around my name. I'm the king of my world, can have anything I desire but that has a huge cost. I'm lost in the fame. But you found me. At my worst, even. Me, the ordinary man, the man I really want to be, and I think God had something to do with that."

He felt her hands cling, her body curl to him and asked to be comforted. He did his best, needing her, wanting her, holding her as close as he dared.

"You like the way I kiss you and you love my strong but soft hands because you like the way they touch you. But you're still angry because I lied to you."

"Yes," she answered softly. "Right now, the strongest feeling I have for you is anger and at times it feels like hate."

His gaze captured her own, held it, and looked as far as she would let him see.

"You're afraid, and you hate *that*," he made a statement. "But we're going to play through those nerves and my obvious first quarter fumble during the quarterback sneak. You know someone said there's a very fine line between love and hate," John warned as his hand stroked her cheek. "Hate me, but don't be afraid of what's happening between us."

She pulled away, as if to deny what she knew he'd seen in her eyes. Then he smiled that smile that made her heart skip a beat and jumped to his feet as if they'd just finished a board game instead of a very serious discussion as he drew her up to the couch. "Basketball is on and I know you're ready for a nap. Neither of us slept at all last night so it's time. Girls," he called the dogs up to the couch as he got a blanket and turned on the television and said, "Cuddle up."

It wasn't a question so there was no reason to answer, especially since he'd already gathered her into his arms. As the dogs settled in and John secured the blanket snuggly up around her she heard him sigh then whisper into her hair on a soft kiss, "King me."

13

The morning light illuminated the modern stain glass windows, enhancing the beauty of the colors even as God's word exposed the dawning edge of darkness she'd found herself in again when she woke up this morning. She was back to not knowing what to do. How to act. What to say. Was she still angry? She just didn't know how she should feel.

She had been happy last week when John asked her to go to church with him. But this morning she felt the spot light hit her just like the sunlight was shining on those windows as they took their place in a pew in the center of the church.

People are curious.

She realized he knew what he was talking about. She glanced over the church. The pews were filled but not crowded yet everyone was glancing their way. Even the people in the pews in front of them seemed to turn their heads and glance back in John's direction. All this curiosity and attention was adding to her nerves.

John had walked into the kitchen in a suit this morning and launched those butterflies once again. He'd just touched her face, smiled and told her she looked beautiful and it had only made things worse. He'd commented on her suit, it was new. A black boucle wool made into a classic silhouette, but the skirt barely hit her knees and her legs felt too long. She was awkward in the heels. John's sport car took some maneuvering to exit with any grace as he had to literally lift her up and out. She was back to fighting off the fear with a distancing coolness with John.

As they stood for the final hymn, John held the hymnal then they bowed their heads as the blessing and benediction were given. Then he said, "I hope you're ready to meet the congregation. I've always come alone and they're biting at the bit to know who the beautiful woman is I've brought to church." His left hand rested at the small of her back as he guided her out into the aisle. Instantly several men were extending their hands to John in greeting as their wives smiled. They slowly made their way to the vestibule of the church.

"Pastor Conrad, this is my girlfriend, Stephanie Hightower. She's from Louisiana." He smiled down at her as he introduced her.

"So glad to meet you. Where in Louisiana?"

"Caddo Parish near Shreveport."

"Oh, yes. Beautiful country. Lovely lake there. "

"Yes," she smiled and glanced at John.

"It was nice to meet you. I hope you'll come back." He took John's hand and said quietly, "If there is anything else I need to be praying about this week, let me know."

"Peace," John answered the pastor as his hand possessively took hers.

"Good morning, John," a petite, frosted haired blond said.

"Mrs. Merrill," he extended his hand, "Nice to see you. This is Stephanie Hightower."

"Nice to meet you," she smiled warmly.

"Are you ready for the press conference this week?" Mrs. Merrill asked.

"As ready as you can be. Is Coach here?"

"Yes, he's talking with Doc and that group of men." She pointed.

"Mrs. Merrill is married to my boss, Coach Mike Merrill." John smiled.

Stephanie nodded. Several couples quickly joined their circle as John made the introductions. There were the usual superficial questions and answers. John politely excused them from the growing group and walked over to the smaller one around Coach and Doc. A tall and lanky man with thin gray hair that veiled his tan scalp immediately greeted them.

"Doc Lambert this is Stephanie Hightower," John stated with a smile.

"Dr. Hightower, right?" He waited for her confirmation. He smiled at John and added, "The veterinarian." He shook her hand pumping it several times. "Glad to meet you. You sure are pretty. How'd you ever get mixed up with the likes of John here?"

"No idea." She instantly liked Doc and smiled.

"I think we've got the whole franchise here this morning. I guess we all felt a need to thank the good Lord on this beautiful morning. Mrs. Casper," he greeted a woman as she joined them.

"Hello," the well-dressed brunette held out her hand to Stephanie. "I'm Chris Casper's wife, Darlene."

"Stephanie Hightower," she replied back.

"It's so good to finally meet you. I think my prayers have just been answered." She gracefully moved Stephanie a step away from the growing circle of men.

"I'm the coordinating director for Bob and Chris's golf tournament. I've been just knocking myself out trying to find someone to replace Cindy Beihn as a volunteer. You would just be perfect. Are you available? Its three weeks from yesterday. And you know what a good cause it's for." She smiled proudly. "I'll make sure to team you up with John's foursome. Oh, you'll be just perfect." She gave Stephanie I quick once over. "Perfect. You will say yes, right?"

"I'm sorry, Darlene, but I'm not sure what you're talking about."

"Oh, my," Darlene gave a little laugh. "Bless your heart. I guess I take for granted everyone knows about the Dallas social functions but you're from Louisiana I hear. Let me start from the beginning. My husband plays on the team. He co-sponsors a golf tournament every spring to benefit local children who are battling cancer. It's such an important cause," she stated with authority. "And since Cindy Beihn had her baby early, I'm out one volunteer. I thought since you're John's new girlfriend, you might be able to help me out."

"I'd like to help but I don't know my work schedule for that weekend," Stephanie replied honestly.

"Oh?" Darlene's eye brow dropped threateningly low. "It's a Saturday function." She paused giving Stephanie time to reconsider. Stephanie remained quiet. "Well, here's my card. Could you possibly call me this week and let me know? And I don't have to tell you what a good cause it is," she said again. Then her voice turned crisp. "But if John Dake's girlfriend is too busy to help children with cancer, I guess Texas will just have to understand she has her own work to do in Louisiana." She waved at another couple and said quietly, "I just hope his fans don't hear about this."

"I'll let you know tomorrow," Stephanie repeated.

"We have shorts and T-shirts for everyone. Size six?" She asked, her voice cheerful again.

"I'm a four."

"Of course, you are. I'll set them aside. I just know you'll make it. So good to meet you."

And she watched the woman reach out to Mrs. Merrill and turned away as she considered what she was getting herself into? This golf tournament would have her back in Dallas in three weeks. In three weeks... with John. No, she couldn't let that happen. She needed to put some space between them and punish him good for lying to her.

Did you just hear yourself? Punish him... Forgiving meant releasing. He owes you nothing.

"Stephanie this is Coach Merrill." The pressure of John's hand against her back gained her attention.

"Nice to meet you." Her hand was lost inside his. He looked more like a football player than a coach. And that tiny woman was his wife. She looked up at John, realizing for the first time how small she must look next to him.

"We better be going. We're meeting friends for brunch in Dallas," John said.

"So, what did the Saint James Presbyterian Church think about you showing up with a date to the ten o'clock service?" Blair asked John with a little amused smile.

"They couldn't get enough of her." John smiled proudly. "I think Stephanie should have stood by the door with Pastor Conrad and greeted each and every one of them."

Blair and Linda laughed.

"I'm sure they knew how many hairs she had on her head by the time the second hymn was sung."

"These Dallas women can be so nosy," Linda added. "Be glad John's not Baptist. We're the worst."

Stephanie still had not commented. Pride had her indecisive about how she wanted to act toward the Bennetts and Layne for playing John's charade with him. She decided to be quiet. She looked out across the restaurant.

Houston's restaurant was crowded. As they had walked in she heard the hostess tell a couple the wait was over an hour. But John led her past the crowd, just nodded as someone called his name in recognition. A table prepared for them immediately. Then moments later the Bennetts had arrived with Layne and Blair. The group sat in a booth. The long deep seats were burgundy leather. Brad had let Stephanie sit next to Linda followed by John and he had sat next to Layne and Blair across the table.

Blair spoke from the corner. "It's been five whole minutes and you two have managed to sustain from kissing. Are ya'll kissed out or what?"

Stephanie opened her menu refusing to play Blair's game today.

"The salads are very good here," Linda commented.

She decided on one and closed her menu. Brad and John were talking about the press conference. Everyone connected to the team seemed to be talking about it. It must be a big deal.

"So," Blair tried again connecting eyes with Stephanie, "have you had a great weekend?"

With a stone face and an even smoother voice Stephanie answered, "It's been difficult." Blair's eyes flashed between Stephanie and John. Stephanie nudged John, "Excuse me, I need to go to the ladies' room. John can fill you in."

She walked away in a flash of black.

"Excuse me," Linda was quickly following.

"I need to go too." Blair looked at John sympathetically and then in the direction Stephanie had fled.

"What's going on? I can tell you're ready to blow your top!" Blair came straight to the point in the bathroom.

Stephanie turned from the sink and looked at her friend, her sister. "Why didn't you tell me?"

"Tell you what?"

"That John was lying to me."

"About?"

"Did you know he thought I didn't know who he was?"

"Huh?" Blair's face was covered in confusion. "Of course, you know who he is. He's John Dake, daddy's quarterback."

"Stephanie, we'd never lie to you." Linda stepped up.

"Not outright but this was omission. You knew he was keeping that from me," she accused her and saw the strike of hurt in Linda's eyes. "You didn't know?"

She shook her head. And something was forced to let go of her with the revelation and she reached for Linda with a little gasp.

She brought her close. "You should have called me, Stephanie."

"At least called me, the minute this happened. Look how worked up you are." Blair nudged her mother, gathered Stephanie into another hug. "Seriously, Steph. You should have called us."

Stephanie nodded as they separated, and Linda took her hand. "What happened?"

She told them, everything.

"Well, it was wrong, but I understand John longing for normal." Blair cupped her hands together as if she held a priceless object inside them. "I think he wanted to keep your relationship tucked protectively away from the world. He wanted to keep it precious, to wait as long as possible before he had to bring you into his world. Famous isn't always fun."

"And I know John really likes you Stephanie," Linda encouraged.

"He lied to me."

"And you'll have to forgive him."

"I have, but it still hurts."

"Let yourself work through that. Catch your breath then trust the Lord and His will for you both. He'll direct you here."

"And you know we love you." There was a shoulder bump then a soft swat. "You know that."

Stephanie nodded, bumped Blair back.

"We want what's best for you. All of us. Mom, Dad, Me, Layne, Samantha."

She nodded again.

"Don't freak on me here. Don't you dare run off to Louisiana and hide, thinking you can just work yourself to death and this will all go away. He's not going to go away. I know John. He's as determined and stubborn as you can be."

"Take a few days then come have lunch with me Wednesday. We'll talk about your concerns. We'll talk about what all this means, John being a famous man. Give your feelings a few days to settle into place."

"I didn't tell him we're connected," Stephanie told her looking down. "I'm not ready to share that with anyone yet."

"If things work out with John, there will be a time to talk about Samantha."

"Our connection is more than just Samantha," she told Linda. "You're my mom. Brad's my father."

"But the reason for that takes an explanation," Linda added. "And that explanation is painful."

Blair said simply, "Maybe it should be just a simple statement—they adopted us. We're a family."

Linda squeezed her hand and nodded. "We are a family. And I know this must have been difficult for you. Next time you are to call me. Communication clears things up, okay?"

Stephanie nodded. "I feel so much better," she confessed with a sigh. "The doubt was killing me. Forgive me for doubting you and acting ugly today."

"I'm here." Linda kissed her. "And I care. And so does John. We're all learning how to love each other. That's why forgiveness is so important."

"He'll grovel for a few days," Blair gave her famous snort.

"Blair," Linda censored.

"It's good for them, mother."

"Be careful," she warned them both. "You're to submit under not hold it over."

They stood by a column partially hidden from view of the passer byers that drifted down the DFW airport terminal. There were several feet between them as they talked. A fan approached, pen and paper in hand.

"Give me a few minutes," he said loud enough for the curious to hear.

"We are now boarding flight two-thirty-five to Shreveport." The announcement broke into their conversation.

Stephanie reached down to pick up her carry on.

"Stephanie even after everything that happened, I still had a great weekend with you." He caught her hand and rubbed it softly.

"Thank you." She stood posture perfect. "It was all very nice."

"When can I see you again?"

"I don't," she looked down, "I don't know."

He stepped closer to her and just gathered her close, held her in a long hug.

Slowly she pulled away. "I'll be thinking about you this week with the press conference. Praying that it goes well."

"I'll be praying for you too, for us." He nodded. "I won't let you go without a fight." He'd tangled their fingers together, was gently holding on. "The only thing between us now is your fear." She blinked, and he saw the naked vulnerability he'd somehow turned to terrorized distrust as the distance grew and he lost hold of her hand. "I'm praying God will give you courage."

"Mr. Dake." Someone was brave enough to step toward him.

Then another asked, "Mr. Dake can I get your autograph?"

Then someone else said, "Mr. Dake will you sign this?"

She looked back. He was still looking at her as he scribbled his name on one piece of paper after another and she prayed for God to help them as she quickly turned away and walked to the plane. .

14

A girl can do silly things when she's afraid to fall in love. The phone rang Sunday night and she just looked at it. Her heart pounding as she counted the rings. Then her machine beeped, and the light blinked, and she listened to his message. Rewinding the little tape a dozen times before she walked away and went to bed only to jump up when the phone rang again. And she just stood over it as he left the second recording.

She kept herself busy Monday morning at the various barns, but she kept finding herself leaning on a wall or gazing at nothing and thinking about John.

She didn't have the answers yet to the questions that kept circling in her head. She knew she would be met by an inquisitive Mary as soon as she got to the office. She even stopped for lunch to waste some more time. She didn't want to talk, especially about John. She wanted to be by herself. That's how she always solved her problems. Late that afternoon she found herself pushing the jangling door open at the clinic.

"Finally! I've been waiting all day for you to get in. It must have been one great weekend. Go see what you've got waiting for you." Mary nodded towards Stephanie's office.

A huge bouquet of flowers sat in the middle of her desk. Tentatively she tore open the large envelope and pulled out the gray linen stationary.

Beauty
Love and your fears will vanish
In place of the things that terrify you
you will discover delicious feelings
a tender and submissive lover
and all your days
given over to happiness
will leave you with no other regret
than that you wasted so many of them
in indifference.

Pierre Choderlos de Laclos
Les Liaisons Dangereuses

Think about it- John

She read the letter repeatedly. He was quoting poetry to her. Something from *Dangerous Liasons*, that really hit home. And the passage was as pointed as it was beautiful. Each time she read it the verse meant more and more. And there was that fear word again.

The only thing between us now is your fear.

He knew she was afraid. How should she act now—brave, cold, careful?

And how had John Dake the quarterback found something as pointed as this passage from *Dangerous Liaisons*? Dangerous, that was John and a liaison with a man that worked for Brad Bennett should be out of the question, especially after he deceived her. There should be nothing else to consider... end the relationship now while it's nothing.

But it's already something. Something that was missing from her past and now that she made the connection, she realized that falling in love was magical and mysterious and powerful. Even terrified and anxious, it was something she wanted. And if she wanted to pursue this, what did she do next?

She was lost again. In the dark. She needed some time for God to help enlighten her to His plan, she would put some space between them and then maybe start over again, slowly. And see how it went from there.

When a man was falling in love he did stupid things. Like look up poetry and write it on a card. Then call twice in one night and leave messages both times when she didn't answer. And he knew she was home. And obviously, she was still mad. Maybe the flowers would help.

But Monday night she didn't answer the phone again, so he left another message. Then Tuesday he tried again. Maybe her machine was broken.

He called her office on Wednesday. Mary was cheerful and promised to give her the message. She didn't call back. So, he called her house Wednesday night and left another message from his car on the fancy cellular phone. He held the brick size technological wonder in his hand and unscrewed the thick long antennae. Then put it back on, wondering if the phone wasn't working right. He called a friend to test it out. He answered, and they met for a beer at a place where he could come and go through the back door. He wouldn't call it pouting, but he was in a bad mood.

Anger felt better than the restless anxiety. John was afraid that she was seriously blowing him off. That's when he left the really stupid message. "Stephanie, am I dead to you..." It was all about to stream off his charming tongue, flow like lava from a spewing hot volcano of need, but pride came to the rescue at the last minute. It's like when he was about to hit a receiver on a crossing route and suddenly saw the safety shift his hips, take that step to intercept the ball and he pump faked and pulled it back in and then shifted his eyes to the corner and wide open, deep, bam! Touchdown. King me!

"You're afraid and need time. I get it." He gave that pause, the pump fake. "When you're ready to talk, call me."

He hung up. Felt confident she'd call back as he flipped through the photographs Kenny had dropped off from the weekend. He liked the one of her and Bradshaw. In this one she was smiling with baby Celia, both looking beautiful and happy. There were pictures with Roberto, and the soccer team and then just the two of them, walking hand and hand with the dogs. She'd been polite in public, but her smile looked sad and it was bittersweet compared to the one she'd worn the night before. Friday night had been perfect... until she'd found out.

When the phone rang, he jumped on it. But it was Carl, with news that he'd set up the anonymous endowment to the Dallas County Foster Care Program to provide new school clothes for the kids. "Did you know there's over a thousand kids in the system."

"A thousand?"

"This could cost you some money, John."

"I'm astounded there are that many kids in the system, just in Dallas. Take care of them. I have the money. Want to make this a priority."

"But you're not getting anything out of this."

"Carl, it's not about me all the time." His jaw was ticking. "Just make sure they have enough to cover what they need. I want those kids to have new clothes. They've got it rough enough without having to wear hand-me-downs and out of style clothes to school. Make it work. Anonymously." He hung up. Wondered if she'd tried to call when he'd been on the phone. Maybe call waiting wasn't working. He was about to test it when his trainer walked in. They got to work. By the time they were done team JDi was in the house with the press conference so close. When Ryan asked how Dr. Hightower was doing, John just nodded when he wanted to blow up as he told his team, "All I care about right now is getting ready for the press conference, can we all concentrate on that?"

Later that night, when he could have confided in Honey, his best friend, he repressed the frustration and pain a little deeper and the pride just grew. The discomfort causing entitlement to spring up as he looked ahead. He was getting ready to start tossing the ball tomorrow. So, he did it in private first and it didn't go very well. His release time way too long, his arm strength pitiful. His range of motion stiff. The spiral falling short in distance and inaccurate.

When he looked at the phone, he was furious.

Didn't she remember he had the press conference tomorrow?

She stopped at a burger place that had a sports bar for dinner Friday night and thought about last weekend. A week ago, she'd been getting dressed up and right about now John was walking into the Lexington's house, taking her hand and stealing her kiss. She touched her mouth. The feeling just lingering there. She'd been thinking about him all day. Praying that he got through the press conference and it went well. She was here to catch a glimpse of it since she didn't have cable TV. It would be great if you could record these things. She heard some people had VHS machines that could record shows on TV. She didn't own one, would rather read then watch shows on television, especially when she found she could never get home on time to keep up with a series on a certain night at a certain time every week. She picked at her fries as she impatiently waited for the sports segment.

She had called Darlene Casper and told her that she would volunteer for the golf tournament in two weekends if she promised not to tell John. She told her she wanted to surprise him and asked if she could pick up her shorts and T-shirt the morning of the tournament. Darlene confirmed they'd make it work and she'd be happy to keep the secret.

Her head snapped up as she heard John's name mentioned on the news.

"This is the last pass that John Dake threw last season."

She watched the replay intently. She recognized the Dallas uniforms and assumed the man with the ball was John, though she couldn't see his face. The ball had barely left his hands before a man was violently taking John to the ground. Every muscle in her body tensed at the violence. The Detroit player stood up triumphantly and John rolled onto his back on the grass. His bent knees swayed back and forth as his left hand grasp the upper part of his right shoulder. The camera zoomed into a close up and through the face mask of the helmet she saw John. There was a look of undeniable pain on his face that had her slowly sitting back. She could read his lips, "Did we win?" It was a horrible way to lose.

"Ah, baby. I'm sorry."

"That could be the last ball he ever throws in the NFL." The television reporter gave the history of three other players with similar shoulder injuries that never came back. "Today at a press conference, the Dallas team announced that their starting quarterback began to throw again this afternoon after reconstructive surgery on his throwing shoulder. The prognosis sounds good although the first passes were short ones and Dake's usually tight spiral seemed to drift. Coach Merrill has stated that they are confident Dake will be the starter for Dallas in the fall.

"We've heard optimism like this before. Dallas will probably be looking to trade for a stronger second-string quarterback or take a quarterback in the draft come April. Today in the NBA..."

The replay of John's injury kept haunting Stephanie. It played over and over in her mind. She never knew football was that violent and the pain she had read on his face tugged at her emotions. The replay of his injury had crept into her dreams as someone brutally tackled John. The opponent was a giant and he crushed him as John's helmet flew off with his head still in it. The decapitated head rolled across the turf and she watched in horror as she read the question on his lips, "Am I dead to you?" Then the dream segued into pictures. Of her sister. And the man, that did those horrible evil things to Samantha, was looking at her laughing. "I'm dead but I still haunt you."

The nightmare had her bursting to the surface. She gasped as her heart pounded. A cold sweat covered her, and she thought of her sister. Then John, of someone hurting him. Suddenly it was as if the light just turned on. She was no longer lost and she knew what she needed to do.

He wasn't dead to her and life was short. Fragile. Things could happen. Forgiveness was letting go of people's debts.

She called him. It didn't matter anymore what she'd say, how they'd start over. She'd just play through it like he said, and she'd tell him she was afraid, and she didn't know what to do because she'd never dated anyone before. She'd let him know she was ready to play through the nerves, get back in the game. She wanted to make up, get rid of the silence she had put between them. She liked what they had started. She wanted it back and it was time she told him.

It was early and as the phone rang she sank deeper into the warmth of the covers fighting tears. Then closed her eyes and told God she was in the dark here, lost and needed His help to find her way through this conversation. She asked God to give her the words to say as he picked up. But it was a female voice that answered, "Hello."

Did she dial wrong? "Is John there?" She opened her eyes.

"Who is this?"

Hang up! I should hang up. But she was already answering, "Dr. Hightower."

"Jack, it's your Doctor." She faintly heard the voice say.

How many women have you slept with?

Enough.

Adrenaline had her heart pounding. She wanted to hang up. She wanted to do anything but talk to him now. But she'd given her name. It was too late.

"This is John," a sleepy voice said, and she suddenly wanted to get a reaction.

"John, its Stephanie."

The instant he heard her voice, John was up and moving. In an anxious voice he stated, "Stephanie, hold on a minute." He walked toward his bathroom.

"I caught you at a bad time," she said evenly, yet suddenly furious.

"No," he paused, "maybe," he moaned, "yes," he finally said as he paced, staring up at the ceiling and wondering how he could be so stupid, how the timing could be so wrong.

"At least you're being honest with me. I'll let you go. Sorry I called so early."

"No wait! You called for a reason. I know you."

"I wanted to find out if the press conference went okay. But you're busy. I'll let you go now."

"Stephanie, no. Let me explain."

"You don't owe me an explanation."

She hung up.

"What did they want?" Elise asked with a sleepy yawn, but there was a look in her eye, calculating and older than time. He felt the trap, like a net or a noose it had snared him and destroyed something else.

He'd been done with Elise. It had been months since he'd peeled her pretty little fingers off him and he'd do it again. For good this time.

"Never again," he said out loud.

"What?" She made her famous move. Like his pump fake, it was a trick that moved you the wrong way. The sheet she'd draped around her supermodel body dropped just like the towel had yesterday when she'd come out of his pool. Naked and wet and willing to soothe whatever was hurting. Pamper that pride and bam! Touchdown. King me! Pick six, you idiot. Right in the end zone she'd intercepted you and gone 100 yards the other way. Colossal loss.

"You need to go." John glared at the naked woman who suddenly sent a flame of guilt firing through him. He wasn't sure they'd said two words to each other last night. It had been physical, from the visual invitation to the culmination. He didn't know why she was in town, what made her stop by or how she'd even gotten in. She'd been willing and available, and he'd been too weak to resist the temptation with his confidence in the gutter and his heart broken. And in his shame, he needed someone to blame.

She sighed, throwing her long straight blond hair over her shoulder to expose her bare breasts. Her skin was darkly tanned and she smiled. Her perfectly straight teeth and cerulean eyes beamed at John. "Jack," she said his pet name in a patronizing voice as she strolled toward him like a siren. "Come on, don't be mad. Last night was great. Do I need to remind you how good this is?" She pressed her naked body against his as her lips curved into a seductive pout. Then she touched the phone in his hands to try to take it away.

He won't let her have it, tried to shift, and finally possessively pulled. She stayed in step with him. "It was just a reaction, the phone rings, you answer it. Surely your doctor knows a man like you has needs? You were insatiable last night. Come back to bed." Her hand ran down his body in a seductive caress.

"Last night shouldn't have happened."

"Oh?" Her smile could devour a man. He stepped back as she advanced. "You sure seemed glad to see me last night." Her eyes examined his naked body. "You're looking glad to see me now."

He stated with strength. "You and I are over, Elise. Move on. I have."

She looked at the phone he was cradling protectively now, then up to his eyes. Her laugh came first, then the wicked smile of satisfaction. "Oops," she said lifting a brow and looking suddenly sullen. "I hope I didn't make the good doctor mad." A long-manicured fingernail passed over the pulse along his jaw and she pouted, "But I see I've got you furious enough to tick." Then her hand slid down his chest. "And hard enough to—"

He pushed her back. "I said you need to go." He opened the door that went to the patio. "Your clothes are still outside. I've got rehab in an hour. And I'm changing the codes and locks this afternoon. Don't try this again. It won't work."

"Um-hm. Sure Jack," she laughed at him. "See you next time." Her parting smile said she'd be back. Her echoing laughter damned him as he swore to himself he'd change all the locks in the house to keep her out. But that wouldn't protect him from temptation or his own weakness in a bad moment. And that inner voice reminded him this was a consequence of being a fornicator and he'd just cheated on his wife. Again.

There was only one person to blame. He hated himself.

Brad watched as the young man talked to his head coach in the door way of Mike's office. Word had spread rapidly around the building to stay clear of Dake today. They said he was in a mood darker than a Super Bowl loss. Brad strategically hit the hall at the same time John did.

"How's the shoulder?"

"It's healing, sir," he answered flatly.

"Can I have a word with you?" He presented his own office. When they were behind closed doors, he went on. "Word has it you're in some mood today. I know The Morning News was critical in their article yesterday, but we both know you're right on schedule."

"I didn't read it." John stood, tension vibrating from him in waves.

"Something's eating at you. Want to talk?"

"Sure, want to hear how I blew it royally again with Dr. Hightower?"

"Stephanie?" Brad concealed a smile that immediately wanted to shine. "She didn't like the flowers and the letter? I made sure the florist got the card on Monday, right after I landed."

"I don't know. We never got that far in our conversation this morning."

"You talked then."

"After Elise answered my phone a little after five this morning."

"Stephanie called and Elise answered the phone?"

"Yeah, that's about the way my luck's gone lately."

"What did Stephanie say?"

"That I didn't owe her an explanation." John shook his head. "I'd want an explanation! I'm furious. I've been calling for a week and she wouldn't answer. She finally wanted to talk, and I blew it again. Probably for good this time."

"What's the arrangement between you and Elise?"

"She used to be convenient. No more."

"I thought she was living in New York?"

"She was in Dallas last night, dropped by."

"She probably saw the paper."

"She wasn't here to console me about short, weak, passes that drifted."

"I was talking about that photo from the soccer game." He thumbed through a stack on his desk and pulled out a newspaper, pushing it toward John. He tapped the small shot beside the bigger image of John surrounded by a soccer team of small boys. It captured John and Stephanie walking both the Golden Retrievers. She was tucked under his arm and curled into his body. 'John Dake has new girlfriend,' was the headline.

"You can't see her face and Kenny won't release her name," John stated.

"Did you read this article?"

"No, I just saw the photos. I have the originals. Kenny probably sent it in to his guy at the paper."

Brad put on his reading glasses and lifted the paper, reading, "Dake ended his relationship with supermodel Elise Kristopher last year and has clearly moved on. The couple was seen attending the opening of 'The Best Little Whorehouse in Texas' and at Henderson park... you know the rest."

He set the paper down. "That's why Elise was here. All people have egos and agendas. She didn't just drop by, John."

"She was in my pool. Naked. When I got home last night." John thought about the lure of temptation and the trap. "It won't happen again. I changed my gate codes and all the locks today."

"You need to change yourself," Brad made the simple statement.

John nodded. "I know that."

"From the ground up," Brad rose from his chair and came around his desk to sit beside John now. "I was right here once, where you are. And a man I came to respect told me the same thing. I wanted to date his daughter and Robert Montgomery said no. He called me arrogant and said I was greedy to be rich and would soon fall into a trap," Brad had picked up a Scottish burr as he told the story and he confessed to John, "*People who want to get rich fall into temptation and a trap and into many foolish and harmful desires that plunge men into ruin and destruction. For the love of money is the root of all kinds of evil. Eager for it you will wander from the faith and be pierced with many griefs.*

"*But you man of God, flee from all this and pursue righteousness, godliness, faith, love, endurance and gentleness. Fight the good fight of faith. Take hold of the eternal life to which you were called when you made your good confession and I charge you to keep to it, commanding you who are rich, not to be arrogant nor to put hope in wealth or your own strength which is so uncertain.*" Brad put his hand on John's right shoulder now, where the scar was sensitive and the muscle was still weak and the joint sore and he told him, *"But you, put your hope in God who richly provides us with everything for our enjoyment. Do good, be rich in good deeds, be generous and willing to share. In this way you will lay up treasure for yourself as a firm foundation for the coming age so that you may take hold of the life that is truly life."* He sighed as he confessed, "I thought money would prove I was worthy of the honor of Linda Montgomery but her father showed me it was character that proved I was worthy of the honor.

"But you man of God, flee from all this and pursue righteousness—fight the good fight—keep your confession—don't be arrogant or put hope in your own strength—put your hope in God and trust Him to give you the desire of your heart—be rich in good deeds and generous, willing to share—these things build the foundation.

"You have some of these things, start working with God on the areas that are underdeveloped, and you'll need accountability for that. Sometimes daily, definitely weekly." Brad made a suggestion, John should call Layne Lexington, then he gave him another name, his best friend, Honey. "A strand of three is not easily broken. You will strengthen each other if you'll be humble and real about where you are in life and how you're working to transform."

John could only nod.

"Why don't you fly to Louisiana with me tonight? You can surprise Stephanie and talk in person."

"No, the last thing I need to do is push her."

"How about Friday night, I'll be here Friday, you can ride back with me then?"

"Maybe. I'll let you know."

15

"Stephanie there's someone here to see you." Mary's voice echoed out of the intercom box on her desk.

"Okay," she answered. It had been one long, horrible week, and she was emotionally exhausted. It was finally Friday and the last thing she wanted was a late afternoon encounter with Phillip. He'd been calling, trying to schedule dinner. She had told him to call her late this afternoon and now he was here. She could say something came up. But what would really come up? Not a thing. She would end up working late, trying not to think of John or sulking around the house only to go to bed early and fight through shallow dreams that had her insomnia getting her up hours before dawn.

She saw his reflection in the glass window before she actually saw him. *Oh. God.* She called out in prayer as she entered the reception area with a pounding heart.

"Are you busy?" John Dake asked her.

"No," she glanced at Mary, "Come on back."

Stephanie led him to her office and sat down putting her large desk safely between them.

"I hitched a flight over here with Brad for the night. I thought maybe we could talk."

She nodded then asked, "Can I get you something to drink?"

He shook his head no. She walked out of the office then returned with a soda. He was on his feet waiting for her. He stood between her and the desk. Nervously she opened the soda and took a drink.

"Stephanie, I'm sorry about the other morning."

She interrupted him holding up her hand. "No, don't! I don't want to talk about it. You definitely don't have to explain, John."

"I want to make sure you understand that girl doesn't mean anything to me, Stephanie."

"Doesn't mean anything? You slept with her and she doesn't mean anything?" she questioned harshly.

"No, she doesn't," he answered evenly.

She shook her head. "That's sad. That's really sad, John."

"It was a physical thing. That's all, Stephanie. She came over without an invitation, tempted me and in a weak moment—"

"Whatever!" She waved her hand as if to bat at a pesky fly. "I told you, I don't care!" She took a drink of the soda, forced her shaky hand to find security around the cold tin can.

"I just let something happen that shouldn't have. There's no excuse for it. I want you to know it was nothing. That there's nothing going on—"

"Stop!" Didn't he hear her? She didn't want to listen to his excuses. "I told you—" her voice was too loud, and she lowered it, "I don't care. There were certainly no rules broken. We've gone out a couple times. There were no ties, no commitment. We both have our own lives. We haven't made any promises to each other and you owe me no explanations."

"Honestly Stephanie, I was under a lot of stress, you wouldn't answer my calls and the press conference."

"*Stress!*" That's it. Her temper engaged full throttle and she shut her office door, turned around and repeated coolly, "*Stress?*" Her eyes glared, and she took a step toward him. "So sorry I put you under such *stress*. I guess it's my fault, right? You didn't get what you thought you were going to? I gave you a bad case of sexual frustration?"

"No!"

"I wouldn't answer your calls."

"Yeah. No one does that to me. Everyone answers my calls—"

"Command those who are rich not to be arrogant."

"If you're giving me the gospel of Brad, I've heard it."

"I was giving you the words of Paul, to Timothy, on how to deal with rich people." She thrust a finger at him. "I read up on you over the past week trying to get a handle on this."

"Oh, yeah, well where can I read up on you, huh? What to do with a woman when she won't answer the phone. You blew me off. Do you know how that feels? The shutdown. The silence. The standoff, while I wait you out."

"And you waited what—less than a week? I'm sitting there last Friday thinking through every minute of our date and while I'm remembering you, you're hooking up with, *"Jack, it's your doctor?"* Did you lie to her too? Tell her your name was Jack?"

"No, she just calls me that."

"She. Does."

"It's over with us. I made sure this time."

"Over? So, she did mean something to you at some time?"

"It was lust and notoriety. We went out for a while. She wanted more, I didn't. Look Stephanie, I want something with you, more with you. When you didn't even call me before the press conference or after, I thought you blew me off. I thought you didn't care what I was going through. I figured you decided I was too much to deal with."

"Too much to deal with?" She laughed. "Please. You think you're so impressive, Mr. John Dake—professional quarterback with your rehabilitating shoulder injury and your press conference to talk about the current velocity of your spiral." She rolled her eyes as she shook her head. "You know what your problem is? You're so into you—you've got our roles reversed." She jabbed her finger into her chest. "I'm the one that's too much to deal with. I don't care who you are, John. All the superficial things that matter to everyone else don't mean a thing to me." She counted on her fingers as she announced each attribute. "Your athletic ability, status, reputation, money, name—they don't mean anything to me. They certainly won't be luring me into sleeping with you for the notoriety of saying, 'I got laid by John Dake'. You better come up with a new way of doing business when it comes to me—because I'm really not impressed with you. A man's character is what counts to me. And yours is lacking."

"I know." His statement just echoed and harmonized with the one she had made that night in his house when she'd said she had always known who he was and what he did. Now her cutting, criticism couldn't have convinced him more. He knew now without a shadow of a doubt that Stephanie Hightower really didn't care that he was a famous football player. She never would have cared, even in the beginning. And this solid confirmation made his insides glow from her stated reassurance.

This woman was incredible. She was exactly the kind of woman he'd waited a lifetime for. She didn't care... and yet, she didn't care. The irony of it made him laugh.

"You think this is funny?" Her eyes were full of fury.

"That you attacked my character? Hardly. That I was feeling depressed and gave in to temptation at a moment of weakness when I was feeling rejected and needed my ego stroked, I hate myself more than you ever could that I fornicated, committed adultery and cheated on my wife, again." He was walking to her now. Anger ticking in his jaw. "I don't find it a bit funny that all I think about is you. That I want to impress you. And you do need to be impressed and kissed and touched and held and confronted and cherished. You need a man that wants to find the best in himself and gather it together to present to you over and over again. That's what you make me want to do. Be a better man, Beauty. And I've failed, and it hurts."

"Yes, it does."

"But you also need a man that knows how to take that fire of yours and tame it, direct it, focus it. A man like me, who wants you, who needs you. I need you."

"No, you don't."

"Yes, I do." He took her chin into his hand. "I needed you to call me. I needed you to talk to me before that press conference. I needed you to hear that

I'd thrown the ball for the first time and it wobbled and..." He swallowed the rest, a whisper away now and he held her gaze and told her, "I need you," as he kissed her. Then said, "I am a kiss thief and a selfish fool. Acting like Jacob when I'm really called to be Solomon. Go out with me tonight. I want to spend some time with you and talk, explain how I really feel. I want to work this out..." Then his lips pressed to hers and held this time.

She jumped when she heard the phone ring and when she stepped back, he let her go.

"This is Dr. Hightower," she answered as she sat down in her desk chair, trying to regain her breath as well as her composure. He'd caused a brain melt, switching parts of her off as foreign parts of her came on line, took over and ruled. She swallowed, hard. She'd made a noise, when he kissed her and clung. Yes, her traitorous fingers had actually curled into his clothing and clung as she made that ridiculous little female surrendering noise.

She was suddenly terrified. At how he could take her in hand, melt her brain, make her forget and cause her will to just wilt. She watched that smooth swagger settle across from her in a chair like a... badass.

Yes, John Dake was a badass. And that handsome, charming badass crossed his legs, comfortable and smooth, totally in control with that confidence that ruled not just a room or a football field but the world.

God help her, he was relaxed.

She was anything but relaxed. She was a wimp.

A swooning little wilted wimp.

A lying, swooning, little wilted wimp.

She was lying every time she said she didn't care. She cared. She ached. Her heart was shattered in millions of scattered little pieces and for days it had bled with her random unexpected tears.

A badass woman would have struck him, hard. With a tantrum of words as she kept her fists firmly planted on her hips like... Wonder Woman.

Yes. Wonder Woman stood her ground. Wonder Woman didn't ever need a mask to hide behind or a man to help. Wonder Woman just planted those Amazon boots and struck that poise and spoke the truth.

I. Trusted. You. Hurt. Me.

But she wasn't Wonder Woman. And a lying, swooning, little wilted wimp was no match for a badass. *God, help me.*

"What? I'm sorry." She suddenly realized she didn't even know who she was talking to.

"It's Phillip, Steph. Are you in the middle of one of those equine genetics charts?" He laughed.

"You know me, *Phillip.*" She lied with a cute little laugh as she smiled for added affect.

"Are we still on for dinner tonight?"

She looked at the badass sitting across from her. He needed something to set him back on his heels. She thought they called that a blitz. A sack. A blind side hit. And if this love thing was a metaphor for a game then she was going to channel her inner Wonder Woman and plant his *badass* right into the dirt.

"Dinner tonight... I've been thinking about it all week. What time are you picking me up, Phillip?"

She looked down right after she had the satisfaction of seeing John Dake's eyes narrow and his jaw twitch.

"That's what I said. She's going out with him tonight!" John downed the Scotch in one drink and set the expensive crystal glass down with a thud onto the Bennett's kitchen table. "I'm furious, Brad. And she knows it."

Linda tried to hide her smile as she asked John if he wanted another. He'd declined the beer, asking for a whiskey. John took it straight, pouring it himself when she handed him the bottle.

"Did you ask her if she'd see you tomorrow?" Brad asked seriously.

"I don't play second string to anybody. Especially that yuppie Tim guy."

"You mean Philipp?" Linda corrected only to have Brad wave her off.

"Did you talk at all today?" he asked.

"She didn't want to hear my explanation." He glanced at Linda then went on. "She said she didn't care."

"I doubt that, John," Brad said shaking his head. "That's probably why she's letting you know she's going out with Phillip tonight."

"Stephanie doesn't play games."

"She's a woman," Brad corrected, "They all play games, son."

Linda lifted an eyebrow but remained silent.

"I don't think she planned that to spite me." John started to take up for Stephanie then sighed in confusion. "But she sure didn't keep me from knowing about it." He pulled his fingers through his hair and mumbled, "Didn't care. Said no rules were broken." He took another deep drink of the liquor. "She said we had our own lives. Hadn't made any promises to each other. Didn't want me to explain." He finished the drink and shook his head. "Didn't want me to explain why a woman answered my phone at five o'clock in the morning."

"What?" Linda's gaze drilled into her husband. "I thought we were still talking about this quarterback cover up?" Linda looked between the two men knowing this new business must have occurred after she had talked to Stephanie at lunch on Wednesday. "You didn't fill me in on the phone call, Bradley."

"Linda," Brad raised his hand to stop her.

"When I told her Elise didn't mean anything, she almost took off my head."

"That line never works with women, John," Brad shared as if he knew from experience.

"No, it doesn't," Linda echoed.

"I said it didn't mean anything." He looked at Brad. "She said that was *sad*." He turned the empty glass in a circle. "Sad, can you believe that? Then she told me a man's character is what counts and mine is lacking."

"Stephanie has high standards," Linda defended.

"Most women don't," Brad replied, "And that makes the temptation steep."

"Now what is that supposed to mean?" Linda glared at her husband. "You're swinging a double-edged sword, Bradley. You've raised the girls to honor God now you tell John that it's okay to go out and sow his wild oats like a pagan?"

"I never told the boy anything of the kind."

John grinned at Linda. "I think this is the first time I've actually seen Mr. Bennett flustered."

"Okay!" Brad's voice was deceptively calm. "Linda," he nodded at the door and she left the room. "We all have our weaknesses," Brad said slowly, softly. "But the lust of women is something that has to be controlled." He held up his hand to stop John. "Let me finish. This isn't a lecture, so don't jump on the defensive."

Brad gave them both a minute to regroup. "Lust is universal and we all should respect its overwhelming tenacity to entice us, but fame amplifies the temptation, just like money or beauty or power. I know you're under an incredible amount of temptation when sex can come as cheap and disposable as a Happy Meal, but God told us sex isn't like a fast food diet."

"I never meant—" John tried.

"It's wrong," Brad said straight out. "I won't flourish it with a convincing argument. Sex outside marriage is wrong. It's not how God designed it. He intended one man for one woman for life. Within those bonds you can enjoy sex for all it's worth, outside those bonds you've corrupted it for what it was never meant to be—a cheap imitation.

"I know. I wasn't perfect. Before Linda, I didn't act any better. My parents didn't teach me what was right or take me to church. I grew up hard and fast, with a timid mother and a drunk dad. They couldn't care less about me. That's why finding out I had a heavenly Father that cared about me, wanted the best for me, gave His Son to save me. It changed my life. I wanted to do what was right out of gratitude. I wanted to honor God with my life because I was so overwhelmed and thankful for His grace.

"So, I'll be frank with you. You've been given much and you're wasting the part that matters most by giving yourself away so casually. You're mocking God with your disobedience and standing on pride because by having sex you think you're above His law. You're going to reap what you sow—it's a basic principle. You better cool down that hot blood of yours and end the carousing by fortifying the inner man and renewing your mind. You need to repent, John. And I shouldn't have to caution you about what can be the consequences—all the diseases out there, not to mention AIDS."

"I've been careful," he cleared his throat, "Protected myself. It was Elise, Brad. Not some girl I didn't know."

"Elise! You want to marry Elise or Stephanie Hightower?"

"What? Now wait a minute," John raked a hand through his hair and started to pace.

"The point is a girl like Stephanie is not going to put up with that kind of behavior. She won't respect you. She's a Christian woman who lives by God's values. She'll cut you off and move on. She's a perfectionist that's absolutely independent! Do you know what that means son? She doesn't need you."

The words struck home as John's face paled. "She said she didn't care," John thought out loud.

"Fiddlesticks! She cared all right. That kind of intimacy is sacred to her and you were sharing it thoughtlessly with someone else you said doesn't matter. I'll tell you it probably tore her heart in two."

"You think she cares?" John perked up a little bit.

"Yes, I know she does." John's full smile showed up for the first time since he'd seen Stephanie. "And don't be getting all smug about it either! That arrogance is—"

"Yeah, yeah. She told me you were quoting Timothy in your lecture the other day about, 'commanding the rich not to be arrogant.' I thought that was all your stuff. It was really good."

"No, First Timothy chapter six is the life verse I put to memory and recite every day so the old man in me is put to death and the new man lives to honor God. Do you know what that means? To honor God?"

"I'm not sure I do."

"We honor God when we make it our chief ambition in life to please Him, to love Him and to serve Him at all times. Jesus lived this out. He said, 'I honor

My Father. And I do always those things that please Him.' The old man wants to honor himself, please himself, love himself, be served and seek the honor of his fellow man. God says, 'The one who honors me, I will honor.' We're commanded to put God first and others second. We're third in line, John."

He nodded, poured himself a little more Scotch then he asked, "I hurt her again. Do you think I have a chance?"

Brad stayed silent.

"You know I'm crazy about her. And you're right. I want her, just her now. She's so beautiful..." He closed his eyes, smiled. "And her body." He moaned. "She's hot headed and stubborn, downright impossible at times but if I can just get her to believe me, that she's it for me, that I'm serious about her, then I can redirect all that passion," he smiled up at Brad. "Can you even imagine—"

"Did you hear a word I just said?" He looked at the glass of Scotch and pulled it toward him. "Are you drunk?"

John waved him off. "I heard you. I'm going to stop the carousing. I just want Stephanie." His wicked smile met a father's scorn.

"Watch it, son." The words were a warning, the tone dangerous, threatening like a peacemaker in a lawman's hands.

John's smile melted away into confusion under Brad's icy gaze. His violet eyes were hard and penetrating, they seemed to narrow on John's very soul, striping him of his confidence.

John's logic, mixed with alcohol, started putting one and one together in a bizarre combination that added up to something he didn't like.

"Watch it?" John questioned, standing up to confront Brad. "That's a pretty strong warning to be coming from a man who's simply financially backing a veterinarian. Or is there something else going on between the two of you?"

Brad took a step toward John. Fire seemed to flash between the two powerful men then Brad stated, "There's definitely something else going on between the two of us. I'm her Father."

16

"Her father," John shook his head. "Died when she was little."

"I adopted her and her sister, Samantha, eight years ago."

John sat down, closed his mouth, swallowed. "You're. Her. Father."

"Yes," Brad answered, he paced, took a minute to collect himself. "And I've just breached a sacred agreement telling you." He faced him. "She hasn't been very comfortable with the relationship but legally it was the best thing for her and her sister at the time."

"She told me she was taking care of her sister and going to college."

"Yes. She wouldn't let me help her with anything but Samantha. She wouldn't take any money for school, any help financially for herself, or my name or connections." Brad pressed his lips together firmly. "She's asks us not to disclose our relationship with anyone, so we've honored that. She's very close to Blair. She's allowed Linda to assume a mothering role, me to be her mentor. But I'm also her protector, and as her father, I won't allow any man, even you, to stand here and tell me you want to seduce my daughter."

John held up his hand, shaking his head. "I'm sorry. Forgive me. I meant no disrespect to you or to her. I don't want to seduce her, Brad."

There was silence, Brad just looking at him. Then he told him, "Stephanie is a rare mix of strength and incredible vulnerability. She's been through too much in her young life." Brad paused, looked away, then said with firm emotion. "You need to take care with her, son. Tender care. I'm counting on it now—that the man I know is there, inside of you, is ready to make a real change, to honor God and her with pure intentions as you develop a relationship. If you can't, if she's just a beautiful woman, a challenging pursuit and this is lust, seduction and conquest for passion—then out of respect for who I am, and our relationship to each other, I'm asking you to move on and let her go."

His entire history with Stephanie flashed quickly by—he recalled every conversation, every touch, every feeling. He reflected on the empty nights he'd spent with strangers, the pleasure he'd shared with lovers and recognized how meaningless it was now. Shallow, so shallow compared to what he had with Stephanie.

John realized there were distinct moments in your life that stretched out and proclaimed they were turning points. Knowing his life had just changed course, John stated, "I can't let her go." He looked into the fierce violet eyes of Brad Bennett. "I can change, Brad and I will honor God and her. I will."

"Thanks, Phillip," Stephanie stood with her back to her front door and her hands clasp firmly in front of her. "I enjoyed it."

"The night doesn't have to end." He stepped to her and her back pressed against the door as his hand rubbed up her arm. He was trying to draw her to him and her hand moved to his chest to block the move she knew was coming. "I'm really tired," she told him turning her face away and pushing a bit.

He frowned, leaning back on his heels. "Where's this going?" he asked her. "We've been seeing each other, and you've never asked me in."

"We're friends. We had dinner."

"Friends?" He sighed, his eyes sparked with impatience before he looked away. "Okay."

She explained kindly, "Friends, who share an interest in horses."

"I'm interested in other things too." It was like a dance now, the way he shifted to get close and she stepped aside to find space. And his hands were sticky, tangling with her hair, and his voice was hot and the words a bit impatient as he demanded now in a warm whisper by her ear, "Ask me in, Stephanie."

"No." She stood her ground as he stared silently at her.

Then he smiled, "I respect you."

"Good."

"So, you can ease up on the hard to get and let me in." He was looking down at her, his hand back to that stroking motion up her arm like she was some kind of spooked horse. Then she felt it, that little awareness that this could turn dangerous as his knuckles brushed her breast. It made her mad. Good and mad and she could deal with anger because heartache had her head booming, her nerves stretched to their limits.

The satisfaction of this date had ended the moment John walked away from her. The contrast of her feelings between the two men was so obvious it made her impatient to be away from Phillip and she caught his creepy hand as he smiled. "If you let me in, I promise you'll like it." Now there was a charming plea.

"That's not going to happen with us. Ever Phillip. We're friends—"

"Friends." The word mocked, his eyes swept her. "There's more here. You wanted to see me tonight."

"Yes."

"You were flirting it up on the phone, were glad to see me when I picked you up, we had a great night and I want to take this the next step, but you're pushing back, issuing a challenge with that never word. It's now, honey." He ducked down and she dipped away.

She had her key in the lock and was telling him, "Really. It's not."

"You're not serious."

"I am. Good night."

She quickly went inside, locked the door. He was mad. Fine. She'd flirted on the phone. Big mistake. Her heart was beating fast from the getaway and she sighed, rubbing her head, dropping her small handbag on the entry table. She just shivered. Disgust sent her to the shower. She bathed and put on her warm flannel dog pajamas.

She needed some aspirin and a numbing night of dreamless sleep. She'd purchased a bottle of Tylenol PM just for tonight. She walked through her dark house into the kitchen and opened the refrigerator for water. That's when she felt it—the instinctual warning—the presence of another person. Everything slowed down as it registered.

Someone's in my house. Phillip?

She froze with the cold air slipping around her body and the light of the refrigerator dim within a too dark house. Thoughts clicking.

Her gun was in her bedroom. She'd always thought that was where she would need it, not here in her kitchen. She had knives. She thought of Samantha, cut up and bleeding and something inside her roared. In a single move she yanked her butcher knife from the block and braced on the balls of her feet as she faced the threat with a growling war cry, "You'll have to kill me first!"

"I just might."

"John!"

He was sitting at her kitchen table, slouched down low in a chair, a bottle of beer the only weapon in his hand. The moonlight put his face in shadows. "If you let that yuppie wimp even touch you, I just might kill you, Dr. Hightower because I do care."

She heard her own breath, sharp and fast as she stared at him. "You're in my house." There wasn't enough air for her adrenaline to rush through her lungs. "You're in my house!"

"Yes. You told me where you kept your hide-a-key the day High Hopes was born, and I came here to get your coat. And I'm furious. You lied to me."

She turned and slipped the knife back in its block with shaking hands as she turned her back on him. He was talking but she couldn't hear anything but the wailing rush of her blood. She'd thought he was Phillip, or someone else, someone worse, who she was going to have to fight off. Her hands took the counter's edge, her knuckles white, her memories places she never wanted to see again as the copper taste of terror came into her mouth and she thought about her sister. The horrible things that were done to her by a very evil man. There were bad people in this world. And you could be in the wrong place at the wrong time and horrible things could happen to you...

Her breath was fast, her body a frantic tremble. As the adrenaline quickly tanked, her head boomed.

"Steph—"

"You scared me!" She interrupted him, her name the trigger, her fury now an explosion of words. They bulleted at him in a hiss, "Don't ever do that! I could have hurt you before I even knew—"

He chuckled, and she erupted.

"This isn't funny!" she wailed now and there were tears, hot and uncontrollable. "I could have thrown that knife at you before I even knew who you were. Or shot you. I have a gun!" She stabbed the air toward her bedroom. "Loaded and ready. And I know how to use it! You have no idea what I could do to you—"

"Hey!" He was up now.

She was pointing at him. "No idea what I've lived through. No one better ever mess with me or my sister again! Not you, not anyone! I'll fight to the death before I let someone hurt us again," she choked, taking in a deep breath to only scream, "Don't ever do that again! I could have killed you before I realized..."

"Okay. Okay. Shh, I'd never hurt you."

Was that her voice echoing through the house? Was she the one screaming? His eyes were wide and worried, searching her face. What had she said? Shame made her turn away from him, breaking into a box of medicine, yanking off the plastic cap cover. The pills shook like a percussion instrument in her hand as she tried to break the seal. She jerked out the cotton, capsules spilling around her as she palmed two into her mouth.

"Stephanie—"

"You scared me," she said again in an even flat tone, now cool and collected as she drank the icy water.

She felt him close, too close now. She crossed her arms tightly around her trembling body when he turned her to him.

Her eyes were haunted. And she was spooked, like she'd been that first day when she'd seen him hit the tree. Terrified, like she'd been when she woke up and saw him sitting by the bed at his cabin, flaying back towards the headboard. He scared her, and it made him sick inside.

When those green eyes filled it so distressed him that she was instantly gathered close. She was tense, and he realized the adrenaline was tanking as her body jerked in uncontrollable spasm in his arms. He apologized, soothing her with stupid words. When he tried to pull away, she clung suddenly, her hands fisting in his shirt, her body nestling to him, asking to be held.

"You s-scared me." She was trembling. Silent sobs that just rocked against him.

"I never should have done this," he told her, surrounded her. "I could have waited on the front porch or in my truck. I never meant to frighten you. God knows I'd never hurt you or you never would have pointed out where your spare key was kept. You trust me, Stephanie and I'm sorry I didn't respect that trust."

There was silence. Finally, he just said her name.

"Someone h-hurt my s-sister." Was whispered, then a tiny sob was smothered to silence as her body quaked and her face pressed into his shirt, fighting to stay in control. "I was her guardian and I didn't guard her." She seemed to collapse, just implode and his arms banded around her tightly to help her stand.

"I'm so sorry," he whispered, holding her as close as he physically could. "I'm so, so, sorry, baby."

Pieces began to fit, the puzzle still far from solved but he knew something horrible must have happened to her sister and it had been the reason Brad had stepped into her life eight years ago.

THE HONOR

Learning she was linked with the Bennetts had put a plan in his half-drunk mind. He'd come over here tonight to wait her out, feeling like he had the upper hand for a change, he was going to point and accuse, "Ah-ha, you've lied too."

He'd wanted to confront her about Brad. Ask questions and demand answers. He realized he'd wanted to bully her back, manipulate, and stipulate. Now he realized none of that mattered. There was so much more to her connection with Brad then just himself and he had no right to violate it. She mattered, and it suddenly stopped being about him tonight and became about honoring her.

He understood now. The knowledge of her family needed to come from her. The story would be shared when she trusted him most, and then it would be a privilege to listen.

Honor her—the meaning of that suddenly expanded. And wasn't he determined to change, to build that foundation. He'd repented and now he needed to keep following through. Take that next step and in faith trust God to meet him there. He prayed for help and immediately it seemed he was no longer acting in the natural but the supernatural took over, making him more than he was alone.

"I'm sorry I hurt you," he told her. "I've been such a self-centered fool. I had no right to come into your house. I was in the mood for a fight and I was determined Phillip wasn't spending the night. I was stupid—"

"Phillip was never spending the night," she just sighed. "I told you, I've never kissed anyone. I was serious. I thought you believed me."

He closed his eyes. His arms closed around her just a little tighter, his heart beat just a little harder and he understood Brad's words.

That kind of intimacy is sacred to her and you were sharing it thoughtlessly with someone else you said doesn't matter.

Honor her. He realized she'd honored him all her life. Waited and separated herself from what he and the world took so cheaply for granted. How true could love be, how pure, how lovely, how honest.

In that moment, he saw and understood the simplicity of intimacy. It wasn't lust and passion and physical gratification. It came from bearing scars and fears and tender dreams. It was a love that shared the heart and the soul and honored the body and put someone else ahead of your own interests.

"I've made a lot of mistakes," he confessed. "And I need to ask you to forgive me again." She was still clinging to him, holding him even as he held her. "I want to start over, make some promises to you. I want to be honest and build something with you, slowly that will last. I want you to know you can trust me, depend on me, that I care about you, so much. I want the best for you and yet all I've seemed to do is hurt you. I need to do better—I need to be a better man. You need to know I'm going to try. I want to honor you with that, my very best. I'm going to change. Work on my character. I need to honor God, so I can honor you. Lead..."

He swallowed, silent now as his soul was revealed to even him. She was it and he needed to change, or he was going to lose the gift of her. John prayed now for the strength to follow through. He could never do this alone. And she would need time.

"I won't ask you to answer now, you can think about it. Can I call you this week, see how you're doing and maybe you'll answer the phone?"

She nodded. She was weak, suddenly exhausted. He felt it.

"I'm better than all this, Stephanie. I'll show you, if you give me a chance."

Her tiny hand surprised him, slipping free to find his own. She squeezed it, then clung tightly to his fingers as he turned it over to lace with her own.

"Pray for me, for us," he whispered on a kiss to her brow. "And I'll be praying for you."

17

Brad found her by the golf ball washer near the number one tee box. Someone from the golf club staff had whispered discreetly that a Stephanie Hightower needed him. He'd been surprised, that she was in Dallas at an event like this. Then immediately concerned. Quickly moving in the direction the staffer pointed after he told him, "Find my daughter, Blair Lexington and send her our way please."

He found Stephanie with her arms crossed. She looked like one of the cheerleaders wearing tiny white shorts and a little blue T-shirt.

"What's wrong?"

"Is Linda here?" She was tucked into the corner of the little shed. Tense and shifting her feet as she held herself tightly and just glanced at him before she looked out over his shoulder at the crowd. She looked cold, uncomfortable and embarrassed.

"No, but Blair is coming." He stepped closer. "Honey, what's wrong."

"I knew better. Shouldn't have come. I gave her my word I'd volunteer today but I can't do this. Wearing this." She was that odd mixture of anger and anxiety. She swept her ensemble with a wave only to cross her arms and curl her shoulders into a slouch as her feet shifted again and she moaned, "I'm stuck with no way out again." She looked up and he saw that she was also angry with herself. "After everything I've gone through I should be more flexible—"

"I never bought into the idea of being flexible," Brad told her calmly. He didn't understand exactly what had gone on here, but he knew she was in a crisis and God was ready to help her in the middle of it all with some encouragement. He needed to get her mind engaged so she could work through this intellectually. He challenged her, "Flexibility really means we compromise or yield to the influence around us. God calls us to adapt instead. Adaptō in Latin is to fit to or adjust."

She looked over his shoulder again. "But Brad—"

"Stephanie," he called her name as he called her to refocus her attention on him. "We're called to adjust our testimony to the culture or the context we find ourselves 'stuck in' without compromising our convictions. Paul says he became all things to all people that he might by all means save some. He adapted for the gospel's sake."

"These shorts aren't going to win anyone to Christ."

"You don't have to wear that outfit to volunteer."

"They locked me out of the locker room." Now he saw the hurt. He'd seen it before in Blair's eyes when girls at school had done something mean and she confirmed it as she told him, "I think she might have done this on purpose. Darlene Casper meet me at John's church, used guilt to get me to volunteer for this. I told her my size, but she said it was too late to get it. She only had the maternity size for Neil Beihn's wife I'm substituting for, so she gave me a pair of the cheerleaders' shorts and their T-shirt. My mistake was coming outside dressed like this, but she just swept me along. Pointed to a place to wait then left me standing here." She waved toward the course as her lip began to tremble. "And all his friends are here. And I just can't do this."

Blair walked up and snorted before she chuckled. "I didn't know you tried out for cheerleader, Stephanie."

Brad frowned as Stephanie said, "Not. Funny."

"Oh, it really is." She just giggled, and Stephanie's lip firmed as her eyes darkened. Panic shifting to outrage. Blair pushing just the right buttons as she said, "Who talked you into that get up?"

"Darlene Casper."

"Ah, she's the captain of the Dallas mean girls. I would have told you being a size four is on the mean girl list of unforgiveable crimes, you've been officially sentenced to show off your little rear end like a Hooter's girl. If you would have called me... talked to me about this, I would have prepped you, but you didn't, so..." It was a rebuke and she crossed her arms. "What are you going to do, sis?"

"Adapt. Give me your shorts, sis."

She snorted.

"And I'll take that advise now with your shirt." She glanced at Brad. "I think my T-shirt is worse than the shorts." She uncrossed her arms and showed Blair.

"Geez. Can you even breath?" Blair stepped up. "We can fix this with a cover up. Daddy?"

"I've got a jacket in my golf bag. I'll be back," Brad said.

"Will this stretch?" Blair's hands took the sides and pulled as Stephanie grabbed the neck. When Blair grabbed the hem, the shirt tore right down the middle to her sternum. And that's when John Dake showed up.

"Stephanie!?" He was all smiles.

Stephanie seemed to shrink and shriek at the same time as Blair just stepped forward and said, "Surprise. Look who found you. Hey, John. Great morning. Aren't you hot in that jacket?" She held her hand out for it with a 'give it here' nod.

He glanced around her to Stephanie, asking, "What are you doing here?"

"Totally freaking out, that's what," Blair was trying to shield her. "Darlene Casper has her dressed like she's volunteering to walk Harry Hines not drive your foursome through this golf tournament."

"She looks..." he leaned to look around Blair and swept her then stepped up, his jacket coming off as he finally realized why Blair had her hand out. "Really cold. Are you cold, Beauty? Because I am hot in this jacket. Burning up here. Was about to take it off. Had nowhere to put it since I didn't bring my golf bag. Can't play golf with the shoulder yet so I'm just riding along." He just covered her as he talked on, the jacket falling past the little shorts to her knees and he was zipping it up.

"Better?"

She just nodded as Brad jogged up with his jacket.

"I got her covered," John made the statement. "You're my big surprise huh? Riding with my foursome for Cindy Beihn?"

She nodded.

"You look good in my jacket."

"Little big, ask me," Blair was adjusting it. "Looks like a dress. Can't see those adorable little shorts at all. Sure you don't want Daddy's jacket?"

Stephanie just cut her a look.

"Okay, Property of #7," Blair read the imprint on the team jacket. "Go get 'em." And she hugged her close and whispered, "Just smile and let your light shine. Relax. You got this."

Brad smiled at her and winked, "Good adjustment. We'll see you at the clubhouse."

"I'm obviously not playing today but Roger graciously took my place. Have you ever met the Hall of Famer? Let me introduce you." He took her hand and led her forward. "You can still drive me around. We'll get to spend the day together." And he smiled, told her softly, "God answered my prayers," he whispered. "You're here, and I feel blessed. I couldn't believe it when I saw you."

"Darlene recruited me after church. She wouldn't take no for an answer and I gave her my word, so I kept it and came today." She watched his smile fade slightly. "I thought maybe God was working because I'd never come back on my own but then I thought it must be the devil when I got stuck in this outfit." She told him what had happened.

"God is working," he assured. "And He's got you covered today so we can play through the rest together, right?"

"Yes." She gave him a little smile. "We can play through the rest together."

John led her forward into a growing crowd of players, fans and famous people. She wasn't sure exactly what she was here to do but it seemed like Blair's advice covered it. Smile and shine as she thought about what Brad had taught her about adapting. She asked God to help her be free of herself and aware of others. He answered as she realized John was nervous too as a group surrounded them.

"Who's this?" A tall black man extended his hand. It was huge and so was his smile as he said, "You're not here with number 7?" He was trying to draw her forward away from John. "He can't play golf at all now. You come ride with me and mine—"

"Dr. Stephanie Hightower this is DeShawn."

"Doc, is it now? Girls got brains too."

"She's smart enough to know she doesn't want to ride along with a receiver at a golf tournament." He'd tugged her gently back as his left arm came around her.

"He's just jealous of my technique," DeShawn told her.

"Grip it and rip it," John taunted back.

DeShawn started laughing and waving people over to meet her. They were gathering into a huddle now and John kept her close as he called out names and introduced her to teammates. Then Darlene Casper moved into the group holding her clip board and asking everyone to line up for a photograph.

"I see you found John, but we need you in uniform for the pictures."

"She's in uniform, property of number seven," John replied and just gave his famous smile as he turned them away from her. They lined up for the group photo. Then another was taken with their foursome plus John before they got started. When they were alone on the cart heading to the first tee he apologized, "I'm sorry about all this."

"It's not your fault."

"Indirectly it is."

"John, it's okay."

"The last thing I want is you mad again."

"I'm not mad, I'm adapting," she shared what Brad had taught her.

There was silence and he ended it with a soft plea, "I just want a chance. I tried not to push you or call too much this week, but I'll beg if that's what it takes to get another chance."

"You will?" She'd been watching the golfers, now she looked at him and smiled, "Really?"

"Yes," he answered without a trace of humor, "I will. You matter. Very much. And I know humility is attractive and honesty is what rebuilds trust."

"Honestly, all I've done for two weeks is hurt over you."

"I've been praying, really hard, that you'd forgive me. That you'd give me a chance to show you how much I care. There is some character inside me that can be redeemed for you."

"I know," she whispered, encouraging him because she saw that he also hurt. "You are a good man, John."

"I'm going to start living like one. I've asked two men for help and accountability. One's also in the spot light, he's a Christian and a family man and he understands the pressure I'm under. The other is my best friend, he knows me. I've spent time with both of them this week and developed a game plan. It might take a lifetime, but I had some long talks with God about it this week, I'm hoping He'll help."

"He will." They looked at each other, she saw all that he was offering.

"Don't be afraid," he whispered, seeing.

"I had some long talks with God about that this week, I'm hoping He'll help."

"He will."

She'd come today to keep her word, but her obligation turned into a time to heal. They'd been able to talk in between holes and having other people around and the event going on made things easier. Now it was over, and the locker room was open. She had her own clothes on and the little shorts and T-shirt were in the trash and John Dake was waiting on her outside the locker room door.

"Thank you," she said handing him the jacket.

"I invited Layne and Blair over," he told her. "And some friends."

"Okay."

"You'll come, right?" She saw it again. The little hesitation. He wasn't used to this, asking and waiting for an answer when most people just did what he said automatically. She wasn't used to this, saying yes, but she did, and he smiled.

John's sunken TV room had a capacity crowd tonight. Couples sat intertwined with each other as they watched the football mishaps video after a dinner of barbequed ribs. The whole room was chuckling as a segment of fumbles played before them. It was amazing to Stephanie how slippery a football could be when it became loose on the ground.

The men continually called out names of familiar players and pointed to the screen. The scrutiny became uncontrollable when the Dallas team was involved in a film clip. Several times John reran certain segments or played them in slow motion. A guy named Paul high-fived John when a clip came on with the two of them.

"If you can't go to the Super Bowl at least you can make it on Steve's films," Paul laughed. "Let's see that play again."

"If memory serves me right, you and John were in the Merrill doghouse for weeks over that play," Leah, Paul's wife announced as everyone laughed.

"Who's Steve?" Stephanie tilted her head toward John and whispered in his ear. They sat on the floor in the loud crowded room and although John held the remote, she seemed to be holding most of his attention. His fingers had been playing in her hair and now when she came this close to whisper, he held her there with a soft affirming sound of approval, telling her she smelled good before he answered.

"Steve Sabol. He does NFL Films. He puts together these clips at the end of every season for a special. I've talked him into sending me a copy for the past couple years. Do you like it?"

"I like seeing you do your job."

He chuckled. "Beauty, tonight I'll have to show you some film of when I'm really doing my job, to the best of my ability, not running around the field like a kid after a greased pig. Anderson, put the second tape in," John requested as the first ended.

Stephanie didn't like tape number two as much. It was play after play of hard bone crushing tackles and catastrophes. Her body became tense as she watched, and Bradshaw moved all the closer onto her lap, but the men still seemed to love it and comments flew across the room.

Stephanie recognized the clip she had seen at the sports bar during the report on John's surgery. Her whole body tensed as the huge man tackled John. To her dismay John played it in slow motion saying, "Right there, crunch, pop!" each time his right shoulder hit the turf. When he replayed it again on full speed, she looked away.

"I can't believe it doesn't bother you to watch this, John," Blair said.

"Oh, it bothers me. Not a lineman in sight." He complained, and several players retaliated. Paul plucked the remote control from his hand, freezing the screen as they dissected the play and positions of everyone in view. Brown was blamed, then McNichols. John continued to rib his offensive line then had to take it when his throwing accuracy was put into question. Finally, the blame fell on the absent Neil Beihn, who had failed to catch the ball as the tape moved on.

"Hey," John whispered as he touched Stephanie's chin. Her head was lowered and turned away from the screen talking to Bradshaw. She lifted her eyes to look at him.

"You getting bored?"

"I don't like watching that play," she answered.

He studied her face for a moment before he told her, "Your eyes are so green." Then he announced as he turned the tape off, "The girlfriend just reminded me that we've got a basketball game about to start. She's a diehard Spurs fan and unlike football, we're serious about our basketball so—get lost."

"John," she gasped but the group was laughing, and they were all getting up, and heading out. In moments, they'd said their goodbyes and they were alone.

"I can't believe you do this," Stephanie said. She was in awe as she watched him throw a ball deep into the end zone. Within a mob of players one of his own came up with it in the high light film for a touchdown.

"That's called a Hell Mary. The play originated with Roger Staubach."

She just nodded, petting his dog. "Look at that mean look on his face, Bradshaw." She giggled as she knelt inches away from the big screen television trying to take in every detail. "I mean you said you did this, but I can't believe that's really you. You make it look so easy. I mean, look at you. That's you. I don't think I realized till this second that you really do play this... this football game thing. And you're really good at it."

"Am I?"

"In the middle of all those guys trying to take you down you made that pass." She smiled at him over her shoulder. "I'm really impressed."

"So now you're finally impressed?" And he tackled her gently, taking her to the floor as Staubach barked and Bradshaw jumped around them and a play ran in the back ground. "Taking you down is called a sack."

"I'm sacked," she answered.

He smiled as he held her. "I should have pulled my brag tapes out a long time ago. Kiss?" He asked her now and it made her smile, nod, wait for his lips to softly press against her own as the roar of a crowd announced another touchdown from the television.

He was looking into her eyes when the kiss broke. There was silence for a while, John just looking at her before he swallowed and told her, "I don't know what to do here, Stephanie."

"What's it called when you get the ball back in football?"

"Ah... change of possession."

"Is that like starting over?"

Now he smiled. "Definitely, when the score is tied."

She nodded. "Forgiveness means the score is tied at zero. You want the ball back?"

"Yes. But I'll warn you, I'm really competitive, like to win," he told her, "And I'm known for my fourth quarter come back, so I'm going to give it my all and be honest. Honor you."

"I like your honesty, it helps me," she told him sincerely.

"I want us to talk. I need you to tell me what you need."

"I needed your jacket today. Thank you."

"I beat Brad out." There was his competitive smile then he told her, "I know you're close to him and I'm glad he's there for you, helping you 'adjust' when you get handed a pair of cheerleader shorts."

She nodded again, swallowed, still holding on to him, still looking into his eyes she said, "Can we talk about that?"

"The shorts? Personally, I thought they were..." She touched his lips with her fingers, shook her head even as he grinned. Then he kissed her fingers and said, "Talk to me," shifting so that they were side to side now.

"Brad Bennett's my father," she confessed. "He adopted me and my sister, Samantha, eight years ago."

"I know," John told her and he saw the surprise in her eyes, the subtle pause as she tried to regroup and take the information in. John shifted his hand, laced their fingers together. "I could just let you talk it out and act like I didn't know, Stephanie, but we're being honest now and that means even in the difficult things." He pressed another kiss to her hand. "Brad told me the night you went out with Phillip. I was angry and whining into my whiskey at his house about your annoying one-of-a-kind habit of twisting me up into a knot. When I pushed a little too far, he pushed back, put me in my place. He told me he was your father. That he'd adopted you and your sister. Then he said I had a choice, I could change—honor God, myself and you or I needed to walk away. He made it very clear he'd stand between us, protect you, without my word that I was going to do this God's way. I gave it to him, Stephanie. And you need to know, that it was me, not Brad that deserves your anger over the revelation. Your father was protecting you."

Her lip began to swell. "Why didn't you tell me?"

"I broke into your house to do that. I thought I finally had the advantage. I was going to confront you with it." He shook his head. "Even after I made that promise to Brad, I was still acting like the old John. But then, I scared you and I realized," now he felt his own body react as emotion came to the surface and the words became soft and slow. "Sometimes truth is a sacred thing that isn't shared until a person can trust you with it."

"I should have told you the day you told me you played football. I just couldn't. I felt too betrayed."

"You needed to trust me, Beauty. I understand that now and it's an honor to listen to you share the truth about your life." Looking into her eyes, he kissed her hand again, cradling it in his own, understanding suddenly another layer of her need to feel secure he shared more of his own heart. "I need you to know, when Brad confronted me about my intentions with you, I made a decision. I can't let you go, Stephanie." And he vowed, "I want a committed relationship with you, exclusively with you, building trust, and getting to know each other on a deeper level. Is that what you want?"

"Yes."

"That means we're dating, not casually, this is serious. I want to call you my girlfriend, be a couple. I want people to know we're together," he stated. "I want to honor you and work together to honor God."

She nodded.

"We're starting over. There's still a lot of things about my life you'll need to deal with. John Dake, quarterback, isn't always easy to live with and I want to give you time to get to know me. You might not like everything that comes with my life—"

"You're forgetting, I'm the one that's life is hard to deal with. Stephanie Hightower, foster kid adopted by Brad Bennett after her sister was abducted."

He was quiet.

"My sister was abducted." She was staring into his eyes. "That's why Brad's my father. I was Samantha's guardian but I," now she shook her head, "I didn't do my job. I didn't keep her safe." Her hand seemed to grip his now as she said the first hard words, "I was studying." There was a long pause, another breath. "I'd been at the library," suddenly there was emotion and she didn't fight it, "When he lured Samantha over to his car with, 'Hey pretty girl, can you help me?' I was at the library. While I was there, studying physiology he'd already raped her the first time. And I got home, and it was late, after midnight, and Samantha was already tied up with barbed wire, bleeding and left alone in the dark, and I got..." she swallowed hard. "Irritated, because she wasn't home where she was supposed to be. I had to call her friends, talk to their parents, and no one knew where she was." The next words were broken phrases. "While I was... mad at her... he was... hurting her. And she didn't come home. All night. And then... it was morning and I had a test. I went to class..." A long pause now as she swallowed back emotion. "I was going to take the test... and it just hit me. I walked up to the professor and I asked to be excused, when I told him why, he... helped me. Because I didn't know what to do."

"You were young. Alone."

"I was worried they'd take her away from me because I didn't know where she was, then I didn't care anymore, as long as she was okay. She was missing, and Layne told Blair. She came that day with her parents, but even Brad couldn't find her. For six days..." The story stopped. She shook her head. "It should have been me he hurt."

"He hurt you too."

"No," she denied. "He took Samantha. He did..." she closed her eyes. "Horrible things to my sister."

"And you hurt for her. You hurt because you couldn't prevent it, help her or find her."

"Richard found her." There was a sudden smile. "He was there, out in the hill country with his dogs, shooting photographs during a storm. God led her to Richard. He found her and he's never left her." Now she nodded. "Brad took over as her guardian. He and Linda made sure she had everything she needed to get better. She's better now."

"And you? Are you better, now?"

"I finished Vet School, started working. Brad helped me get the internship in Equine surgery and the Association hired me."

"You're very good at what you do, Stephanie, but that's not what I asked you."

"I keep that part of my past in a compartment. Things you try not to think about anymore." She tried to smile, and he frowned.

"Have you talked about this to anyone?"

"They call it survivor's guilt. I worked with a counselor. Brad made sure."

"You understand it's not your fault."

"I understand, I'm not God, He allowed it. He allows things we don't understand, so by faith, I leave it with Him. That's what I mean by compartmentalizing it. I choose to dwell on how grateful I am instead. I'm thankful that He allowed my sister to be found, rescued, and strong enough to survive what others didn't. Because Samantha survived that evil man was found, sentenced and punished. He was executed, and my sister is alive. She's in law school now because she wants to help other victims and I'm so proud of her."

John nodded. "I'm so very sorry, Stephanie." His thumb wiped a lonely tear away and she moved toward him, into his arms to receive his condolences.

She held onto him as he held her.

"Kiss?" With her nod he kissed her tenderly.

"I want you to meet her."

"I'd be honored."

"Easter?" she asked him. "I'm going to Austin for the weekend and I'd like her to meet you too."

"Then we'll go. What else?"

"I'll be nervous; it's been hard since everything happened, but maybe you can help me be brave and just... play through it and find normal again."

"Absolutely. What else can I do?"

She'd snuggled into his neck then she surprised him as she asked, "Do I still have a place to stay here?"

"The bedroom is only yours."

"Does it come with Bradshaw?"

He chuckled, "Sure."

"Tired?"

"Not at all," he answered.

Then she stole his line, "Can we cuddle for a while?"

John Dake smiled, looking up he told God, "King me."

18

Easter came late, arriving the last Sunday in April with spring weather and the soft green of life. Samantha Elroy smiled, glancing through the plantation shutters, watching the shady Austin street for the first sign of them. Stephanie was coming, and she was bringing someone with her. Her sister had a boyfriend.

It made her giggle and she covered the ridiculous little girl sound quickly, glancing to see if Richard had heard as he played the piano. His eyes were shut. His head lowered, the sweep of raven hair curling in a way that was carelessly handsome. A Renaissance man, dressed in jeans with his shirt untucked, playing a disorderly jazz that poured across the width of both ebony and ivory keys on the piano so that his hands seemed to dive and dance. But his posture maintained its formal elegance, his tall, lean body graced with a regal heritage he could never disguise with casual clothes or grass roots jazz music. Her fiancé was a royal snob and the thought made her chuckle again because in truth all Richard did was give his money away.

He glanced up at her, his lips tilting; his brown eyes warm with the knowing of her. The jazz music was a kind of joke, a dare she'd made, that the baby grand wouldn't know how to play if the music wasn't over two hundred years old. He'd showed her she was wrong, and he could be current. Playing Queen's *Bohemian Rhapsody* then moving into a little *Tom Sawyer* by Rush and now some bluesy Dave Brubeck jazz. She couldn't believe she was longing for the classic calming of Bach again.

"You win. Please, for the love of New Orleans let them keep their jazz there and return to the classics."

He finally stopped and gave her a boyish smile. "I never win."

"Please."

She waved him off only to hear the beginning notes of *We Are the Champions* accompanying his quiet agreement, "You're right. I always win."

He was sixteen years older and they'd been together for eight years. Without saying a word, she knew Richard was teasing her in his subtle way. Telling her he was delighted in her excitement. Thrilled with her joy.

Her friend and protector had watched in silence for days as she prepared for this visit with her sister, perfecting every detail of her house for the holiday weekend. Today he'd tilted picture frames and unbalanced the bouquet of spring lilies every chance he got. She glanced at the vase, leaned over and rearranged it drawing the flowers up for the right proportionate height. She refused to look at him, merely straightened the signed Ansel Adam's and marched on to the kitchen for a glass of water with her beloved dog ever her shadow. In moments she was back at the front windows, pretending to study a law book in the harsh constrains of a Frank Lloyd Wright chair with Nick curling up near her feet. Then the case caught her interest and she was consumed in the application of the law until she heard Richard's voice.

"Nick," he called the Belgian Malinois who obediently came and stood beside the piano as his alert eyes stayed on Samantha. She glanced out the window, saw the car.

Samantha's gaze jumped to hold Richard's.

"Your sister is here."

She nodded. "Do I wait?" she asked him, her heart pounding. "Or go outside?"

"We should go outside," he smiled. The nobility of his birth touched the words with the soft French accent. His smile bloomed as he stood and took her hand. "Come and show your love to Stephanie. Forget the man."

She was up, her long legs taking her quickly through the door. She swept her sister into a hug, fierce and tight as she got out of the car. "I've been a wreck," she confessed as they clung to each other.

Stephanie held on tight. "Me too."

They broke apart laughing.

"Where's—" Samantha looked up, she connected with intense blue eyes, familiar and famous blue eyes. She gasped and pointed. "That's Dad's quarterback."

"Yes," Stephanie nodded.

"Yes?" she asked then shook her a little as she repeated, "Yes? You never said his name was John Dake."

"You never asked what his name was." Stephanie grinned, taking John's hand as she introduced them.

Samantha glanced at him. "What in the world are you doing with my sister?"

John smiled, it almost knocked her over. "Rattling her," he pulled Stephanie off balance into his arms. "Every chance I get."

Samantha smiled. "I like you already."

"Richard," Stephanie stepped forward into his embrace.

"*Amour vous rend encore plus belle*," he stated.

"Do you speak French?" Stephanie asked John.

"Love does make you even more beautiful," John replied with a grin of satisfaction at Samantha. "Your sister was translating for me."

"This is Richard de la Bovier." The men shook hands. Then Richard's hand rested lightly on Samantha's back like a proud father stood over his child. "He's a French Aristocrat," Samantha explained. "His father is the Comte de la Bovier and holds several other titles equally as pompous sounding. His family has royal blood. Someone back there squeaked out of Paris with their head intact and their pockets full."

Richard said straight and smoothly, "Samantha is after the emptying of them."

Samantha smiled. "Most definitely."

"It must run in the family, so is Stephanie," John added casually.

"John."

"Don't worry, we know her too well. She won't take a thing, has to be sick to death with Mono to give anyone an inch of room to help her. She's the worst."

"Then we're well matched. I met her at my worst." John kissed the top of her head. "Count myself blessed she's still hanging around as I try to grow up."

"Come inside, John." Richard led the way as John followed.

The sisters stood where they were, smiling. Then Samantha wrapped her arm around Stephanie and said, "I'm going to kill Blair for this."

"She can keep a secret, imagine that?"

"I'd never believe it." Samantha whispered, "Did Blair do this or Brad?"

"Would you believe neither? We meet on our own."

"I'm so glad you came," Samantha said hugging her tight. "I want to see you rattled and beautiful with love."

"I wanted to share it with you," she told her sister and together they followed the men into Samantha's house.

This Easter was the first holiday Helen Dake had ever spent alone. It was a day she'd been anticipating. Her son was a man now, with a full life and a heart on the edge of love. There was another woman seeking his time, his devotion, his life and she feared this one was the scissors that would finally cut the cord between them.

She already felt the tearing away, just as she had when he'd been a teenager. But during those hectic days she'd helped him to stand and separate, knowing it was her final job perhaps, to give him the wings to fly from her nest. Now she wanted to hold tight—as wrong as she knew it was—and hold on to him, feeling that he was all she had left.

If only Paul were here...

How many times had she thought that? She fisted her hands on the worn cover of her Bible as grief asked for a pity party and the Easter Cantata praised her risen savior's name. She looked at the man with the sparkling white robes that portrayed Jesus in this dramatization. His resurrection had been her hope, that one day she'd see Paul again. Christ's love had been her assurance, that He would provide for her, be her husband and help her to raise her son. His peace had filled many lonely hours, comforted her when she grieved, encouraged her when she struggled.

For twenty-five years she'd held on to that, martyred her love for Paul because it had been deep and so rare she'd thought it could never be repeated in her lifetime.

But today her devotion was more bitter than sweet. Somehow, she knew very soon her son would leave her side to take a wife, raise a family. She would have a new role in his life, as she should, and God had been preparing her, stirring her spirit so that it was restless and unsatisfied. Today she knew it was time to leave the Hill Country. She glanced over the faces of the faithful here in her church. So many she loved and loved her. Doubt told her she was too old for changes, but she'd never lacked courage before. With God's help she'd excelled in her career as an educator and a principal, managed a good size ranch and raised a boy into a fine man. She smiled, she wouldn't face this new challenge alone. She would go to Dallas and see what God had for her there. She would open her heart, her mind, her will and see what God had for Helen Dake's future. She pressed her trembling lips into a smile as she stood with the congregation and applauded the choir.

"So, how was Easter, Samantha?" Blair asked, balancing the telephone between her cheek and shoulder as she stirred the spaghetti sauce.

"Oh, it was interesting," Samantha answered. "Although I'm not sure I'll tell you just how interesting since," her voice rose several octaves. *"You never told me he was John Dake!"*

"Did I forget to mention that, Sammie?"

"It was almost time for them to leave before I stopped gawking. He's just—"

"I know," Blair finished and they laughed

"I really like them together. He does something to her. Takes the edge off." Samantha explained. "And he can't be in sight of her without touching her somehow. It's sweet."

"It's sickening," Blair added. "They're lovesick, I swear they kiss every second."

Samantha laughed. "They must just do that to irritate you. He was far away the gentleman here."

"What did Richard think?"

"They're destined."

"I knew it!"

"John told Richard he has some things to work on and he needs some time to prove to her and himself that he can change. He's given Dad his word and Layne, apparently, that his intentions are serious."

"Layne? Hmm, he's said nothing to me."

"Don't get mad. Layne's just being protective, Richard is the stealth spy. He poured whiskey and apparently John just spilled it all out with a few drinks as they commiserated over the two of us. Apparently, John wants Stephanie to have some time to make sure his life is what she really wants since he's got the famous thing going on and I'm having to deal with the Comte de la Bovier himself."

"How is the Comte?"

"As critical as ever. Richard can never do enough to please him but on a grateful note, our sister is finally happy." Samantha's hand stroked over the fine fur of Nick as her body relaxed. "I just hope she doesn't do something stupid to mess the whole thing up."

"Are you coming to Florida?"

There was silence. Then Samantha smiled. "Richard told John I would."

"Great! And Richard?"

"We're still discussing it." Samantha surprised her again. "He wants me to go alone."

Blair covered the shock with wit. "Let's just hope Stephanie shows up."

"What?"

"She's still stalling. Something about work."

"She has no idea we're coming. John wants to surprise her."

"I can't wait!" Blair said. "We're going to be together, the three of us, in Florida for a week."

"You better get to work on her and make sure that happens, Blair."

She hung up and instantly called Stephanie.

"So..." Blair asked.

"Yes..."

"Spill it, Steph."

Stephanie laughed. "It was great. I shocked Samantha silent with John."

"I can just imagine!" Blair laughed softly.

"She wanted to kill me for keeping him a secret."

"I got an earful myself," Blair added.

"So, you already know everything?"

"I wanted to hear it from you."

"And what did Samantha say?"

"She thought John was terrific. She said he couldn't be in the same room with you and not touch. I told her you guys kiss so much it's disgusting."

"Please," Stephanie countered.

"It's the truth."

"This from the married woman having all the sex she wants."

"Umm," Blair sighed. "I do have the advantage but remember Layne and I dated six years."

"Yadda, yadda," Stephanie replied.

Blair probed. "So, things are getting a little serious between the two of you with this exclusive commitment."

"I guess," she paused, "We haven't been apart for even one weekend this whole month."

"Have you finally given in and told him you'd go to Florida with him?"

"Blair," she moaned. "Not you too?"

"Look Steph, I don't want to twist your arm into going but, Layne and I are coming for the long weekend. He hosts this Memorial Day party every year for the team and his friends. You know how much he wants you to be there as his hostess."

"He also wants me to meet his Mother the weekend before. I think she was a little upset that he spent Easter with me and Samantha."

"Well, that's a good point, you took him home this weekend."

"Yeah, I know. But, after all the time I was off with mono, I hate to ask someone to cover me for another week."

"You belong to an association for a reason. You've got people to cover for you so you're out of excuses."

"Okay, I'm out of excuses."

"Good. Call John and tell him you're going, it will make his day."

"Blair, you're something. I think you should have been the lawyer as persuasive as you are."

"I have thought I missed my calling at times, but the wife of a politician is just as important," she said laughing. "He has risen, sister!"

"He has risen indeed. Happy Easter, Blair."

"Call John. Right now, and tell him yes."

And she did.

19

John leaned in close as he pointed out the airplane window. "That's Captiva Island and there's Sanibel."

"They look so small."

"They are. You can literally walk out the front door of my house to the bay side and turn around and walk out the back door to the ocean."

"Really?"

"Really." He touched her nose. "You are too cute."

"Can I take your drinks? We're about to land," the flight attendant asked.

He swallowed the remaining half of the fluid. "Okay, you can take it."

Stephanie lifted a brow.

"What?"

"You're drinking whiskey, neat. I think you're nervous."

He frowned. "You've got my tell?"

"Um." She kissed him. "I think I might. Just play through it, number seven."

"Okay, I am nervous so give me your sweet little hand Beauty and let's go meet my Mother."

Helen Dake was a beautiful woman. Her hair was a light ash blond. It was all one length and the chic style was swept back away from a striking face. Her eyes were the same vivid blue as John's and her skin glowed with a healthy warm tan and a rosy blush flushed her checks.

Beside her stood her sister Louise. She sported a visor on her short golden hair and stood several inches shorter than her elder sister. Both women had huge smiles on their faces when they finally spotted the couple.

"This is Dr. S.B. Hightower." John introduced, smiling down at her.

She extended her hand. "Please call me Stephanie."

"My mother and my Aunt Louise."

"I want you to call me Helen."

"And call me Louise."

"You can call me hungry, because I'm starving. I'm taking the three of you to dinner at the Mucky Duck as soon as we drop off the dogs," John said leading the group towards the baggage area.

His beach house was beautiful. Three levels with a basement. Every room had a view of the ocean. Her bedroom was downstairs by the pool beside his mother's room and the other guest room in their hall held Louise. John was in the master suite upstairs. They'd eaten at the island favorite then come home to play cards and the conversation had been relaxed and lively but this morning she was nervous.

After her early morning swim, she'd come inside to find Helen Dake waiting with a fresh cup of tea and breakfast. Her warmth and hospitality seemed genuine although Stephanie knew John's mother was conducting an interview behind her version of a Mr. Charming smile.

Linda had warned her. This was Helen's only son and she was fiercely protective. She thought of Samantha and understood. She remembered Linda telling her to just be herself, to extend Helen some grace and give her time to adjust to their relationship.

"I'm so glad you could come. I've heard so many lovely things from John." Helen sat beside her at the table. "I could hardly wait to meet you."

Stephanie smiled. "I was looking forward to meeting you too."

"Did you have a nice Easter with your sister?"

"Yes. I miss her. She's in law school at the University of Texas."

"She's engaged?"

Stephanie took a sip of tea and nodded. "A Frenchman."

"Tell me about your job. It sounds exciting."

"I have a clinic in Caddo Parish, Louisiana. I can treat both small and large animals there, but my specialty is equine. I work with several barns around Shreveport and consult with horse breeders. My love is genetics. That's what I eventually want to do, breed horses."

"Did you enjoy the golf tournament? John told me you surprised him."

"I was glad to help. They raised a lot of money for those children. It was a good cause."

"There's always a good cause wanting John's help."

"Yes, he's told me. It's hard for him to say no."

"It's important he prioritize. He can't do everything, or he'd never have a moment."

"He told me you're a great help with his foundation."

"I enjoy it."

"Is it hard to decide what to focus on?"

"Most things are personal in some way. John has his convictions. The military and children. Recently he's become passionate to help orphans. He just set up an anonymous endowment to make sure foster children have new school clothes. We've been working on naming that new project since we also just agreed to be a sponsor for a local news' segment called Wednesday's Child. They highlight a child up for adoption each week and from that John also agreed to promote CASA—the court appointed special advocate volunteers. They stand up on behalf of abused and neglected children because they want them to have a future brighter and more hopeful than their past. Better Days is what John has been calling it with JDi but Kenny thinks we need a name that links with John's now that he's made the investment a priority."

She blinked, startled to hear the information. "He's very generous."

"Have you meet his team, JDi?"

"Yes, ma'am."

"They were formed to protect my son. They congregate and help insulate because the media will either have you believe John's their hero or the villain in their story. I make it a practice not to listen. It doesn't hurt when you don't hear it." Helen patted her hand. "And I hope you'll let me know if I can do anything. The season escalates his fame and the pressure. Since he went pro, he's never played ball and had a serious girlfriend there to watch. I hope you'll sit with me at a few games, we'll cheer him on together."

"I'd love to."

"I've got four season tickets and friends I invite to certain games traditionally. We've got a fun section of loyal fans."

"My parents want me to sit with them for a few games too."

"Oh? Are they fans?"

She smiled. "Big fans. My sister and I were adopted by Brad and Linda Bennett eight years ago. It's not common knowledge."

"Oh."

Stephanie saw the shock, John hadn't told her. She gave Helen a moment to adjust to the news, taking a few cards from the deck they'd used last night and putting them in order. 3, 6, 7, King as she said, "They tried to get me to come to a football game for years while I was in school, I never had the time. Maybe if I would have..." She smiled now looking up at Helen. "John's videos dazzle me. I'm still trying to understand the game. Brad gave me a book on the basics. It's helped."

"You'll catch on." Helen encouraged.

"I want to do my best to support him, any advice?"

"It's off season so he can be consumed with you right now." She smiled. "But from July to February it will all be about football. If you understand the nature of his job, then you'll be more understanding of the pressure he's under. So, my best advice is try to be flexible, sometimes plans must change, but the season doesn't last forever. Spring will come again." She encouraged.

"I know John would love for you and Louise to stay longer."

"I appreciate that, but I need to get back to work."

"She sure does," John said looking apprehensively at his Mother as he leaned down and kissed her good morning. "I only approved a week's vacation."

"Ha! This principal retired last year. I only volunteer for JDi." Helen smirked accepting his kiss. "Coffee?" she asked, already getting up to make him a cup.

"Playing forehead poker with my mother?" he whispered. "She's lucky in cards."

She put the three on his forehead and held up the six to her own. He nodded, and she ask the question, "Why didn't you tell me about Better Days?"

"Matthew Six." He reached for the next cards and she stopped him.

"I knew what the cards were. These are a 7," she dealt him, "And a King," she turned it over in front of her.

"You don't need cards to ask me a question." He switched the cards. "And I would have been dealt the King, Beauty."

She smiled. "Your question?"

"What inspires you?"

"God."

"He used your story to inspire me. I think He honors his own through their stories that honor Him, don't you?"

"Jesus promised, '*I will not leave you as orphans; I will come to you.*' I used to remind Samantha." She covered his hand and John quickly linked their fingers. "I like the name. Better Days. You're going to inspire a lot of disadvantaged children to hope."

"I wanted to do it in secret."

"You can give in secret," she encouraged him, "No one has to know how much money you contribute, John, but your name can draw needed attention to a group of people that are too often overlooked. Make your good work public in hopes that it becomes contagious. "*Religion that is pure and undefiled before God, the Father, is this: to visit orphans and widows in their affliction, and to keep oneself unstained from the world.*"

"I could use some help."

"I'd love to help with Better Days. It would be an honor to give back."

After they said goodbye to Helen and Louise, they spent their first day alone on the water in a sleek speedboat. He showed her Captiva and Sanibel and the small private islands close by. They stopped at the sand bar, spending an hour wading hand in hand and searching for shells. The area was famous for it and she had handfuls she carefully tucked away in a bag John had bought her.

As the sun set they swung in a hammock as Jimmy Buffet music serenaded them. They were tangled tightly together when she whispered, "Your eyes are blue."

He grinned, blinked. "Are they?"

She frowned, nudging him, trying again. There was suddenly so much inside her she needed to express and finally the courage was there to trust him with the knowledge. Her hand touched his cheek, her gaze watching as his eyes focused on her own. "They're dark, no clear and crisp really, like the sky when it's hot."

His fingers stroked across her face. "Your eyes—

She covered his lips, smiled softly. "Want to look at you, talk to you. I mean," she exhaled. "Let me talk."

He smiled, she watched her finger tracing his mouth. "Do you have any idea what you did to me the first time you smiled?" She studied him. "You were leaving the clinic. You had a hat on and you snugged it down, like you were tipping it at me then this smile developed."

"You said my name." Her eyes came back to his. "I liked my name on your lips."

"You distracted me."

He grinned, pressing his lips together. "Shh, sorry."

"No, in that moment when you first smiled at me. You distracted me, for the first time in my life, my thoughts, my... body, I stopped... breathing. I think my heart even stopped for a second, then it raced and butterflies, there were suddenly these flutters inside me." She shook her head. "I didn't understand, that first time, what happened. Then you were there, at the house for dinner and it happened again. Only it was worse, because I realized I wasn't just distracted but attracted. Not by just your smile, or your eyes or... the whole way you were put together." She smiled now. "Although you are put together very nice and that certainly, well... caused some of those butterflies, but there was just something else." Her hand was stroking his chest, her gaze looking deep. "Something there, that I... " She shook her head, trying to find the words. "It was something inside you that connected to something inside me," she finally told him.

"Ditto," he stated simply.

She smiled.

"Butterflies?"

Her gaze narrowed a warning.

He laughed, squeezing her tight. "A guy's got to love that, Beauty."

She nipped his lips then whispered, "I'm not good at this."

His hold gentled, cherished. "What?"

She nestled to him, clinging. "Telling you... what you mean, how much this matters."

He whispered her name, lifted her face so she was looking at him. "You've told me that since the beginning with the way you do this." He hugged her close. "Cuddle, nestle, need. The way you silently need me makes a need in me rise up and take you even closer and I love that."

She smiled helplessly.

"You've touched a desire I never knew I had—to be needed, not for my fame or talent, but just for myself. And after all the fumbles at the beginning, you've given me the chance to be trusted. Now you're in my arms, giving a voice to your heart and freedom to your feelings and your hands." He patted her hand that rested on his chest.

"You've got a lot of muscles number seven. And you've been showing them off all day in that swimsuit."

He laughed, "I've been showing off? Have you seen yourself in a bikini?"

"This is the very special John-Dake-only-bikini by the way."

"John Dake only?"

"Rhonda helped me out. She said I could not spend the week in my black Speedo one-piece."

"Thank you, Rhonda," he whispered into her neck.

"John."

Now he grinned.

"You're making me nervous."

"Sorry. Shh. I'll stop." Then he whispered, "Why am I making you nervous?"

"This was a big deal, stepping out in this. I'm not like a lot of people."

"I know and that's why I'm so attracted to you, Stephanie. You got this bikini and it's just for me. I love you in it, just like you're attracted to me. You like my hands, my eyes, my smile, you've mentioned my muscles. It's all part of me. You're modest but you trust me enough to be safe stepping out in this because you know that I'm going to honor you. That makes this John-Dake-only-bikini even more special."

"You're comfortable with your body. I've spent years covering mine up because I needed to be seen as smart and capable."

"Can't you be smart and capable and sexy and pretty?"

"What does God think about sexy?"

"I don't know." He joined hands with her. "I've never thought about that. What do you think?"

"I think sexy has a place, but it's not paraded out in the world. It's private and it's for the married or its tempting us to sin."

He was silent.

"I sound like a prude, don't I?" She squeezed his hand. "I worry sometimes what you think of me and it makes me nervous because I want you to like me."

"I do like you. I like the way God created your mind and your spirit and how you honor God with your life. I also like your body in this bikini." It was black, a simple classic style that tied at her neck and on her hips. "We're getting to know each other, and things are still new. So, when you took that cover up off this morning I said, 'Wow... her stomach is really white.'"

She busted out a laugh. "Well it hasn't seen the sun since I was twelve."

"So, I smothered you with sunblock."

"Three times," she reminded him still smiling.

He pressed a kiss on her shoulder. "You still got a sunburn. Not good. You'll have a bath tonight with my mom's special stuff. I'll have to take better care of you."

"I'm okay. I can—"

He shook his head as his lips stilled her words. His kiss deepened as her heart accelerated. His gaze was fierce as he broke the kiss, his hand sliding over her cheek to rake into her hair.

"I want you to know something. I know you're smart and capable and very independent, but I want to take care of you, so you need to start getting used to it, Stephanie. I don't want you to fight me every time I try to give you something or do something for you. I want to lead, protect and care for you. I need to practice, and you need to practice letting me, okay?"

She smiled.

"Okay," he asked again. He was serious, and for the first time there was a tone of authority as he told her, "It shows me you trust me."

"I'll work on it."

She could already hear the rumble of the water as she walked into the master bathroom and watched John pouring a gallon of milk into the tub.

"What's this secret potion that you're conjuring up for me?" Her voice was full of amusement. Millions of tiny bubbles were growing with vast speed to challenge the rumbling milky waters.

"Vinegar in a milk bubble bath. Mom says it takes the sting out of the worst sunburns. It may burn a little at first, but it will be worth the first few minutes of discomfort. I don't know how many times I've come back to this tub after too many hours in the sun, I swear by it. Unfortunately, you usually forget too quick the next morning the discomfort you had the night before. Get in and I'll be back from my run in plenty of time to watch the basketball game together."

"Take the girls."

He saluted her as he walked away.

She pulled the cover-up over her head, taking off her bikini and dropping it onto the vanity. In the large mirror she saw the clear contrast of pink and white skin in the sun tan lines on her skin. Her stomach was flamingo pink, her legs and arms just rosy. She tested the top of the bubbles with her hand. It was unusually hot for a bath. Slowly she slid into the water. "Ahhh!" Her stomach screamed in protest. Was he crazy? John had said there would be a little stinging sensation at first, but this water was sizzling over her stomach. She forced herself to relax. Slowly, the water began to soothe, and she closed her eyes as she sank deeper into the thick milky depths of the bubbles.

"Stephanie, are you in the tub? Can I come in for a second?"

"I'm in and cooking. This is hot." She opened her eyes. Both dogs beat John into the bathroom and paced in front of the tub excitedly. He had changed into a pair of shorts and wore a shirt with a washed-out emblem from college on the chest.

"I'll add some cold water." He turned it on, "I brought you some things. The wine you like and here's my Walkman, its waterproof, so it can't shock you and don't worry if it gets wet." He placed ear phones over her ears.

"Umm." She closed her eyes as she turned on the music. She smiled and thanked him softly. "This is wonderful. Thanks."

He turned off the cold water then waved. She followed him with her eyes as she sipped the cool white wine and he and the girls left the bathroom for their run.

The ending of the CD woke her. The wine and the heat of the water had enticed her to doze. It felt too wonderful to just relax. Blindly, her arm reached over to the edge of the tub feeling for the Walkman. She jolted as she touched flesh. A hand. John's.

"Hey, Sleeping Beauty." He intertwined their fingers.

She took off the headphones. "How long have you been watching me?" Bradshaw rose off the ground waving her tail and rubbing against John.

"Just for a minute. You're buried in bubbles," he reminded her. "And the water is milky. I can't see a thing, but it looks relaxing."

"It feels great. Thanks for taking care of me." She smiled at him, squeezed his hand.

"Thanks for letting me. Need anything? More wine?"

"Back rub."

"Hmph..." The word was indecisive.

"You can't see a thing and there's more than enough room. Get in," she moved up, wrapping her knees with her arms, giving him the back half of the huge tub. He was looking at her and she smiled. "Keep your shorts on and rub my back with those famous hands of yours. I trust you," she told him.

Now he smiled, stepped in behind her. The dogs both stood at the edge watching them now. "Want a bath?" John asked the girls.

Staubach sat down. Bradshaw bowed low.

They both laughed.

"Like my tub?" he asked as he started the back rub.

"It's big as a swimming pool."

"They call it a soaking tub. My mom ooh'ed and ahh'ed when we first looked at the house."

"It's wonderful. I don't relax like this much."

"That's what vacations are for." His hands were gentle on her shoulders.

"That feels good." She closed her eyes and dropped her head down as he massaged her back, soothing over the muscles, long and deep strokes that made her sigh. "Did you have a good run?"

"Great run." He rested his chin on her shoulder and told her softly, "I shouldn't be in this tub, Beauty."

She looked back at him, palmed his face, told him sincerely, "I trust you," as she whispered a kiss to his lips, her hand brushing over his cheek, into his hair. He looked into her eyes. Those deep green eyes were lazy and full of him. She rotated, turning her whole body towards him, taking back his mouth.

"You're tempting me," he told her. "I should not be in this tub," he growled into her ear, caging her with his arms, pressing her back against the slanting side with a dangerous look. He nipped her lips.

She wrapped her arms around him and narrowed her eyes seductively. "Umm, probably not."

"I better get out," he told her between kisses. "You're naked..."

"Yes," she told him, and the willing word jolted him.

He rose out of the tub so quickly the water rocked in waves. "The game is about to start so I'm going to get a quick shower. I'll meet you downstairs." And he ran.

Like Joseph with Potiphar's wife on his heels.

What just happened?

She blinked, thinking it through then pulled the drain from the tub and rose realizing sometimes you shocked yourself with your actions or words.

Who was that woman in the tub?

Get in. That feels good. Yes.

There was astonishment and guilt and disappointment, and the mixture confused her. She wrapped herself in a blanket of a towel, picking up John's lightly damp shirt and running shoes. Then she saw herself in the mirror. Her, Stephanie Hightower, clinging to a towel and holding his clothes. She took a shaky breath.

Lord, what's wrong with me?

She didn't know what just happened. So, she just stood there stunned.

Then she heard the dogs. He was coming back, and she was still standing here like an idiot, naked, wrapped in a towel. She ran out of the bathroom. Out of the suite. Out to safety. She wasn't ready to face him yet in the hall, so she fled through the glass patio door onto the balcony and raced down the spiral stairs that would take her to the first floor. She never slowed her pace. Moving down the narrow and steep steps of the spiral metal staircase, she flew with the armful of clothing.

Then she was slipping. And bouncing. Hard. On her tailbone. Banging down several steps. Terrified she was about to break her neck she grabbed the railing with her hand as clothes went tumbling with his athletic shoes to the ground below. Finally, she stopped, in a tangle of terry cloth.

That was one way to clear her head. She sat there for a minute, her eyes welling with tears. Pain screamed from her bruised bones and the soft palms of her hands felt like they had just slid across a paved parking lot.

"Was that your version of a spanking?" She looked up at stars twinkling across a summer sea. "Was that your way of clearing my head?" She caught her breath; felt the emotion rising like a burn as the tears came. "Or was I just foolish and clumsy? I tempted him."

She moaned.

Closed her eyes. "I'm in the dark again here. I'm not sure what just happened but I think I wanted more than You've said I'm entitled to. Help me, please, to honor You. You promised that when we ask for wisdom and understanding, You will give it to us and the supernatural power to overcome temptation. Please help me. I love You, God and I'm falling deeper in love with him."

"John, they're getting ready to start that basketball game." Her voice lofted up to him from the first floor as he sat on the bed. The dogs were running in and out, dashing around his legs, springing up to paw at him.

"Okay girls, I heard Stephanie. Bradshaw, go on," he commanded, trying to think through his game plan after what had just happened.

He should never have got in that tub. Stupid! She'd been naked, and he had no business tempting either of them. That single choice to get in the tub, could have changed everything and he didn't want to change the balance of their relationship. Dishonor her. Sin.

He raked both hands through his hair. He was almost positive the whole thing was innocent. She just didn't realize, and he needed to lead. He definitely didn't want to make her feel like what had just happened should draw some uneasiness between them, but he was uneasy. They were alone, in a beach house, with a dozen beds. He thought of the hammock, their embrace in the surf, the playful innocent touching that had happened when they showered off the sand on the patio today. Desire was strangling him, spurring him on to old behaviors that would lead them into deep waters of trouble. He shouldn't have let his mother leave. They shouldn't be alone. He'd vowed to honor her. How? *God, help me...*

He looked at his hands as he ended the prayer. It was natural to clap. Break the huddle. Trust God like he did the offensive coordinator with a play call. He knew how to lead. A team, the offense. Knew better than to retreat when a pass rush was coming at him. You had to step up into the pocket. Go against what your flesh was demanding. Obey your training. Was this really any different? Just slow down. Focus. Be intentional. Take control. Communicate. Lead. Protect.

I can do all things through Christ who strengthens me.

The words were suddenly there. He repeated them giving himself instructions as he got up and went downstairs.

"John! You'll be mad if you miss the jump start of this playoff game." She yelled unaware that he was behind her.

"It's called the tip off." He tugged a long damp curl. "Do you want anything?" he asked.

"A soda would be great."

"One can of poison."

He handed the opened can to her as he walked over to sit in the large leather recliner. She had the newspaper, was doing a crossword puzzle as she watched the game in the other recliner.

John concentrated on the game as he complained about the officials. They always had a way of complicating a good match with bad calls. The buzzer sounded for the first half and a parade of commercials started.

"What an incredible first half, huh?"

"Who's winning?"

"Who's winning?"

She met his amused gaze with a smile.

"Chicago's ahead."

"You want some popcorn?" She was standing up, he held out his hand and when she took it he pulled her down into his lap.

"I want to talk."

"About?"

"Can we talk about the bathtub?" he asked, and she just nodded. "I want to be honest. Need to be more careful." He held her gaze and said sincerely, "Protect you. Okay?"

She nodded.

"I want to be in control. Not the power kind of control," he explained. "But self-controlled. I want to maintain mine... with you. To do that, I need to be careful, thoughtful. I don't need you naked in my arms. Even covered with bubbles," He smiled softly. "You're too beautiful and I stop thinking, start responding then you start asking and before we know it..." He shook his head. "That's not deliberate or slow or honest or careful. We'd regret it."

"I shouldn't have asked you to get in the tub."

He stroked her face. "I want to honor you, Stephanie. I shouldn't have let my mother leave. We don't need to be here alone."

"We're okay," it was a question.

"We're definitely okay." He assured but he also confessed, "But we jumped off sides. So, we confess it, go back five yards and start the play over."

"John, I'm sorry."

"God, forgive us and help us now," he prayed out loud. Then he looked at her. "We're being honest, and I needed this talk, so you knew that I'm struggling. I'm not rejecting you, I'm honoring you. Do you understand the difference?"

"Yes." She nodded. "How can I help? No more bikinis."

He frowned, "I loved that bikini."

"I'll sit in my own chair."

"We're seriously cuddling here for the rest of the game, Beauty."

"Okay."

He pressed their foreheads together and whispered, "You can't say yes. Or please. Or invite. Or give in or over. You say no."

"No."

"That's my girl."

"And if I want to say yes, or please, or give in or over, you'll say no." Now she snuggled closer. Her hand over his heart. "Like you did tonight. You did it. You led, just like you should have. You stopped, got out of the tub and then you ran." She patted him. "From Jacob to Joseph, number seven. I think your character is starting to show and that is soooooo attractive to me."

He smiled. "You wanted popcorn. I'll get it." He was up and off to the kitchen. Started the popcorn then he turned on his socked feet a complete 360 and spiked the dish rag like he was in the end zone. Then John pointed up to the ceiling, "Thank you God." He set that imaginary crown on his head as he announced, "King me!"

"What. Was. That?" Her eyes were wide, her smile breaking into a laugh.

"Ah..." He glanced at her then just smiled as he confessed, "Touch down celebration thing I do."

"You were practicing a touch-down-celebration-thing-you-do in the kitchen?"

"I might have been celebrating." He slid over the tile on his socks, taking her into his arms as he grinned.

"Celebrating?" Her eyes were sparkling.

"Sooooo celebrating," he mocked her enthusiasm with a kiss. "You—such a godly woman. Thinking. I'm..." He just shook his head. "It's a God thing, Beauty. It's all Him, in me. I started hearing Him, cooperated. We were having a king me moment together."

"A king-me-moment?"

He glanced at the popcorn popper, held up his finger. "Yeah. It's what I say when I score a touchdown. King me." He emptied the kernels into a bowl.

"Like in checkers, when you get to the other side?"

"It's more like a praise thing, Beauty. I tell God the success is all You. You gave me these skills, anointed me, set the crown on my head. I feel like the king of the world in that moment. It's the sweet spot. You know, when you do what you know you're born to do and things just..." He shrugged. "I don't know, it's hard to explain. It's just what came out when I was in college and I kept it going."

"Wow."

"What?"

"Just wow. I get it." She nodded. "I sooooo get it. King me."

Now he smiled.

20

John couldn't hide his smile as they waited for the jet to connect with the jet bridge. She was going to be shocked since she thought they were here to pick up his best friend. He'd been able to keep this a secret and the anticipation had him fighting to keep the smile off his face. He didn't have to wait long. Samantha came off right away. Her features were similar to Stephanie's in many ways, the heart shape face identical. But there were distinct differences in the sisters. Samantha's hair was silky straight. It moved like fluid as it brushed past her shoulders in an even length—thick and inky dark. The green of her eyes was gold, large and exotic. She was tall as Stephanie, her long legs moving with the same graceful gait but there was a tension in her body as well. As her eyes checked and double checked her surroundings. He saw the fear and the courage she was struggling to keep as she proceeded forward into the airport, searching for them. If Stephanie didn't see her in another moment, he would call her name.

"Samantha!" she suddenly gasped, grabbing John for an instant before she ran to her sister. There was that female thrill that hit a high note as they hugged. Stephanie all astonished smiles, her sister smiling back. They were adorable and excited, and he was the proud mastermind behind it all.

"Samantha's here!" she told him. "Did you do this?"

He pocketed his hands. "Surprised?"

"Shocked." She turned back to Samantha. "Where's Richard?"

"At home. Nick came."

He watched Stephanie cover the shock with pride. "Great, the girls will love him."

"Hi, John."

He carefully drew Samantha close and hugged her lightly. "I almost didn't recognize you behind those lawyer glasses."

"Oh," Samantha reached up and removed the very contemporary black frames. "I was trying to study a little bit but this obnoxious cowboy across the aisle kept bothering me."

"Oh?"

John covered Stephanie's concern with a grinning, "Obnoxious cowboy, really?" as he glanced toward the door where the rest of the passengers were coming from. "You won't believe this, but my best friend is on this flight."

"You're kidding?" She looked toward the door.

And they all watched a cowboy saunter out. He wore starched denim the way some men wore tailored suits. His cowboy hat straw and his boots sporting a shine. Three flight attendants were prancing on their toes in kitten heels to keep up with him. They all seemed to be talking at once as the man just looked ahead at John. Giving a nod and a grin that broke into dimples before he tipped his hat and waved good bye to the girls.

Then he swung his carryon bag behind his back, so he could extend his hand.

"You obnoxious cowboy," John said as they shook hands. "Beginning to think you missed the flight but I see you got detained."

"Sorry to keep your famous self waiting so long out here with two beautiful women."

John tugged him into a tight hug and when they broke apart he said, "This is Samantha, Stephanie's sister. Samantha this is my best friend, Honey Cooper."

"Nice to meet you."

"I think we already met counselor." He smiled until a dimple danced within his left cheek.

"I guess we did."

"I never got a chance to tell you how pretty you are though."

She didn't reply.

"If I know Dake. I'm sure it runs in the family." Honey looked at Stephanie.

"James Hunnicut meet my Stephanie."

"My friends call me Honey." He took her hand, drew her into his arms for a tight hug. "I've been wanting to meet you. John's gone on and on about how smart you are." He tucked her close and told his best friend, "She's gorgeous. You forget that in the description, brother John?"

"He knows I call you Beauty. Pick up your bag, Hunnicut. Nick's waiting."

"Nick?"

"My dog," Samantha answered.

"And we're losing daylight; I want to get out on the water." And the four made their way to baggage claim.

"Can you see it?" Samantha asked, leaning out over the back of the boat beside her sister. Stephanie had a snorkel and mask on and she was looking into the water's surface searching for the Manitou that had crested the water and swam by.

She shook her head, surfaced and took out the snorkel calling out to John as she looked across the water. "Do you see it?" There was no answer. "John?" She looked over her shoulder. He was standing next to Honey. Smiling. "Do you see the Manitou?"

"It's hard to look for a Manitou when you are fanny up over there, Beauty."

Samantha laughed.

Stephanie said, "Really. You are horrible."

"Guilty." He pulled his mask on. "Let's take a look."

He came close and she pointed. "He's was over there."

And in a move, they were in the water. And she was in a panic. Surfacing and reaching, then grabbing on to him with all four limbs as she gasped, tried to climb him.

"Hey." He pulled her in tight. "I have you." Their mask knocked together. She saw his eyes, felt his arms around her. "The boat is right there. You have a life vest on. I have you, Dr. Hightower."

"I do dogs and horses. I don't like water and fish."

"Okay."

"Especially when the fish are bigger than you."

"Was it bigger than me?"

"It was huge," she told him softly now, "I'm scared, John."

"Okay. Manitou are gentle. Play through it for a minute. I'm right here. Okay?"

She held on to him.

"Have you snorkeled before?"

"No."

"Ah, we should have practiced first in the pool before I took you into the game. Sorry." He gave her a few instructions about the snorkel, taught her how to clear her mask.

"I've never been in the ocean like this."

"Hmph, I didn't know you'd be scared."

"It's more about control," she confessed.

"Do you want to get back in the boat?"

"I..." she looked around. "Can practicing letting you take care of me, I guess." She was clinging tight. "Please, don't leave me."

His arm was around her. "It's peaceful, quiet in the water."

"Mysterious," she said. *"There is the sea, vast and spacious, teeming with creatures beyond number—living things both large and small."*

He nodded. "So, if God would take as much care creating what's hidden in the ocean as He did with what we can see on land, there must be a lesson here. Want to look around? We can stay on the surface above it, okay?" He tucked her to his side and they put their snorkels in and looked under water.

She could hear her breath, huffing in and screaming out. Her hand griping tight to him. He pointed with their joined hands at some small fish. She just nodded, looking out into the clear water for something big and scary. There was a splash, then another. Samantha and Honey joining them. She watched her sister swim. She had on fins and beside her Honey was pointing at the small colorful fish. She let John lead her. They swam together. Slowly she got comfortable with the snorkel and the soft pulsing tide that skipped over them as they swam and searched for fish together.

Finally, they surfaced, pulled up their masks. He kissed her. Smiled. She kissed him. Then Honey whistled. He was pointing at the Manitou.

John's arm was around her. "He's like a Labrador. Goofy and gentle for a big guy. And curious. If you're still, he'll give us a look. Okay?"

She could only nod. Trust him. Watch as the Manitou swam closer to Samantha and Honey moved between her and the fish. The Manitou snorted, and Samantha laughed, leaning on Honey and bobbing in the water, both of them smiling. Then the Manitou sank slowly into the water and swam off; a giant shadow moving off in the clear water.

She exhaled. Her sister calling out, "That was awesome!"

"John said Captiva Island is the best place to find seashells in America." Stephanie picked up a conch shell, bleached white and the size of her palm. She handed it to Samantha as they walked along the ankle-deep water of a sand barge and the guys snorkeled some more.

"It's beautiful here. I'm so glad John asked me to come."

Stephanie hugged Samantha to her side. "I'm so glad you're here."

"This is the first time I've seen my big sister with a real tan."

"Well, this is the first time I haven't felt totally guilty about laying around doing nothing but relaxing."

"I think John is the best thing that's ever happened to you, Steph."

She raised her eyebrows and scrutinized Samantha a moment. Part of her wanted to object, to say, 'hey wait a minute. I'm a Doctor, a vet and a good one. That's the best thing...' but her face softened realizing her sister knew almost better than she did. "Maybe so," she answered.

"Maybe?" Samantha smirked, and Stephanie finally had to smile. "So, how does it feel to be in love, Stephanie?"

Stephanie looked out across the ocean. She wanted to tell Samantha everything she was feeling. Try to put a voice to this chaotic swirl of emotions, to give these feelings richer words than happiness and love. To tell her about the trust she was learning and the hunger and the ache she was fighting as her love for John deepened. And even try to explain about the little seed of fear that was there as she let herself depend on someone again and give away some of the control.

"Stephanie?" Samantha drew her back. "I won't fall apart or have a panic attack just because we're talking about men."

"I know you won't," Stephanie insisted touching her sister to emphasize her statement.

"You can talk to me just like you would Blair. You don't have to avoid certain subjects or try to protect me. I know you've always felt like you had to do that." Samantha could read the uncertainty in Stephanie. "Besides the panic attacks, I'm okay now, Steph."

"I know," Stephanie confirmed quickly, finally looking at her sister again. "I know you are and I'm so thankful."

Samantha's voice became serious. "It wasn't fair that you felt like you had to be my parent, provider and protector. You did everything you could, and I feel so guilty for the burden you were under and then the years we were apart when I went to France and left you here alone."

"Don't feel guilty. I wanted you to have those opportunities. A new start at such a great school. And you were with Richard in Paris. He knew how to help you. I wasn't trained or prepared for what you were going through, but God knew who was and He provided it."

"Don't feel guilty either. I know you do. I think we both need to let the guilt go. If I let go of mine, will you let go of yours?"

"Yes." Stephanie hugged her and whispered, "Yes, I will."

They held onto each other for a long time. And Stephanie just let herself give into the tears as she told her, "I'm so proud of you, Samantha. I think my baby sister has grown into a wonderful woman. I love you, very much."

"And you love John, right?" Samantha was smiling, in fact it was a bold, knowing grin.

Stephanie closed her eyes. "Samantha."

"Stephanie," she echoed. "Is it so hard to say you love him? The man is crazy about you. Just the way he talks about you says enough. He thinks you're special or something. So, tell me how it feels to be in love."

"Wonderful." Stephanie smiled. "I wish I had the words, there's so much inside me about how I feel for him. So yes, I love him and I'm in love with him and I'm caught between terror and exhilaration most of the time."

"There's no fear in love," Samantha reminded her. "And you need to stay in the moment or you'll lose the joy in today." She hugged her close. "You're in love. Don't wait too long to tell him."

Two days later the girls were circling with excitement as they came back into the beach house after another day on the ocean. Stephanie gasped as people started singing. Linda was holding a cake and Brad held balloons as they came out of the kitchen. Blair and Layne carried brightly wrapped packages beside them, grinning as they sang along until the famous song ended.

"Is it your birthday?" John was shocked.

Stephanie just nodded.

"You weren't going to tell me?" He'd narrowed his eyes.

The room was quiet. She could feel heat flood her face and shame started riding up her neck as she searched for something to say. She glanced at her family, the armful of gifts and telling silence. Then she looked at John. He was lifting a brow, waiting with empty hands.

"I should have told you."

"You should have told me."

"But you would have made a big deal out of it."

He pinched her chin and lifted her mouth up to him. He kissed it smiling. "I'm going to make a very big deal out of it, Dr. Hightower and you're going to let me now. Happy Birthday!"

"You knew."

He only smiled.

"Surprise!" Blair hugged her tightly then Layne had his turn.

"Happy birthday," he whispered.

Honey was snapping pictures as Brad and Linda embraced her and she saw the table. Spread out like a Mexican fiesta.

"All this is compliments of Senora Hattie," John said hugging Stephanie as he grabbed a nacho.

"Transported via mom and dad's flying picnic basket," Blair added.

"You look beautiful with that tan," Brad told her touching her face. "Having fun?"

"The best time. Thanks for coming." She kissed him.

"We wouldn't miss it."

"Everybody sit down. I'm hungry," John exclaimed as everyone found a seat. "And there's nothing more shameful than a cold enchilada. Will you bless the food please, Brad."

The grace was said, and the food was served.

"I'm so glad you guys are here. Thank you, John. You've brought my favorite people together." Stephanie leaned against John, squeezing Samantha's hand as she raised her glass. "To boyfriends. Old friends," she looked at Layne, "And new friends," she smiled at Honey. "Parents. Sisters. You're the best and I love you."

"Happy Birthday," the table answered.

As dinner ended John set down a small box. It was long and narrow, light blue with a white ribbon. "Open it," he urged her. And her heart was throbbing, her pulse fluttering in her throat and John casually put his arm around her shoulders. "I get to make a big deal of this, remember."

She untied the little bow. Opened the box to find a black box embossed with a famous name. It was hinged and hard to open, and inside a bracelet sparkled with emeralds and diamonds from its bed of velvet.

"It looks like a whole lot but it all has meaning. Twenty-five diamonds for every year and then five emeralds for the months I've known you." He picked it up off the velvet and laid it over her wrist, clasped it shut. The shape forming to her arm and lying surprising flat.

She turned into his neck, just held him tight. As tight as she'd held her sister a few days ago. Love so warm and right and healing some lonely, hurt part of her heart for a moment that she didn't want to fight it. She clung to him, praying just her savior's name as she was overwhelmed with joy.

"Happy birthday."

She just clung, still hiding in his neck, humbled by the blessing of this moment.

"Do you like it?"

Now she had to engage. With a new kind of courage, she looked up at him. "John, I love it." Then she smiled. "Thank you."

"She's accepting gifts!" Samantha exclaimed. Suddenly the table was filled with presents.

"What! Wait. No," she frowned.

Samantha laughed. "Too late. John finally broke your stubborn tradition. You're letting us bless you this year."

"I brought seven years of gifts," Layne told her, stacking them up.

Linda gave her a dress. It was like a water color of ocean water. Dark green and blue silk designed into a halter style sundress. She wore it that night with her new bracelet and Samantha's perfume and Blair and Layne's pretty earrings. The group going out to the Plantation Resort to dance. She loved having her sisters together, her family here to celebrate and she began to embrace it because John made her realize tonight was special. She was happy, and the joy just rose and overflowed from her heart as she celebrated.

His hand felt warm and secure as they strolled down the soft sanded beach late that night with the dogs. She leaned gently against his side, listening to the soft rhythm of the tide. The sky was cloudy, and the night was midnight dark and hung with humidity. A gentle breeze whisked by intermittently to cool the air.

"It's so wonderful here. It must always be hard for you to leave."

"It's definitely my escape from reality, and you're going to have to keep coming back with me. It seems like you've been able to forget about work and enjoy yourself."

"I gave Mary an oath that I wouldn't call the office." Her smile faded. "You know, I think this is the first time I've actually just relaxed and done nothing since..." She stopped and looked away thinking. "The summer before my mother died."

"How old were you then, Stephanie?"

"That would have been, the spring I turned thirteen."

"You were so young when your life must have turned upside down."

"I guess I was. I never really felt young. My mother was a single mom, so it seemed like I was always the big sister, taking care of Samantha."

"Who took care of you?" he asked gently, tucking her hair back away from her face.

"I did," she said firmly.

"Is that why it's so hard for you to let me?"

"I'm learning to let you." She smiled up at him. "Snorkle. Sparkle." She held up her bracelet. Smiled. Then said sincerely, "I love this, John."

"I'm glad." He just held her.

"I'll take good care of it—"

"I don't care if you deliver foals with it on. It's sturdy. I made sure. And it's special, I wanted it to mean something not just be some bracelet. We've come a long way in five months."

"I loved the whole day," she told him, and she wanted to tell him more, that she loved him, was in love with him, was it time? But he was suddenly frowning. "John?"

"I wish I would have called off the party or trimmed it down, to just a few close friends, your family. I've loved this time with you." He shook his head. "Our time alone is about to be over with the weekend party tomorrow."

21

It started early on Saturday morning. John's team from JDi arrived with a troupe of workers. A tent went up, and the beach was scattered with bright colored umbrellas and lounge chairs beside a beach volleyball court. Beverages were put on ice by two bartenders and a barbeque was smoking huge briskets and slabs of ribs. A cover band was coming, and Kenny and Rhonda were deciding which location they liked better—the one from last year or from the year before—they decided poolside was best and cleared the space. The kitchen had a chef and three assistants already busy on the side dishes for the day and two security guards were here to rotate from house to sea. By mid-morning the beach and pool area were crowded with an array of people. Stephanie couldn't believe so many would come all the way to Florida for a party. Several boats arrived from the South Seas Plantation Resort via the bay, and the volleyball court was the hot spot with a tournament starting.

There was nothing for her to do. But watch. And try not to wring her hands.

"You okay?" Blair asked as she approached her with Samantha.

"I was looking for something to do."

"I think it's all done." Blair smiled at her. "Your girlfriend job is to meet and greet not hide and work. I'll make sure to introduce you to everyone I know today. If I don't, it's because I don't know them, so introduce yourself." She frowned. "And don't look at me like that. You're the hostess of John's little party, FMJD."

"Blair, don't call me that."

"Future Mrs. John Dake," Blair explained to Samantha.

"Sounds appropriate." Samantha grinned. "Since you're the queen of his world."

"And I doubt the king will be around to introduce you," Blair added then turned serious, "I'm sure the guys will be in that sandbox all day, playing volleyball in that four-man tournament."

"Well, I think I'll leave you in Blair's good hands and go even things up." Samantha headed over to the volleyball pit.

"I thought she might leave this morning with mom and dad," Stephanie said softly.

Blair took her hand, uniting them. "She's out to prove something to us and herself. She's okay and overcoming her fears."

"Still, I know this is hard for her," Stephanie commented watching as the guys welcomed her instantly. She smiled as she watched John and Samantha join up with Honey and Layne for a team. "And hard for me not to hover."

"The guys will watch out for her and I'm right here for you."

"I know," Stephanie smiled. "Hover on, sister."

"Players' wives at three o'clock. And there's Cindy with the baby. Come on, I'll introduce you. John's close to the Beihns."

Stephanie glanced toward the volleyball court, watched John's team as she sunned beside Blair by the pool. It was a great day; the sun warm, the breeze cool, the band stringing together favorites. John was having fun, playing with his friends. She was relaxing, just taking it all in from the sidelines as the party continued to grow.

She was praising God for the joy when they walked in. Three women, famous for different things, seemed to strike a poise on the patio. They were wearing heels and beach clothes. The tallest peeled off a tight little dress to reveal her angelic body in a small bikini. Most of the world had seen it before, blown up in lingerie shop windows and highlighted in magazine ads. The supermodel was also known for her long platinum hair and she moved it over a shoulder as she swept the scene. The pop singer beside her was already stepping out with the actress toward the music. Their hips were swinging, the volume turning up a bit as the band saw they had dancers. People began to move with them, gather there on the sandy dancefloor.

The women were smiling. The men were laughing. Suddenly the volleyball game was over, or it just stopped, because the crowd was drawn toward the music, everyone dancing or singing along and the party really started.

Stephanie slipped into a long sleeve denim shirt, snapping it shut as Blair told her, "You know about Elise."

"Who?"

"John's ex."

"Oh."

"The blond. Supermodel," she answered at the same moment the blond waved at John and called him Jack.

Jack it's your doctor. The memory of that voice came rushing back. That blond, supermodel, that Elise girl, a girl that John said meant nothing, was certainly something. And she was here, the life of the party. Suddenly Stephanie was walking. Her heart pounding, hurting, maybe breaking again. Emotions just chaotic. Her mind fighting to think. She didn't know what to do, headed toward a bathroom, silence, privacy, darkness, safety; when one of the JDi team stopped her. "Dr. Hightower, need anything?"

"A drink." She just answered, forced a smile because she suddenly felt caught off guard and embarrassed and lost. She caught hold of what she could manage. Anger. It took her to the bar.

"John's girlfriend needs a drink." Kenny announced. "Can you do the honor, Will?"

"Yes, sir. What can I get you?"

The bartender was busy, but he turned to her with a smile, gave her his attention as he filled drink orders.

"Scotch. A good one."

"I've only got Jack Daniels out here." He held up the bottle.

"Then water," she answered.

"Sure."

Was it a question? Everyone else was drinking icy margaritas, wine or beer. And here she stood, white knuckling the countertop of the bar, asking for water, about to bolt from the edge of the party. She didn't belong here. She swept the crowd. Beautiful. Famous. Powerful. Popular. Party people. John's friends. This was John's world. She glanced at Elise, dancing in the center of it. The real queen was right there.

"The top shelf Scotch is in the house," Kenny said softy with a smile.

She smiled back. "I'll get it." She turned toward the house with the new excuse.

"There you are." She was taken into John's arms. Kissed. He was smiling but it was tight because his jaw was ticking, and she couldn't see his eyes because he had on sunglasses, but he glanced toward Kenny and gave him a nod. Began to lead her away from the crowd, toward the water, tucking her under his arm, his voice soft in her ear. "Take a walk with me, Beauty." He nodded at a guy as they passed. "Hey Williams, glad you could make it. I got a slab of ribs with your name on them."

He kept them moving. Greeting people but not stopping. Holding her possessively close as he purposefully continued on. "The blond with the long hair, up by the band, is an old girlfriend of mine."

"Elise," Stephanie said evenly. "She was the girl that answered the phone that morning."

"Hey, John. Great party." They had to stop for a minute, John quickly moving them on after the short conversation with a teammate.

"I haven't seen her since that morning, and there is nothing going on between us."

"Great party, John."

He just nodded, smiled, kept moving them. "I just want you to know I have no idea why she's here. I never invited her and I'm going to tell her and her friends to leave."

"It's your party," she stated.

John felt her stiff fury. What had he been thinking with this party? His old life corrupting his new one. This wasn't getting anywhere. They needed to go somewhere private, where they could talk this out. He walked up to a jet ski and started it.

"Let's take a ride. Get on." He ushered Stephanie behind him and they were flying across the bay. John beached the Jet Ski on a small private beach. He held out his hand to help her off and she bluntly refused it, getting off on the other side.

"I knew you'd be upset." He walked in front of her, cutting her off as she walked away.

"Upset?"

He pulled her to him by her arms. She was stiff. "Beauty, you're angry."

"I'm not," she countered, slipping loose.

"You are and if I don't confront it you're going to pull back and shut down. I need you to practice talking this out, so we can work it out."

"Hmph," she mocked the word he used when he was short on words.

"Stephanie, I didn't ask her to come. I swear it. I don't want anything to do with her."

"You've already told me, remember? You've told me all the girls you dated mean nothing to you afterwards. Even your mother said you'll be consumed with me until July, then things change, I'll need to be flexible or you're done."

"My mother said that?" He stepped back. Frowned. When she crossed her arms and nodded there was only silence. His past came between them again and the upcoming future pushed them even further apart. "I won't let Elise start something between us, when she's no threat to you at all. Don't let her do that or my mom. I'm committed to you." He waited on her, prompted, "Stephanie. We need to talk about this. What are you thinking?"

"I'm thinking about high school. Worse, this feels like the drama from middle school."

"The modern world is often just that immature."

"Well in high school I wasn't at your parties. I didn't sing, dance, and drink with friends. I lived with five different families. I studied or worked or worried about my sister." She shook her head. "So, she is a threat," she told him. "I understand why you were with her. She's incredibly beautiful. And famous. The life of the party. I understand." She gave him a little nod.

He shook his head. "Big hat, no cattle," he stated. "That means she's all show, shallow," he reached for her hand. "You're substance, real, spiritually mature. More beautiful inside than even you are out. And your life isn't a party, it's a life of purpose. That's priceless to me. Do you understand that? And this isn't a short-term fling, Stephanie." His thumb soothed the skin beneath her bracelet. "I'm committed to you. Talk to me, please."

"Okay... You slept with her. She's had something of you... that I anticipate and cherish." Her voice had gone raw and soft. "She shared with you... what I haven't, what I want. It hurts, John."

The revelation was a crippling wound of regret he couldn't change. There were no excuses now, no way to lead her or them out of this, but his soul told him there would be forgiveness.

"I'm sorry," he told her. "Forgive me." He closed his eyes and prayed the same words, meaning them fully, finally coming into line with God's law and understanding his full rebellion. He didn't want to live that way anymore, was ready to change and honor God and her. And in time his past would be past to them, today lived well would only make tomorrow better. "Stephanie." He opened his eyes, took her hands and in faith he stated, "I'm not that man anymore. We're going to have better days."

"I know," she agreed, nodded but her eyes suddenly filled, "And I'm turning into the girl I used to be. I'm an outsider in your world. Scared. Insecure. Feeling overwhelmed. Lost and alone."

"No. I found you," he told her. "The moment I saw Elise, I came and found you. Kenny stepped up immediately, he had you. Team JDi knows how much you mean to me. You're part of us now. Not alone. And spiritually, Christ is always with us as we try to be in this world but not of it, right? We'll help each other do that together as we honor God. You're not alone anymore so don't let her make you feel isolated."

"I feel jealous. I hate that woman. I'm feeling all these horrible things, feelings I've never had before... Competitive, like if I don't step up, right now, I'll lose you. That I need to learn how to drink, dance, be fun, seduce you."

"No, that's a lie."

"She makes me feel inferior and awkward and a prude."

"That's a lie too."

"And that makes me want to believe I better strip down and seduce you, prove it. I feel entitled to intimacy with you. Me! I'm the one that's saying, 'Let's go.' And you're saying, 'No.' Have you lost your mind?" There was a little laugh. "See, I'm losing my mind. My heart is so full with my feelings for you. I want you. Physically. Now. Today. I'm watching all those people and I'm thinking I've been an idiot, missed out, never even lived. I'm boring and self-righteous and ridiculously naïve and prude. Why can't I be like her? Why does everything have to be so serious and hard and reserved? She's free."

"That's another lie."

"Is it?"

"Give me a verse on what God says freedom is."

She could only shake her head.

"Come on, Stephanie. You know one, it's in here." He touched her chest.

"*Where the Spirit of the Lord is there is freedom.*"

"You're free. We are free from all that worldly deception. Right. Give me another verse."

"*Don't use your freedom to indulge the flesh; rather serve one another humbly in love.*"

"Do you hear the truth?"

She gave him a nod.

"Don't you know yet?" He took her hands, squeezed them, then gently followed her arms up until he held her face. There was silence. Looking into each other's eyes. Then there were three words, said almost simultaneously by the two of them with courage and trust and sincerity.

"I love you."

She wanted to kiss him, hold him but he held her just there, apart from him, looking into her eyes. And he wasn't smiling. His voice was serious with that edge again, of command as he told her, "I want you to know that I don't want sex. What I want is your love and the intimacy we're building, and the care we have for each other, the respect, the need, the longing and the love. I love you," he repeated. "I think we might have a lifetime to work out the sex when we're free to do that, until then we're going to do this right." He smiled, soothing her. "And because its right, we have to be united, believe God will help us and help each other because the world doesn't honor this kind of freedom or love. So, forgive me for my past," he said softly. "That it can haunt me and hurt you. I wish I could have believed, obeyed, known what was waiting for me. I'm sorry, Beauty."

"If you forgive me, for losing it sometimes, running scared, thinking I'm still on my own, alone."

"You're not alone. I found you," he reminded her. "I'm going to honor and protect you because I love you."

Now he gathered her to him and she kissed him, pressing up, presenting her heart to him. He held her there for a long time, close and protected. "I'm afraid," she whispered. "This means something. You mean something. It scares me to death how much this means and what I could lose again."

"Play through it because we're going to win," he told her confidently. "The whole world might try to oppose us, but I'm not afraid. There's no fear in love. I want to show you, that I'm worth your trust. We need to walk through the football season together. I need to prove to myself that I can be more than just a quarterback that love can endure the ups and downs and—"

"I love you." She smiled as she said it. "Don't be afraid of the future, right? There's better days ahead."

He smiled back, promised, "I'm going to bring you back here one day." He looked at the tiny island, the crystal water, the private beach. "Make love to you right here." He picked up a shell. It was a common Whelk, a white fan with a squared base. He pressed it into her palm, closed their joined hands around it. "We'll come back every year and remember this was the place we first told each other I love you."

"And I'll have you pick up a shell for me to keep and I'll put them all in a bowl to remind us."

He smiled. "I want to fill that bowl up with a hundred shells." He brought her close, held her near.

She smiled, joy coming suddenly with the hope he'd given her.

"I love you," they said together then simply stared into each other's eyes and let a few moments of silence hold them there as they smiled. Then he took her hand and together they reentered a world that was constantly working to dishonor love.

They returned to find Honey by the dock. The girls and Nick sitting with Samantha. He was snapping pictures with a camera, grinning as she made faces and he announced the title of each masterpiece.

"*Darling and the dogs,*" Honey stated.

"We've been waiting on you," Samantha called out, taking her sister's hand. "We've been challenged again."

"Let me guess, croquet?" Stephanie teased.

"Volleyball. We can make it five on five. Play with us," Samantha demanded.

"*Angels on the beach,*" Honey announced, snapping a picture of the sisters.

"One more picture and that Nikon is going in the water, Cooper."

"I can't help myself, my camera likes beautiful things."

John's arm wrapped around Stephanie. "Point it here, Hunnicut."

Samantha stepped back, smiling as he snapped several pictures.

"*The mighty has fallen.*" He zoomed in close, capturing the two of them for eternity in a picture John would always treasure. "*A lovesick beast and his Beauty,*" he announced. "No rebuttal, Dake?"

"I am in love," John answered, kissing Stephanie.

Honey rested the camera on his shoulder, grinned. "Don't say?"

"Umm, so far gone you'll have to tear me away from her."

"When is that volleyball game starting?" Stephanie grinned.

John pouted. "Play with us."

"Not my sport. It kills my wrists." He lifted the one that wore his bracelet, kissed it. "I'll practice cheering from the sidelines."

He tucked her close, pulling Samantha against his other side. Honey snapped another picture. "*Two angels and—*"

"Give me that!" Samantha snatched the camera and clicked off a picture of Honey.

"Cowboy with heatstroke!" She squealed when he lunged then dashed away, three dogs and Honey chasing her down the beach.

"He's been sweet to her," Stephanie stated.

"He's a good man."

"Did you tell him about her?"

"No. She'll have to do that, it's not my story to tell," he assured her.

"She's had fun and Honey's helped."

"Beneath the charm he's got a sensitive spirit, and a kind of chivalry that demands he defend. He's watched over her this week without any prodding from me, just comes natural to him." He kissed her. "Like me loving you."

"I love you too."

"I'll never get tired of hearing that."

22

Big hat, no cattle. His phrase came to her as she spotted Elise alone by the bar and with a prayer she approached her. She was a beautiful woman. Symmetry cloaked in couture styling. Her hair pale blond and thick and straight to her waist without even a tangle in this humid evening. Her eyes were blue and sharply narrowed as she approached her.

"Hello. I'm Stephanie."

"Can I get you anything, Dr. Hightower?" the bartender interrupted.

"I'm fine, thanks." Then she politely asked, "Elise?"

"Vodka martini. Won't you join me?"

Stephanie just smiled. "Enjoying the party?"

"They've been better." She accepted the drink. Smiled at the bartender as she took a long sip. "Thank you. So good. You don't drink either?" Her brows were slightly lifted with that sinister smile shinning behind her knowing eyes. "How sweet." She looked off to the volleyball court, watching John play. "You're a doctor then?"

"I'm a veterinarian."

"Interesting."

"You model."

"Yes." She drank some more. "Third in the world right now." Elise watched the game again. "John's used to keeping company with people of equal status. He always thought ordinary people would never understand the lifestyle of famous people. Do you find it intimidating?"

"What did you find so intimidating about it, Elise?"

She laughed. "I make three times what John does playing football. I'm hardly ordinary."

"Money can't—"

"Buy you love," she interrupted singing the tune. "To the Beatles then." She toasted her.

"Solomon said it originally. In the Bible."

"The Bible?" She swept her. Then laughed. "Oh, bless his heart." Then she laughed harder. "Now I know he'll be back. By October no doubt. He just can't help it. You're rookie green." Then she whispered the words with a chuckle. "You'll learn quick enough. Jack doesn't like it sweet. And he hates rookies. He needs veterans. On the field and in his bed." And she patted Stephanie's back and strolled away as she bid her, "Good luck next season."

Stephanie just blinked. The warning an insult that froze her until the bartender said, "Mr. Dake, need anything, sir?"

"Water please," he answered as he turned her a step away to privacy and whispered, "Don't talk to her."

She looked up at him. John had that edge of authority to his voice. "I know you can take care of yourself, but I want to protect you. So, whatever she said, don't listen to her."

But she did listen. At the oddest times she would hear Elise's words. They would circle in her mind and mix with her emotions and tempt her to act. She'd find herself responding. Pushing John's boundaries or pulling back emotionally. Overwhelmed with the feeling of being in love and not knowing how to show it. Anxious that suddenly this mattered. More than perhaps anything in her life. And she was rookie green. Sweet. Inexperienced.

"What's wrong?" John asked her.

She shook her head. It was early, and the sunrise was exquisite on this Memorial Day morning. There was an unbelievable calm across the water, a subtle peace along the island. They walked the dogs one last time down the beach. This had been the most incredible week of her life and it had nothing to do with the things in life that once were the only things that seemed to matter.

She wanted to be a vet, a specialist in horse breeding. That's all she'd ever wanted to become and now she was becoming something surprisingly more. She was in love. In love—something that had never seemed important was now the most important thing in her life. John loved her, and she loved him. And... she was intimidated by her lack of experience.

"It feels like you've pulled back from me." He glanced at her. "Emotionally. You do that when you're not sure what to do. And I have to woo you back, warm you up and disarm you." He tugged her to him. Locked his arms around her. "Last night you wouldn't let go. This morning you're steps away. Are you mad about last night?"

She shook her head. Remembered John's quiet authority when he told her good night, that he'd see her in the morning. She'd clung to him, wanted him to stay with her. Anxious and wary to let him go. John strong and secure in his honor had walked away.

"How could I be mad?" She kissed him, leaning into his arms to be held as she said, "It was a great week." She looked at him. "The best week. I'm sad. We leave today."

"I'm going to see you in a few days at the lake. Spend as much time there as I can this summer before training camp starts."

And he did. Through the month of June, they spent leisurely time together out at the lake and at the Bennett's house in Louisiana. Now July had arrived. The last days ticking down before John started training camp. The Bennett's were having a political fundraiser at the plantation. The Presidential election was next year, and the primary season was already started. Layne was in the thick of things as he prepared to run for congress.

When they arrived, the party was in full motion. The house was open to the large back lawn where red, white and blue decorations were draped and hung. A

Dixie land band played as they walked through the buffet line, filling their plates. They sat at a table with Samantha and Richard and Layne's parents, the Lexington's. Brad blessed the food then stood towards the end of the meal to say a few things to the large group of friends that were gathered.

"Linda and I couldn't be happier to have all of you here and Layne, our son-in-law, wants to say a few words tonight."

Layne stood and gave a short speech before he smiled down at his wife. "Blair and I are proud to announce that we are expecting our first child at the end of November."

Brad was back on his feet at once shaking Layne's hand as Linda hugged Blair.

"That's great!" John smiled at Stephanie.

"I can't believe she kept this a secret," Samantha exclaimed.

Blair was grinning at her sisters as they came to the table.

"This is so quick," Mrs. Lexington said as they greeted their son and daughter-in-law.

"Layne didn't want to wait to start a family." Blair smiled at her beaming husband.

"Family is mighty important for anyone that's politically minded. Need to be a family man—beautiful wife and kids—people love that. This is great son." Layne Lexington senior put his arm around his son's shoulder. "Right on schedule."

"So, this is why Layne was bringing you glasses of milk and forcing you to eat all that fruit in Florida." Stephanie frowned at her. "I can't believe you didn't tell us."

"Me either. I just wanted to wait, to make sure everything was okay, since it's our first."

"Are you feeling okay?"

"Great." She flattened her hands across her stomach and pulled the red material tight. Her tummy curved out in a small compact swell. "It's hard to believe there's really somebody in there."

"We're so happy for you both."

Stephanie wrapped her arms around John as they stepped back to let friends congratulate the couple. "I'll be an aunt in November, wow!"

"Umm, you'll make a great aunt."

"She's already half way through. Time is flying."

"I can't believe my vacation ends Monday and I'm back at work." John gathered her closer, whispered, "I'm anxious to start, but dread not seeing you."

Her fingers were playing in his hair, finding the soft curls along his neck. "John," She lifted up, kissed him softly. "I love you."

"I love you," he answered. His body suddenly tense as someone called his name. He tucked her close, accepting a handshake, smiling.

"I thought this was supposed to be a small gathering?" John whispered into Stephanie's ear as yet another of the Bennett's guests approached John for a little one-on-one and he was forced to turn his attention from Stephanie. She squeezed his hand encouraging his tolerance then someone stole her attention calling her name.

"Congratulations on the baby," John extended his hand to Layne and the two shook hands.

"Thanks." Layne smiled. "We're excited."

"Blair's feeling well?"

"Normal stuff." He glanced toward his wife. "Been a little sassy lately."

John chuckled. "That's hardly new."

"How's Stephanie?"

John watched her. She was classy and considerate, listening to Mrs. Lexington and another older woman as she stood with Blair. Excited for her sister. Beaming and happy tonight. "Great."

"You start back next week?"

John put his hands in his pockets and nodded. "You and Blair were apart for a while when you dated, right?"

"Four years. Helped us actually."

"Oh?"

"She was younger. Had high standards which I respected and valued. In the beginning she was firm with her resolve of purity, then we fell in love and it reached a tipping point. I was the one that had to say no, protect her and honor our commitment to wait. It's emotional for them, physical for us. So being apart made it easier. When the times together got too hard, it was time to get married."

"Hmph." John nodded.

"She's in love with you. You've reached that tipping point." Layne looked at him. "And the test. How are you going to display your love? Honor and protect or indulge impatience and take advantage of her weakness to you and fail to lead. They want to be led. It's how God created us. They don't know it. Usually don't show it. In fact, regularly resist it, but when a man leads with love he earns the respect of his wife and that's what a man wants. Respect. So, lead well and it all works. "

Layne's words were a charge that rang in his ears as he drove back to her house. Stephanie was touchy-feely tonight. Her fingers in his hair, lingering over his arms, tracing muscles and clinging close to him. John liked her like this. Soft and willing and needy. She wanted to be alone. So, they'd left the party and it was hardly midnight and he knew they were headed toward trouble. The weeks apart looming ahead, her emotions possessive and passionate.

It's emotional for them, physical for us.

John knew they were past the tipping point. She was going to be asking. And she did. In a whisper. "Stay with me."

In the silence he heard their breathing, their hearts beating, desire building. He held her gaze, seeing such love there, knowing she was his destiny and together they'd share the future. This was right, he rationalized even as his voice said firmly, "Stephanie, I'm too weak." It was their code of accountability. She should take a stand, be strong, help him. But she couldn't. "Stephanie," he moaned now, knowing. "This is a decision we can never go back from. It's wrong. It will change us and that's why I'm so uneasy tonight, because I see the change that's already ahead. The season is starting, I'm anxious how we'll adjust to that. There's a sudden need to possess you and assure myself. And you want to be assured emotionally and loved physically... and that's not why we should do this. We need to wait."

"So, what should we do?" she asked. "Should I send you home." Tears were filling her eyes. "When I want to keep you close, not lose a minute when we'll be apart for weeks?"

He shook his head.

"Will you sit here in the car, holding me till dawn?"

"I might." He smiled now. "Because we aren't going in your house. We don't need to be alone."

They stared at each other again, breathing and thinking.

John confessed, "I saw you standing in the airport in this dress and I..." he sighed, moaned. "I could see myself unbuttoning every single button and that two second fantasy put my mind on a dangerous course."

"So, if you did that, unbuttoned this dress and we spent all weekend making love until you had to leave Sunday night, how would we be anything but closer and deeper in love?" She stroked his face. "If you need to possess me and be assured that this is real, let me say, this is real. I can make it through days apart, missing you. I can adjust to your schedule, be flexible through the season, give more than I take while you play ball because I know how much you love me, John. I know now. I trust you. There's not a thing you don't tell me, not a fear I won't share with you. We've learned that."

"I can wait," he told her firmly. His smile broke and glowed in the moonlight. "We are, going to wait."

"What?" She sank in his arms. "That was supposed to assure you—"

He laughed, kissed her. "It did. I love you. And that means I'm doing this right, protecting us and leading." He began to drive.

"Where are you going?" she asked.

"To your parent's house. We're going back for strawberry shortcake. I'm going to get a huge piece, tuck you in my lap and feed you. We'll find your sisters, have a good family chat in the kitchen, listen to Miss Sassy tell us her stories, let Brad go proud thinking he had something to do with us falling in love and drink some of that new Cabernet from Richard's vineyard. We'll go up to the theater with Samantha, put in a good movie and you can fall asleep in my arms." He kissed her. "Okay?"

He quickly drove them back to the Bennett's. They walked in the kitchen, hunting for the cake.

"I thought you guys left with the rest of the crowd?" Blair asked as her family turned their way. They were gathered around the kitchen table relaxing.

"I didn't get any cake, little momma," John said giving her a kiss. "Did I say congrats by the way?"

"Yes." Blair handed him a double serving with a lifted brow.

John took Stephanie into a chair, resting her on his lap, feeding her the first bite. "Samantha, want to watch a movie with us? You and Richard were saying Brad had the summer block buster."

"Sure." She looked at Richard, nodded. "We can do a midnight movie."

John nodded, eating. "This is great, Linda."

"I'm glad you're enjoying it." She smiled at Stephanie.

Blair plopped down beside them and put her chin in her hand. Her violet eyes were narrowed and studying them. "We were just talking about you two." A slow grin formed.

"Oh?" Stephanie asked.

Samantha moved to their other side, her elbow was on the table, her chin in her hand as she leaned in from the other way. "Yes, we were having a very involved conversation."

"Gossiping about?" Stephanie's brow lowered.

"How lovely it was watching you," Samantha quoted her mother.

"How sweet Stephanie's young man is," Blair quoted her mother-in-law.

"How close you danced." Samantha grinned.

"How lovesick and—"

"Lip locked you were all night," Blair finished with a snort.

"We were assuming all manner of decadent behavior must be going on right now back at your little house, sis."

"But someone assured us, we were letting our imaginations run wild."

They looked at Brad. "And I guess he must have been right since you're sitting here."

"Eating cake!" Blair's snort turned into a giggle. "Good night, get out of here and don't feel guilty for wanting to be alone."

"Anyone with eyes can see you only have eyes for each other."

"We can see you after Monday, Stephanie."

"We know John's starting back this week."

"Go on," Blair nodded toward the door.

"No." John shook his head. "We really want to be here."

Stephanie smiled. "We need to be here. Right here, with all of you. Chatting, eating, watching Harrison Ford, catching up with Richard, talking till dawn like we always do."

There was a beat of silence.

"Ohh!" Blair suddenly sat up with her brows in her hairline.

"Ohh!" Samantha echoed, grinning at Richard.

Blair crossed her arms and gave her father a look. "See, my imagination was not that far off, Daddy."

"Do you have a goal for this season?" she asked him softly. They were pool side. She was in her John-Dake-only-bikini. He was fingering one of the bows at her hip as they lay facing each other on a double chaise lounge chair. They'd told each other they were going to get some sun. They'd been up all night, had a huge breakfast. John suggested the shaded deck of the pool, this chair. They were cuddling their way into a nap when she'd asked the question.

His answer was simple, and he said it closing his eyes. "Win."

"Every game?"

"Yes."

"You're tired."

"I'll never get tired of this." He'd slipped his thumb through the loop of the bow. Palmed more fanny than hip as he drew her closer. "Of you." His hand swept up her back to her neck, settled her to him as he whispered, "I love you." Then in a breath, he snored.

She smiled. Wondered if he snored at night. When she'd know that kind of thing. If he'd wait a season. Two. Could they wait that long? Did he want to get married? Have kids? Blair was pregnant. She smiled. Fell asleep.

"You want to win every game so that means the Super Bowl," Stephanie stated, holding his hand as they walked the dogs the afternoon before he left. "Do you think it will happen this year?"

"Every championship season is really a destiny. The small things that all add up just seem to go your way. And there's a chemistry and timing when the team peaks, gets on a hot streak and then there's the injuries, your key people have to stay healthy."

"You're healthy, John."

He nodded, intertwining their fingers.

"Your body is in the best shape of your life, you've told me that. I know you've worked very hard to be ready for this season. What do I need to do?"

"Be yourself. And pray. I covet your prayers."

"To win."

"To honor God. That will cover about everything."

"Specifically, what do you need?"

"Hmph," was his answer.

"I want to know. If you need something."

"Okay." He just kissed her.

"If I need to do something for you."

"Like?"

"Anything."

"Like?"

"I don't know. I've never dated a famous football player before."

"You've never dated anyone before and I love that." Now she was in his arms. "You're just mine. All mine. You don't need to do anything but be who you are, I love that woman. She doesn't let me get away with much and that makes me a better man."

"We won't see each other much. I understand the schedule."

"You'll come to Dallas, stay with Blair when we play at home." He kissed her.

"Blair?"

"We stay at a hotel, even before home games."

"Okay, but the girls—"

"You're keeping the dogs for me until the season starts."

"Brad says each week starts a whole new process. You'll study the new opponent, watch hours of films, sit in strategy meetings and run plays and practices for that specific opponent. Your job is as much mental preparation as it is physical. And both parts take a lot of time. You only have Tuesday's off and I work on Tuesdays."

"We'll see each other. I promise."

"And the press is another big issue. Your mother told me not to read the papers."

"Good advice."

"Do you read them?"

"No, the JDi team takes care of the media for me."

She nodded.

"You're worried."

"No." She sighed. "But you're not saying much. I thought you would. You'll be gone six weeks."

"We'll talk every day." He smiled at her. "I left a few things in your kitchen."

"Oh?"

"Cable subscription for the games. A new television. And an antique chest to put it on that you'll need to refinish which will take you some time."

"John. Dake."

"A bed for the girls. A new lap blanket for you. A few books. And a nice piece of jewelry."

There was a sound of outrage, high and hot as his fingers rested on her chest. "It should rest right here. Close to your heart. Don't be mad. I'm about to leave for six weeks." He kissed her again.

Then she told him, "I had a speech."

"Oh?"

"About being supportive."

"Let's hear it."

"You left stuff in my kitchen, Dake." She was frowning.

"I love you, it's part of the package deal, girlfriend. Now let's hear the speech."

"Hmph."

He drew her closer. "Please, I really need it."

"I was going to say, it's all going to be okay but maybe not."

"Give me the speech. *John, it's all going to be okay...*"

She looked at him. Sighed. "It is. Your job will keep you busy and so will mine but we'll figure this out. It's just a new rhythm. And I wanted you to know that I'll be supportive. I'm here for you and I know if I need you, you'll be here for me. I know our time together will be cut back, but it will be more treasured." She kissed his lips lightly, tucking their fingers tightly together, "I know what we have together has been built on a strong foundation. So, trust what we are to each other, trust God. I will be praying for you."

"No wonder I love you." He drew her into his arms, held her close and strong to his heart. "That's all I could ask for."

John sighed when he left her. It was a deep long exhale of relief.

He'd made it through the weekend. He wasn't sure how they'd remained pure. It was supernatural for sure. Little moments clicked by, sensual little clips of memory that should have taken him down. To dwell on any one of them wouldn't be wise. He made a phone call to Honey. Confessed how hard it had been. Agreed it was a good time to take a break at training camp. Shared that he'd told Stephanie she wouldn't be staying with him in Dallas anymore. He hadn't explained the real reason like he should have but he would. Later. He would tell her the temptation was just too much now. He would lead. Protect her. And it was getting harder. She was definitely past the tipping point. In love with him, trusting him, wanting him. Layne was right, that was the real test. How would he lead now that she would follow?

Honey asked him that if God got him through *this* weekend couldn't He be trusted to get him through any weekend in the future. Yes. The answer to that was a simple yes. And he smiled, a new kind of smile because he couldn't explain it, but he was suddenly stronger, more confident. The feeling like a hard-fought victory. With Christ's help, John had won.

"King me."

23

Stephanie searched for her old habits, trying to find the way of life she'd known before John. But her routine was ruled by her heart now, not the independent spirit and determination to succeed alone. She realized breaking that prideful attitude was a side miracle of this. She did need Linda and Brad, her sisters, friends, and work associates. Having a community around her gave her the added strength to be adaptable and balanced. Life wasn't just about work and reaching goals anymore. Success wasn't graded by her solo achievements. All of this she noted in her journal, taking time to go back and read over the past months and clearly see the explosive growth God had orchestrated since she met John.

God was so alive in her life right now. It seemed He'd taken her hand and ushered her into the land of Goshen—a place foreign but overflowing with blessings. She marked off the weeks that John would be in training camp and made specific goals for herself. For her body she would swim every morning at the Bennetts but instead of heading off to work, she incorporated time to come into the house and share breakfast with her parents. She accepted the invitation from Linda to join her in a women's Bible study. She played Bunko with a group of Mary's friends on Thursday nights. She volunteered at the community center Tuesday afternoons and spent a week with the children at Vacation Bible School sharing her love for God and fostering theirs.

She finished refinishing the antique chest and watched her new television, hungry for the sports update on John's team. Every morning she spent an hour with her God and every night she anticipated the long conversation with John.

As busy as she was, the emptiness still found a way to make her long for John. It was Samantha who encouraged her to come to Austin. The plan excited her. She would surprise John for once. Her sister picked her up at the airport and they enjoyed a holiday of shopping and lunch that Friday together.

A small private college was the campus for John's training camp. The grounds around the sports complex were crowded with fans, the stands filled with people in team jerseys and hats. The children watching practice, holding pens and paper as they anxiously waited for the final whistle to blow.

She watched among them, just as transfixed. There were tall towers holding coaches and cameras. Players in white collided with players in blue, producing grunts and whistles, and snapshots from the eager press photographers scattered among them. Activity spread across the hundred yards of green and she watched John in the center of it all.

He wore shoulder pads and shorts, the number seven boldly blue on his white jersey. His legs were tan, his wrists guarded with bands of white. His face was a mask of intensity, his eyes a jolt of blue.

Samantha nudged her. "The kids are making a move." The veteran fans seemed to know something and were gathering along a fence as a security officer faced them on the other side. Her sister handed her a pad of paper as she smiled holding the leashes of Nick and the girls. "Get by the kids, he seemed to migrate to them when I was here last week with Brad."

Stephanie made her way with the pack. A team ball cap covered her hair, her baggy short overalls layered over a team T-shirt. Excited anticipation seemed to vibrate around her. Kids were jumping, squeezing to the fence and maneuvering into position. Player's names were called out as fathers hoisted sons onto their shoulders for a better view.

A wave of lineman came by first, grabbing paper and pens, scribbling their names with the wounded hands of warriors and the grunts and smiles from trench dirty faces. A little girl beside her squealed out Teddy's name and she watched the large man's smile break wide and beautiful as he answered.

"Who's calling me?" he barked, stomping over with a scowling but funny face. Hundreds answered but he found the little girl and took her autograph book. "Whatcha name, princess?" he asked her with his smile beaming from his dark face.

"Greta," she answered. "You're my best player. Look!" She held up her bear who wore a handmade jersey with his number.

"Let me see." His beefy hand took her treasure. "You make this for him, Greta?" She nodded.

"Want me to sign it too, here on the back?"

"Yes!" She jumped.

"You take good care of him and mind your momma, now. Okay?"

"Yes, sir!" She was still jumping as he handed her bear back over then signed his name quickly on several pieces of held out paper before heading off.

There was a sudden press as she heard, "Dake!" screamed out. He was fifteen feet down the fence, smiling at kids as his pen flew over paper. He reached four deep to sign a boy's baseball hat, dropped down on a knee to talk to a toddler, threading paper back through the holes of the wire fence to eager hands.

From the other direction, Dewayne the running back was coming down the fence. His name was shouted as people suddenly pressed the other way. She felt like she was swimming upstream when the little girl with the bear yelled, "Mr. Dake! Mr. Dake." A boy twice her age pushed her back, squeezing to the fence and Stephanie grabbed her hand.

"Here, Greta." She smiled, lifted her up. "Keep calling him," she encouraged.

"Bigger crowd every night," the security officer mumbled in John's ear.

"A few more minutes," John answered, scribbling and smiling as sweat raced down his back.

"Get off the fence!" the officer commanded as a little girl's voice called John's name.

He wiped his forehead, glanced down the fence line at the ocean of paper waving for him. You could never get to everyone.

"Mr. Dake!" The little girl was leaning over the top of the fence, smashing a teddy bear with Deux number on its jersey to her chest. She was cute and determined.

"Off the fence there!" the officer shouted, pointing at her.

"It's okay," John told him handing back another autograph book and heading toward her as he continued to sign down the fence line.

A boy was standing weak and pale beside his mother who waved desperately to him. Beneath a ball cap he hid the effects of chemo, and his gaze watched him with doubt. He took the mother's paper. "What's your name?"

"Jacob Painter."

"Jacob," he repeated. "Did you know I hurt my shoulder?" The boy nodded. "I had surgery and had to spend my whole off season trying my best to get better. It was tough." He looked at him. "It's tough, getting better, isn't it?" The boy nodded again. "My friends prayed for me and I think it helped. Can I pray for you?"

"Yes," he answered this time.

John wrote the word Jacob on his forearm with the marker. "Will you write to me and let me know how you're doing, Jacob?" He nodded again, and John put his hand on the boy's shoulder, praying for him silently as he said, "Have faith and don't give up."

He touched the mother's arm, smiled at her tears of gratitude. "You too." He winked as the crowd yelled, waving papers.

He never knew what to say to people like Jacob, but he'd learned to open his mouth and just trust God to speak the words. He hoped he never lost the awareness of what his words could mean to someone, how a simple gesture of kindness could change a person's life. And so, he signed his name here and there as he moved to the little girl with the bear who was calling his name. He took her book as she jumped up and down and told him her name was Greta.

"Greta. I like that bear, he looks like Teddy Deux."

Then a flash caught his eye, diamonds and emeralds in a familiar pattern. The bracelet circled a slim wrist extended with a pad of paper that had 'I miss you' written in bold letters. He took her paper, scribbling with his head down and handing it back. But he held her hand, pulling her to him as his pen rode over paper two deep, three deep, four deep. They were eye to eye, her grinning back to his glorious smile before his mouth covered hers in a kiss.

"Come here!"

"I can't," she laughed, then imitated the officer's bark, "Get off the fence."

She squealed when he picked her up and brought her over, laughed when he yanked her close and kissed her again. "My girl's here!" he told the crowd. "Isn't she pretty?"

"Smart," she corrected.

"And really smart. Always got A's in school," he told the kids. "Now she's an animal doctor. Hard work pays off. Umm," he kissed her again, waving to the crowd as he began to walk with her tucked beneath his arm. "I've missed you. I can't believe you're here. This is great."

"Surprised?"

"Very," he answered, stealing another kiss. "Pleased, proud, and possessive too." He growled, hugging her fiercely.

"Um, you're sweaty." Her teeth were on his neck, then her tongue, a little lick as she stretched up high on her toes and held on tight to him. "We missed you. So much. I brought the girls."

"Where?" He began to look.

"They're with Sammy and Nick." She pointed. He waved to her sister, smiling. "Can you come over for dinner? Brad said you were off tonight."

"Tom!" He waved the security officer over. "Will you tell that pretty brunet with the dogs I'm coming over for dinner and bringing her sister? That we'll be over in half an hour."

"Sure." He nodded, jogging off to do it.

"I'll shower and change, and we'll head out." He turned her baseball hat around backwards and kissed her again. "I have missed you!" His smile was dazzling. "And you are looking too cute in that fan gear."

His dormitory room was small. One bed was covered with the paper work of his profession, playbooks. There was a small stocked refrigerator, a television on a desk, three sets of athletic shoes lined up in front of the closet and her picture by the phone. His Bible was on his neatly made bed, she picked it up as she took a seat to wait for him to shower. Secured to the inside front cover was a small photograph of the two of them and beneath it was the statement, "Honor God. Stephanie. Yourself."

He had changed since they met, just as she had.

Her fingers caressed his words.

Honor God. Stephanie. Yourself.

He came out in shorts and a T-shirt. Smiled, glancing at the Bible in her lap.

"Doc leads a Bible study in the morning before breakfast."

She nodded, standing. "Israel's battles, you said."

He brought her close and gazed into her eyes. "If I wasn't so hungry, I'd never move."

"I cooked for you." He growled when she told him his favorite. "The cake is homemade."

He kissed her. "You're a good woman, Beauty. A very good woman."

He held her hand through dinner, stroking it as he ate three servings of prime rib and declined the beer for milk. He wanted to know about Samantha's summer job with the Austin DA, how her law classes were progressing and what Richard was doing in France. He told her Honey was in California, winning rodeos and working off his temper because he'd failed to win Cheyenne Frontier Days again, getting bucked off in the final round. It was the only major rodeo he didn't have a buckle from. They shared a huge serving of cake, then Samantha said good night when she excused herself.

Stephanie sat in his lap in her sister's back yard as John tossed tennis balls to the girls and kept her mouth busy kissing him between throws. Night was becoming a dark and private blanket around them.

"Umm, your body," he mumbled as he drew her tighter against him. "These overalls are dangerous."

"They're baggy," she laughed, "I'm hidden in here."

"They're baggy." His hand roamed inside. He laid her down under a blanket of stars. Then she shrieked because he was tickling her. And she was bucking as the dogs barked and circled, Bradshaw kissing both of them. John grabbed the loose ball and sent it off with a sideways toss that had the girls sprinting off as he looked into her eyes.

"I missed you" She reached up, brought him down into her arms. "So much."

"I love you. So much." And he closed his eyes and just gave in to the moment.

24

In the grass on a hot summer night it had been an old fashion make out session that had her blushing now. They'd both let go and taken things farther than they'd ever gone before. John had flicked on a switch inside her and she was suddenly aware of her body like never before. There were no longer butterflies fluttering, but a sharp, building ache. It was desire, in its purest form. It could start with a thought, or a flash of skin on television. It came when she heard his voice or daydreamed about him. She loved him like no woman had ever loved a man before. Love like this needed to be shared in intimacy. It was too deep, too right, too intense. These feelings coloring everything with their beautiful demand for more.

Yes, she wanted more, needed more, ached for more. She filled pages of her journal with the reasons as weeks turned to just days, then hours, then minutes and she was here. Waiting no more. In moments she'd see him.

John stood in the driveway as Blair pulled up. They locked eyes and Stephanie didn't even remember getting out of the car before she found herself in his arms.

Blair honked the horn and waved to the couple as she pulled away and the dogs ran around them barking to play with John. He gave them some attention, asking, "Did Steph take good care of you? Huh, girls? She's the best, you're lucky dogs. There's new treats on the patio."

Her eyes looked up at his hair. It was short. Very short. The sides were clipped, shaved over his ears and the top had been left just a little longer. It stood straight up like a flat top from the fifties. "You like it?" he asked as he ran his hand over the short cut.

She looked around to the back of his head. "Your curls are gone." Her eyebrows dropped.

He took her hand and kissed the palm before he ran it across his hair. "It feels really soft. I thought you'd like it."

"It does feel soft." She smiled. "I'll have to get used to it." She looked back around to where his curls used to sit at his nape and pouted. "I liked playing with those curls."

"It will grow fast, Stephanie. I didn't know you were so attached to my—"

"Curls," she stated firmly. "You had curls back there." She touched his neck softly.

He smiled again. "Even my *curls* got to be too much in this Texas heat. I wanted it all off."

She cocked her head and looked at him. "I like it. Love you."

He kissed her, long and deep, murmuring poetry back to her.

"You're okay staying in for dinner?"

"Of course. if we go out, the town will mob you."

He nodded. "I've got steaks. Hattie made a salad and some other stuff. It looks good."

He pulled her close as they walked into the house. Then she saw it. A huge framed portrait of herself was waiting in the kitchen. In the photograph, Stephanie's head was turned, and she was almost in profile. A soft smile was on her lips and her eyes were a deep green as they looked up at him. You couldn't see John's face, just his arm and his body, muscular and golden tan, holding her. Curves and edges fit into the strength of him and a sparkling bracelet across the wrist of her hand that rested on his forearm added a crown of color.

"Honey called it, *'Beauty in my arms'.*" John smiled. "I wanted you to see it before I hung it in my bedroom."

"That was taken down at the dock."

"Right after I told you I loved you for the first time," he said, looking at the photograph. "I love that picture. I love the memories of that week and I love the woman in it." He stroked her face and turned her toward him. "I look at you, there, and I think about that island, the shell I gave you." His gaze connected with hers. "You wanted me there, for reasons the world tried to sell you. I told you what we had was better than what the world offers."

"I was afraid, jealous, possessive," she confessed as he interlocked their fingers together. "I thought sex was the answer. You showed me it was love."

"I love you."

They stood there, their hands clinging, a safe space between their bodies as their cheeks pressed together.

"Are you hungry?" she asked softly.

"Starving," he answered, then added, "For you, honestly. You need to help me here, Stephanie." He said again, "I'm really weak. I touched you, in Samantha's backyard, it was a mistake... it's all I can think about now."

"Me too," she confessed.

"Stephanie," he squeezed her hand. "You're not helping here."

She looked into his eyes and shook her head. "I'm too weak to help. I love you, John. Want you. We've taken our time to get here and you've honored me, shown us both that you could. We laid a foundation, built on it. I trust you and I want this. I want to make love with you tonight. It's right."

"It's right?" He just looked at her.

"It's time—"

"To call for back up," he told her picking up the cell phone. "Layne. John. Ya'll come over. I've got steaks. See you in a few minutes." He looked at her, saw the hurt. "I love you, Stephanie."

They stood apart, looking at each other.

Then John said, "I got you this." He held up the cell phone. "It's yours."

"Mine? No. I'm not walking around with a cellphone attached to my hand. Who does that? The president, that's who. No one else is important enough to need a phone wherever they go. Phones belong in homes and offices, not cars. It's over the top. Normal people just carry a beeper."

"I have the same phone."

She shook her head.

"You're important to me. When I call, I want you to answer."

"No."

"Stephanie."

"My job is important and so is yours. If I call in the middle of practice are you going to call timeout and answer me?"

"No."

"Okay. See."

"Just keep it in your Jeep. If I beep you and you're out of the office but available to talk, you can call me back on the cell phone. That's a compromise."

"You'll beep me first?"

He nodded.

"And I can use a normal phone."

"Stephanie, it's selfish but I want you when I want you."

"Yes. You called for backup."

"You know it's the right thing to do."

"Yes. It makes it easier for us."

"Exactly." He held the phone out.

"We were talking about sex."

"I was talking about the cell phone."

"You were not."

They were grinning now, and steps had brought them back together. John said, "Indulge me."

"You'll have to show me how."

"We're talking about the cell phone."

"Sure."

"God help me you're—"

"Don't say stubborn."

"Sexy," he answered and showed her the features on the phone. The ten stored numbers in its memory. How it turned on and off and accepted a phone call and fit into the recharging cradle. "I want you safe."

"So, it's about safety."

"No, it's about me. Not having a lot of time. And you, taking my phone calls if I need a five-minute conversation and you're available to help me play through my current crisis. My mom has one too now. They're more common than you think."

"How does she like her new house?"

"She seems happy here in Dallas. She left almost everything at the ranch. Is shopping for new furniture." He nuzzled her with a kiss, whispered, "I'm protecting you. Okay?" as he brought them back to the present.

She nodded.

"Being the guy you want me to be."

There was a little moan.

"None of that." He fingered her hair back. "We worked hard to get here. So, you're going home with Blair and Layne tonight." He kissed her little frown. "You're mad but you know I'm right."

"Hmph," she mocked him. "I guess I wasted money at the lingerie store."

"Girl." He frowned. "You're going straight to hell."

And she linked their hands, gave him a smile. "Thank God for Jesus."

"Thank God for Jesus," he said sincerely.

"Don't you want to know what color it is? Lace or satin—"

"Stephanie." He stepped back.

"You knew that forehead poker game would come back to haunt you, Dake."

"Hmph." He took another step back. His gaze tight to hers.

"It was lace, green, had little ties—"

In a move he had her in his arms. Her mouth silent until a little sigh escaped. Then she saw his eyes, the dark endless blue of them and his tone was that soft authority again, telling her, "I want you in white. The first time. And not lingerie. That can come later. I want you in a wedding dress. I'm serious, Stephanie. That's the game plan. And to win we have to have a strategy. The offense of planning and the defense of knowing when we're in over our heads. Tonight, would be too hard. For both of us. Agreed?"

"We're here!" Blair swept in. "I brought some extra steaks. You boys go get the grill going. Baby's hungry and my sister apparently needs a lecture." She snorted giving her husband a look.

Layne cut through the sarcasm with a simple statement, "Blair this is serious. *Flee fornication.*" Layne looked at Stephanie now. "Your purity is beautiful and pleasing to the Lord. It shows a spiritual strength. Don't make your man weak, little sister." It was a charge and the gentle rebuke rang in the room as he ushered John outside to the grill with a hand on his back.

Helen Dake considered three different shades of lipstick before she settled on the coral. She carefully applied it then slipped the tube into the small handbag. She'd even replaced her old standby bag for ball games, with an updated chic little backpack. She'd replaced a lot of the old standbys in her life for new over the past three months. She had her new house, close to John, close to her office, far away from the past.

She'd simplified her possessions, releasing herself from memories, stepping out into the future. She took a deep breath and gave herself a nod. Another season opener, perhaps the first game of John's greatest season. Stephanie would be here today, a new fan, perhaps his greatest fan. Change, it was constantly coming.

She was ready.

She drove herself, meeting friends for lunch near the stadium. Her good friends Suzanne and Bob Bass would sit beside her today. They parked in the special section of the reserve lot and made their way under a hot Texas sky to the stadium.

People were everywhere. Some gathered around a van or the open trunk of a car as they tail gated before the first home game of the season. Twosomes, foursomes and groups of friends were making the long walk from the outer parking areas toward the stadium. Inside the gate, vendors peddled souvenirs. Helen stopped to buy a program then they walked down to their seats on the Forty-five-yard line.

There was an anxious lift to her heartbeat as her gaze carefully scanned the crowd. She recognized many of the fans in this section, they'd cheered together for four seasons now. She wondered if he would come alone, or like her bring friends. She wondered if he would come this year at all.

She took her seat, spotting her son on the thirty-yard-line warming up. John looked loose but wore the edge of restlessness, ready to play, to cut through the drama and get to the game. She'd sensed that before, felt that a bit herself. How did a woman cut through the drama and play ball after so many years watching life pass her by on the sidelines?

She saw the four empty seats a row down from her, thought of the past four years. She could clearly remember Angela Sullivan. She'd been vivacious and lovely and Texan to her booted toes. Her husband wore a Silver belly cowboy hat over his salt and pepper hair. Dylan Sullivan was tall, with strength over his lanky frame. He'd played ball in the sixties for the Oilers, now the linebacker owned Ford dealerships across North Texas. He was subtle for a salesman, with intelligent dark eyes and a slow smile. He'd fiercely loved his wife and lost her too swiftly to brain cancer three years ago.

They'd shared a lot of conversations during ball games. Helen grieved with him, watched him try his hand with someone knew, watched him come back last season alone. He'd asked her to dinner and she'd politely declined. She'd seen him at the Cattle Baron's Ball this year and accepted a dance. They'd shared a drink and an evening of conversation. He'd told her he was going it alone now. He asked how she did it so successfully. He'd looked away and told her the loneliness could kill a man.

Perhaps that's when her heart had changed, to hear such pain and understand it. She'd taken his hand and given it a reassuring squeeze. His gaze had linked with hers and a tiny jolt had stolen her breath at the look in his eyes.

"I'm looking forward to the season starting," he told her, pressing a chaste kiss to her cheek then he'd walked away into the summer night.

Now he walked down the aisle and tipped his hat to her. "Helen," he greeted. "Nice day for a football game."

"Hello, Dylan. You remember my friends Bob and Suzanne Bass?"

"Dylan Sullivan. Most call me Sully." He winked at her. "Only Helen's brave enough to call me Dylan." Bob stood shaking hands with him. "How have ya'll been?"

"Great. You?"

"Blessed." He glanced up at the Texas sky. "Could get hot."

"We brought our fans," Suzanne waved her paper one.

Dylan smiled, taking his seat one to the left and below Helen's. A pair of reading glasses was dawned, and he opened the program. "Any news on this Bama rookie, Helen?"

"Heard he's fast."

Dylan nodded then glanced up, smiled. Stephanie Hightower stood in the aisle with Cindy Beihn. Her beauty somehow glowed, perhaps intensified by the excited anticipation in her eyes.

"Hello, Mrs. Dake."

Helen stood and took her hand. "Can you sit for a minute, meet my friends?"

"Of course." Helen introduced her to the Basses then Dylan. "Dylan used to play linebacker for the Oilers."

He waved her off. "Before football was physical."

Helen laughed. "That's why he moves around so well."

He grinned. "Got me there."

They all sat back down as Helen stated, "Stephanie is dating John. This is her first game. Excited?"

"Yes." She smiled. "A bit nervous too." She glanced out to the field, watching John warm up.

"Our boys looked good last week," Helen stated with a natural smile wide on her face. "Didn't you think Cindy?"

"Yes, I'm ready for some more of that this afternoon."

"How's the baby?"

"He's fine. He's getting so big. I'll bring him once we get through this heat." Cindy smiled as she fanned herself. "Seems like we're either running around half naked or covered up in blankets in this stadium. And little Neil would be a little cranky I'm afraid."

"I can't wait to see him. I hear he looks just like Neil," Helen stated.

"He does," Stephanie confirmed, realizing people were waiting in the aisle to claim their seats.

"Good to see you." Stephanie surprised her with a tight hug.

"You too. Enjoy the game."

Once the girls were out of sight Suzanne Bass stated, "Oh, Helen, she's gorgeous!"

"A looker all right," Bob commented. "'Course I've never seen John date an unattractive girl." He grinned at his wife.

"She's a veterinarian," Helen told them. "Specializing in horses."

"Do you think they're getting serious?" Suzanne asked.

"She's very independent, and career driven. We all know John gets rather single minded during the season. He's told me they're taking it slow, whatever that might mean." She smiled.

"She's darling," Suzanne added.

She found Dylan watching her over the top of his reading glasses. Slowly his smile came, tilting to the right. She lifted a brow. "Watcha think, Dylan Sullivan?"

"I think I'm smart enough not to get between a grizzly bear momma and her cub."

She swatted him with her program. "He's hardly a cub."

"They're always cubs." He winked.

She identified with the protective possession she'd always felt for John. He was her one, her only, her beloved. She watched the subtle changes in him this year; the injury, the determination to be better from it, the spiritual maturing of his character. She'd listen to his words about this woman, then seen for herself the wonder of love in her son's blue eyes. Stephanie was the one, deep in her soul she knew this and was working hard to accept it. But acceptance amplified her loneliness and created a frightening need. Her gaze stayed on the field, her body ever aware of the man below her.

She had no idea what a woman over fifty did to attract a man. It had been another lifetime ago. Fear bolted through her system and she pressed her dry lips together. Sensed when Dylan rose and made his way to the aisle toward the middle of the second quarter. She glanced at his empty seat, at the three businessmen who sat beside it talking about the newest Ford truck.

How did a woman let a man know she was interested?

That thought bred a hundred others and she didn't notice Dylan take a seat beside her with a frozen lemonade. He placed it in her hands.

"Oh! Thank you."

"It's a good day for a cold drink." He took a spoonful of his own. "How was your summer, Helen?"

"I bought a little house here."

"Lovely house she means," Suzanne corrected. "And where did you find those cool drinks?"

"Second gate to the right," Dylan answered with a smile.

Suzanne tugged Bob up. "We'll be back."

"What part of town is your new house?"

"North of the airport in Grapevine. You still down the road in Southlake?"

He nodded. "Practically neighbors. There's a nice little restaurant on Main Street in Grapevine called Mason's. Good home cooking."

"Yes, I've seen it."

With his gaze on his treat he said, "Maybe we could share a meal sometime."

"I'd like that."

His gaze came up to hers, his smile following. He nodded. "Your boy looks well mended."

"He's worked hard."

"Girl helping or hurting?"

"Helping, I think."

"Bittersweet thing when our children fall in love."

She could only nod and their gazes lingered, then slowly fell away.

"Liking the city life?" he asked, eating the icy drink.

"Getting used to it."

"Like the girl?"

A small smile curled around the spoon. "Getting used to her." She dug out another spoonful of ice. "She's more brains than beauty."

"Must be a genius then."

Helen laughed.

"Always been partial to blonds myself."

"Arlene was a brunette and she was lovely."

He shrugged off the lady he'd dated two years ago. "Like I said," his gaze scanned her hair. "I like blonds best."

"Where does silver fit in?"

His brow creased. "Silver?"

She nudged him with a shoulder. "As in old gray hair."

"Your hair is blond, Helen."

She laughed. "Put your glasses on Dylan, my hair is silver."

His index finger very slowly moved the fall of it back from her forehead to tuck behind an ear as his gaze studied her eyes. She felt the thickness fall in with the swing of her bob.

"When you move I can hear your hair. Like wind through a field of wheat. You've got beautiful hair." He smiled now. "And it's blond, Helen."

"Oh," she said, transfixed by the look in his eyes.

"This is wonderful!" Suzanne said, sliding past with a container of the frozen lemonade. "Nothing like a cold drink on a hot day."

"Or a good plate of Mexican food," Dylan added.

"Oh, that does sound fabulous. Where do you like to go for Tex-mex?" Suzanne asked.

"Esparzas," he answered.

"Doesn't that sound good?" Suzanne sighed against Helen with a whisper.

Helen's heart was racing, her gaze on the marching band on the field, her thinking trapped in a mad circle of giddy nerves. He likes my hair. He touched me. He likes my hair.

"Helen?"

"Huh? Oh... yes?" She quickly spooned a heap of ice into her mouth.

"Dylan asked if you wanted to join him for dinner at Esparzas."

"I know the owner. We can walk right in and sit down, avoid the wait," Dylan told them.

"I'm with Suz—"

"They're invited."

"Better be. I'm craving enchiladas! Oh, here come the boys." Suzanne cheered loudly as they stood. "And we'd love to go." She answered for Helen.

"Stephanie," Cindy nudged her and pointed to the field after the game. "John wants you."

"John?"

"Yeah, right there." She walked with her down to the last row by the field. Several of the players were speaking with friends and family from field to stands along the wall.

"Stephanie," John called out with a smile. The wall surrounding the field was at his shoulder level and he reached up to take her hand as she leaned down to him.

"John, you were great!" Stephanie stated with excitement.

"So, you liked the game?"

"I love watching you play."

His hand reached into her thick mane of curls and rested at her neck. His thumb stroked over her jaw bone. "I love having you here."

"I was tense every time you were on the field. I hope I get use to this."

He pulled her head down to his mouth and planted a soft kiss on her lips. "We're eating with Neil and Cindy, okay?"

She nodded, and he jogged off the field for the locker room.

"Mom." John called into the phone impatiently. He'd tried her at the new house, then the ranch, finally the cell phone number. "Where are you?"

"John. Good morning—"

"Have you seen the paper?" He paced in his kitchen. "The Dallas Morning News, page two in the sports section." He glanced at Kenny, calmly drinking coffee and waiting for John to decide how he wanted to handle this publicity.

"No. I don't read the sport section and I've warned you—"

"John Dake with his new shoulder, new haircut and new woman could take Dallas to new heights this season," he read the headline. "They got us after the game, Mom. Look at the paper."

"I, ah. I'm not at home. I'm in the car."

"Just come over, I want to talk about this."

"I, ah... can't right now."

"Are you at the ranch? Get the paper, Mom."

"I'm in Dallas. Meeting someone for breakfast. They caught a shot of you with Stephanie?"

"They caught the back of my new haircut, got a full frontal of Stephanie leaning down toward the field." There was a growl. "She's going to be furious. *New heights* of fury over this."

"It's a great shot," Kenny voiced.

"She doesn't do this." He rattled the paper at his publicist. "Show cleavage."

"It's the angle. She's leaning down," Kenny said the obvious.

His mother advised, "John, this is about you—"

"The shot is of Stephanie." He described the photograph that showed the back of him. The word *Dake* was clearly visible under his short haircut. His hand was resting on Stephanie's neck, his thumb stroking her face and she was smiling leaning down at him, her blouse falling open. "My new woman and her spectacular body. She's going to hate this. She prides herself on her intelligence."

"Then tell the reporter she's a veterinarian."

"They're calling Kenny for her name. We're not revealing it."

"Because of the Bennetts?"

"No. I want to protect her until she's a Dake. And even then... Yeah, Kenny, I know it's pre-season, but we won the game. And I had that great pass to Beihn in the first quarter. Can you believe this Mom! Don't they have better things to run then my hand caressing a woman? I mean good night, I know its Tuesday, but there are tons of things to write about beside my love life and new haircut." John paced across his floor.

"You framed that picture up for them—calling Stephanie down to the wall, kissing her publicly while half the stadium was still lingering around. John, you know how Dallas is, they're interested in you—you personally. You might want to have Stephanie stay home for the next couple games to let this cool off."

"What?" His eyes ran across the headline again. The brief article talked about his arm, his performance in the first quarter of the game and the team's optimistic season. *Dake doesn't seem to be playing with the same risk taking and toughness as before his injury.* "You don't bullet every ball, sometimes it's about touch. Floating a ball over the top of a guy and letting it drop into his hands over the middle. Beihn got us forty yards on that play. I'm playing exactly the same way as before my injury!" he told Kenny and his mom.

"I said you might want to have Stephanie stay in Louisiana until—"

"No. She's coming to Dallas next weekend for Atlanta. We'll be apart enough. I'm not letting the press keep us apart any more. She's sitting with you. You know what to look out for and what to do if one of those reporters starts noising around. Besides she gets nervous when I'm on the field, you can talk her through all that, teach her about the game and trusting me while I play it."

"But, I ah..."

"She's coming Mom and she's sitting with you." His finger traced Stephanie's face in the picture. She looked gorgeous. "There's too much going on right now. I'll talk to you later Mom, I've got to call Stephanie and spin this a little so she doesn't get upset."

Helen Dake looked through her car window as she ended the call. Dylan was patiently waiting. Opened her door. "Good morning, Helen. Everything okay?"

"Yes." She nodded, the nerves firing up. "John," she explained, "The press apparently got a picture of his girlfriend. You know how relentless they are."

He held out his hand, helped her out, held on a minute as he told her with a smile, "Not really, back in my day they listened to the games on the radio."

She laughed, squeezed his hand. "We're not that old."

"Black and white TV then." He squeezed back. Smiled. "No one knows who I am."

"That lie was so smooth I'd think you sold cars."

"I do."

"You're a hall of famer and I'm a huge football fan. Buy me a paper, number 54." She pointed toward the dispenser. He bought a paper and they ordered breakfast, found the article. "Hmph." Helen Dake gave the familiar sound.

He took his first sip of coffee as he looked at the photograph. "They did catch them but he's famous."

"And people are fascinated." She looked at him. "That's the reason I encouraged him to hire a team. Funded JDi after he won the Heisman and I saw what was happening, the media frenzy, the invasion of his privacy and what would happen to his life when he got drafted by Dallas of all places. My husband left John an inheritance," she told him, "So I used it to put people around him who were wise to the system and could help him navigated through the fame. You must think I'm a stage mom."

"No, I think you're a businesswoman and a wise mother who wanted to protect her son."

"I was a widow who wanted to protect her husband's legacy. Make sure John honored his name. And he has," now she spoke the truth, "And neither of them needs me overseeing that anymore. John can handle that. And this," she tapped the newspaper. "Or Kenny will." She smiled. "And I'll find my place."

He tapped the table by her hand. "There's a place here."

"He said something about her being Mrs. Dake."

"I was talking about here, by Mr. Sullivan."

"That car salesman?"

"He used to play football. I heard you liked football."

"Love it actually. He wants her sitting with me Sunday."

"You or us?"

"Us."

He smiled. "Good because I gave my tickets away."

"Good because I'd like you to sit with me, meet her and my son."

He covered her hand. And the food came. The waitress saying, "Oh look at that John Dake," as she saw the paper. "He's so hot."

"He hardly played a quarter, barely broke a sweat on Sunday," Dylan said the words in a way that had her knowing he knew exactly what 'hot' really meant. And so did the stranger at the next table.

"His new girlfriend is the hot one. That babe's got some rack—"

"Hey." Dylan cut him off. "That talk isn't for breakfast or ladies." His look struck the younger man, his voice low and slow and held the kind of quiet authority that had dominated offenses in the early seventies. He'd held a record for sacks and a reputation for being as nice off the field as he was lethal on it.

There was silence and Dylan let it settle the room. Then he said, "I'll say grace." And he bowed his head, blessed the food with the room watching. And Helen Dake fell in love.

25

It was the third pre-season game they called the dress rehearsal, meaningless but still a time to iron out strategies and test out new ideas. This was also the last game before the final cut down to the fifty-man squad. Players in the grey area would be striving to perform to their potential and coaches were making critical roster decisions. The combination of the Texas heat, Helen Dake and the press, made Stephanie tense and edgy. She was glad when Cindy arrived before the game to sit with Stephanie and Helen.

"So how is *John Dake's new woman?*" Cindy asked with a grin and Stephanie felt the heat flame her face.

"Fine."

That had been the question of the week. John had paged her Tuesday morning with a code to call ASAP. She'd stopped an examination with an apology to her client as she slipped out of a stall to call him back on the cell phone in her Jeep and listened to John apologize, explain and then go into tactical lecture mode that she was now sitting with his mother.

She glanced at Helen Dake. She hadn't mentioned the article yet. But her friend, Dylan smiled and said, "Dr. Hightower, I thought it was a great article. Sets the stage for the new season. New hopes. New Heights. Helen, do you know much about this Miller boy?" He leaned toward her and the two of them looked at the program, began to talk.

"Neil said John was concerned you'd be upset."

"I'm not sure what I am," she answered. "It's the first time I've been in the paper."

"It was a great shot."

She glanced at Cindy. "I'm now wearing T-shirts. No blouses. Or bending over walls."

"Orders from number seven?"

"No, my own, but John does want me sitting here with his mom."

"They're great seats. Her boyfriend is cute," she whispered.

And Stephanie glanced at them. "He's not..." And then she suddenly realized, he was.

Late in the first quarter John was sacked hard and Stephanie grabbed hold of Cindy's arm and waited for John to come out of the pile up.

"He's okay," Cindy reassured softly as Stephanie's eyes stayed riveted on the field. "Just stay confident. You don't want to ever be a sideline story if the camera finds you."

"What?"

"They show Mrs. Dake sometimes. When John takes a big hit. They know where she sits."

"He's fine," Helen told them confidently.

"And probably done for the day if they don't convert. The quarter is almost up."

Stephanie sighed with relief when John put on a baseball hat on the sidelines. He was done. And when the game was over he just glanced up and smiled at her. They had dinner with the Beihns and she had a late flight out of Dallas. The team would be out of town for two weeks, the season opener in New York. They were going over the logistics, Stephanie assuring him she'd be fine.

"I'm going to miss you," he said it as he kissed her. His eyes were open, the color a darker blue. His words slowed and deepened with authority. "Need you to know that, if I get distracted this week preparing. We need to win these first two conference games."

"I understand." She kissed him back. "You need to win all your games."

"You'll sit with mom for Buffalo with Cindy."

"And Dylan. Don't forget your mom's boyfriend." She saw confusion first, then shock had her softening the revelation with a grin. "I found out where you get your cuddling gene."

"My mom was cuddling." There was a tick in his jaw. "With Dylan Sullivan." Now a frown. "In this heat."

"They just lean toward each other and smile a lot. It's cute."

"Cute?"

"I like him."

Then the classic "Hmph."

"He calls me Dr. Hightower. Your mom calls him Dylan. His friends call him Sully."

"What does he call my mother?"

"Helen," she answered simply. "There was a sweetheart once or twice." She kissed him. "I'll take better notes next time." She soothed him. "It's okay, John."

"Hmph."

"They went to dinner tonight. And were meeting for breakfast—"

"Breakfast." The word wore a frown.

"She seems really happy. We'll have dinner with them next time and you'll see."

"John."

"Mr. Sullivan."

There was a firm handshake before the girls broke it up. Stephanie by his side. His mother standing opposite him, switching sides suddenly for the first time in his life, as she stood beside the tall, wide shouldered hall of fame linebacker. He'd heard stories about Dylan Sullivan, that he was a force of nature back in the seventies. As ruthless and powerful on field as he was charismatic and charitable off. They said he was a good guy, but the man sold cars.

"How long have you known my mom?"

"Almost Five years?" Dylan looked at Helen.

She nodded, stated, "Since your rookie year, John. We met at a game."

"We were never formally introduced." He smiled. "Just came to know each other over the season."

"He was married back then." Helen grinned.

He grinned back. "She was friends with my wife."

"You're divorced." It was more of a statement than a question that John voiced.

"Widowed."

"His wife was lovely. Dylan has two married daughters and three grandchildren."

"Want to see pictures?" His wallet was already out. "They're beauties." He showed off his family.

"Oh, they are beautiful," Stephanie was smiling. "All girls."

"Little angels," Helen told them more.

Dylan chuckled. "They're on their best behavior for Helen but they're about perfect."

"So, you've met them?" Stephanie asked.

"Several times. They've been to the ball games," Helen told him, "And we met for dinner while John was out of town. We were glad the team was back at home today."

"Three wins is a great start."

John stayed silent. He was stewing as he studied the man and he knew it was ridiculous, but he wasn't going to make this easy.

"Is this serious?"

Helen laughed as Stephanie censured, "John."

"Is it mom?"

"I'm serious," Dylan answered, looking right into John's eyes. "I'm in love with your mother. She's a little overwhelmed."

John looked at her. Saw that she was but then her eyes sparkled, and her smile came, and she surprised him, "I've been swept off my feet." Then she laughed. "It's wonderful really. He's wonderful, John." She was actually blushing now as she praised him, "And you've played great. Three wins in a row. What a start. Don't you think?"

"Great start."

"Really great start," Stephanie added.

"Are we going to eat?" he asked his mother. They were at her house and she had brisket. When the meal was served, Dylan said grace. He knew where the glasses were stored and the hot sauce his mother always kept homemade in the refrigerator was kept.

"Play through it number seven," Stephanie whispered to him. And he reached out for her, his hand knocking off her napkin.

"I'll get it." He ducked down to retrieve it and saw his mother holding Dylan's hand under the table. He put the napkin in Stephanie's lap and his hand cupped her thigh, held there. It grounded him as they talked around him and he seemed to float, his emotions static, his body stiff and muscles aching after a long, hard fought game.

He let Stephanie handle this, stayed quiet. Ate and drank and grunted out his responses until they finally said goodbye and left.

"I want you to stay with me. Sleep with me tonight and never leave."

"That's not who we are," she answered him. She was looking out the window, but her gaze came slowly to him and those pretty eyes had darkened. "And you're upset about your mom."

"Yeah."

"It's okay, John. Your mother is happy."

"They're serious."

"Seems so. You're sulking. What can I do?"

He drew her to him in the car. His hands possessive as he kissed her and repeated, "I want you. Tonight. Stay."

"Okay."

He growled her name and cursed and nipped an ear and set her back and away.

"This week is going to be long."

"Monday night against Miami."

"Then were at Phoenix. What have you got this week?"

She went through her schedule. One of her papers had been printed in a periodical this summer and the Thoroughbred Breeders Association had invited her to speak at a symposium in Florida.

"I'll miss you." They looked at each other. They'd found a routine now in the coming and going. A flight time in and out. A place to pull in at the airport close to her gate and an agreement that it was crazy for him to try to go in with her. They said their goodbyes at the curb in the car. Tonight, she held him and softly assured again. "Dylan is a great guy. Once you get to know him this will be alright. You want your mother happy, not alone. Right?"

He nodded. And they kissed goodbye.

John beeped her as she prepared to speak at the Thoroughbred Breeders Association symposium. She glanced at her watch, then the crowd in the hotel ballroom. She had minutes, maybe moments before she was called to the podium.

She was nervous. She'd never spoken in front of so many people before. There were hundreds of them, from around the world. John just wanted to tell her good luck. So, she went back to her notes and smiled when they introduced her. Brad had helped her with the ice breaker in her opening and it got the desired chuckle, then she moved into her talk about pedigrees and the theory of nicking; that certain equine blood lines have an affinity for one another.

The applause startled her a bit at the end and so did the number of people who had questions or comments. She didn't have enough business cards and apologized to the man standing before her, telling him she'd run out.

"He knows who you are." The stranger held out a white card. "He would like you to call him. Tonight please. To schedule a consultation."

Stephanie took the card and watched the man walk away to join a group of five others. They all had dark hair and well-manicured beards.

The card had a name, Prince Faisal. Below it was the words, House of Saud, and a string of digits made up the phone number.

When she got to her hotel room she called John.

"When I beep you're supposed to call me back, Stephanie. What took so long?" There was noise in the background and John was telling someone to hold on. "Where are you?" Then he told Kenny he knew it was live. "I really need to talk to you, but I have an interview. I'll call you back." He hung up.

She was hurt. Then angry. Then picked up the phone and called the number on the business card for Prince Faisal. "This is Dr. Hightower."

Immediately she was connected. Then quickly absorbed in the conversation. The prince had been involved successfully in horseracing for years. Now he was concentrating on breeding and studying the various theories. He talked about outcrossing and then moved into her theory of nicking when John beeped her the first time. She silenced it, only to have the beeper rise up again in an impatience vibrating dance across the desk. That's when Prince Faisal paused. His voice formally polite as he insisted he had gone on too long and she must have many vying for her attention. Would she call him when she was back in her office to schedule an appointment with him? The beeper went off again. The read out said only 911 as she agreed to call Prince Faisal in two days. Then she called John.

"What is the emergency, John?"

"My mother is engaged." There wasn't even a pause. "He came over today to talk to me about it. Had a ring. Three rings. From Tiffany's. Loaded with diamonds. That interconnect or symbolize something. And he sat me down and said a lot of stuff, but I can't remember any of it because I think this is way too fast."

"What did you say?"

"I don't know. He hit me with it like one of his sacks. Rang my bell and knocked me out. I don't know."

"You're upset."

"Yeah, I was when I couldn't get you to answer. When I need you, I need you. Were you in surgery?"

"I'm in Florida. Had that speech today, remember?"

There was silence. Then he said, "Right. Sorry. See, I'm off. Sorry, Beauty. How did it go?"

"Fine."

"You're mad."

There was silence. Then she said, "No, I understand this is a big deal to you."

"This is crazy. Why are they rushing this? They hardly know each other." She was about to remind him they'd known each other five years but John just went on. "And in the middle of the season, she does this. She knows better. They could have waited till February."

"John—"

"I've got Monday Night Football to prepare for, she knows that, and he should know better, he played the game."

"John—"

"And then you don't respond, and I take it to practice and Curtis, the rookie left tackle that replaced the injured veteran, well the stupid kid backs up right into me. Thud! I'm down and my O-Line is coming to arms, fighting each other while I'm lying in the dirt. We can't be doing that this week. I got up and threw my helmet, cursed the lot of them. Felt like an idiot. My head is screaming, Beauty. And I'm beeping you. With no answer. Then I've got a live radio show interview, acted like a grizzly bear, Kenny on me about my answers and attitude."

"What did you say?"

"I don't know. Need you here."

"Sorry."

"Want you. Take tomorrow off."

"I'm in Florida."

"Sorry. Right. When are you here?"

"Monday afternoon."

"Saturday," he argued.

"John, we talked about this, remember? I'm going to catch up on Saturday at the clinic. Come in Monday and take Tuesday off. We've got Tuesday together."

"Right."

"You okay?"

"My head hurts and I'm obviously a little irritated."

"Take some meds, hydrate and sleep. We'll talk in the morning."

"Love you," he said before he hung up.

Orchids were waiting on her desk when she got back from Florida. She opened the card expecting an apology. Instead the card read,

Looking forward to working together.

Faisal.

She called John. "I got flowers today. From a client. I thought I should tell you."

"Hmph."

"You want me to tell you, right?"

There was silence. Background voices. JDi was around.

"John?"

"No. I don't need to know right now that someone is hitting on my girlfriend."

"It's from a client."

"What did the card say?"

"Looking forward to working together. Faisal."

"Faisal," he repeated. And she heard Carl then Kenny before John repeated, "Prince Faisal? He's a Saudi prince."

"He raises race horses."

"A prince from the House of Saud sent you flowers."

"He's just a client I met in Florida."

"Florida, huh?... Hmph. Why did you need to tell me? Do you think I should tell you what some fan offered me in Miami? Or how I got propositioned in the parking lot last night on the way to my truck? Huh? Do I need to tell you every time some woman... Kenny is shaking his head. Telling me no. I don't. But do I? Huh, Stephanie?"

"You're mad and I was being honest."

"Don't turn this on me. Not today. I've got Monday Night Football. Prime time, honey."

"Honey?" Her voice turned into a crisp warning, "You need to stop, right now, or I will be mad, *Baby*."

"I don't have time for this today, Stephanie. Throw the flowers away and stay away from that Arabian prince. You've obviously got enough clients already since you have to work this Saturday."

"I took Tuesday off, so we could be together on your day off."

"You took Tuesday off because my mom is getting married. She said she called you and Honey."

"She did, but I was already taking Tuesday off—"

John cut her off. "I need you to listen." There was a pause, the background voices fading away. "I know it's your rookie season. I need you. To remember. What you promised me. It's October. I need you. Sweet. Supportive. Submissive. This week especially. I need you. Strong. Sympathetic. And please God, not sexy. Don't you tempt me, Stephanie. I mean it. Did you hear me?"

"Yes."

"Good." There was an exhale. An expletive. "I've got a headache. Need to get to work. I've got to be first in-last out. It's on me to lead this team. It's all on me. Do you understand me?"

"I'll be praying for you."

"I need it. I love you."

He hung up. And he must have told Kenny to send her flowers. Or Carl. Because they came within the hour, an extravagant bouquet of roses and this time the card was signed, John. And he always signed it 'Love, Mr. Charming', called her Beauty. Only sent roses on Valentine's Day until now.

And it was October. And Elise's words mocked her. "He'll be back to me in October. You're rookie green. Jack doesn't like it sweet. And he hates rookies. He needs veterans. On the field and in his bed."

And the anger left her to be replaced by anxiety.

"Stephanie, ready for lunch? Wow," Linda smiled. "Look at those roses. John?"

"Carl or Kenny. He had someone send them."

"Oh. And the orchid?"

"A client. Would you like it? I'll kill it. Really." She handed Linda the plant from Faisal, lead the way out for their weekly lunch.

26

"You decided on the Adrienne Vittadini sweater dress." Rhonda circled her as she came into John's kitchen, nodding at the dress. "It's ready-to-wear but I thought the colors and shape would look great on you and it's appropriate for a wedding."

"Thanks so much, Rhonda. What do I owe you?"

She frowned. "By now you know how this works."

"Do I make it out to JDi?"

"Put that up. Please." Rhonda closed the check book. "Really. We've got it. A girl at Neiman's did me a favor. They want your future business and I was thrilled you called me to help find something for Mrs. Dake's wedding today," she explained, then whispered, "Really, anything can set him off right now." She looked back toward John's master suite and slipped Stephanie's wallet into her opened handbag. "Just smile. Be agreeable. Let the guys handle him since he didn't sleep well."

"He didn't sleep well?"

"It was a rough game with that rookie starting on the offensive line. Eight sacks and they knocked him down over a dozen times. Plus, three interceptions; that's what's eating at him. Monday Night Football and he had three. You were there, saw it."

"Yes." Her body was still tense. She'd ridden home with him and Honey from the stadium. Slept in her room, at his house, since Honey was across the hall, an obvious chaperone. Honey had helped her through the violent game last night. When the hits kept coming and the sacks took John down or worse, when he was slow to get up. Honey would just keep talking. Hand her the popcorn. Remind her John was tough. That interceptions happened. This was a rivalry game. Monday Night Football amped things up. And when things went bad he'd just cheer, 'Alright, alright, Dallas, let's go now.'

"We won, thank God. Imagine if we lost on Monday Night." She made a scary face. "We'd live with that for a season."

Stephanie was about to ask what it was like, to lose but Rhonda had moved on, handed her a greeting card. "He wants you to sign this. I already wrapped the camera. That was a great idea. We were at a loss. Everything we suggested for a wedding gift, he didn't like. Then you say camera and he's happy."

"I brought a gift and have a card with it."

"Oh." Rhonda frowned. "He won't like that. He wanted you to sign this card with him."

"I got them a camera bag. I showed him last night."

"I doubt he'll remember. He got his bell rung. Twice Kenny said. That makes him double grumpy. And mean. He gets a bit mean when he gets concussed."

"He has a concussion?"

"Probably. He never lets the team doc know. I stay out of it, let them handle all the athletic stuff." She handed her a pen. "Honey's here so things will be fine. He totally gets how to deal with John. And he loves you. John wants your name on the card."

Stephanie signed the card. Rhonda smiled, sealed the envelop and tucked it below the pretty bow on the fancy wrapped box. The dogs preceded John and Honey, racing into the kitchen and sweeping around Stephanie as Rhonda picked up a lint brush. "It's weird. The girls are shedding. Its fall and they should be growing a thicker coat. Instead, they're shedding." She went to work on John's pants.

"Weirder still, most people get married on the weekend, in the spring or summer after they've known each other a while. Not on Tuesday. Huh, girls?" The dogs made laps around them as John greeted her with a kiss. "You look pretty. In pink. You've never worn pink before."

She held his face, studied his eyes. He looked tired. His neck clawed with a bright red scratch over his suit collar. His hands banged up with cut knuckles. "How do you feel?"

"Great." He smiled. "Three interceptions but we won last night." He tucked her to his side. "You ready? That the gift?"

"Yes." Rhonda handed it to Stephanie. "She signed the card."

"Hunnicut."

"Alright, alright." He jiggled the keys. "Let's go, I'm driving."

"You okay?" she asked softly as they walked.

"Great."

"Your hand is cold." She turned into him holding it to their hearts. "And hurt. You're hurt."

"I'm fine. You're here." There was a kiss. "Just stay right here today and make sure I play through this rush of an inconvenience."

"John," she stopped him.

He waved her off. "I'm fine. It's happening. Today. What can I do?"

She looked up at him. "I'm not sure you're ready to hear this but I need to say what God tells us to do."

"Okay."

"*Honor your mother and your father, for this is the first commandment with a promise; that it may go well for you.* You don't have to love him yet, or even like him, but you do need to honor your mother and respect him. God promises it will go well for you. That's how we have to play through this today."

Honey held the door. Stephanie held the gift. And John just held on to her as they walked into the mega-church and looked for the parlor the wedding was to be held in.

A woman appeared in the hall. "You're John Dake!" Her smile was wide as she pointed at him. "Well, goodness be! It's such an honor." She was shaking his hand. "Such an honor. What a win last night—"

"Thanks." He smiled. Squeezed. Stepped back.

"We're here for a wedding, ma'am, in the parlor," Honey stated, his hand a gentle gesture to guide her forward and away from John. "Could you point the way?"

"Of course. The parlor is right down here." She led them forward as Honey compliment the church.

John drew Stephanie in close again. His hand curling around her waist to catch her ribs. The sweater dress, a weave of pinks, grays and black, had a little jacket over a tight bodice and a slim skirt to her knees. The fabric was soft beneath his hidden hand and he could feel the delicate ridge of her ribs and the weight of her breast if he turned her just right. He curled his sore fingers there into her softness, something driving him to old habits that felt utterly rebellious today.

It's because of the pain. He hurt, all over and the short at-home rehab session this morning had been rushed.

His head felt hungover. He'd hardly slept with three interceptions last night! On Monday Night Football. When the whole league was watching. He'd replayed the game, focused on the imperfections, how he could have played better. *Thank God we won, or I'd really be grumpy.*

And this head ache wasn't helping. *Who could smile with this throbbing mind stealer?* He'd be better off alone today. He wanted to look at film, solve problems and move forward as he got a jump start on the game plan for Sunday during this short week. Instead he was here, looking for a parlor in a mega-church holding on for dear life to Stephanie.

He felt about eight. In a smart pout with a secretly dark mood that was waiting to break out and say or do something really stupid, like a flagrant foul. He'd heard the whistle. And Stephanie had thrown the flag.

Honor your mother...

Hmph. He wasn't eight anymore.

Or eighteen—trying to cop a feel of his girlfriend's breast in a church, *really?* He shifted his hand, down and away. *Holding her ass isn't any better, Dake.* He took hold of her hand. And those intense green eyes cut him a look. *Yeah, she's so got your number, Seven.*

She wasn't going to indulge him here, today, probably never, anywhere. And that's what he wanted. Why he fell in love with her. Right? Hmph.

Yes, she's right, he sighed out the truth.

Like last night's poorly played game, they won in the end. That would be the stat that stuck. They got the 'W'. God's grace not luck.

Stephanie was right, and he loved her unwavering wisdom. She never nagged him with her opinion but cut straight to the truth. *God says.* That's why we're going to play through this the right way, because God says that's how you honor me, yourself, your girlfriend, your best friend, your mother and yes, your new step-father.

So, are you going to hide your hand under her sweater and rebelliously misbehave and pout or are you going to obediently show some honor so it will go well for you, Dake?

Times up. You're here. The Parlor. The playing field. A spiritual battleground in a private war.

She squeezed his hand. Gave him a soft beautiful smile. She thought he could do this. The decorative cross that greeted them, shining out from a bright stain glass window, reminded him he was never alone. Game on.

I can do all things through Christ who strengthens me.

They walked into the parlor. It was a homey room, with sofas and chairs, a fireplace and that large stained-glass window. His mother stood there with Dylan and a man holding a Bible. She smiled, moving toward them to take John into a hug then she greeted Honey.

"Mrs. Helen."

"Stephanie." Helen was all smiles. "You look beautiful."

"You look beautiful." They hugged; cooing to each other over their outfits like females could do at these kinds of occasions.

He slipped his arm around Stephanie and drew her back, told his mother, "I didn't think the groom was supposed to see the bride before the wedding."

His mother laughed, blushing as she said, "We're calling this just a simple ceremony that's makes the legal paper work official." She fiddled with her hair, sweeping the room with her gaze. "We'll stand and say the vows then all go to lunch. We're just waiting on Sandy, Dylan's youngest... There she is." As she said the words she took John's hand. "You need to meet his girls."

"Yes, Ma'am. Probably should."

Stephanie nudged him. *Okay, little slip there, like an incomplete pass. Let's huddle up and try again.*

He squeezed her hand. "Mom, introduce us." He gave her his smile, saying, "Hunnicut, come meet the sisters."

It was a circle of introductions and niceties; smiles and nods, shifting feet and shaking hands as most of the attention was cast onto Dylan's three young granddaughters. Then the Pastor said, "Well, it looks like we're all in position. Should we make this official?"

"Helen?" Dylan asked.

"I'm ready," she answered.

Then the groom smiled, holding out his hand. "I've been waiting two years for you to say that."

His mother accepted his hand, said the simple vows and made the important promises after Dylan.

John watched the man, his words sincere and strong and certain, his eyes only on his mother, and as she spoke, they sparkled. Seeing their emotion of love, something squeezed John's heart and he drew Stephanie closer and glanced at the cross as the pastor read the classic verses about love.

He'd known he was loved before, but now he believed. His mother was a blessing. Having a friend like a brother another. Now this beautiful godly girlfriend the last strand of three that surrounded him with love. As they all bowed their heads for the prayer of blessing, and he felt his best friend's hand rest upon his back and Stephanie's fingers curl into his own as his mother kissed her new husband, John silently praised again, "King me."

John knocked on her door, calling out, "Stephanie."

"Come in." She stopped packing and looked up. Smiled and held out her hand to him again because he'd seemed so needy today. So, lost and tense and trying so hard to just hold it all together and play through it. She'd been so proud of how he'd come around and tried to celebrate the occasion today. "Hey, did you get some aspirin for your headache?"

He nodded and brought her close, whispered, "Thanks for today."

"Sure." She held him to her.

"Sorry if I was—"

"Don't apologize. You overcame, and I watched it happen. I'm really proud of you."

"I think I've been frustrated." He was gathering her up higher into his arms.

She dropped her head back and looked up at him. "You didn't have much time to process this, John."

"I'm edgy."

"Umm."

"A bit... immature."

"Hmph," she said, lifting a brow because his hands had been roaming. Down over her hips then up beneath her arms, fitting back to her ribs, his thumbs a sweeping caress of the sides of her breasts. She waited now, looking into his eyes for him to say more as his hands did another lap—down to pull her close—up to sweep her breasts. "What can I do?"

And there was a growl. A step as he swept her off her feet in a gentle tackle and they fell to the bed, bounced as he repeated, "I'm frustrated." He buried his face into her hair. "Want you. Here. Now." Another growl, weaker, his body gathering her closer. "I need you... to say something now. Speak truth again."

"It's okay." Were her words.

"My mom got remarried and now..."

"You feel alone."

"No." His hand was moving again. Over her body. "Frustrated." There was a sigh. "I held her back from being happy. It was all about me. For too long. I realized that today."

"She is happy, John and the timing was perfect for them."

"It happened too fast for me. I didn't have time to adjust, and that's about me again." He rubbed his forehead, squeezing his eyes shut. "And they'll be gone. Two weeks in Europe. She's never missed a game. And that's about me again. God I'm selfish."

"You're tense." She soothed him. "Take a breath, baby."

Now he laughed. "A breath's not going to help this, babe."

"Oh?" She brushed his hair back. There was fire in his eyes and she interpreted the smoke signals now as she saw his desire and her tone changed. "Oh."

"Oh. Yeah. To be honest, I need a release and that used to mean sex."

"Okay." She nodded, thinking she should be praying but instead she just asked him, "What can I do? To... help. Just tell me what to do..." her words just fell off as he rolled away. "John?"

The yarn and catnip pillow was over his face. There was a curse. Mumbled but she understood its frustrated tone.

"John."

"Stephanie," he countered, throwing the pillow. It tumbled through the air and landed in the nearby chair as he sat up. "You're not going to do anything. I'm certainly not going to give you lessons today."

"Lessons." The word held hurt as she remembered Elise's mocking laughter about her being rookie green and sweet with inexperience and how much John hated that.

"Yeah." He rolled up to his feet off the bed, towered over her. "I'll teach you everything I know once we're married but not today. And you need to stop tempting me."

Anger just erupted, sputtering at his self-righteous down the nose look as she found her own feet. "Then keep your immature hands to yourself, Mr. Charming."

"For the record, stop wearing pink clingy sweater dresses with little jackets where I can hide my immature hands." He waved at her breasts.

"Really?" There was a clear warning to the word as she crossed her arms, narrowed her eyes and said it again. "Really. And for the record, I don't care to *learn* everything you discovered from Elise Kristopher, supermodel."

"Hey." He pointed at her. Then wagged his finger. "Not today."

"And the idea of you—teaching—me." She shook her head. "Coaching me up. Please." And she mocked his finger wag. "No."

"What? That's pride talking. Yes, I will coach you up. Provide, protect, cherish, love. Didn't you listen today to the vows?"

"I thought we'd figure it out together. I didn't know that you had it all figured out already. How many women were there anyway—"

"Stop. Don't you get mad." Now he pleaded. "I can't do it. Charm you out of that anger today or tomorrow." Now his hands lifted in surrender. "I love *you*, you're it, not any of them."

She was still frowning.

"Look, I know I deserve it but I'm no good today. Stuck on myself. Would love a good fight but you'll tear me up with that brilliant intelligence. Quote me scriptures and add a few pie charts on my statistical bad behavior while you calculate the Vegas odds on my self-indulgence starting this again tomorrow. I can't be at odds with you this week. Okay? And that's about me. Again. I'm selfish. I'll work on it. But please, keep that promise you made to be here for me and give me some grace."

She exhaled and nodded. Walked half way to meet him as he came toward her. They just looked at each other.

"Sorry," he said.

She nodded.

"Say it back."

She lifted a brow. "I love you. You're the only one for me. How's that?"

He thought about it for a second and nodded then lifted her close to him and whispered, "Even better, Beauty," on a nipping kiss as his hand settled on her ribs and his thumb swept her breast again. "Catnip," he teased.

She teased back, "Yarn. You said you liked this dress."

"It's what you do to this dress. Lord, help me."

And she closed her eyes, quietly prayed, "Lord, help us. It's October and things are... happening around us that are difficult. We're anxious and frustrated. And how we used to handle that in the past, You're asking us to try it Your way now. Help us to trust You and empower us to play through it in faith for victory. We love You and each other and want to honor You always. Amen."

"Thanks, Stephanie."

"Better?"

"I will be once I finally beat this headache."

27

It was a new sound that escaped from her heart and held the tones of fear and frustration as John took another brutal hit and was tackled to the turf. Stephanie wasn't the only one that had gasp, the crowd was on their feet, but the shuttle pass had Dewayne picking up over fifteen yards as the stadium burst into a loud ovation. Stephanie kept her gaze on John. She held her breath, squeezing Cindy's hand. He was slow to get up, just lying there for what seemed long haunting minutes.

She was terrified. Something cold and wild rising up from her soul from the repeated violence against John. It was becoming hard to watch. Her body twitching with the tension as fear mounted to an anxious terror.

The helmet clashing echo of these hard hits was flipping an odd emotional switch inside her. Maybe it was the violence or the repeated cycle of seeing John, a man she thought was so physically strong, be brought low. Or it was this love deal. She was really in love with him, head over heels kind of change your life love and all she could do was watch. Him struggle. Get hit. Again and again. And he expected her to sit here and cheer?

She needed to pace. Wished she'd sat with her parents up in Brad's box so she could just walk out the tension and keep watch out of the corner of her eye while she prayed. Because she felt suddenly, desperately, out of control of everything.

"We should sit down." It was Cindy Beihn that gently drew her down beside Kenny and Rhonda in Helen Dake's seats.

"They know who you are and where you sit now," Rhonda offered her some nachos.

She shook her head, felt sick, her gaze watching Neil Beihn offer John a hand as he helped him off the turf. The two jogged up field to the new line of scrimmage. But John kept on going, into the other team's huddle where there was bumping and shifting and obvious words said before San Diego's nose guard waved toward the Dallas bench.

It was Kenny that said, "Ut-oh."

Then Rhonda added, "He doesn't know where he is."

It took two refs and a Dallas Offensive Linemen to get him headed off the field with the trainers. John sat down on the bench, leaned over and threw up. And that new little sound came out of her again, a gasp-cry-moan that had her lip trembling with emotion.

Kenny leaned toward her and held up his program to shield their faces as he told her, "He'll be okay unless he sees you crying. Then he'll be all over me for letting you worry. Blink or wipe those pretty eyes now. He's a tough guy, rock solid and he's had a great game, adding to an incredible season. You're a big part of that, part of us at JDi, so he needs you to smile and nod. Clap when a play is over and cheer on the backup quarterback now. Wash, rinse, repeat until the fourth quarter ends. Okay?"

She just nodded. Clapped as the back-up quarterback took the field and Kenny said, "Here we go now, Eleven."

She kept her gaze on John, he was arguing with one of the trainers. He'd taken his helmet as two men in suits were trying to distract him. He'd pushed away from the team doctors, following the trainer with his helmet like it was a game of chase with a drunk. John weaved in and out of players as they cleared a path for him. It was a coach who pulled him up short. Guided him the opposite way back to the bench.

"They'll keep him out," Kenny said reassuringly.

"They better," Cindy insisted. "He's clearly got a concussion."

"Was he concussed last week, Kenny?"

"He had a head ache, but it was a crazy week. Monday Night Football. Tuesday wedding. Short week for this late Sunday game."

"He was grumpy," Rhonda whispered.

"Focused," Kenny corrected.

"Focused on being grumpy."

"Rhonnie."

"She knows what I'm talking about, Kenny." She ate a nacho. Looked toward the field. "His hair is finally long enough to curl again, Stephanie."

"Umm," Stephanie nodded, seeing the curls spring up because both of his hands were threading through it in frustration. And he seemed to be holding his head. Then he was looking around and arguing with the coach again. The coach was keeping a hand on his jersey. When Dr. Lambert tried to talk to him, John shook his head.

"He never goes down easy," Kenny stated but there seemed to be a compromise because as the fourth quarter began, John was walking with Dr. Lambert toward the locker room.

"Where are they going?"

"To evaluate him."

Rhonda took a deep breath. And Cindy said, "It could be a long week."

"Let's hope it's only one long week. Helen's gone," Kenny reminded them.

Cindy patted Stephanie's leg. "Looks like you're up, FMJD."

"What?" she blushed.

"Blair told me." She smiled and mouthed it out, "Future-Mrs.-John-Dake." Then she leaned closer and told her, "It fits. You'll need to stay tonight. Do your duty for the team."

She paced in his kitchen. The dogs keeping step with her. Her gaze kept glancing at the clock. He should be home by now. But he wasn't. Cindy had dropped her off after the game. Offered to stay. But she'd told her JDi would be here. But they weren't. And Hattie was off on Sundays.

Stephanie was alone, for another hour.

Finally, Staubach barked and darted off. Bradshaw just circled her legs as they both walked toward the back door. John came in last behind Kenny, Carl, his manager and Ryan his personal trainer.

"Hey, girls," Kenny was talking, greeting the Goldens. "Staubach."

"Staubach," John said and petted her as she rushed around him.

"Here's Bradshaw."

John repeated, "Bradshaw."

"Hi, Stephanie." Kenny gave her shoulder a squeeze.

"Stephanie." John turned toward her and seemed to look right through her. She reached for him, concern rising with a dozen questions she wanted to ask the men, but John took her hand, held tight as he said with his normal loving tone, "Hey, Beauty."

"We've been waiting for you," she said as the dogs circled and brushed them. "I see that."

"I'm staying tonight," she whispered it as her arms went around him, needing to hold. "You okay?"

"We won, right." It sounded like a question, so she nodded as he hugged her. "You smell good." There was his smile. "Feel even better. You're staying."

"He needs to hydrate," Ryan directed him. "Get some nutrients and minerals back in his body. Have a seat, John."

The phone rang, and John looked at it.

"The phone," Carl said. "Stephanie will get it."

She answered it. "Hello."

"I need to talk to him."

She recognized the voice. Elise Kristopher. She looked at John and took ownership, turning away. "He'll need to call you back."

"Look little doctor, I want to talk to Jack—"

"I'll let him know you called." She hung up. Held the phone tightly as her anxiety kicked up to another level with more questions she couldn't ask him right now. She stepped back, feeling dizzy from the onslaught of feelings. Worry and fear twisting around a hot jealousy, the need to confront him suppressed by the need to comfort and care for him.

Then the phone rang again. Twice. Before John barked, "That's not helping my headache!"

"Hello," she answered it again, bracing herself as John held his head in his hands. "Honey." She was immediately relieved.

"Alright, alright." John held out his hand for the phone and she gave it to him.

As John talked to Honey, Kenny told her quietly that John had a concussion and a severe headache. Both light and sound were bothering him. The team doctors had done a thorough evaluation and finally released him with instructions. The team had a handout on what she needed to watch for and she quickly read over the list.

Symptoms include:
Changes in the ability to think, concentrate or remember.
Headaches.
Blurred vision.
Changes in sleep patterns: not being able to sleep or sleeping all the time.
Changes in personality: becoming angry or anxious for no clear reason.
Lack luster interest in your usual activities.
Changes in your sex drive: intensified or no interest.
Coordination: dizziness, lightheadedness or unsteadiness in standing or walking.

Call the Team Doctor or 911 if the player has:
A headache that intensifies or does not go away.
Weakness, numbness, or decreased coordination.
Repeated vomiting or nausea.
Slurred speech.
Extreme drowsiness or you cannot wake them.
One pupil that is larger than the other.
Convulsions or seizures.
A problem recognizing people or places.
Increasing confusion, restlessness, or agitation.
Loss of consciousness.

The best medicine is rest.

"We give him memory cues. They help keep him calm until his brain comes back online. He's out of it, but don't worry, we'll take care of him and he'll see the doctor again in the morning."

She looked at him. "I'm staying." Then she looked at John, said his name, told him, "Tell Honey, I'm staying."

He looked at her, confused and she told him, "Tell Honey, Stephanie's staying since your mom is out of town. I'm staying with you."

"Huddle up... No, he says cuddle. I like to cuddle with you." Again, it sounded like a question.

"And the dogs. We'll find some basketball to watch."

"No television," Ryan told her as John listened to Honey. "His brain needs to rest. Dr. Lambert, the team doc, he'll call every three hours. John has to talk to him. Then get up and take a walk, get some water. Doc usually tells some story that takes about five minutes then he can go back to sleep. Tomorrow the doctors will check him out again and see how he's progressed."

"You've done this before?"

"Two years ago. The protocol is preventative."

"Beauty." John was looking at her as he sat the phone down.

"Finish your drink, John," Carl suggested. "Are the Meds helping?"

John didn't answer. Just drank the water.

"Want some ice for your neck?"

"No." The word was flat. "I'm iced out." He was up, holding the counter, Kenny moving in as they all watched him take that first step. "Going to lie down. Boys hit the road. Stephanie's staying."

Ryan opened his mouth to argue but Stephanie said, "I've got him." She slipped her arm around him and they walked toward his bedroom. "Sit down," she told him as they neared his bed, "I'll get your shoes off." He was in a team sweat suit and he took off the jacket as she slipped his shoes and socks off.

Kenny walked in. "You good?"

She nodded. John just looked at him.

He handed her the concussion handout and a pad and pen. "In case you need us." The men's phone numbers were written down. "We're heading out, John. Doc Lambert will be calling in a few hours. Good night."

The phone rang, loud and shrill like the bell at the end of a boxing round. John was tangled up, in beautiful, warm, bare limbs. He ran a hand back over edges and curves as someone talked. It was loud this close to his ear. He pushed away.

The phone. John.

Right, right. Nothing made sense. But he reached toward the sound and it cleared as he sat.

Hey, John, you awake? It's Doc Lambert... I need you to get up, take a little walk to the kitchen. You up? Walking?

He pushed away, saying, "I can walk. To the kitchen. Stay," he said. But they followed him, all of them, tails and hands and wet noses.

There should be two white pills on the counter with a glass of water, see them?

They were in his mouth and he drank. Set the glass down only to have it handed back again. And he set it down. But there was still more to drink. He stopped her hand, held it.

She's right. You have to finish all the water. Then you can rest. Get back in bed.

Bed... oh, yeah. He pulled. Her in closer. Smiled into her curly hair. That smell. Soft. Warm. It felt good. Umm, so sweet. That's what he wanted.

John... Dr. Lambert's on the phone.

"Shh!"

I'll let you go.

Let's go, John.

There was a gentle tug. He dug in. Tugged back.

No. Here. Now.

John.

Now. Here. This time. Right here. Yes... Right. Here...

The phone.

The words had him reaching, muscle memory knowing what to do. "Hello."

He combed his hair back as he sat up, the room glowing with the early dawn sunlight as Doc Lambert's words began to register through the dull thud of his headache. He had to get up. Take a walk. Drink water. In the kitchen. Take some pills.

He turned as a gentle hand stroked his back. "Stephanie's here." He just blinked at her. Her hair was tussled and wild around her pretty face. He brushed it back. Over a bare shoulder. She was holding the sheet up to her chest.

He shook his head. Closed his eyes. He couldn't think. Rubbed his head. Things were mixed up.

John, are you up, walking?

"Give me a minute."

He looked at the huge portrait on his wall. Stephanie. Wearing his bracelet. Wrapped in his arms, like the sheet. He looked back at her. Touched the emerald bracelet. Tugged the sheet. He should smile but he frowned. And something started to boil, and it was deep, from the bowels of his gut he erupted, "Get. Up."

It growled out of him as he stood up. But she was still there, in his bed, on the phone now. Her words were unclear because it was like a storm in his head, a down pour of pounding thoughts all collecting at once into a flood. But he knew. Sensed the truth because his body told him with that loose, light, relaxed exhaustion—that was quickly being taken over by a clenching rage—what had happened. His body told him everything.

"We had sex."

She blushed. Holding phone and sheet. And the dogs were up and circling at his tone as she hung up the phone

"Out!" The word just snarled in a hard command as he pointed.

But she dove under the sheets, came up struggling into his T-shirt before she rushed out of his bed, to the door, let the dogs out.

"No. You. Get. Out."

John's face was tight, set like stone. And his jaw was ticking as he pointed to the door. His eyes were wild, no longer dull. The color bright. The pupils, even pin pricks, were directed right at her as the angry words rang out in the room.

Her hand was on the door knob and something irrational was telling her to run and get away from him. Now. She wanted the dogs back. Between them. She needed to get the phone, call for help. See remembered the handout, 'Changes in personality: becoming angry or anxious for no clear reason.'

She stepped back, wiped her sweaty hands on the shirt, swallowed as she tried to think. Instincts had her circling out of the corner, like she was with an unpredictable stallion. Her hands held out, trying to make herself bigger and increase her balance even as the stance was the universal sign of surrender.

"John, you have a concussion," she said calmly.

"And we had sex."

She felt the heat hit her face in a blazing blush. He was just standing there as naked as Michelangelo's David.

"I have a concussion and we had sex. How did that happen?" Immediately his entire body changed, his face went from rage to dread as he stepped toward her. "Did I do something to you?" He had her in hand. So quickly. He was just holding both her arms as he stared into her eyes with some kind of horrible self-damning terror. "Force you? Are you okay?"

"No. No." She was just shaking her head. "It's okay, it just... happened."

"How? How did it happen?"

Another flash of heat hit her, and she was painfully aware of... Shame. The feeling overwhelming her suddenly, with the need to hide, flee, be alone. She pulled down on his T-shirt as she tried to find the words, avoided his eyes.

"The dogs." She tried to move toward the door.

He wouldn't have it, held her tightly. "I need to know what happened."

"It just... happened."

His jaw ticked off the seconds as they stood there. "I don't remember, *it* happening."

"You have a concussion," she said, and it was ridiculous, and she knew it and he was furious again.

"If I didn't force you, then did you seduce me into *it* while I had a concussion?"

She blushed, and he pushed away. She'd never seen him so furious as he demanded, "Start talking, Stephanie."

"You were hurt. And I was..." Her voice was trembling. A new kind of fear washing over her as he waved her on.

"You were what? Naked. How did you lose your clothes?"

"The concussion. You were out of it. Wanted them off." Now she waved her hand, pointed, "In the bathroom. You took them off and put this on me." She tugged on his T-shirt.

"And you must have been saying, 'John, stop. I'm not that kind of girl. And you have a concussion.'"

"You were hurt." Now her eyes filled.

"I was out of it. Don't remember anything. My God." He was turning in a circle now, his hands in his hair. "I can't believe you did that. To me." Now he glared at her. "You raped me."

"I did not!"

"Then what do you call it? Huh? What would you have called it that night at my cabin, when you got drunk, passed out; if you would have woken up naked with me in that bed? If I had taken advantage of you when you were drunk and didn't know what was happening." His fist went to his heart. "I sat in a chair, watched over you, and protected you that night, because I would never have done that to you, then or now."

"Well you did it with a hundred other girls. Supermodels, singers—Elise called last night by the way."

"They weren't you. You were my 'it' girl, Stephanie. You were special. We were special. Now look at you." He waved at her. "You had high standards and integrity. Quoted scripture and lived it. I don't even know who you are anymore. Standing there naked in my T-shirt. Jesus." He sat down, held his head in his hands and she was terrified.

"I'm sorry. John." She just gasped, came to him as the tears started pooling in her eyes. "I thought," she reached out and he reacted.

"Don't touch me." He pushed her back. "I don't want you near me. And don't *even* cry."

"I know your head hurts. And you're out of sorts. Still have a concussion. The doctor's list," she picked it up and he snatched it away. Read it over and looked up.

"Just has more proof; that you knew how bad off I was." He tapped it. "I can't think, remember anything about the game or this weekend. My head is killing me. And my sex drive has certainly changed. I've been celibate for almost ten months and only you know how many times we had sex last night. After a hundred girls, I know it was plenty. My God, what did you do?"

She could only shake her head as a tear ran down her face.

"Well I'm going to make sure I never forget this." He snatched the notepad and pen. Writing as he spoke out loud the words:

"Stephanie took advantage of you while you had a concussion." The pen scored hard into the pad of paper with harsh strokes.

"She disrespected you.

"Dishonored God.

"Broke your heart.

"And that's why you broke up."

Now the pen scribbled off his famous name before he tore the page off and stood.

"I want you out of my house. I'll never speak of this, so tell them anything you want about why we broke up."

28

The sound was like a rhythm. The rubbing of charcoal to paper sweeping back and forth across the page that played into the silence of her house with the ticking of the clock. Three weeks was about to turn into four and she'd uncovered another word today. The notepad she'd taken from his house was engraved with his sentences. And at last the ghostly white of his signature was revealed with the shading coverage of the pencil.

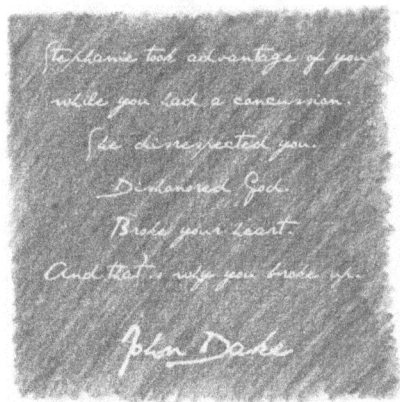

They were over.

She'd thought he'd call. The second day. Maybe the third. Then in a week. Or after his concussion healed; and he could think clearly. He'd call her. They'd talk. He'd forgive her eventually.

For three weeks she had just sat here—when she wasn't working herself to exhaustion—in the quiet darkness alone in her house. Waiting. That fragile hope giving way as the days passed by to a condemnation that was brutally cold. It had frozen her. Her prayers unnaturally awkward, just His name, *God* called out in a whisper as words dried up.

Days of lies catching up with her. The ones she'd told to herself, and people close to her. That everything was... Fine. Okay. Work was busy. They were both just busy. And he was off last week but she was speaking in Kentucky and didn't they see him on TV, he'd gone back to USC to watch a college home game. And the team played in New York this week.

What else could she do, call him? What would she say? Shame had her disconnected. She was the only one to blame and she deserved his anger and the break up. What she'd done was unforgivable. She was the definition of a hypocrite; saying one thing with passionate zeal and then doing the other, in secret, where no one could see, even John.

And she wondered if it all didn't come down to her pride. Not wanting to be the rookie, green, unexperienced. Being in control when John couldn't be and yes, manipulating him. Or maybe it was fear, being terrified that he was hurt, and she could lose him, or that Elise was still around with so much more to offer. Fear had been the tipping point. Because it couldn't be love. Love didn't do that to someone.

Yes, he had a right to send her out of his home. To break up. To never want to see her again. And she was lost again. Displaced, though she hadn't physically moved. She feared she would. She was preparing to run. It was the pattern life had taught her after all. Starting over. Moving on. Her mind was making plans. The exit strategy taking form and shape. There were job offers and options. She thought she was settled. After she'd finally made it, become who she'd always wanted to be, but Dr. Stephanie Hightower still didn't know who she really was at all.

I don't even know who you are anymore. His words rang through her soul and intensified the shame and caused a nervous energy that had her tense body twitching and unsettled with fear. She was as lost as she'd ever been since the day her mother died.

She looked at the clock. It was time. She slipped the shaded note pad page into the front of her Bible and carried it to the television, turned it on and tuned in to the game, then took a seat. She was holding tight to her Bible. The cover cracked, the binding stretched over time so that it gapped a bit. Like loose clothes on a lean body, the book was comfortable worn. It was all she carried out of the past, what she held onto to navigate her future and what she clung to now in the heartache.

She tunneled her index fingers in the gaps between the binding and the leather spine and tap, tap, tapped on the sewn and glued volume of pages, holding on to the Bible every time John got the ball. He was almost through the first quarter; so far so good after being off the field for two games and then the bye week last week giving him more time to rest.

Her first sight of him back in uniform had her emotions rushing up to the surface. He was back. Healed. And she was here. Heartbroken. They were broken up. Over. Yet strangely back in their places. He the famous superstar, her the lonely outsider. All she could do was rock, hold her Bible and watch him play.

There was a long pass and the camera followed the ball, the commentators calling it a post. Then a touchdown. But she didn't care what was happening in the end zone. Just wanted to see what happened to John at the line of scrimmage. In a moment he was back in view, celebrating with teammates. Happy. Whole. Back to being who he was without her.

King me.

She released her breath. Watched the extra point go through. The quarter ended, and Dallas was up on the New York team by four. She squeezed the Bible, held it to her chest as her body twitched with the tension and her mind began to combat the heartache with rational defenses. It was never going to work between them anyway. Elise was right. She wasn't part of his world. Was rookie green, inexperienced, a loner and an outsider who rarely knew how to deal with people or a social scene.

Pat Summerall was talking about St. Jude's. They were showing children being treated there and a black-tie fund raiser from the weekend. And he was talking about John's growing charity work for foster kids. How he'd made sure all the Dallas kids had new school clothes.

She was crying. Because he had really cared about her. Wanted to help those kids and hadn't even told her until she mentioned it. Then he just gave her a curious kind of humble smile and said she'd inspired him to do something that could really make a difference in a person's life. He was such a good guy. A good man. Giving to those kids because he knew how much they needed it. And what had she done but ungratefully taken.

She had raped him.

She stood up because the truth was still so startling it shook her soul. The twitching energy the kind that couldn't be contained so she paced. Her thoughts condemning, her sin so dark with pride and twisted up with fear it couldn't be overcome when she remembered what she'd really done. There in the dark. How selfish she'd been. How seductively controlling. It was unforgivable. And if she dwelt there, in the dark pit of it; the sin was a damnable soul destruction.

She forced her mind away and headed for the kitchen, thinking she'd try some hot tea or just dry toast. She felt sick with the constant self-hatred. Then she heard his name from the television again and turned to see.

John in a photograph with six other people at the black-tie gala they were calling 'the Friends of St. Jude's'. The woman next to him was Elise Kristopher.

I told you so was there in her confident poise and over bright smile as she clung to John with a hand on his arm.

Stephanie slowly walked toward the TV as it showed a live shot of the supermodel now at the football game. She was wearing John's Dallas jersey. Smiling and pointing at another woman, sitting next to her in the New York owner's suite, wearing the New York quarterback's number 5 as they pretended to banter about which quarterback was better.

Stephanie hurled the Bible into the TV.

There was no crash. Just a thud. And a flutter of pages. And another new sound. It came out of her soul like a war cry as she rushed the television and shoved it off the cabinet to the floor.

Now there was a crash.

Then, she just took a breath staring at the mess. There should be ugly tears that rage a face with snot. And emotional spit that dripped from your chin. Instead, there was a hollow hardness of condemnation.

You took advantage of him. Disrespected John.

And now you throw the Bible.

You dishonor God.

She knelt.

God. I'm so sorry. Help me.

The Bible was open wide and askew. Its cover had taken the most abuse. The pages were shifted high at an awkward angle. She carefully tried to adjust them all back into place, held the leather cover and shimmied it a bit to line it back up. Then held it by the spine and let gravity hang the pages in place as she gave it a little shake. That's when the first photo fell from its hiding place.

It was a square, with scalloped edges. Her mother's handwriting had scripted out,

Sam and Maria
September 1967
16:13

She turned it over and there in the faded Kodachrome image was her mother, Maria and a man in an army uniform. They were in a nightclub, with drinks on the table. The man behind her beautiful mother both handsome and so obviously up to no good with that smile on his face and his hand planted there. Fingers fit into ribs around her mother's slender side. The cut of the short 60's style empire waist dress only exaggerated the fullness of her breasts and the length of her legs. *Sam. July 1967* at military time of 4:13 p.m. Stephanie had been three years old. Didn't remember a man named Sam.

Curious, she further pried the gaping slit of cardstock cover from the lip of leather and another photograph fell out from between the layers of the Bible's back cover. This one was a smaller black and white of a couple. The woman was her grandmother with the man in the white of a sailor's uniform. The back read,

Gloria and Mario

December 1942

1:42

The year before her mother was born, during World War II where her grandfather had died in the Pacific. Taken at 1:42 p.m.

She slipped her finger between the layers of the cover and found one more picture. The last photograph was the same size as the first one. She read,

Stephen and Maria

July 1963

144:2

Stephanie flipped it over. The color was dull, but the man had the same green eyes as his army uniform. She studied Stephen. Her father. Looked at every detail. His dark hair was military short, but it had a certain wave to it, maybe he had the same curly wavy hair. And his face was handsome, his expression a shy joy from a serious stance. He looked proud, standing the way he did. Tall with shoulders back, militant, like there was an honor to wearing the uniform. And her mother was held close, tucked within his arm, like John often held her. And the poise spoke, 'this girl is mine, the one I'll give me life to, the one I honor to hold here.' And Stephanie knew now, the embrace was protective, possessive even, but also secretly powerful. Because only the woman held like that knew how much at times the man needed her.

Stephen Hightower had loved her mother. She wiped away the tears. Looking again at his eyes, his hair, his face before she held the little photo to her heart.

She'd never seen a picture of him. They'd been lost during a move; her mother had told her. Before he'd died in Vietnam.

Why were these photos hidden? Here, in the Bible? Why was the time written on them? And did her mother or grandmother mistakenly put the colon in the wrong spot on 144:2 or did it mean something else. Some code. She rose and went to her desk. The troubling questions brewing her thoughts away from her heartache and self-hatred. She flipped through the three photos, and then laid them down.

Mario.

Stephen.

Sam.

Then she added one more. Removing her favorite picture from its frame, she cut the photograph down to the size that matched her parents. On the back she carefully wrote.

John and Stephanie.

The time and date were stamped in the corner she'd cut off and she added them to the back.

May 1991. 1:03.

And she tucked the four photographs into their hiding place and closed the Bible.

She looked at the clock, noted the time. This was the moment she knew in her heart John was done. She felt the shift from shock and denial through that bout of anger when she'd knocked the television over. More anger would come, more temper and heat and exhaustive fury at herself, John and God. And then the self-preservation rationalizations as the pain grew ripe, to head off a complete breakdown. She would begin to engage a plan of action to rise out of the depression and move on with the reality of this new life. She understood the stages of grief all too well, but it didn't stop her from picking up the phone and putting those bargaining exit plans into motion.

After what she did, John had every right to hold it against her. He'd moved on and God help her, so should she.

"John Dake." She curled her hand onto his arm.

"Mrs. Lexington, how are you?" He had the nerve to smile.

And Blair had to hold back from taking the man by the ear and demanding answers. Layne had warned her off. In fact, he might have told her to stay away from him and give them some time to work it out, but she just couldn't help herself. Her sister wasn't talking, hadn't said a thing in four weeks other than that she was really busy at work. Was avoiding their mom for lunch the past three Wednesdays when she hadn't missed since they began the tradition. And Samantha said all Stephanie wanted to talk about was the speaking engagements she had scheduled and her consulting work in genetics and how busy she was right now. They were lucky if they could even get her to answer the phone. But John was in Blair's cross hairs and she would get to the bottom of this because something was very off.

"I'm surprised you recognized me dressed like a football player," he joked about his Halloween costume being a team jersey. "Trick or treat?"

She looked over the little spectacles of her Mother Goose costume as he reached into her pumpkin of treats. "It's little books. Most of the kid's here at Cook's Children's Hospital can't have candy."

He nodded. "That's why the team brought toy footballs. How's the baby?"

She patted her belly. "Four more weeks. How's Stephanie."

He looked away with eyebrows up. Held up his hand as if he were answering someone's request.

No one was calling him, and she called his bluff. "DeShawn just stepped in." Her grip tightened. "I want to talk to you."

"There's nothing I can tell you, Blair. Talk to your sister."

She snorted. The sound pure outrage this time as her eyes narrowed. She knew they were heated now, a weird dark purple about as telling as John's ticking jaw. Her emotions were hardly in check and it took a strong self-control to rein in her tongue, but she cared nothing for that at the moment. "Is your brain back online after that little sack-fest the other week?"

"I played Sunday. We won. By ten."

She swept him. Toe to head. "Who cleared you to play?"

"Doc Lambert."

"Ah." She made a clucking sound. It was sarcastic. "Obviously he didn't see you last Friday."

"Friday?"

"Standing next to little miss supermodel at the St. Jude's benefit. That girl is some kind of eye candy poison. You just look at her and go brain dead."

He stopped her. "I wasn't with Elise."

She snorted. The sound just a cover up for a very bad word. "It sure looked that way on page six of the Post. And so did the sight of her at the game, wearing your jersey next to Phil's wife. I never thought you'd do something that low so the only thing that made sense is that your brain was still numb. Was it?"

"I can't control what Elise Kristopher wears or what she attends, Blair."

"After everything that woman said to Stephanie—"

"She's a liar."

"Oh? Elise got something right. Its October isn't it, and all you obviously care about is football. Good luck with that." And she walked away before she said anything else.

John watched her go and frowned, clenching his jaw to control the, 'hey, come back her and listen.'

She didn't know anything. Had no idea how low Stephanie could go. And neither had he. What Stephanie did, came out of nowhere. Like a blind side hit. And he might be cleared from the concussion, but it was going to take the rest of the season for him to be over what happened.

And who said Stephanie had even seen the picture from the St. Jude thing Blair was so upset about. He'd been ambushed in that shot; was talking to the New York quarterback when suddenly they'd been called on to poise. And there she was. He'd said maybe a single word to Elise. About as interested in her, or any woman, as he was in playing the Detroit defense again. Much less interested in doing something intentional to hurt Stephanie. He just didn't care right now. A coating of numb over the intense anger and hurt that had him withdrawn. Focused on the job. And winning. Working night and day, while pressured on all sides to win, after the team had taken two losses in a row with the backup while he was out.

He didn't care what Blair Lexington thought. He was here for the kids.

Neil Beihn's son was dressed like a pumpkin. He tickled him, and the baby laughed.

Cindy smiled. "Is Stephanie coming in this weekend for the game? I haven't heard from her."

"No." He kept his attention on the baby.

"You didn't scare her off, did you?" She had to chase after the little football Neil dropped.

"What do you mean?" he asked, helping.

"She was a mess during the San Diego game. Her little lip would just tremble when you got hit. Her whole body tight with tension. Kenny had to talk her down when you took that last hit. I seriously thought she was going to make a run for you. But Rhonda told me she lost her mother in a car wreck. And her dad in Vietnam. The fear of losing you too probably comes out when the game gets too violent. I'm sure it must be hard for her. It took me three years to get used to Neil playing ball and I still turn away at times. The game can be violent. Make sure you talk to her about it. And don't be surprised when she gets," she blushed a bit and looked at her son. "Well, if she needs to check you over to make sure you're really okay. She loves you, John."

Cindy's words were circling as he drove home and watched the smallest of the trick or treaters begin to hit the sidewalks with their parents. He had full size Snickers bars at his house. And the girls had their jerseys. Terry Bradshaw and Roger Staubach's numbers on their replica colors to wear tonight. Hattie had the night off to be with her family. But Kenny was here, dropping off the box of football cards so he didn't have to sign autographs.

"What's up?" he asked as John entered the kitchen and the dogs swept around him.

"Got the cards?"

"Think five hundred will cover you." Kenny grinned.

"Hope so." There was a chuckle as he went to the refrigerator for a drink. "I left the gate open, so they can get up the drive to the door. There are kids on the streets already."

"Last year it seemed they came in buses."

His head was still in the refrigerator when he asked, "Cindy said you had to talk Stephanie down at the San Diego game. That she was a mess?"

"Yeah. But you know how huge that hit was. It scared me too when you walked into the defense's huddle."

He looked at him now. "I need you to call her."

"Oh?"

"Spin that St. Jude photo with Elise. Clarify I wasn't there with her."

"Okay."

"Do it like you handle all the news guys. Business talk. Call now."

"Sure."

John took the phone, looked at the time and dialed the vet clinic. "Ask for Doctor Hightower." He handed him the phone. Held his gaze as they waited.

"Can I speak with Doctor Hightower?" *She's not there,* he mouthed.

Leave a message, he mouthed back.

"She's in California. And you're not sure when she'll be back." Kenny lifted a brow.

John gestured immediately for him to hang up. California meant Prince Faisal. That had his jaw clenching when he wasn't supposed to care at all. He turned away for ice, let it drop, drop, drop into the glass as his jaw clenched down, down, down.

"I saw you took her portrait down."

John just nodded. Drank. It seemed to haunt him, so he'd put it in her bedroom, facing the wall. Closed the door.

"Can I do anything?"

He shook his head, said, "I'll see you tomorrow," as the doorbell rang and he grabbed the box of cards as the girls began to bark. They sat on the front step together and handed out Snickers bars and his rookie card to the kids, shook hands with their fathers and smiled at their mothers as they honored him with their praise.

An hour later Dylan showed up. His step-father smiling as he took a seat beside him. "Your mom sent me with our overabundance of candy." He had sticks of Sweetarts. "Our neighborhood didn't open the gate and we've only had a few kids stop by," he explained. "Have you been busy?"

"Given away about half my stash."

They talked between groups of trick or treaters. Then Dylan said, "Oh, here comes one of my angels."

The little girl was three and ran right into his arms. "Grandpa!" She was dressed like a ladybug, her little pumpkin overflowing with candy.

"Who is this?"

"It's me." She smiled, lifting up her mask. "Jennifer." She looked into his candy bowl. "What do you have for me, grandpa?"

"Well, what do you say?"

"Trick or treats!"

He presented her with the Sweetarts stick.

"Hi, Uncle John. Trick or treats. Are these your dogs?" She laughed as they greeted her with kisses.

He got the girls to sit down so she could pet them then handed her two Snickers.

"Thank you," she told him then came closer. "Whatcha got there?" She pointed at the box of cards.

"Football cards. Do you want one?"

"Yes, please." But her hands were full, and she wasn't sure where to put it as he held it out.

He smiled and tucked it into her pumpkin. "There you go little ladybug."

"Thank you, Uncle John. Look Mom!" She held up her loot. "Big candy." She tried to get the long stick into the small mouth of her pumpkin with the two Snickers. "Momma, it won't fit."

"Daddy can hold it."

"But don't eat it," she warned sweetly.

"There's plenty more, Ladybug," Dylan told her.

"I can only take two. Momma says. And I'm not sleepy, Grandpa, but my pumpkin is full."

"It's past your bedtime," Sandy told her. "This is our last stop."

Jennifer sat beside John on the step. "We saw the new Grandma."

"Bee, remember?" Sandy asked her daughter.

"Bee loved my costume. Gave me a book with the candy. Hey! She had the same candy, Grandpa!"

"Did she?" he asked with astonishment as they saw another group of children making their way up the drive.

"Okay, little ladybug, let's go. Kiss and hug," Sandy told her and she kissed her Grandpa, hugging him tight. Then she hugged both the dogs then kissed and hugged John.

When it was just the two men again Dylan asked, "You're good with the kids, is that something you want?"

"In the future."

"Helen says, you and Stephanie are taking it slow."

John just nodded.

"And you think me and your mother rushed it."

It wasn't a question, so he remained quiet.

"We couldn't take it slow or we would have sinned. So, we did the right thing and got married before temptation overtook us. I wanted to honor your mother and she honored me, that left you out and I'm sorry."

"Oh? She told me she was having a very hot affair with a brunet with a spectacular body."

He chuckled. "She told me that story. We weren't having a hot affair... yet."

And that was a little too much information. "Your granddaughter was cute."

"We were trying to come up with a name for your mom. The kids were calling her the new grandma and it didn't settle with any of the women. I was teasing that she was the Newbie and then it changed to Bee and that stuck with everyone. So your mom is now Bee with the grandkids. I know this all takes some time to get used to," he said as another group arrived.

"Dylan Sullivan!" A dad was pointing at him as he walked up the drive. "That's Sully the Hall of Famer."

He stood to greet him. "Hello, how are you?"

The man just began to tell his two sons all about Sully's career.

"Dad," one of them said, "That's John Dake."

The man looked at him now. "Well, trick or treat!"

When it was dark, and a group of young teenagers made their way out his gate and Sully left, John sat alone. He didn't like being alone until just recently. Now he didn't want anyone too close.

He felt... betrayed, was the only way to describe it. Cheated. After he'd worked so hard to do this right. And tricked. When he'd wanted to honor her, he'd been dishonored. He was like Jacob, waking up in the honeymoon tent with Leah instead of Rachel.

Hmph.

Wasn't he more like Solomon? Raised up to be a king. Finding her working in the vineyard, pretending to be normal as he wrote about love in the Song of Songs. Maybe the vineyard girl tricked Solomon too somehow when she got to the palace. And maybe the reason we never heard about her again was because brokenhearted Solomon moved her into the harem and forced himself to forget her. Just went on back to his life and wrote Ecclesiastes, it's all really vanity and all that 'heavy is the head that wears the crown stuff.' King. Me.

Hmph.

Maybe he was Jacob... deserved the Leah trick. After Elise... and the 99 before her. No, he was definitely feeling like Solomon... the over indulged prince. Thinking you found normal, your 'it' girl, but it wasn't normal after all, just chasing after the wind. King. Me.

Hmph.

The anger had sizzled down to a simmer and left him feeling confused and even defeated, and he hated that feeling. That feeling made him get focused, and focused John was a winner. And winning was what mattered most. And that truth was selfish and made him see there was more than he understood under all this.

He didn't want to deal with Stephanie right now. She was right, she was too much to deal with, might cost him his edge or get in his head, or worse break his heart. And that had him back to being Solomon. With the Sovereign power to put her in the harem/female doghouse for a while—a divine timeout 'it' girl. I will deal with you later.

Gone to California, huh?

Well go. Go. On. Don't. Care.

Hmph. Liar. Shouldn't care. Should. Not. Care. That she never even called you. Hasn't begged your forgiveness. Not once. Never. Even. Called.

He looked at the moon and felt lonely tonight. Remembering, all the times they'd talked on the phone. How he could tell Stephanie things, like the TMI about his mother and Sully, or how cute the little kids were or how awkward their parent's praise could be or a stranger's concern. They really seemed concerned about his concussion. And she'd been afraid that night...

Hmph. The sound had Bradshaw back up close for a pet. As he stroked her John realized he'd never stopped to consider what Stephanie might have been going through that night when it all went down. He'd been consumed with himself.

"Hmph," he said again as that truth just settled on him and he realized he was right back to the root of things. He was selfish. Then to no one in particular he stated, "It is October. And all I care about is football. And why did you indulge me like a prince when you knew I'd end up so selfish? Hmph?" He stood up, wondering if that was a statement or a soul question as he gathered the leftover cards and candy. Then he told himself, "Good luck with that, Dake."

She was running fast. At a sprint now to get away. Stephanie made a phone call, just showed a little bit of interest and he wanted to hire her. The offer involved little veterinarian work and a lot of genetics. He wanted to utilize her breeding ideas and that required a move to California. She said she needed two weeks to consider the offer. Working for Prince Faisal would involve travel. He wanted to send her to Ireland first, then England, eventual to Dubai. She needed a passport. And to get her passport she needed a copy of her birth certificate.

Stephanie took two weeks off and drove down to El Paso. She learned she'd been born at the county hospital, not Fort Bliss as she assumed. Her mother would have had military benefits being married to an Army Lieutenant, but the legal document showed there was no marriage. Her father simply listed as Stephen Hightower and her mother as Marie Xavier.

She'd spent three days in El Paso trying to find his service records, but the veteran office had no death certificate from Vietnam, nor any record of him serving. A woman named Betty had told her flatly after studying the photograph of him, "I see a soldier with a pretty woman but that doesn't mean his name was Hightower or Stephen. If you could see his name tag in this photo you might have more to go on, but your mother is blocking that out."

"Why would my mother lie on a legal document?"

"Maybe she didn't know his name."

"They had to know each other, she was pregnant."

"And that problem is older than time. It might have been the 60's but being pregnant out of wedlock wasn't groovy. It labeled a single woman as loose and made life difficult in her community."

Her mother had moved, near Fort Hood in Killeen to raise her shortly after she was born. Four years later, Samantha was born there, but not at the military hospital or even in Bell County. She'd been born at the county hospital in Coryell County near Gatesville. There a woman named Tracy accepted the fifteen dollars for a notarized copy of Samantha's birth certificate. Stephanie took the document and read just one entry, her mother's name was still Marie Xavier not Hightower or Elroy. Then she placed it inside the manila folder full of research. She knew the drill now, what offices to visit, who to ask for and what documents she needed to see. There was no Sam Elroy ever enlisted at Fort Hood.

She got in her Jeep. Just sat there, holding the steering wheel. Her mother had lied. Stephanie's surname was a lie. There was no Stephen Hightower. No wedding licenses. No death certificate or service record anywhere with Stephen Hightower's name on it. Nor was there any evidence of a Sam Elroy. And she wasn't certain there was even a sailor named Mario Xavier who died in World War II either if she took the time to look back and find her grandfather. But she didn't have that time right now to start fact finding and deliberating on a generational curse.

After almost two weeks of acting like Nancy Drew she'd reached the same dead end. No one was alive to tell her what went on, but she was beginning to put the pieces together and understand how it could have happened. A single girl, and a soldier leaving for war, and that last desperate night together where you dismissed everything you believed. She thought of John, and that last desperate night together where she had dismissed everything she believed, gave in, took over, and controlled everything to suit her purposes.

She felt sick. Saliva pooling in her mouth. She needed to eat. Found a small café on Route 36. It was crowded but a booth had just come open in the corner. Nothing on the menu looked good. The smell of coffee just a little too strong like something was burnt. She was about to rise when the waitress finally showed up. She ordered soup and asked for crackers and hot tea.

Beside her three young women were talking over lunch. "It's not the flu, Mitzi." One whispered, holding a young toddler on her lap. She said to the other woman, "Mitz has been on a Saltine diet for over a week. Jolly Ranchers helped me through the first months. Kept the saliva down so it didn't build up. That's what triggers vomit. Sugar worked better for me, but Mitzi wants salt. The flu doesn't want anything. Believe me, you're pregnant."

The waitress was back with her food as those last two words rang out. She prepared her tea as the toddler slapped a white sack, with Eckerd's drugs printed on it in bold bright blue, off the table to the floor. Stephanie quickly leaned over, pushed the pregnancy test back into the sack as she picked it up. Then handed it to one of the girls who said, "Thanks," as she handed it to Mitzi.

Stephanie tasted her tea as Mitzi asked her friends in a whisper, "What am I going to do if this test is positive?"

"Join the club," the young mother told her. "You're not the first girl to get pregnant before a soldier ships off to Iraq." She told Mitzi, "The sooner you accept it the sooner you can make a plan and start taking better care of yourself. You can't keep a pregnancy a secret, it's going to show itself."

The other woman finally spoke. "I warned you not to give in to him. It happens, a lot right before they ship out. You kinda freak, ya' know? Want to hold on tight and just have that night in case they don't come back. But most of them come back. Report in married to some high school sweetheart, and then they move out of the barracks into married housing. Jeremy's daddy never looks twice at me."

The other woman assured her, "But we've got our soul sisters."

She watched the three girls walk towards the front and thought of Samantha and Blair. She should call them. They could talk about this. But what would she say? How could she tell anyone what she'd done? She was too ashamed. Getting sicker by the minute as she thought about it.

She paid the bill, made a quick stop at Eckerd's and went back to the hotel. The next morning, she took the pregnancy test, started sucking on a Jolly Rancher as she forced a multi-vitamin down.

Then she drove by the duplex in Copper's Cove where she grew up. It was a tiny place. On a little cul-de-sac, tucked away and hidden. The one home she remembered, where her single mom had done the best she could to raise them and protect them. And Stephanie had been loved and taught the Bible and prayed over and when the childhood life she knew was lost, she'd grieved... for home and a godly mother. There were some sins you could hide, and others revealed themselves to everyone.

Looking at the manila folder full of documents and facts that pointed out a sin her mother had hidden, Stephanie began to understand more about fear—fight and flight; and sometimes both. How things could just... happen and why a mother does what she does to protect her children.

She met with Linda that Wednesday and made the official apology to the family. She said she was sorry and the words meant more than just missing a few of their lunch dates. She told her she'd been given a great opportunity and had needed time to think about it alone. She acted excited as she announced that she'd accepted the job from Faisal and was already packed for California. It was easy to cut the ties. This was her dream job, she told them all. When they finally asked her about John Dake, she told them the truth, "We broke up." And the answer to why was a simple lie. "We wanted different things and we're both moving on."

29

Brad stood in the middle of the Dallas empty locker room with the team's head of publicity. Two of his men were at their side and three policemen stood in the open door softly discussing the logistics. The distant cheering of the fans amplified then lulled with the soundtrack of stadium music between the plays as the game clock ticked down. Dallas was ahead in the fourth quarter in this crucial conference game but that was the last thing on his mind. Brad looked at his watch for the hundredth time and held tight to his mobile phone as he repeated the same simple prayer. He also asked for wisdom, he was going with his gut here, trusting that God was directing him and kept his gaze on the door. No one said anything. There was nothing to say. They just waited for Brad's instructions to be quickly put into action.

Dylan Sullivan breeched the door first. The man knew his way around a locker room and he escorted Helen inside and beside her was John's best friend, Honey Cooper.

There was no, 'hello, how you doing, or what a great game' today. Helen just asked, "Brad, what's happened?"

"Stephanie." Her name was said softly before he swallowed and added, "She's been in a car accident. Outside of Tyler. She was headed to Amarillo on her way to California. They air lifted her to Parkland, it's a level 1 trauma center and her injuries are life threatening. Linda, Layne and Blair are already on their way. I'm flying down to Austin to get my youngest. We don't want Samantha by herself since her fiancé is in France."

"I can go to Austin." Honey Cooper stepped up and reminded him, "Samantha and I met in Florida, Mr. Bennett. We became friends, still communicate. I'll get her here, so you can get to the hospital and be with your family."

He blinked, then went where he felt God was directing him as he told one of the men, "Get Mr. Cooper to the jet at Addison Airport."

"What can we do?" Dylan asked sincerely.

"I'm not sure how John will take this, but I told the coaching staff the situation. I thought it best if you were here to tell him what happened when he gets off the field. After that it's up to John."

"I'm going to get him now," Dylan stated.

"Now?" Helen asked. "But the games not over yet."

"Now," Dylan answered and jogged out.

They'd failed to convert but the field goal was good. They were up by ten now. With four minutes to go. John resettled his ball cap and watched special teams take the field for another kick off as he held his helmet. The defense would get a stop. He'd be back on the field with plenty of time... "Sully?!"

"Great game, John."

"Thanks, but we still have four minutes left."

His stepfather had a hand on him now, turned him away from the field as he said quietly, "There's been a car accident. Stephanie was careflighted to Parkland. It's life threatening." John glanced at his coach. "The staff has been told, but it's up to you. What you do."

"I have to go." He was jogging. Fast. And Dylan Sullivan, bad knees and all, was keeping up. And Dylan knew how to shed shoulder pads and cut through tape when they got in the locker room. When John reached for his clothes, Sully directed him to shower.

"Get it now. Quick." And he didn't argue. He'd seen the look of emotion in his mother's eyes, she was unusually quiet. Her husband doing all the talking. Telling him the little they knew. Where Honey had gone, and that Brad had left for the hospital to meet Linda, Layne and Blair.

He was in and out with a quick rinse. Dressed in a hurry, throwing his jacket on over an unbuttoned shirt as he grabbed his bag.

"This way," a man from the team led them out and he noticed security was holding a small group of reporters back as he exited the locker room.

"John! Hey, Dake! Where are you going? The game's still on and Washington is coming back... Dake, we need you! John!"

He didn't answer. His mind was a blank. Everything was running together but somehow also clearing up. He couldn't separate the sound of his name from the pounding of his heart, but he knew exactly how he felt, he loved her. And the love of his life was being threatened.

Regret roared and pummeled that numbing frozen block of ice around his heart with brutal strikes. She's been hurt and she's alone. Somehow you're to blame for this. You selfish, football focused fool, you could lose. Big. Lose everything.

Silently, he let strangers lead him, following Dylan, trusting him as a sea of police and security guards surrounded them. Their honor guard walked them out into the corridor that led to the parking lot. An officer opened the door and John followed his mother into the back of an Irving city police car.

"Let's go," Dylan directed the officer from the front seat. Sirens blared, and the car sped away with a second car following. "Helen you need to get someone from JDi on the phone. Get them up to the hospital so I can talk to them, that way John can just talk to me. I'll take care of things. Intercede with her family and your people. Okay?"

He nodded.

"We're not going to let this become a press circus."

Helen agreed, "Absolutely not."

"And if you want to see her, I'll ask Brad to allow it."

"Allow it?" John blinked, realizing as he said the words.

"The hospital won't tell you anything or allow you in the ICU. You're not family."

"And we broke up," he finally told them. "While you were gone. Her family might not allow me anywhere near her now."

"Brad wanted you to know what happened, John," his mother reminded him. "He made sure we were here for you and Dylan knew what to do. He didn't wait to tell you."

"I figured I'd want to know if the girl I loved was in a serious accident, so I could make the decision myself, so I came to tell you."

"Thanks, Sully." Then he told them. "I do love her. I thought we could work it out later, after some time had passed. In the spring. I was selfish."

"God's got this, John."

He nodded as they tried to encourage him, looking out the window, he just nodded hearing only, God's got this. John realized he did not. In fact, he couldn't control anything. If he'd be allowed in the ICU or anywhere near her. He needed to tell her, he loved her, and he was sorry. That he forgave her and...*God, please forgive me.*

He looked at the window. It was raining. Long tears falling down the dark pane of glass as he looked at the reflection of his face.

The lobby area of Parkland was crowded and as they walked in people noticed him.

"Mr. Dake! Do you have another concussion? Is that why you left the game early?"

"Just keep walking," Dylan told him. The police were still flanking them, one of the officers leading the way. And John felt the nerves hit him, as he saw the group of her family ahead, huddled together tightly and he was now an outsider. Would they tell him anything? Not let him see her or make him leave. And what if it was bad news. Horrible news already that someone was about to tell him.

He took hold of his mother. Her hand was cold, but Dylan's was warm on his back. And his voice was steady as they stopped, and he asked Brad Bennett, "How is she?"

"John." It was Linda who spoke first. Just his name with a smile that welcomed him then Blair was in his arms. Her pregnant belly between them but she hugged him tight and thanked him for coming as Layne reached out and shook his hand.

"How is she?" he asked Layne now.

He looked worried, holding his wife close but he answered, "She's still in surgery. Care Flite got her here and into surgery before we arrived."

"She had what they called, 'a hot abdomen.' She was bleeding internally and they're telling us it's..." She was shaking her head.

"Life threatening," Layne finished quietly. "That's what they told Brad when they called with the news at the game in the third quarter. Thank God, Stephanie had your cell phone in the car and the first number the DPS officer called got them connected to Hattie. She gave them Brad's number and they called us at the game."

"How did it happen?"

"We don't know the details yet and the doctors haven't been out to give us any updates."

"Let's sit down," Brad told the group and everyone found a place.

John looked around the surgical waiting area decorated in warm colors of yellow and brown and took a seat where he could see the door. A sit com was on a television and a single phone hung on the wall. There was a narrow window and he noticed that it was still raining as he stared out on the parking lot. There was small talk about Blair's pregnancy, then she asked about the game. Had they won? He didn't know. They thought they did. He didn't want to talk about football and asked if they'd heard from Samantha. Brad's mobile phone rang, and he was up, walking off. All John could do was watch him. Wait to hear the news as he watched the door.

A pattern began. Brief conversations interrupted by phone calls. There would be silence as Brad walked away to talk and then he would come back and make a brief statement.

Dr. Lambert had come, and he was going back to the Operating Room.

A Sheriff called from the accident site. A truck had hit her Jeep, it had rolled and one of the horses was dead. The other had been taken to an emergency Vet Clinic in Longview. The officer also had some of Stephanie's things at the county office.

Word came that Samantha had landed.

Then Brad announced someone from JDi was here and Dylan went out to the main lobby to update them.

Then Samantha and Honey arrived, and everyone stood as she was embraced by her family. She looked at him and they both just nodded. The awkward silence broken by Honey as he asked what would become *the* question, "How is she doing?"

There wasn't much in the way of answers yet, but what they knew was repeated. Then Samantha added more information. "She was going to stop in Dallas." She was looking at her parents, then she glanced at him. "And drop something off at John's house. I talked to her before she left for just a minute. She wanted to get on the road. Knew there was rain ahead. The last thing I said was, 'please stop being so stubborn.'" Her voice caught a bit, just hitched up before it fell silent. She looked down as she told them. "She was going to sleep in the horse trailer in Amarillo at a rest stop. Do you know which horse was killed?"

"No. I'm waiting on the Sheriff to call back with more details." Brad had taken hold of her hand. "Is Richard coming?"

"I left a message. It's the middle of the night in the middle of Africa."

Brad gave her a hug and then Linda joined them. It started a chain reaction and she went around the circle until John held her close.

"I'm glad you're here," she whispered.

He just held on, tighter and wanted to say so much but all that came out was a name. "Richard?

"He's at one of the orphanages his foundation supports. Dad made sure I wasn't alone. Sent Honey to bring me here. He was at the game, he said."

He was nodding, as she stepped back and glanced at Honey. And Blair was there to take her hand as Samantha stated, "She said she needed to return some things of yours. Had you talked to her?"

"She said you broke up." Blair made the statement. like a question.

"That's not important today." It was Brad that answered.

John knew he had less than a heartbeat to say something, but the words were just stuck in his heart, squeezed by the ache there. And Dylan stepped in again and said, "We're all here because we love Stephanie." John nodded, looking at the window and seeing the long trails of rain crying down the glass.

It was two more hours before the surgeon came out. He was flanked by a man in a suit that was introduced as Dave Evans, one of the hospitals administers, and beside them was Dr. Lambert from the team.

"She's in recovery," Dave told the group.

And as the surgeon requested to speak to the Bennett family, Doc Lambert said, "Come over here for a minute John and let's talk while Dave and Dr. Werner speak with her family."

He led him into a private corridor as John asked, "How is she?"

His face was serious as he began to speak. "Stephanie's had a severe abdominal trauma. She's a little thing. Just a drip of water and when a person doesn't have a lot of meat on them, their organs don't have as much protection. The car must have rolled because she was bruised up pretty good in her insides. She had a ruptured spleen and there was a lot of internal bleeding.

"Thankfully, there were no spinal injuries and no swelling around the brain. Dr. Warner says her nervous system looks good. She had a compound fracture of her right arm and it was broken in three places. An orthopedic took care of that. She had a bad laceration on her forehead. There were several minor cuts, bumps and bruises. She'll look pretty banged up by the time you see her. But the serious stuff is on the inside. Her body has undergone a tremendous trauma and she's going to be in a lot of pain."

He reached out and gripped John's shoulder and immediately John knew that wasn't the end of it. He was preparing him for bad news. "Now, when a body goes through a trauma like Stephanie's just has, well, it takes everything that body has, to fight for itself. It's like this, the brain sends out a survival signal—that the most important thing to that brain is saving the person it's responsible for and it cuts off everything else that isn't life supporting. It's like an athlete, when you perform at a high physical level, all the blood goes to the major muscle groups, heart, lungs, and the brain. Things like the stomach get cut off. Now we don't know whether it was the accident itself or the trauma afterwards. But she lost the baby, John."

His mouth just opened as his heart paused. His mind trying to make something of the words he'd just heard but his eyes blinked from the sting and his heart already understood as it grieved. She was pregnant.

Was. Pregnant.

"I'm so sorry, John. By her injuries she did everything she could to protect it. Her body fought a tough fight not to let go of that little baby. The doctors said it was touch and go for a while just to keep Stephanie alive. Everyone in there was pulling for her and the baby. They did all they could. But her body had just had enough. And they both couldn't survive the trauma.

"I know she was just weeks along, but it's still a loss just the same. It's never easy to lose a baby. But if it makes it any easier, you and Stephanie can have lots of children. An Ob-Gyn was in the surgery. I talked to her. She says all is fine. The main thing is, Stephanie is alive."

John nodded his head.

"She's going to need you. Prayers and positive thoughts. Lots of laughter and encouragement. Now I know you can do that, right?"

John nodded again.

"Okay." He patted John's arm. "She should be in recovery in a little bit. They plan to keep her sedated for the pain control in intensive care until she's stable. I won't lie to you. These next twenty-four hours will be crucial for her, fifty-fifty. But she's got a good chance. I know a fighter when I see one. I'll try to sneak you into recovery for a minute or two."

John's voice was hoarse. "Please. I need her to know I'm here."

"Thank you, doctor," Brad said again as they shook hands and walked several steps away from the family.

"They'll call for you when they have her in recovery. You can see her there for a moment then visit in pairs when she gets moved into ICU."

"We appreciate all you've done so far."

Dr. Werner nodded then he glanced past him to the family as he lowered his voice. "One more thing. She lost the baby. The trauma, it was just too much to sustain the pregnancy. In this early stage, I believe her hormones had gestation at about seven weeks, the fetus wasn't viable. I'm sorry."

Brad realized emotion had finally shown itself, his eyes full of tears, his mind putting things together and his words could only be expressed in a simple nod of thanks as the doctor walked away.

He kept his back to them, prayers unceasing as he worked with his Lord to handle this one moment at a time. He needed to lead, with faith and show the hope he confessed...

"Bradley?"

She was pregnant. They were the words he whispered as his wife came to his side, then stepped into his arms. "She was pregnant."

"That explains everything." She whispered, holding him tighter as she just gave a great exhale of enlightened understanding.

But for Brad there was anger. "He broke his promise to me, Linda."

"Or he kept it." Now she took his arm, made him walk with her. "Maybe that's what this break up was about. John trying to keep his promise, honor and protect her and Stephanie was making that hard. She loved him, Brad."

He nodded and reached for her and she came into his arms again, held on tight. "I love her," he told his wife in three gasps, then three more. "We love her."

"Yes," she whispered the words. "And we need to remember what love is, how it shows itself, how it honors God. We love her."

"Yes," he agreed. "She was seven weeks along, the doctor said," Brad was thinking out loud now, counting back games and weeks. "That was back—when he got hurt against San Diego."

"And she stayed that night. Didn't go to Blair's. That week I knew something was off, tried to get her to talk about it. Then she avoided me for weeks, running to try to stay ahead of us. She still doesn't trust us."

He heard the break in her voice, the piercing pain that deflated his anger and need to blame John. His time spent in ongoing prayer brought revelation once again. "Linda, she was hiding not running. Hiding because of sin. Sin brings shame. It makes us hide and cover up and blame and lie and run. Sin had her running, but God's furious love stopped her. That pursuing love with its grace and forgiveness," he brought her in close again. "Will heal her and restore the fellowship." As he held his wife close he said, "Father, forgive us. We've failed you too. Many times. And this is a hard place to show you honor but we offer ourselves to Your will. Let us honor you and you've promised to honor us in return. Help us here. Give us faith, hope and love. And heal our daughter. Sustain her life for your glory and welcome her child into your kingdom that we may share eternity together. Amen."

30

There was artificial light that came from behind a wall of stain glass making the room sparkle with colors that seemed to dance far too merrily with life on a rainy evening. He didn't really know how he had found it, but John sat in the small hospital chapel on the second row, alone. He felt compelled to pray, as if her life depended on his constant pleading. But his heart was in his throat, aching there and the prayer was anemic of words as the pain seemed to grow deep in his soul. All he could process was his guilt as he considered the facts— that while he'd been completely absorbed in a football game a truck had hit her Jeep while she was on the way to California, flipped it, killed a horse and they had lost a baby he didn't even know existed. And she had a fifty-fifty chance of surviving the night. Odds so great, coming down to a flip of a coin—heads you win, tails you lose.

Like in an overtime game, when you lost the coin flip and the defense took the field and you were helpless to do anything but wait it out, hope the D could hold off the score so you could get a chance with the ball before the game was over.

Was this game over, God?

There was only silence. He was blind to the game on the field inside her body. He could only see the clock. The tick of his watch that told him she'd survived another second, minute, hour.

Had she heard him? Had he said enough in recovery if they were the last words he could tell her?

He ran the fingers of both hands through his hair and held the back of his neck as he bent over and closed his eyes. She looked so foreign, so pale lying in recovery. Tubes going in and coming out everywhere of her unconscious swollen body, and she was hooked up to half a dozen machines that were monitoring her vitals with an assortment of beeps and colored lines that made her look a bit alien. He was almost afraid to touch her, but he did. He held her hand carefully and leaned close to whisper softly into her ear.

"I'm here, Stephanie, praying for you. I love you, Beauty."

Had she heard him? And should he have said more? Ask for forgiveness? Told her he forgave her? Said he was sorry, so sorry.

God- He just said his name. Let the moan come up from his soul to speak what words could not. He was no longer angry with her, or even emotionally numb. He sat here terrified in the darkest valley of his life as he realized how much he could lose if they lost this fight.

"John." He felt a hand squeeze his shoulder and jolted up.

"Is Stephanie okay?" He questioned as he saw Honey Cooper.

"No changes." He placed his hand on John's back reassuring him as he led him to sit back down in the pew. "Are you okay?"

"Did they tell you? She was pregnant." He got to the point before the heartache strangled the words. "I got that concussion and... we gave in. Maybe she was afraid because I was hurt, or I was unruly or demanding. I don't remember any of it. I woke up and there she was... and I was furious, Honey. Said... things, I can't take back. Broke up with her and just went cold. And played ball. Thinking I'd deal with it post-season. And ... You were right. I should have married her, when the temptation got to be too much. I should have protected her and married her. I was selfish. Thought we needed a season. That she needed a season, to be sure. But it was really about me. I'm always so selfish."

"John, you're being tough on yourself, brother. You love her, and love covers a multitude of sins. Hers and yours. You'll make it through this together."

"I could lose her tonight. Flip of a coin. Fifty-fifty the doctors are saying." Tears came now as he said it out loud. "I can't do anything to help her, even pray."

"I will. *Lord Almighty...*" Honey's words flooded over him as he took John's hand. He just nodded in agreement to the healing and forgiveness, the grace and mercy that he requested. Tears dripping now. Beating the floor like the rain outside beat the windows.

"Thanks." John squeezed his hand not knowing if the word was loud enough to hear.

"John, when we're over whelmed with life we need to be overcome by Christ. He's right here. Praying for you too. Interceding for His Father's will to be done. In her. In you and through you and others. I'm here for you. I won't stop praying and others are praying too. Take faith in that."

Then he sat with him quietly until John spoke again. "I was never going to tell anyone what happened. I wanted to protect her. I promised Brad I'd honor her. I'll need to talk to him now with the baby, but what do I say?"

"I'm sorry still protects and honors her."

"Mr. Bennett." John stopped beside him as Honey walked on to sit with Samantha. He looked Brad in the eyes as he said sincerely, "I'm sorry."

The words were barely out, and Brad embraced him, held on tight. Then he said, "We want you to go in first, with Samantha. She's been moved to ICU now and they'll let us visit in pairs."

A nurse led the way into the ICU the first-time John was allowed to go back with Samantha. Patients recovered in small individual cells with glass walls. Twelve of these cells stood together to form the intensive care unit. In the small cubical, one chair sat in a corner and another at the side of the bed. Complex machines and graphs surrounded her. A large tube was fed into her mouth, a catheter was taped to her neck, her left wrist was laced with an IV line and another catheter and tubes fell from her abdomen draining fluids.

Her face was swollen and bloated. Her skin had a glistening sheen to it and it looked as if there was a layer of fluid beneath the top stratum of her skin. A greenish bruise covered her left cheek like a rash and a stark white bandage was taped to her forehead and a cast with metal pins protruding was on her right arm.

John sat down in the chair at the left-hand side of her bed and pulled Samantha down into his lap protectively. Neither said a word as they sat there in silence and slowly became accustom to this new sedated Stephanie.

John softly stroked the top of her fingers. Her flesh felt cold and unusual. He gently took her hand and wrapped it in his warm hand then took Samantha's hand and placed it on top of Stephanie's.

"We're here for you, Stephanie," Samantha said in a hoarse whisper. John watched the numbers and lights of the machines at work as they silently kept watch that first hour. Blair and Layne came the next hour, then Linda and Brad before Samantha and John went in for the second time. And between their visits the nurses came and went setting the cycles. The sun was beginning to brighten the room when the new nurse arrived to introduce herself. It was their cue to leave so she could work. John leaned close to Stephanie and brushed a kiss near her ear as he told her again, "I won't leave you. I'm staying right here until you wake up. I love you, Beauty."

John returned to the section of the seats he'd chosen for his own. The ICU waiting area was filling with people this morning. Families of the sick finding sections to congregate in as they waited and kept watch. They noticed him as he walked through. He saw the recognition and the respect. He might be famous, but they were all on common ground here. Suffering a great equalizer. All sharing a measure of fear at the unknown the future would bring to anyone within the small sequester cells of this ward. The worry followed him like a shadow he couldn't shake and just when the anxiety was about to overwhelm him, Dylan or Honey would sit beside him. They didn't have to say anything. They were just here with him. Praying and occasionally saying something that helped him get through the next moment or hour.

"She made it through the night." Dylan handed him a cup of black coffee. "Let's celebrate that."

Samantha popped the top on her soda and Honey taunted, "Who drinks cold soda in the morning?"

John stood up and paced to get away from the conversation as he threw away his empty coffee cup. His body was stiff. Muscles reminding him, it was time for rehab and treatment, nutrients and calories. He had a habit of being grumpy on Monday mornings. People interpreted it as focus, but it was a cover up really. He hurt on Mondays. And he'd been indulged. By his mother, team JDi, teammates and trainers.

Stephanie had always let him be honest. From the shoulder surgery and into the season, he'd just told her the truth. Admitted he hurt, was grumpy, weak or selfish. She'd always listened and encouraged him to be more other-focused than self-focused. He'd begun to change. He suddenly remembered her arguing during the quarterback cover up that she was the big deal, not him. She'd said she wasn't the normal one because her foster-care childhood made it hard to trust and too easy to be independent and self-reliant and fearful. She'd changed too. Until the concussion, when they'd both jumped back into their old habits.

God, you can't mean this, to take her away, after all the transformation you've accomplished in us through each other...

He watched a young mother pace with her baby and felt guilt not loss, anger not sadness as he saw the child. They'd lost their child. Their first...unborn. His jaw was clenched making the blood throb there in an angry tick until he gasped and pleaded with God.

We were wrong but please, don't punish her for it. She's honored you, her whole life, through so much. Please don't take her now when we are so incomplete. You can't take her from me...

He rubbed his forehead, there was a tension in his soul and his head. His heart a battlefield of selfishness versus sovereignty. And the coffee was kicking it all up a notch. His emotions were building up like a storm suddenly in this push and pull spiritual battle of needing God to fix it and being suddenly furious with what He was allowing.

"Hey, John—"

He interrupted Dylan's soft compassion as the words erupted to the surface. "She didn't deserve this, Sully." There was anger. Rude and loud like a fool.

And a hand was on his arm and they were walking as words just spewed out of him and people turned to look.

"There's a room full of people and all eyes are on you, John."

He cursed them all with a wave of his hand.

"Hey!" Sully manhandled him farther down the hall. "I'll walk you right out of here if you can't control yourself and start dishonoring your good name."

"Really?"

"I've taken down the best. Staubach. Bradshaw."

"They're dogs."

"Not in my day." He reminded him. "In your anger don't sin."

"You sound like Stephanie. Quoting Scripture. She never indulged me."

"No, your mother handled that duty."

"Did she send you?"

"I told her to stay put. She listens to me since we're newlyweds."

"So, you want to play dad here, Mr. Linebacker."

"Love to. Dads know when to step in and protect. I'm protecting you from yourself, John. This is overwhelming. And I know, because I've been here. Add to it that you're tired, your body is tight, and it probably hurts because it's Monday. Right?"

"You might have been here but I'm not sure you know how sore a quarterback gets. You played defense."

"I've been here because my first wife died of aggressive brain cancer," he just replied. "For the first time in my life I couldn't fix something with strength or smarts, my competitive edge or even prayers. I was angry. Sound familiar to you now?"

"Sorry, Sully." John wiped at his face. "I'm in a mood obviously. Vacillating between pleading with God and being furious with Him."

"And it's understandable but you need to work through it. After the doctors do their rounds and give us an update, I'll get you over for some treatment. You can check in with the coaches, get the game plan and refuel. Get a workout in and release some of that anger then we'll come back over and see how she's doing. How does that sound?"

"No, I'm not leaving her."

"Your mother will stay here, and it will do you good."

"No."

"You're only going to get stiff, sore and surlier."

"No." He crossed his arms.

"And more belligerent if you don't work this anger out." Sully frowned.

"What's going on?" Helen stepped between them.

"We're discussing how you indulge me." John stepped beside his step-father.

"Really?" She looked at Dylan.

He advised, "With wisdom and love."

"I know charm when I see it, Dylan."

"He thinks he can take me, Mom. He also claims you do what he says by the way."

Her gaze moved from Dylan to John. "He's my husband. You're my child. You're not too old to do what I say."

He blew out a breath and confessed to them, "Look, Stephanie is still critical, and I can't leave. If anything happened and I wasn't here, I couldn't live with myself."

"Well, you need to eat. And there's got to be Physical Therapy at this hospital somewhere where Ryan can come do some treatment on you. We can find some ice, sit you in it and cool you off. You can't throw a temper tantrum in here, John Paul. And you're clearly angry."

"Hmph." He unclenched his molars, tried to relax his jaw.

"The world is watching how you handle this."

"Not today." He was right back to grinding his teeth.

"This is a public place."

"I don't care about my image." His whole face was throbbing now from the angry beat in his jaw.

"How about God's image?" His mother asked him. "You honor Him, and you honor her. It does matter how you respond. Even if the worst happens, it matters. *Honor me and I will honor you.* Remember that promise."

His body went tight and his eyes burned as he looked down. "I'm not sure I'm up to it right now, Mom."

Sully stepped in closer. "It is a high calling but to whom much has been given, much is expected. His Spirit will help you be up for it and His grace is sufficient for your every need, even your anger."

"And there's no VIP pass from suffering. Play through this," his mother also encouraged. "I know you can do it, John, if you let God help you."

"I can't leave until she's stable. I can't. She's been alone most of her life. I promised her in there I wouldn't leave her. And I have to be here, close, praying through this until she's okay." He looked up at them. "Everything else is going to be sidelined. Including the anger and the pride along with the game of football. I'm not leaving her."

"Okay, but you will eat. Eggs, oatmeal, toast. I'll see if they have some chocolate milk. And you're going to have to rest at some point." She gave him a nod. "I'll be back with breakfast for both of you." She swept Dylan. "I could hear your stomach growling from across the room."

"God love her," John looked at Sully and they both just laughed. It rang into the room and John stopped, frowned at the ICU audience following his every move now.

Dylan put a hand on his back and whispered discreetly, "Famous can often be inconvenient but it's part of the package deal."

"You're right about that. And most of the other stuff," he confessed to Dylan as they walked back to their seats in the waiting room.

"Not always right. If it was me, I wouldn't leave her either, but I played defense. I don't know about you offensive guys now—"

"It's so much easier to just hit somebody, isn't it?"

"And it takes a certain kind of man to stand tall and take it when the hits keep coming."

"Oh, I never just take it." He smiled. "Hunnicut on the other hand, he lives in the dirt."

"What was that?" Honey responded.

And the banter lifted his spirits as he smiled at Samantha and took a seat.

"Do you think she looked better?" Samantha asked as they walked out of the ICU toward the waiting area. "Blair thinks she looks better."

"Her color is better."

"Last night she was gray. I asked Cindy, but the nurses won't tell you anything. Just ask the question back to you—do you think she looks better? I want straight answers. There's already too many questions."

"The doctors will tell us more."

The group was standing when they came into the waiting room. Blair was wiping away tears and Samantha took her hand as Brad said, "We got an update on the details of her accident."

"What happened?"

"We might never know what led up to the initial accident. The rain caused slick roads and limited visibility. But when she was hit, the trailer jack knifed, and it caused the Jeep to roll."

Blair told them. "The mare is dead but High Hopes made it. And the DPS found the kitten, banged up pretty good but it was in a small carrier so it was protected. Thelma has it. She went to the DPS office. She also brought a box." She looked at John. "It has your name on it."

It sat in the seat next to him. A brown cardboard box. The flaps folded closed and untapped. His name written on top in her pretty handwriting. He couldn't open it. Just rested his arm on it and curled his fingers over the edge. Held on.

When the doctor came after his evening rounds John picked it up. Held it under his arm as they got the update. Still critical but holding her own. Organs functioning. Vitals consistent. They were cautiously optimistic but were going to keep her sedated another day.

It was good news and there was a sigh of relief. And plans were made. Brad told Layne to take Blair home. She was objecting, and Linda stepped in. "You have to rest. We want you to get a good night's sleep for the baby. You can come back in the morning."

"We're going too," Brad stated.

Linda just looked at Brad and he took her hand. "We all need to sleep and shower. Start to rotate shifts now that she's stabilized."

"I'll stay tonight," John immediately offered.

"With me," Samantha added taking his arm. "Cooper can get us some food, so no one needs to worry about bringing us dinner." And she began the hugs. With Blair first then Linda. It took a while before they all got on their way and then John and Samantha sat down alone as Honey went to find them food for dinner.

"What's in the box?" Samantha asked.

"I don't know."

"Will you look?"

"After dinner. Okay?"

She nodded. "Brad said the coaches sent you the playbook. You haven't looked at that either. Haven't even touched it."

"It doesn't matter right now."

"But it will on Sunday."

"I've got a backup."

"The team needs you to win. He lost two when you were out."

"I need to be here, and I told them that today."

"Stephanie said you wanted different things. What did you want?"

"It doesn't matter anymore."

"Maybe it does." She'd crossed her legs like an Indian up on the sofa and got comfortable as she settled in for a talk.

"Maybe you need to head over to Blair's and get some sleep too."

"Maybe you need to," she bantered back.

"I've got a house here."

"Who's feeding your dogs?"

"Hattie. Who's feeding Nick?"

"Richard has a Hattie in Austin. He's rich too." Now she smirked. "So, what did Stephanie want that you didn't like?"

"I'd have given your sister anything."

"Then something's not adding up." She looked at the box. "Show me what she was returning to you."

"Geez, you're a lot like your sister."

"We had the same mother." She smiled. "Different fathers that's why my hair is straight, and she got the green eyes and curls."

"Your mom must have been some lady."

"She was a great lady. Loved the Lord Jesus Christ and us." She nodded. "The box. Open it up."

"You've got a little Blair in you too, Sassy."

"What can I say, I'm the little sister." She patted the table in front of their chairs. "Put it here and open it."

He did. Holding the flaps closed for just a minute before he opened one, then the other and they looked inside.

"That's mom's Bible." She reached first. Grasping it as she asked, "Why would she give you this?"

"I don't know." He looked inside. "There's a file." He lifted out a manila folder. Her handwriting was on the cover in various places with phone numbers and addresses, names of cities and offices. The tab said, Mom/Me/Sammy.

"CDs. Kleenex. A bag of Jolly Rancher's, that's weird. And this is her purse," she pulled it out, unpacking the box. "And here's a mobile phone, and a..."

"Tiffany box," John finished. "The bracelet I gave her for her birthday."

"She never took that off."

"And the cross necklace that matched from when the season started."

"I'm sorry," Samantha said. "Put those in here." She opened the handbag. "She's going to want those back."

"She might not."

"You're both horrible liars. When you're ready to talk, you will. It looks like Stephanie's personal things from the Jeep got put in your box by the DPS officers at the accident. What's in the file?"

He opened it and they found an assortment of paper work.

"Her birth certificate?" Samantha asked, leaning toward him to see.

"Yours actually." John handed it to her then said, "And hers."

Samantha took it too.

"Some printouts." He flipped through the wide green and white striped computer paper with the holes on either edge that was printed with columns of names and dates from 1962.

Samantha took that too, opened the accordion linked printout. "What is she looking for in these reports?"

"Don't know. But here's a photocopy of an old photograph." He held it up for her to look at as he asked, "Who's this?"

"Our Mom and some... guy." She took it to study.

"She's on this one too."

She wanted that copy as well.

He pulled yet another from the folder. "Who's this?"

"Our grandmother." She took the copy. Then looked at him as he studied a piece of paper, "What's that?"

"This is mine." He pulled the paper out of her reach.

"And this?" She picked up a small note pad. It was shaded with a pencil but she could see the white words left behind from the sheet on top. "Stephanie took advantaged of you—Hey!"

He'd snatched it away. "That's mine too. You got your stuff."

"John."

He'd sat back, looking at the note pad. The careful meticulous shading from corner to corner that revealed his hateful words.

"John?"

"Yeah." The word a soft shaky breath as his eyes filled.

"You okay?"

He just nodded.

"She copied one of your photos too." Samantha held it out, so he could have it.

"It's from Captiva." He put it on the table, still holding tight to the shaded sheet of paper.

"John and Stephanie. May 1991. 1:03? What does one colon zero three mean?"

"The time it was taken, maybe."

"Why would that be important?"

"Got the grub." Honey was back. "Fried chicken. I was looking for Barbeque but... What's all this?"

"It was in John's box." She held up the copy of the photograph of her parents and her golden eyes were glistening with emotion as she looked at Honey.

"Let me see, Darling." His voice was gentle, and he set the food aside to sit beside her.

"This is my mom and dad." She showed him. "Stephanie found these photos somewhere."

"Sam and Marie. You're named after your father." He smiled at her. "Sam."

"Sam," she repeated looking at the photo. "I've never seen him before."

"You've never seen these photographs before?" John asked, looking at Honey. His friend wore compassion and had looped an arm around her. And John was glad Honey was here since Richard still hadn't arrived from Africa.

She was still studying her parents as she told them, "Mom told us the photos had been lost in a move."

"And Stephanie found these." Honey was looking at the other photos. Each sheet had the front and back of the photograph copied onto one sheet of paper. They were talking about her family as John began to read over the notes on Stephanie's legal pad.

"I took this photo." He held up the sheet and looked at John. "At 1:03 apparently."

"Maybe." John was flipping a page on the legal pad, following her notes, seeing her logic.

"On the photo of Stephen and Marie, the number isn't a time. It says 144:2."
Samantha showed him.

"Huh. Is that a code for something?" Honey asked.

"Stephanie thought it was a Bible verse," John told them.

Samantha picked up the Bible. "Must be in Psalms."

"It is. Psalm 144 verse 2." John looked at Honey. "It's where Stephanie
thinks she got her last name."

Blessed be the Lord my Rock,
Who trains my hands for war, and my fingers for battle—
My lovingkindness and my fortress,
My high tower and my deliverer,
My shield and the One in whom I take refuge,

"Her birthday is written here in the margin with the word Hightower."
Then Samantha looked at her parent's photograph. "Mine has 16:13, that could
be anywhere in the Bible."

"Stephanie thought Elroy came from Genesis 16:13."

She turned there and read,

Then she called the name of the Lord who spoke to her, You-Are-the-God-
Who-Sees; for she said, "Have I also here seen Him who sees me?"

Samantha repeated, "El Roi, the God who sees me." She just blinked. "She
has my birthday written beside these verses."

"What about your picture. 1:03, John?" Honey asked.

"From Psalms again. She says, 'He crowns my head.' Will you read it?"

"Praise the Lord, O my soul; all my inmost being, praise his holy name.
Praise the Lord, O my soul, and forget not all his benefits—
who forgives all your sins and heals all your diseases,
who redeems your life from the pit
and crowns you with love and compassion,
who satisfies your desires with good things
so that your youth is renewed like the eagle's."

He put the legal pad down and showed them her notes. "On this page she was working on names. For the baby."

"John—Joanna, Joanne, Johanna, Johannah, Jonnie. Joanie. Jo. Those are the first names. Then she went to Psalm 103 and chose Crown for the last name. John/Johnna Crown, she wrote right here." He showed them.

"But your last name is Dake."

"It seems that's not how your family does things. Your first name is after your father and the last name comes from the Bible. Did you know?"

"Know? I'm still not sure I understand what all this means," Samantha answered.

"Did you know she was pregnant?"

She looked up at him. "Oh. Not until Linda told me. Stephanie wasn't talking much the last month or two to any of us. Just working, speaking a lot and consulting. She just told us you broke up last week, but we all knew something had happened weeks before." She glanced at Honey. "Do you know?"

"Know? I have no idea what this means?"

"About John and Stephanie?"

"They broke up."

She just stared at him. "You know and won't say."

"You know your sister, Samantha and you also have a legal mind that might make more sense of all this than John can understand."

"Here, read this." John handed her the legal pad.

Samantha flipped the page of the legal pad and read through the notes, picked up a birth certificate, then a photo. Then she opened a Bible and read before she turned back to a page in the legal pad. Finally, she said, "Based on our birth certificates and the county and service records; my mother was never married. It also seems she; hid the surnames of our fathers, didn't know them, or maybe needed to protect them or us. 'The 'why' remains a mystery', Stephanie wrote. But our mother's faith does not. Despite her choices or the consequences Mom trusted the mercy, grace and faithfulness of God. Despite her unfaithfulness or our fathers', she lived forgiven and trusted in God's character to bless her children and honor their fathers.'

"It seems Stephanie understood my mother was claiming these verses as much for our fathers as she was for us. Stephanie's Psalm about the High Tower is a song of war. It starts, 'Blessed be the Lord my strength which teacheth my hands to war, and my fingers to fight: My goodness, and my fortress; my high tower, and my deliverer; my shield, and He in whom I trust; who subdueth my people under me.'

"Mom also put a star by verse 12. 'Then our sons in their youth will be like well-nurtured plants, and our daughters will be like pillars carved to adorn a palace.'" She looked at John. "Pillar and High Tower have the same symbolic idea—safety is found in one place alone, the Lord."

"The name of the Lord is a strong tower, the righteous run into it and they are safe," Honey added.

Samantha flipped over to Psalm 103. "And here she has written John's name in the margin at verse two and she meditates on the word 'crown' in her notes. Stephanie writes, 'Crown is defined as a wreath or garland, or any ornamental fillet encircling the head, especially as a reward of victory or mark of honorable distinction; hence, anything given on account of, or obtained by, faithful or successful effort; a reward. Anything which imparts beauty, splendor, honor, dignity or finish. The topmost part of anything; the summit.' Then she states, 'Though I deserve to be orphaned, outcast and ordinary-God forgives, heals, redeems, crowns, satisfies and renews me instead. He will bless my children's children. Psalm 103.'

"I'd conclude that she was claiming this Psalm and particularly this verse for you and the baby and for her future. That God would honor you with not only the reward of victory but His love and compassion that make everything right."

"King me," Honey stated looking at John.

He just nodded.

"King me?" Samantha questioned.

"That's what I say. When we score a touchdown." He stood as his hands placed the imaginary crown on his head. "King me."

"Makes even more sense if that's your touchdown dance."

"I don't dance."

Samantha smiled at him. "If you rest now, I'll stay with her then we can switch, is that okay? I need to talk about all this with her." She picked up the Bible and smiled. "I'm going to read to her too. She'd like that, and I believe she can hear us, John."

John rested his head back on the seat and closed his eyes as he lounged in a stiff slump. He could hear the muted sounds around him, feel the air cycle on and off from overhead. His body was sore, and he shifted off his left hip. In moments, he was falling into a shallow sleep, aware of the room but resting. He thought of Florida, their time together there. He remembered walking up to the house after a day on the beach. Sun kissed and gritty with sand, they'd stopped at the outdoor shower on the back patio. She'd been in that black bikini. He could remember her body, the gentle curve of her hip, the little dip of her lower back. There'd been sand there and he pulled the rope to engage the shower and wash it off. He'd been smiling when she gasped, the water cold on sunburned skin. He'd caught her by the waist, held her there as he pressed his chuckling kiss to her neck. "We don't want sand in the house." That's what they'd told each other as they assisted the water to rinse the sand free with their hands. He could remember his hand on her skin, riding dips and edges and curves. Following the length of those legs down to her little feet. She'd picked them up and he'd cleaned them off. One at a time. Then looked up at her as he rose. Her body slick and cool and pretty with color. Then she'd washed him, finding her own pleasure in touching his body until the water was silent and their kiss just held.

It had been intimate and honoring. He could see the love reflected in her eyes. And he'd wanted her that day, as his wife, pure and cherished and fiercely his forever.

31

John read her Psalm 103. Then meditated on it out loud, remembering how God had forgiven him, honored and blessed him with so much love and compassion. "You're one of His greatest blessings to me, Stephanie." He kissed her hand, held it as he laid his tired head down on her bed, just watching her as he prayed silently now. Words flowed as he recounted God's goodness to him and all the blessings in his life. His memories of Stephanie and the spiritual changes she'd help initiate in him and he in her. He fell asleep and dreamed of her. Chasing her only to catch her and have her melt away. Joy turning to a fear that had him jolting awake.

But she was in the same sedated state, sleeping with the many machines keeping order. He softly kissed her hand and told her, "I love you so much. Please wake up, so I can tell you how sorry I am, how forgiven you are, how much I love you, Beauty."

John was too tired to notice the unusually high pulse rate that suddenly became displayed on her monitor. It slowly tapered back to normal as the room grew silent and he fell asleep again.

There was an eerie mist that clung to everything around her. It was the purest of whites. Totally void of anything tangible. An absolute brightness that led her nowhere yet held her firmly in its soft embrace. She drifted, resting comfortably in the stillness until something began to draw her forward. Soothing sounds, a familiar voice with assuring words and that secure feeling. *Grace*—she was accepted. *Accepted*—she was loved. *Loved*—He was here, with her always, she was never alone or outside or orphaned, and nothing could separate her from this Love. *Love*—welled up in her, Spirit to Spirit she was full with the truth of it. And it rang out now, touching her heart, then calling her to reach out, to touch others.

Love.

The word rang out. A simple command. But soon complex. His voice merging into other's. His Word inside her as she heard a voice. Soon it was quieted to silence and she struggled to listen, to seek. She began to find her way. There were other noises now. Imperceptible sounds that slowly became recognizable ones. Something hissed in a constant rhythm, while a beep and a drip kept time. She concentrated on those sounds and the rhythm seemed to melt the numbness. As she became more aware, gradually she could feel again, and the sensation grew until it became acute. Pain absorbed her body and thrust her into consciousness.

She gasped as something strangled her breath only to force it upon her. The pain was everywhere as her lungs expanded. Like a growling heat, her body warmed up like a kettle on the boil, her mind coming back online. Senses engaging. Sight blurry. Just like her hearing, she blinked repeatedly for the light to yield sight and her brain to analyze recognition.

All she wanted to do was scream as she saw her surroundings, but a machine was doing that for her. An alarm venting angrily as strangers rushed into the room. They were speaking but she couldn't understand, too overwhelmed by the pain and her loss of control. She wanted out. She wanted to run.

She had run.

The truth tolled. She'd been running... driving to California. And God stopped her. Grace. Acceptance. Loved. Love.

His Love was furious. The truth overwhelming. He had pursued her to stop her. Free-will would have one second chance.

She tried to get herself free, but she couldn't move. She tried to breathe in more air. She needed more air. She wasn't allowed to breathe. That hiss was attached to a machine that was forcing air into her lungs. Breathing for her. She screamed for him, *God.*

I AM here...

And she clearly heard her name. "Stephanie." A familiar sound attached to an unfamiliar face was quickly in focus. "Stephanie, it's okay. You don't need to be afraid. You're in the hospital. We're taking care of you. Nothing is going to happen. You need to relax." A soft hand took hold of her own and the contact was like a lifeline. "I'm right here. You're on a machine to help you breathe. You're in a hospital in Dallas. Blink if you understand me."

She blinked with both eyes.

"You were in a car accident; do you remember?"

It flashed. That thrust of time, her life rushing by as metal screeched and bent. And the Jeep was flipping, skipping over concrete in an angry scream until it slammed to a stop. She had hung upside down. Saw his name, John, written on a box and her Bible opened, words on a page. **God is love.** Blood dripped from her body onto the paper and her hands clutched protectively over her belly.

My baby. She tried to move her hands, wanted them over her belly now but she couldn't get them to move, started to panic.

"It's okay Stephanie. You're okay now. Try to relax. Are you in pain?"

She tried to nod, blinking rapidly, hearing the rhythm pick up of beeps and the whoosh building. Stephanie moaned in her chest, it was the only sound she could make.

"I know you want that out."

Stephanie's eyes blinked rapidly but a soothing warmth slowly flowed over her body and the potent pain killer had her floating away again.

"Stephanie." She heard her name, it came to her with the even rhythm. There was no hiss, only a beep and the even drip and she could breathe.

Something was making her feel all right. They were holding her hand and saying her name. She could feel the warmth around her hand, and the cool air on her arm and the weight of her legs. Her eyes sought the light again. They blinked rapidly as she tried to focus and found her sister. The gold of her eyes. "I'm right here, with Blair. You're okay, sis."

Blair leaned closer, "Getting better every hour."

She tried to move her free hand. Saw the cast and felt the pain pitch and burn inside her arm. She moved her other hand, placed it protectively over her belly. It felt numb and blotted and was beginning to hurt. Stephanie tried to clear her throat. It felt dry and raw. She had to speak. She had so many unanswered questions.

She squeezed her sister's hand and in a faint voice choked out a soft "What," followed by a raspy, "happened?"

"You were in a car accident. Rolled your Jeep and the trailer. Do you remember?" Blair asked.

Stephanie nodded then whispered, "Horses?"

Samantha told her, "Runabout was killed Stephanie. I'm so sorry. But High Hopes made it. He's doing fine."

Runabout killed.

"You had a ruptured spleen and internal injuries. You broke your arm in three places."

She saw the cast and pins. No wonder she couldn't move it. She looked back up at her sisters.

"You were very critical. I thought we might lose you."

"I'm pregnant," Stephanie whispered so softly that no one else would have understood it.

Her sister moved in closer, said solemnly, "You lost it, Stephanie."

"We're so sorry."

Runabout was killed. Her baby was gone.

She closed her eyes again. Tears rolled down her face. There was nothing that could make them stop. She felt her sister's hand softly stroking them away as they reassured her. It was too much to take. She didn't want to think anymore. She drifted off again.

"Stephanie." Her name was said with love and called her to wake. Again, she felt the warmth of a hand covering her own. And she recognized the voice, wanted to see her. She opened her eyes and Linda Bennett smiled at her. "There you are."

"Hey, sweetheart." Brad was beside her. "How you feeling?"

Stephanie attempted a smile.

"Only two of us can see you here in ICU but they're going to move you today. We've got a private room for you upstairs. And I hear they're going to let you try to eat something once you get there. The Doctors say you're improving every hour. You're going to be fine."

"I was pregnant," she whispered it to them. "I'm sorry," she said next. The grief all rolling together to choke her. The apology about too many things. And the emotional pain flowing now as Linda stood from the chair and leaned toward her to kiss her face.

"We love you." It was Brad's voice as Linda wiped her tears, crying herself and nodding as he spoke. "There's nothing you could do to make us stop loving you, Stephanie. You're our daughter and we love you."

"We love you," Linda repeated. "And John does too."

Then she told them what she'd done. In sound bites and through retching tears but Linda soothed her, and Brad held her hand and they both told her again when she'd said it all. "We love you. And John loves you."

"And Jesus loves you even more," Brad told her. "He forgives you, Stephanie. You need to receive that forgiveness and forgive yourself."

Her father's words were an invitation that she carried into sleep as Stephanie squeezed Brad's hand and closed her eyes again. She met Christ in those words and pleaded for His agreement and she heard His soft assurance that it was already done. Now she needed to believe and receive and forgive herself.

She could feel her family, holding her hand. Touch an assurance that she wasn't alone. A mysterious power that diminished fear and pain. She'd experienced it first in the caring touch of the ICU nurses. Then in the companionship of fellowship she felt with her sisters. Then the encouragement of her parent's care and wisdom. And now, it came in the strong assurance of his commitment.

"I'm here, Stephanie. And I'm not leaving this time until you wake up and I see those pretty eyes..." His rich voice lured her to the light again. She felt his hand holding hers. "Sleeping Beauty, can you wake up for me?"

John smiled at her.

"John."

"It used to be Mr. Charming," he said moving closer.

"Hard to talk."

"Then just listen. I love you." His eyes were sparkling yet sad, his voice soft but it held that firm authority she'd come to admire when he led with conviction. "Forgive me, Stephanie. I'm so sorry for what I said and did that day. That I didn't call you—"

"No. Me. It was... all me."

"No. It's all on me."

"Me."

"Me." Now he grinned but his voice was also firm. "It's on me. I'm supposed to lead, and I didn't do that very well."

"You were hurt."

"No excuse."

"Concussion—"

"Healed. And I should have called you, forgave you. How many times have you forgiven me? Hundreds. So know now, right now, I forgive you. It's forgotten. And I'll never bring it up again. Or hold it against you. Ever."

"But—"

"Stop. You can talk about it later if you need to, when you're stronger. But right now, know I love you. I'm here and I'm not leaving."

"What day is it?" She frowned. "Your game."

He shook his head. "No. You matter more than any game. I'm not leaving until you're better."

"I'm okay."

"Yes." He smiled. Kissed her hand. "I'm thanking God for answered prayers. You're going to be fine. They're moving you to a room. And they've still got you pretty sedated, so I'll be telling you the same thing over and over again to make sure you remember. Now, close your eyes and rest. I love you and I'll see you in a little while upstairs, okay?"

It was a blur. Of motion and noises. She was in and out as they moved her on the bed on wheels up the elevator and down halls, around corners, to a new room. It was private and full of family and flowers. No one walked in empty handed. Everyone smiling as the light conversation floated around her. She was trying to keep up, her gaze moving from person to person, seeing the collective relief on their faces.

Honey was here for John, and his mother had been here with Dylan. Blair and Layne with Samantha since Richard was still in Africa. Linda and Brad were taking care of all the arrangements, talking to their pastor as he spoke with pastor Conrad from John's church. She was drifting only to blink her eyes and look back at John. He would smile. She wanted to reach for him, but he was standing on her right, by the windows, leaning against the wall. He looked relieved like the rest of them, but his smile seemed propped up on an exhausted face.

Samantha asked her, "Want another sip?" She held the Sprite with the straw close to her mouth, and she drank.

"John looks tired," she quietly told Samantha.

"He hasn't been home. Hardly slept. Honey stayed here with him. And me," she added. "We made Blair go home to rest."

"He needs to rest."

"What's that?" Blair asked moving in now.

"She says Honey and John stink." Samantha held the glass up again for her to drink as she looked at the two of them. "You guys need to clear out and go shower. Rest."

"I think we all need to clear out. Let Stephanie rest," Brad suggested.

"I'm going to stay this time," Blair told the room as she took the cup of Sprite from Samantha and pulled her up from the chair. "You stink too, sis."

"No."

There was a snort. "Tell her, Honey."

"Well now."

"Alright. Alright," Samantha mocked. "I'm going."

The room cleared. John stopping at the end of her bed. "You okay, Beauty?" She nodded.

Blair said, "Go get a good night's sleep and maybe you can come back after practice tomorrow."

"I'm not playing this week."

"What?" Stephanie asked.

He repeated it.

"But... you have to." She watched him lean back, stare at her. "It's Philly. Don't miss because of this."

"This is you."

"I'm okay," she assured him.

"She sure is," Blair added now. "Just needs to rest."

"The game is in Philly," he reminded her.

"And it's important. A conference game."

Blair stood. "I'm, ah, going to go get you some more Sprite." She left the room.

"What are you saying? You don't want me here?"

She reached for him now and he took his hands out of his pockets and accepted her hand. "You're tired. I see it."

"You're in pain. I see it. Don't like it. Do you want me here?"

"I feel guilty—"

"Don't." He sat now, in the chair beside her. "Do you want me here?"

"I want you to rest."

"I can rest in this chair. Do you want me here, Stephanie?"

"I don't want you to miss a game."

"I don't want to play games." He reminded her of her own words as he leaned forward. "I want you to know without a doubt I love you. Want you. Forever. Do you?"

She just started to cry. And he cradled her hand, then moved in, leaning toward her he took her face, whispered soothing words. Hoovering over her because there was no way to hold her. "It's okay," he repeated it, again and again then he pleaded, looking into her eyes. "Please, let me stay. Tell me it's okay. What do you need?"

"You, to know, that I'm so sorry."

"I know you are." He nodded and said it again, then again. "I forgive you. God forgives us. And you can show you believe that by honoring Him with gratitude. You're alive. Right?"

She nodded. "Thank God, yes." Then asked him, "Kiss?"

He smiled. Softly brushed her lips then the kiss held, deepened. When it ended they were looking at each other again as she told him, "I need you. Forever. Don't leave me."

Blair walked back into the room and John said, "We just decided that I'm staying."

"Can you stay... this weekend, Blair? So, John can play."

"Of course." She handed John the soda with a smile. "I'll see you both tomorrow."

They watched her leave the room and they were alone. "Look, Beauty, I'm supposed to have the advantage here. You being drugged and weak and needy should not be able to make a chess move like that and have me at checkmate. I don't want to leave you to play football this weekend."

"I need you to play... or I will feel horrible. Don't make it worse."

"I need you to know football is not the most important thing in my life anymore. What would it matter if I won every game for the rest of my career, I almost lost you."

"You don't have to prove that to me."

"After what I said to you and did, I think I do." He was up now, pacing around her bed. "I was a jerk after that concussion. Selfish and arrogant. I never considered what you were going through when I played a hard game or what it was like when I got hurt. And after it happened, I thought I could just put you off and finish the season. Keep football first and deal with us later. Now I know so much better."

"Really?"

He looked at her now. She had that gleam in her eyes, but her words were for him now instead of against him. "I think you didn't know what to do with me. How you would deal with us, the intimacy. I betrayed you, John. I did take advantage of you. After everything you'd done to honor me, I let fear and insecurity and pride and selfishness say yes, yes, yes and yes. I wanted the sex, on my terms. And after it happened you were right, it was wrong in every way. Your only protection was to break up or ultimately you would have given in and hated yourself and me. I ruined any chance for us."

"I should have married you this summer. After Captiva and before the temptation had us going farther and farther." He prompted with a lifted brow, "Austin. In Samantha's backyard. I didn't protect you. Honor you. Then... that night when I got the concussion." There was pain in his soft words, "You were pregnant."

"Yes." And her eyes filled with tears.

"Would you have told me?"

"I don't think so."

John just nodded, his own eyes filling as he told her, "I didn't give you a reason to think you could trust me after the way I responded," he patted his chest like she'd seen him do when he overthrew a pass, "That's on me too, Stephanie."

"No." The word was a lament. "I was running scared when I should have been fighting hard. For us, for our family." Her hand had been over her belly again, now it moved, shaking as it took his hand, squeezed. "Forgive me."

"I do."

"I wanted you." She patted his hand now. "My way."

"Out of fear," he told her. "I never thought about what you were going through."

"Out of pride," she confessed. Her hand trembling as her words tumbled out. About being rookie green and inexperienced and how Elise said he hated that, and she'd called that night, made her jealous and she just took control and seduced him, and it was all on her.

"Stephanie." He'd taken her hand. "You're smarter than this." He was looking at their joined hands as he softly said, "That night, it's like a crazy dream, that turned into a nightmare, where you can't wake up."

"It was a sin. My sin, and it destroyed us."

He looked up at her and said, "My savior lives. He won. Overcame. All of that is under His feet and forgiven." Now he squeezed her hand. "And He has our child." He nodded, brought her hand up to his lips and pressed a long kiss there. "Can we honor Him and live forgiven and agree to forget that night?"

"Yes." She nodded. "I want to forget that night."

"It's forgotten, like a dream drifts away."

"It was more like a nightmare."

"Hmph. I know I had a concussion, but I was that bad, huh?" There was a grin. "Even with yes, yes, yes and yes."

"John." She blushed but tears gathered, and he leaned toward her to wipe them away again.

"I want you to laugh about this soon. It's going to be our very private inside joke, okay."

She closed her eyes and surprised him, "It was a nightmare, but it had been what, ten months of celibacy for you?"

He chuckled. "There you go."

And she opened her eyes. Smiled. Squeezed his hand. "Seriously, no one knows about that night, but Honey, and I only told him when I was sitting in the chapel a few nights ago, praying for your life. I'll always protect and honor you, Stephanie. I want to make your dreams come true. What are they now?"

"You, winning games. Me, cheering you on."

"I can work on that with you." He interlaced their fingers. "Next week."

"Sunday," she demanded, squeezing his hand. "Win for me in Philly."

"Hmph. What else?"

She was quiet, just looking into his eyes. He pulled something from his pocket. Emeralds and diamonds dangled and glittered as he draped them around her wrist. "Remembering the reasons behind this bracelet might help you dream with me. Psalms 103. *He crowns us with love and compassion.* Samantha and I read through your file. And I want to talk about it more with you later, but I need you to know something now." He frowned, "No daughter of mine is going to be named Johnna." He smiled at her and her eyes just filled again. He kissed her hand, brushed the skin beneath the bracelet with a sweep of his thumb. "And you know I prefer Scotch, so Crown for a last name, well that reminds me of Crown Royal and that's whiskey, Beauty." He smiled at her. "I think Dake is a better last name, don't you?"

"Yes, Dake is a much better last name."

"I thought so." Now he whispered, "We'll be having boys by the way."

"Will we?" It was a dare now.

"A houseful to guard that beautiful daughter," he told her as he took the cross of emeralds from around his own neck and carefully put the necklace on her. "Dream with me, Beauty," He whispered looking into her eyes now. "We both want God's will to direct us. What do you think He's calling us to do?"

He sat on the bed and waited. "Hmph, nothing to say? You want me to lead."

She nodded. "When I tried to... it led us into trouble."

"Okay, let's see if you agree with me. I need a wife. A beauty, inside and out. Who fears the Lord, is wise in His ways, knows I'm called to lead so she's supportive, my helpmate and what I cherish more than anything else in life."

There was emotion now and he let it come to the surface as he told her, "Because all these blessing are nothing without having her beside me."

There was a ring in the palm of his hand now, with a diamond that dazzled almost as brightly as his famous smile as he looked at her. "Stephanie, would you do me the honor."

She was shaking her head now. "John. No."

And he kept her gaze. "No?"

"Not like this. Because of the accident."

"Just like this. Because of the accident. God intervening. To stop you from running. And show me it's time to step up and stop waiting. There's no time to wait. And you are right, it's the only way we can do this God's way now. Honor God and each other. I love you. So much. Want to be with you. Now not later, not one minute later, by tomorrow in fact, or as soon as we can make it legal, I want us to marry. I want to bring you home. Take care of you. We can celebrate our marriage publicly later; however you want to do it, I'll make it special for you." He held out the ring. "Trust me. It's now. Stephanie, will you do me the honor of being my wife?"

32

Lights brightened up the sunken area of John's game room. The producer had chosen to film the interview here. It would be aired during the pre-game show of the Super Bowl. He told John and Stephanie to get comfortable as he positioned the bright lights and the cameras around them. She sat on John's right with her legs curled up beneath her and Bradshaw by her side on the sofa. John's arm was behind her, his left hand clasping hers as it rested on his leg while Staubach sat at his feet. Then Rhonda moved in to style them. She'd made sure the colors of Stephanie's sweater, woven in navy, green and heather gray, complimented John's woven button down. She straightened John's collar a bit then moved some of Stephanie's hair over her shoulder before she stepped back and told them, "You look great together." And Kenny gave a nod.

John leaned toward her and said softly, "Just play through it, Beauty," before he kissed her.

"Mr. Dake?" the famous sports journalist asked, "Are you ready?" as he sat across from them.

"Mrs. Dake?" John kept his gaze on Stephanie as he used his new favorite title for her. Her hand was cold, and he stroked it, his fingers sliding out from beneath the emerald bracelet to allow his thumb to nudge her ring. He loved seeing it on her finger. That brilliant piece of ice, emerald cut and just a little flashy, said she was his wife.

She'd said yes. In a gasp of love and agreement to trust his plans and their dreams. They'd said simple vows the next day before he left to play against Philadelphia and he won that game for her. And now, holding his hand, she'd said yes to telling their story.

And her trust just made the need to honor her only increase all the more. He whispered, "I love you, Beauty," and brushed her lips before he gave her a smile and she squeezed his hand, smiled back.

Then he turned to Al and gave a nod, but the cameras were already rolling. The questions began, about the Dallas season. John had answered these before and his calm attitude helped Stephanie relax and the interview moved forward smoothly until they were discussing the upcoming Super Bowl and Al was bringing in John's stats.

"John you've had a remarkable season. You're about to play in the Super Bowl for the first time and you'll be heading to the Pro Bowl as the starting quarterback from the NFC Eastern division next week. What's made this season so successful?"

"I've said before that football games aren't won by individual efforts alone, so I always want to honor my team. We do it together and we have coaches and a front office that support that effort. God also has a time for everything and it seems this was my year. It started bumpy, I was injured but then I met my wife, Dr. S.B. Hightower, and things began to change."

"She's a doctor?"

"Stephanie's a veterinarian," he corrected. "And a devoted Christian. From the very start her faith began to increase mine and prepared me for this season."

"You were the NFL Man of the Year award winner for your work with CASA and Foster Care kids in the Dallas area."

"Yes, it was a huge honor, but Stephanie inspired me. She and her sister were in the Foster Care system for several years before they were adopted, and it was a cause I became passionate about. My foundation provided school clothes and shoes to over a 1000 kids in Dallas. It was a unanimous donation until I began to see that making it personal could help these kids go even further. I began to work with Wednesday's Child to highlight these kids who are longing for forever families. I also encourage others to the call of being advocates. CASA, court-appointed-special-advocates, is an organization that links foster children with adults who can help them navigate through the legal system, so they never stand alone. God calls us to care for the orphans."

"And Stephanie's forever family is someone you know well, correct?"

"Yes, Brad and Linda Bennett adopted her."

"So, you met through football so to speak?"

John smiled. "We met through my dogs. She treated Bradshaw." The dog looked at him when she heard her name and Stephanie just gave her a stroke. "They fell in love with her and I quickly followed."

"And you were recently married?"

"Yes."

"You left the Dallas-Washington game early for a family emergency, was that Stephanie?"

"Yes, she was involved in a serious car accident outside of Dallas."

"And Careflited to Parkland with life threatening injuries," he expanded with confirmed details.

"Yes, it was serious," John answered without elaborating.

"We were told that it was extremely serious. That you stayed at the hospital all week and only played in the Philadelphia game because she requested it, John."

Now he smiled. "She said she wouldn't marry me unless I went to Philly and won."

"And you almost had a perfect game there."

"Yes. I was very motivated, but don't make me out to be a hero. I would never have left the hospital unless I knew she was okay." He paused. "I respect my teammates, but football is my job. It's not my life or my God."

"And when you scored during that game you changed your victory routine a bit."

"Yes, since I played high school ball I always said, 'King me,' and put the imaginary crown on my head in the end zone if I scored a touchdown. Now I also take a knee and lay that crown down. God has blessed me. He's crowned me with my athletic ability and resources and only when I lay them down and offer them back to Him are they eternally used to honor Him and others. God used Stephanie to help me understand what honor really means."

"So Stephanie, will John be this season's MVP and win the Super Bowl?"

"He's my MVP," she answered, looking at John. "And there's no doubt in my mind we won't win the Super Bowl."

John ran the ball in for the last touchdown of the game and said, "King me!" as he pointed to the sky then placed that imaginary crown upon his head, then he took a knee and laid the crown on the turf. He looked up to where his wife watched, their family celebrating in the Bennett's box and he was overwhelmed with gratitude. God had crowned him with love and compassion. He had raised his life up from the pit. Forgiven his sins. Satisfied him with a beautiful godly wife and renewed his strength after last year's injury to find victory. Like a crown, he was on top and his soul sang, 'Praise the Lord.' They would win the Super Bowl today. Then this moment would pass away, but God's love, His overwhelming furious, pursuing love would remain. Love would be passed on, to his children's children.

With seconds remaining in the game, John took the last snap and took a knee. He bowed his head and set down the football, the tool of his craft no longer his treasure. And in that moment, with his head bowed and his heart honoring God he realized the victory formation required you bend the knee.

Honor Me and I will honor You. Dying brought the abundant life. Surrender brought true spiritual victory.

His Lord's name was on his tongue. The Lord Jesus was who he honored when they asked him their questions. His teammates were who he pointed to when they tried to single him out. And his wife was who he swept up to share the celebration of victory. As she ran into his arms he said, "King me."

ABOUT THE AUTHOR

J.L. Kelly is an American speaker, Bible teacher & author of Christian novels that combine compelling story worlds with unforgettable characters in tremendously moving novels. Her writing is dedicated to the Lord Jesus Christ in thanksgiving for the many relationships that have inspired, redeemed, sustained, challenged, encouraged and transformed the life God has invited her to humbly fulfill for His glory.

She believes words are powerful. "Writing is a great privilege and carries a responsibility with its creative expression. I pray for inspiration and the right amount of balance in creating deep and compelling characters in a story world that is authentic and yet hopeful. My books are founded on relationships—spiritual, friendships, and family and forged through the real and raw stories that take place as sinners are saved by grace and sanctified through the Word of truth."

J.L Kelly's characters are connected from one book to the next. Ones you love will show up again in another story and like old friends, she hopes you're glad to see them. Ones you don't like might catch you judging them. Every good story needs an antagonist and we've all been that from time to time. We need grace for the proud and the hurting. She hopes you're open to changing your opinion of some of her 'bad guys' as they are transformed. We should never assume the arm of the Lord is too short to save any character. After all, we were all at one time that "character".

Her mission is to share the Truth in love. Reviewers agree that J.L. Kelly books are sometimes intense and might not be for readers who are looking for the classic sweet Christian story where characters do everything right. Unapologetically her style is to write it real—meaning closer to real life, tackling issues with universal importance in a God honoring way. Her characters will never be perfect, but they will proclaim to you the love, grace and mercy of a perfect God.

BOOKS BY J.L. KELLY

The Glory is the story of Samantha Elroy. She was rescued. Survived what other girls did not and she doesn't like to talk about it. That was then. Now she is working as an attorney, helping victims of crimes find justice. She's satisfied, settled and safe. So getting swept off her feet by a danger junky cowboy is totally out of the question. Honey Cooper could give an engaged girl a panic attack with his swaggering, slow talking charm. Not to mention his probing questions. And she's done with all that. So why does she keep thinking of Him? And why does God keep pushing them together?

In a world where fear is a sin that paralyzes and thanksgiving is faith's courage to trust beyond what can be seen, **The Glory** is the victory we realize when holiness comes to expression.

For the once afraid victim doing the hard work of turning evil's wounds into victory's scars.

For the dangerous who fearlessly pursue God's purposed plan.

For the suffering who long to experience God working out for them a weight of glory amidst these light momentary afflictions.

The Glory is the transformation story of how God deposits something of His moral beauty and majesty into the soul of a believer and how this holiness comes to light through thanksgiving in the metamorphosis.

A parable of how God is the saints' glory and so they are His.

The Glory is the journey of the worm, wrapped in the substantial weight of affliction and grappling with the paradoxes of faith to emerge from the cocoon of oppression the transformed butterfly.

The Glory is the prequel of The Glory Series.

The Secret is the story of Jillian Montague.

She's Irish and an actress and she's fallen for the Dake Family in a way she never expected. Intuitive, Jillian's learning their secrets; those sacred things people keep from knowledge or view of others, sometimes even themselves. Quarterback, Jude Dake has shared a confidence. Dr. Ellen Dake's mystery is about to be solved. Stephanie Dake and her sisters divulge their spiritual secret and Jillian realizes that handsome smile isn't the only secret-weapon John Dake's handed down to his boys. Jillian's learned sports broadcaster Dylan Dake's infamous destruction has left a trail of heartbreak and coach Dwight Dake's search for success has found her out.

Jillian's a witness to the conflict of how holding onto secrets forms a triangle—involving one and excluding another—that precariously separates and distinguishes friends. In the end the secrets they try to keep divide and breakup the very relationships they long to protect. And the most dangerous secrets of all are the ones you hide from even yourself. But God, always sees into the darkest depths of the heart and everything secret will be revealed in His timing so that we can be forgiven and free, redeemed and reconciled.

For anyone with a secret they've hidden away under shame.

For anyone who longs to have the courage to be more than their secret.

For the one who knows a secret has divided a relationship or stolen their joy.

For all of us who long to know the secret of living a life of faith.

The Secret is a story of spiritual discovery. There is a secret to faith, of love and finding hope. The parable of a woman with a secret will remind us how you can think you really know someone but everyone has secrets. The dark are covered up. The holy are beyond understanding. And the lesson of our secrets is this; we all think we keep secrets; actually they keep us. God longs for us to be free.

To find out about new book releases
or retreats where J.L. Kelly will be speaking

Follow JL Kelly on Facebook
https://www.facebook.com/J.L.Kellybooks

Her blog at
http://4jlkelly.org

Website
www.JLKellybooks.com

And Pinterest
http://www.pinterest.com/4jlkelly/